ÉILÍS NÍ DHUIBHNE was born in Dublin in 1954. She was educated at University College Dublin and has a BA in English and a PhD in Irish Folklore. She has worked for many years as a librarian in the National Library of Ireland and is a member of Aosdána. The author of eleven novels and collections of short stories, several children's books, plays, and many scholarly articles and literary reviews, her work includes *The Bray House*, *Eating Women is Not Recommended* and *The Dancers Dancing*. She has been the recipient of many literary awards, among them the Stewart Parker Award for Drama, the Irish American Cultural Institute Award for Prose, several Oireachtas Awards for Irish language fiction, and three Bisto Awards for novels for young people. Her novel *The Dancers Dancing* (Blackstaff 1999; new edition 2007) was shortlisted for the Orange Prize for Fiction in 2000. A collection of essays on her writing, *Éilís Ní Dhuibhne, Perspectives*, edited by Rebecca Pelan, will be published by Arlen House in November 2007.

'We have all met Ní Dhuibhne's Anna, walking down Grafton Street, waiting at the school gate in her smart car, toying with food in an expensive restaurant. She is as omnipresent as she is foolish. She is also touching, vulnerable and all too human. This is the real achievement of this novel.'

ITA DALY

'Hugely enjoyable. I laughed aloud and cried. Ní Dhuibhne is Chekovian in her mixture of comedy and tragedy.'

MARY ROSE CALLAGHAN

'This is the Celtic Tiger novel we've all been waiting for – searingly perceptive and wickedly funny in its stylish dissection of the rotten heart of contemporary Ireland's chattering intelligentsia. Does what Messud's *The Emperor's Children* did for ennui-driven New Yorkers. Even better, Ní Dhuibhne's heroine delivers on all the pathos and wit you'd expect if Anna Karenina were a spoiled Killiney housewife with literary aspirations. Brilliant.'

KATE HOLMQUIST

FOX, SWALLOW, SCARECROW

ÉILÍS NÍ DHUIBHNE

BLACKSTAFF
PRESS
BELFAST

ACKNOWLEDGEMENTS

Many thanks to the excellent editors at Blackstaff Press.
Thanks to Pat Donlon at the Tyrone Guthrie Centre
at Annaghmakerrig, where some of this novel was written.

First published in 2007 by
Blackstaff Press
4c Heron Wharf, Sydenham Business Park
Belfast BT3 9LE
with the assistance of
The Arts Council of Northern Ireland

Typeset by CJWT Solutions, St Helens, England

Printed in England by Athenaeum Press

A CIP catalogue record for this book is available from the British Library

ISBN 978-0-85640-807-6

www.blackstaffpress.com

To Ragnar,
with whom I have had many
good discussions about books,

and for Olaf,
who reads Russian novels

Before any definite step can be taken in a household, there must be either complete division or loving accord between husband and wife. When their relations are indefinite it is impossible for them to make any move.

Leo Tolstoy, *Anna Karenina*,
PART SEVEN, CHAPTER XXIII

'But that's how it is – people are different. One man just lives for his own needs, take Mityukha even, just stuffs his belly, but Fokanych – he's an upright old man. He lives for his soul. He remembers God.'

Leo Tolstoy, *Anna Karenina*,
PART EIGHT, CHAPTER XI

One

From the new glass bridge which spanned the inscrutable waters of the Grand Canal, the tram purred downhill and glided gently into the heart of the city. Like a slow Victorian roller coaster it swerved through Peter's Place, passing chic apartments, their balconies rubbing shoulders with almost equally chic corporation houses, genteel vestiges of democracy that had contrived to survive in this affluent area. Then it swung nonchalantly onto Adelaide Road – the modernised version, all windows and transparency, where once there had been high hedges and minority religions. 'Next stop – Harcourt,' whispered the announcer. Her voice reminded Anna of Marilyn Monroe's. 'An céad stáisiún eile Sráid Earcair.' The seductive tone always unnerved her, even though she presumed it had been designed to soothe her and her fellow passengers. That the translation was in Donegal Irish made it even more eerie. It was like a voice from fairyland or the world beneath the wave, from some place aeons away from the land of the Luas.

The passengers did not look as if they needed soothing. They had been seduced already. They were in love with the tram. Confidence and well-being crowned them like an aura, one and all, from a toddler wearing cheerful denim and mini mountain boots to the old ladies in beige raincoats and cute little Burberry hats. This was the Green Line, the track that connected the

1

middle-class suburbs of south Dublin with Stephen's Green and Grafton Street: the fashionable shopping area, the theatre area, the restaurant area, what they were now calling 'the museum area'. The tram was a novelty and people were still very pleased with it, pleased with its sleek design and its efficient frequency. It was the first fashionable form of public transport to be introduced to Dublin in about a century.

Travelling by tram, at least on the Green Line, had a bit of cachet. Being seeing on it was not necessarily a bad thing, whereas being seen on a Dublin bus, even a most respectable bus like the 7 or the 11, was an abject admission of social and economic failure. Only the young, the old and the poor used the bus. But any successful citizen in the prime of life could travel on the Luas, confident that neither their reputation nor self-esteem would be tarnished: doctors and architects, solicitors and designers, all used it, at least at weekends. (You often needed your car for work, of course. Your briefcase was in it, and a clean shirt or blouse.) Once Anna had even seen a government Minister fiddling with a ticket machine – the machines were tricky. He had looked vulnerable and naked, somehow, without a big black car surrounding him; he had looked like someone who had rushed out of the house in his pyjamas to put out the dustbin. You knew he was not going to do this very often, that the next day his car would be parked in the garden of Leinster House, along with the cars of all his colleagues, blotting out what was once one of Dublin's finest lawns, which some Irish government had covered with black tar. But it was telling, Anna felt, it was touching, that a ruler of the land would, even once, leave his car at home, do the environmentally desirable thing, that such a busy and important man would stop polluting Dublin, even for one day. On the Luas.

She sighed. Thinking about the government, or about politics, or the environment, always wearied her. What was the point? What could she do about any of the country's problems? She swept her annoyance about the car park outside Leinster House out of her mind with one swift stroke, like an energetic housecleaner. Brushing problems under the carpet was a skill she had long ago perfected, especially if they were other people's problems. Instead of worrying about the ills of society, she amused herself by observing them.

A father and daughter sat opposite her. The little girl was called Nellie, the sort of name one heard on the Luas. Nellie, Katie, Sally, Lolly. Emma and Emily and Rebecca, you could meet anywhere, on the DART, on the bus to Ballyfermot. Regency elegance was out, hillbilly homeliness was in, for the moment. Would the names of the fifties, of the grandmothers, now so outré they could hardly be pronounced and had not been seen in the Birth columns since the time of the Howth tram, be next? Would Ann and Margaret, Marian and Lilian, be queuing at a station near you? Elizabeth? Or Imelda or Concepta or Assumpta, those Dublin names of the 1950s, so unfashionable now that their owners seemed to have vanished off the face of the earth?

'Look, Nellie, see the dog!' said the father, pointing to a nondescript mutt that was sniffing at the bins outside one of the old Harcourt Street hotels. He had made such comments several times, directing his daughter's attention to objects of interest in the passing scene. A boat on the canal, a girl on a bicycle, a marmalade cat. Would Nellie really be excited by the sighting of a dog? Yes, indeed she would. She responded with delighted smiles and happy exclamations. Nellie, a porcelain princess, dressed in a pink empire dress trimmed with black velvet ribbons, wearing pink silk shoes, was one of those little girls who might have been cut out from the pages of a fashion magazine. They were numerous on the Green Line. The father, too, looked perfect, in the style of the perfect young fathers of Dundrum and Ranelagh: living practically in the city centre, they reminded Anna of the younger sons of country squires in BBC costume dramas; they were trim and neat, and wore clothes that suggested the hunt, or at least the village horse-show – fawn cords, tawny Norfolk jackets. This father was devoted to attending to his daughter. They always were. She seemed delighted in his company. They always were.

At the last stop, Stephen's Green, Anna alighted in the stream of passengers flowing onto the street. People seemed to falter momentarily when they got off the tram and took a minute to find their bearings. They bumped into the crowds waiting to board. Long lines waited at the ticket-issuing machines, which was where the beauty of the new tram system failed: there were not enough machines to cater for needs, and bad temper ensued.

3

As Anna got off the tram, an altercation was breaking out in one of the long lines; an old lady with a walking stick had jumped the queue. Most people ignored her; they were accustomed to minor injustices, and the ethos of the Luas, Green Line, did not permit you to raise your voice or become embroiled in unseemly squabbles. But someone did not know the unwritten rules and was shouting in a loud voice, which had a working-class-estate accent.

'Hey you, get back to the end of the queue!'

He must have strayed in from the north or the west, since there were no working-class estates on this line.

The old lady hobbled on, pretending not to hear. Maybe she was deaf.

The objector, a middle-aged man in a tracksuit, followed her and confronted her. 'What the fuck do you think you're doing?' he said.

At this point the driver got out to intervene. 'Fuck' was not a Luas word. 'What's going on?' he asked, with a dry smile.

The man in the tracksuit squared up to him. 'She jumped the fuckin' queue. I've been standing here for ten fuckin' minutes and along comes madam and sails right up to the front.'

The driver looked at the old woman. She was dressed in a beige trouser suit and wore a small white sunhat. Her face was wrinkled but sunburned and her eyes were wide with surprise rather than indignation.

'What age are you?' asked the driver.

'I beg your pardon?' she asked, cupping a hand to her ear.

'Do you not have the free travel, missus?' he asked.

'Of course I do,' she said, hearing this time.

'You don't have to get a ticket. Just get on.'

'I didn't realise ...' she said. 'I never got the Luas before. I live in Greystones. I'm just going to visit an old friend in Dundrum, she's my daughter's godmother, you know, and I – '

'Well now you know,' said the driver. 'You don't need a ticket on the Luas. You can just get on.'

'Any time of the day?' she asked suspiciously.

'Any time of the day or night,' he said. 'No restrictions.'

'Isn't that wonderful?' said the old lady. 'I can't go on the bus during peak times, which is a nuisance because, you know, my memory is not what it used to be and – '

'Excuse me, missus,' said the driver. 'The tram's due to leave.' He nodded and went back to the cab.

The old lady climbed into the nearest coach.

Anna left the scene as the man in the tracksuit swore again and went to the back of the line. The commuters continued to squint at the screens on the ticket machines and tried to decipher their invisible instructions. The tram moved off.

Anna walked by the Green towards Grafton Street. The wide pavement was relatively uncluttered and she strolled easily down to the traffic lights at the Boer War memorial gate, where the jarveys parked their horses. The path under the darkening trees smelt of leaves and earth. There was a definite hint of autumn in the air, and of horse manure. It was a potent mix that stirred the soul uncomfortably. Only a few leaves had turned and the days were still exceptionally warm. But inexorably the evenings were drawing in and everything, the deep ochre mellowness of the sunlight, the silence of the birds, the brown and purple velvets and tweeds in the shop windows, reminded her that winter was on the way.

Autumn always saddened her, when she noticed it. But it had its compensations: the season of mists and mellow fruitfulness was also the season of book launches, openings and first nights. She was on her way to a book launch in the House of Lords, which this autumn was top of the league of fashionable locations from which to fling your latest work into the public domain, and watch it sink or swim, like a witch in the murky ducking pond of the book market. To the House of Lords they flocked this autumn, the glitterati and the celebrities, the literary journalists and social diarists and the elusive press photographers, and the derided wannabees, whom clever event organisers kept on their guest lists, since at least they could be guaranteed to show up.

Tonight Ireland's most important poet was publishing a new collection of essays. It was not as big an occasion as if he were launching a new collection of poetry, but it was nevertheless a major event in the literary calendar. The topic of the book was Irish identity, an old chestnut that continued to fascinate – though perhaps the word is too strong – as many people as it had recently begun to repel. But although the rebels declared that Ireland was no different from England or America, and insisted on locating their stories in anonymous places representative of the modern globe, some readers still wanted poems and stories about bogs and farms and derelict market towns in Leitrim and Laois and Limerick. They expected the leading writers to explore the tired old topics. They would be grateful to the Nobel laureate for attempting to satisfy their insatiable thirst for literature about the subject they loved best: themselves. They would all be there. And the people who thought all this Irish stuff was nonsense would be there, too, because everyone liked the Nobel laureate, and because, as well as being nice, he *was* the Nobel laureate and they were privileged to have received an invitation. Everyone who was anyone, and many who were nobody, would be at this event. Even Anna's husband, who thought literature was on a par with skate-boarding, a pastime for children, would deign to attend. She was meeting him outside. They would go in together.

She avoided a horse-manure pat on the edge of the footpath and squeezed between two jaunting cars parked outside the shop that used to be Habitat and was now boarded up, awaiting new tenants. Habitat had moved to an old bank in Suffolk Street; she must see what they had down there, she was often getting little gifts for people in the Avoca shop next door, where they had such pretty jars of pickles and jam, and such unusual toys and clothes for children.

A few people looked at her as she walked briskly down Grafton Street. She was not a supermodel by any means but something about her always attracted attention. Slight, of average height, she had unfashionable curly hair, and a face that reminded older people of dolls of their youth: Crolly dolls, with black ringlets, red smiles, and green dancing costumes. And indeed Anna, the granddaughter of a great Irish scholar, Seán Jack Ó Ceallaigh, had once been a champion Irish step-dancer, although she allowed very few people in on this particular secret. She still moved with a grace and a briskness that marked her out from the crowd, where all the young people walked with a slow, languid gait, as if they were going nowhere. This drew attention to her, apart from anything else.

Grafton Street was busy, but not too busy. She loved its energy, the happy throngs of shoppers, the buskers. There was one group playing Mozart outside Dunnes Stores, and outside Boots that little traveller boy with the freckles and red hair who had featured in a film, that film about the journalist who had been shot at the traffic lights, was singing his signature 'Fields of Athenry' to an enraptured crowd. Anna had heard him about a thousand times. Getting into the movies hadn't got him off the streets, apparently, or even got him to learn another song. His repertoire was limited to one.

She paused at Brown Thomas, which had an interesting window display. The clothes looked like something you'd buy at a jumble sale, prints and stripes and different kinds of material all mixed up together. Their display often looked like that, and very effective it was too, in a window. 'The small free birds fly,' the little boy sang, hauntingly, as Anna decided she would never wear such unstructured, messy clothes. Nobody in their right mind would. 'We had dreams and songs to sing,' he sang, as she tried to read the tiny price tags. Five hundred euro for a blouse that you could, certainly, pick up for fifty cents at any Oxfam shop. 'It's lonely round the fields of Athenry.'

She passed on around the corner to Suffolk Street and into the new Habitat. Someone had told her they had called it Shabbytat in London in the eighties, but over here its products were still desirable. Sofas, they consisted of mostly, and lamps. The sofas were grey tweed, dark red – all that ecru and pastel cotton was finished, there was a return to a 1960s retro look, a return to modernism. The lamps were more attractive, pale cylinders of light that would look great if placed directly on a wooden floor. A vast orange cube caught her eye. Anna wouldn't have minded something like that, as a talking point, for her hall, maybe. But it was not for sale, being part of an exhibition of twentieth-century furniture. How odd to see that caption: '20th century furniture'. It had been the twenty-first century already for half a decade but Anna found it difficult to regard the twentieth century as something that was already history. Already gone. It would always be her century, because she had been born in it, albeit well into its second half. The new century she would never appropriate in the same way. That would belong to people like Rory, her child, a person who had come into the world not long before the new millennium dawned, who would never know what it meant to write a year beginning with nineteen on the top of the letter or on a form. Anna still found the look of the new dates, two thousand and whatever, strange, spurious, as if this new millennium were a just a game, not to be taken seriously. The 1900s had solidity, as if the entire century had carried in it the deep values of its beginnings – the sacrifice of the Great War, the idealism of 1916, the other revolutions, the pain of the early decades of the new Irish state. The 1900s had their feet firmly planted on a ground of nobility and pain, whereas everything about the 2000s seemed flimsy, as if all life, in spite of the disasters and wars one heard about hourly, were as insubstantial as an episode of *The Simpsons*.

And, of course, the 1900s, like the millennium it wrapped up, had one great edge, historically, over the 2000s. In spite of everything, the century had finished. It was rounded off now, packed away, whole and entire and chock-a-block with event. Somehow it was hard to believe that the 2000s would have the same fate. It was difficult to envisage 2100, and only the wildest optimist could imagine that the year 3000 would ever dawn on this earth. But the 1900s had made it. They were a story with a beginning and an end. And to that story Anna felt she belonged.

She passed through the shop: as she had hoped, there was a door leading onto College Green, so it functioned as a short cut to where she wanted to go. She emerged from the calm colour of kitchenware and posters into a maelstrom of eighteenth-century grey buildings, nineteenth-century bronze statues, and twenty-first-century traffic. In the doorway she almost stumbled over a man who was spreading his sleeping bag in the porch of the shop; people who slept rough went to bed much earlier than anyone else. Some of them never seemed to get up, Anna thought, sticking her hand in her pocket and pulling out fifty cents. They were drug addicts and Alex told her not to give them money but she found it hard to pass one without putting something into their begging bowls, or begging coffee cups. Some superstitious instinct warned her that not to give alms would bring her bad luck, and she kept loose coins in her pocket so she would always have something small handy. It was a habit that tended to ruin the line of her coat, but that gave her an excuse to buy another one all the sooner. The small coins she would never have spent anyway – often she had to throw them away, those piles of five- and ten- and twenty-cent pieces, which accumulated in bowls and jars all over the house, and in the bottom of her handbags.

As she crossed the street to the Bank of Ireland she could see Alex. He was standing at the corner of Foster Place, waiting for her.

Two

Anna saw him as soon as she crossed the street but Alex did not see her because he was busily consulting his diary, a frown on his face. He was always consulting something; he never allowed himself a moment's idleness, unless it had been pre-ordained – an hour at the gym three times a week, a half an hour with the newspapers on Sunday morning, that sort of thing. Since he had studied for the Leaving Certificate and discovered that by using his time wisely he would get maximum points, he had never wasted a minute of his time. It was the key to success and to a morally justifiable existence, in his opinion. Some people, those who did not know him, believed that Alex's only motivation in life was to make as much money as he could. But Anna was aware that, unlike her, he was driven by a conscious personal ethic, which was to use every minute of his time on earth to achieve something. Once, he had achieved high grades, and now he achieved high figures in bank accounts. But he did not discount the possibility of other ways of measuring his success, in the future.

Trained as an actuary, he was now a successful property developer. Mainly thanks to his marriage to Anna, who had a minor reputation as a minor writer of books for children, he had managed to acquire a reputation as a man with an interest in the arts, and consequently – unlike Anna – sat on the boards of several cultural organisations, all of which hoped to benefit from his financial expertise and, at some stage, from his money. The meetings were, on the whole, excruciatingly boring; he put up with them because he liked being on the boards. Anna did not know why. They paid him a stipend, which accumulated – he earned about fifty thousand euro in expenses, in return for attending meetings. But he did not need the money, so his motives were not mercenary. So why did he do it? He did not really know himself. She had asked him and his answer was: 'Because they ask me, I suppose.' Once he said yes to membership, being diligent and active became a duty.

As a result of a rigorous regime of physical fitness, Alex did not look like a man who rested often. His body was trim and neat; he was slightly small, for a modern man, about five foot nine, but that was still taller than Anna. His skin was rather sallow, which made him look suntanned and healthy all the year round. His only flaw was his dark hair, or lack of it. It was getting quite thin, revealing very large ears, which no plastic surgeon could repair – not that any had been asked to do so. Alex did not worry about his ears. It was his balding head that bothered him – in winter he had taken to wearing a hat, but it was not winter yet so his bare patch was visible and gleamed in the last rays of the evening sun.

He was dressed in his working clothes, a dark navy suit and snow white shirt. His tie was a dark blue. How neat he looks! Anna thought, as she approached him, walking down the small, cobbled street, a strange street, going nowhere. But other people looked at him and admired his smartness, wondering how any man could have such a sparkling white shirt at this hour of the day. (Alex's secret was this: he put on a fresh shirt every morning at home and every evening at five in his office. On Friday evening he sent fourteen shirts to the dry-cleaners and got them back, cleaned and ironed, on Saturday afternoon. On Saturday and Sunday he wore a T-shirt and an old jumper with sleeves that had shrunk about ten years ago, to indicate to himself that he was not at work.)

Alex smiled cheerfully when he saw his wife and gave her an affectionate kiss on the cheek. She warmed to him momentarily. His manners were impeccable, she had to hand it to him. 'Of courtesy, it is much less than courage of heart or holiness' was a

11

line that often came to her mind when she was pleased by Alex's pretty ways. Hilaire Belloc. She thought. She'd learned it in school.

'And how are you?' he asked.

'Fine,' she said. 'How about you? Had a good day?'

'Yes,' he said. He never told her much about his days at work, considering them not worth talking about. She didn't know what exactly he was doing all the time; whenever she visited him in his office, he was talking on the phone. That seemed to be what his work consisted of. Talking on the phone, and attending meetings. Where he also talked, she presumed (wrongly; he said very little, which was generally taken as a sign of his superior intelligence). 'Will we go in? There's a crush, as you might expect.'

They made their way through a few lobbies and into the big old hall, with high painted ceilings, where Grattan's parliament used to assemble before the Act of Union ended the Irish parliament and brought them all over the water to Westminster, resulting in the decline of the status of Dublin as the second capital of the empire. From this decline the city had now, two hundred years on, recovered so completely that Dubliners believed there was not on earth a more desirable place in which to live, at least in the winter months (all successful Dubliners now had a place in France or Spain for the summer).

The hall was hot and smelt of wine and sweat. It was packed with people, many of whom Anna knew personally and several others whom she recognised because anyone who ever read a weekend newspaper would know their faces.

'The President hasn't arrived yet,' said Alex crossly. That had been one of his main reasons for coming, that the President would be in attendance. He liked to meet her casually at cultural events of this kind, to let her see that even though he was rich, he had a cultural dimension to his personality and deserved his places on all those boards. Apart from her, he had no interest in anyone at this party. He disliked writers in general, although he had not analysed the reason for this antipathy. Alex occasionally analysed his thoughts but never his feelings, unlike Anna, who devoted half her waking hours to this activity.

'No, but Seamus Heaney and Marie have!' said Anna, waving at the famous poetic couple, and pleased that he waved back

12

and Marie flashed her a beaming smile. They were kind; they waved back to most people.

'Hello, Anna.' Lilian Meaney, one of her personal friends, a novelist, came up to her. 'How are you? Do you know Christine Goodman?' She introduced her, although Anna had met Christine several times before at events of this kind, since the same people attended all of them.

Anna liked Lilian best of all the writers she knew. She had a special charm, a gift of intimacy, and she was never petty or malicious, like Anna or most of her friends. In addition, she loved literature and was rather serious about her reading and her writing, and about the way she lived her life. Lilian had published three novels and a few collections of short stories, as well as non-fiction. Her works were respected and two were taught on university courses, she had let it be known, but discreetly, so as not to annoy too many of her friends. Nevertheless most of her books were out of print and she had made very little money from her writing, just like almost all the writers in Anna's circle. At the moment, Lilian was working on a novel about Irish participation in the First World War. This book had occupied her for years, involving much research, and she had confessed to Anna that she was finding the writing of it very difficult. Now someone else had published a novel about Irish participation in the First World War, which was on the Booker short list.

'It's a big subject.' Lilian shrugged. 'I don't think it matters that he did it. My treatment is bound to be different. Anyway, my book may never get finished.'

That she could be so philosophical and resilient was something Anna admired. Much later she would recall this comment and ponder its significance. But now she let it glide off into the ether, with all the other comments that were being made at the launch. The slightly resigned, sad look Lilian's face sometimes wore when she talked about her writing moved Anna, however, and struck a tiny chord of terror in her heart. It was a look that many of her women writer friends wore, a look that suggested they had accepted that they were not going to make it, that they were not going, ever, to enter the golden circle where fiction was big business and writers were surrounded by phalanxes of well-wishing agents and editors and publishers, all anxious to

13

protect and nurture the talent that earned them their living. Anna, however, although she had enjoyed the most modest success so far, still believed she could and would break into one of those circles.

Christine had an absent-minded expression that told Anna she was one of the lucky souls who never worried about worldly things. These people were often poets, never fiction writers, or playwrights, the most mercenary of the lot. Christine was the typical poet, the poet who looked poetic and no doubt lived a poetic life. Her looks were pre-Raphaelite and she wore something commensurate – a flowing dark blue dress, printed all over with some generic, apple-blossomy-looking flower; it was rather like the garments in Brown Thomas's window, but probably bought at an Oxfam shop, which was where most poets shopped, Anna knew. And most of the novelists she knew as well. She herself was exceptional in having money, but it was Alex who earned it, not her.

'We were talking about the drag production of *The Importance of Being Earnest*,' Lilian said. 'Did you see it?'

'No,' said Anna. 'I didn't get around to it.' Typically. Although she went to a good many plays and films, she never seemed to have seen the ones people were talking about. Why hadn't she gone to *The Importance of Being Earnest*, in drag? Because she had seen it about a dozen times before, not in drag, that was why. It had seemed like a good reason for not going at the time, but now it seemed stupid.

'I wasn't sure about going,' said Lilian. 'I had reservations, about the all-male cast and everything. I mean, there are not enough parts for women as it is, etcetera, etcetera.'

'Or plays by women!' intercepted Anita, a would-be playwright who had joined them suddenly. She was one of the large loose circle of women writers to which Anna had belonged for years, who bumped into one another every couple of weeks at a launch or a reading. 'No plays by women, no parts for women, and they spend the whole summer doing a classic play by a man using an all-male cast! Phew!'

Anita Harkin was plump and forthright. She was always smiling, but her smile was mischievous. She dressed in bright colours, to spite all those who insisted on wearing black, she said, and to give the finger to people who thought fat women should dress down. Tonight she was togged out in an orange tent with black dots down the front. Anna thought her somewhat naive, but she was wary of her also and often avoided her.

'Yes, I agree with all that,' said Lilian. 'But even so, it was ... well, just wonderful!'

'I'm sure Alan Stanford was hilarious,' said Anna. He had played Lady Bracknell.

'They were *all* hilarious.' Lilian nodded, smiling at the memory.

So the conversation meandered on, like a wandering dog, taking odd twists and turns that made no sense. This could become boring but mostly Anna found it soothing. The content of the conversation didn't matter much, what she liked was being with her friends.

They started to talk about the forthcoming theatre festival, but most people could not remember what was on the programme, so they moved on to the novels on the Booker short list. This worked better. Anna had read four of the books and Lilian had read one, otherwise nobody had read any of them but they nevertheless had strong views as to who should win. Two of the short-listed writers were at the launch, and they all peered around discreetly, trying to locate them in the crowd. John Marvell, who had written a nostalgic novel about a country childhood, was secluded behind a pillar, looking shy and aloof. He was renowned for his reserve and was often said to be a genius. Jonathan Bewley, author of the novel about the First World War that Lilian hoped would not spoil her novel's chances, seemed to be chatting amiably to Seamus Heaney and the Director General of RTÉ.

'It would be nice to see one of them win,' said Lilian, referring to Jonathan and John, with at least a very convincing imitation of sincerity.

'Oh yes,' agreed Anna, without enthusiasm. She didn't care if they won or not. The only Irish author she really wanted to win the Booker Prize, ever, was herself, Anna Kelly Sweeney. But of course she would never admit that. And the Booker Prize had taken on the characteristics of the Cheltenham Gold Cup; you were expected to support the Irish horses, even though everyone knew they were so good because their owners got outrageously unfair tax breaks. And it always was uplifting to see the Irish horse romp home, as Lilian said. Unlike the horses, however, which often took the cup, an Irish book hardly ever won the prize. Recently, only Roddy Doyle had. And the snobbish critics still looked down their noses at him and pretended it had never happened.

'So why doesn't an Irish woman ever get on that short list?' Anita asked angrily. 'It's always those guys!'

Anna shrugged. She knew the correct answer. Jennifer Johnston had been on it, and Iris Murdoch had actually won the Booker, in 1978. Probably there had been others as well. But people forgot these things very quickly.

'Those guys are not any better than the Irish women novelists,' Anita went on. 'But they get all the attention. Nothing's changed.'

'Who are the Irish women novelists?' Anna ventured. She could hardly think of any apart from herself and Lilian, and they didn't count. 'So many of us write chick lit.'

'Apart from Edna O'Brien, Jennifer Johnston, Clare Boylan, Evelyn Conlon, Deirdre Madden, Anne Enright, Anne Haverty...' Anita frowned, trying to remember other novelists called Anne. There must be more ... Anne Brontë was the only name that came to mind. 'I could go on!' she announced breezily.

'Is there a conspiracy?' Lilian frowned too, because she found it hard to believe there could be. Lilian believed the best of people.

'It's called patriarchy,' said Anita, laughing. 'The guys are seen as more heavyweight. But when you read the books, you see that they are not in the least more heavyweight than the women. Still, they earn the big bucks and get on the short lists and are on the tip of everyone's tongue.'

'I don't know,' Anna said. Feminist ideology unnerved her. She did not know where she stood on it. When someone like Anita reeled off the names and numbers, it all sounded very convincing. But, like Lilian, she did not believe there was a conspiracy against women in Ireland. This wasn't Bloomsbury in 1895, which Anita seemed to forget. It was College Green in the twenty-first century. Apart from anything else, who would be bothered conspiring against women, or anyone, or anything, these days? Conspiring in that way implied a sense of purpose, energy, belief: like religion, conspiracies against women must belong to a past, in which one half of the population was sure of its beliefs and diligent enough to do something about them.

Anita didn't think so. 'They network,' she was saying; meaning, men network.

Anna gazed around the room wondering who she could find to talk to next. She wanted to network too.

'They create golden circles. Look at the acknowledgement lists at the front of their books – the same names on all of them. Important guys, publishers and famous male writers. Not their aunts and children and fellow writers' group members. They never belong to writers' groups, like us girls, but, boy, are they all in some sort of a group. Chaps who help them get along. Men are loyal to one another, it's some sort of atavistic thing, so they won't betray their mates when the Germans capture them and try to make them talk.'

Anna glided off in the middle of the tirade, looking for Alex. She couldn't see him in the sea of bodies, but found herself face to face suddenly with Jonathan Bewley. Since she knew him faintly, she said hello and 'Congratulations, Jonathan!' with her warmest, most hypocritical, smile.

'Thank you,' he said, in a friendly voice, but clearly he hadn't a clue who she was. He immediately turned to talk to someone else.

She turned on her heel, humiliated. Out of the frying pan into the fire. Now she found herself facing Carl Thompson, one of the Irish writers whom she would rather not meet, ever. Many years ago, she had reviewed his first novel in *Blackbird*, a college magazine. The review had not been favourable. Although she realised that the chances of Carl Thompson having seen that review were slim – the periodical had had a lifetime of six weeks, during which it appeared twice – everything about him indicated that yes, he had read it. Probably he had a very efficient clipping agent. He had never forgiven her.

As usual, he looked right past Anna. Damn him! she thought. What do I care? He had a reputation for being calculating. That's what Anita said. He was one of Anita's main bugbears. Anita said that she knew for a fact that Carl Thompson only talked to people who could further his career. Somebody who was a friend of Carl's had passed on this nugget of information to a friend of Anita's, and Anita had duly relayed it to everyone she knew. She added that Carl did not like women, although this was her own theory.

Another woman came along, and Carl welcomed her with open arms, literally, giving the lie to one of Anita's prejudices. He fell upon this woman, hugging her and kissing her. Katherine Molyneux. She was one of the few women novelists under the age of eighty of any repute in the entire country. 'Quirky' was the word most often applied to her and her work. That and 'intelligent'. She could be funny, and she delighted in mildly shocking tactics. Her clothes were always black, and loose – like so many others' clothes – but she might wear a bright pink headband, or carry a ridiculous handbag, to offset the dullness and emphasise the quirkiness. She was wearing a luminous pink headband now, with antennae, for some odd reason, the kind of thing children wore at parties. She looked like a benign beetle with pink horns. Anna would have liked to get to know this woman but she felt shut out from her world, the world of Jonathan Bewley and Carl Thompson. Whenever Anna had met them, they had been locked in a cliquish conversation, dropping names, talking about conferences they had been to and gigs they had done in Australia and America, and generally ensuring that people like Anna felt insignificant and unwanted.

The woman novelist nodded at Anna; she was friendlier than her male companions, but nevertheless there was an impatient *moue* on her face. Anna scanned the room looking for someone who could further *her* career. And who could be guaranteed not to look the other way when she approached them. There must be at least one in this gathering of hundreds.

She caught sight of Kate Murphy, the sister of her sister-in-law, Olwen, and moved as fast as she could in her direction. Kate was a useful contact, as well as being a relation.

'Anna! How lovely to see-ee you!' She beamed and kissed Anna on the cheeks, and looked wildly excited, although they had in fact met only two days ago. Kate worked in arts administration and often attended the same events as Anna. 'Do you know Vincy Erikson?'

'I don't think we've met.' Anna smiled at him. 'Hi, I'm Anna Kelly Sweeney. Your name is unusual. Is it Scandinavian?'

'My father is Swedish,' said Vincy. His hair was fair, curly, and quite long; it looked as if he hadn't combed it for some time. His clothes were careless, too, for an occasion such as this – no tie, and the jacket hung loosely on him, as if it belonged to someone else. But he was saved from looking scruffy by his skin. It was clean and pale, like a piece of polished pine. Anna had to suppress an urge to touch his face, to see how that strange skin felt.

'My sister is married to Anna's brother,' Kate said, laughing as if this were a joke.

'I'm delighted to meet you,' said Vincy. He had a mildly formal style of delivery, and this made him sound bright.

'Have you read the new book?' Kate nodded in the direction of Seamus Heaney.

'No, I haven't had a chance as yet,' said Anna, lying. She had had plenty of chances but hadn't bothered and probably never would. Tonight she would buy a copy and get it signed and stick it on the shelf where she put all the inscribed first editions she had collected over the years. In brighter moments she regarded them as an investment, rather than, more realistically, as dust traps. Seamus Heaney himself it was who had said that an unsigned book by him was now probably rarer than an inscribed copy, and he was probably right.

They were joined by Leo Kavanagh, someone they all vaguely knew, but whose name nobody could remember.

'Hi. Leo,' he said, apologetically, when he joined them, as if he were used to people not remembering his name.

'Oh *Leo*!' said Kate, beaming. 'How lovely to see you!'

It emerged that Leo lived in the country, in Kerry, where he ran a small poetry publishing house and was known for something else was well; Anna could not remember what it was just now. He had a bushy beard, and was bulky and short in a healthy-looking way. Anna guessed he was a vegetarian. He looked as if he ate a lot of carbohydrates. He seemed to be very interested in Kate.

'You're staying in Dublin for a few days?' she asked kindly. She would have liked to see Kate paired off with a good man like Leo. The talented, lovely girls she met all the time who were getting older and not settling down disturbed her. They never indicated in any way whatsoever that they wanted to settle down, but Anna, who had married when she was twenty-five, firmly believed that under the glossy, ever-cheerful exteriors they concealed this old-fashioned desire.

'Yes. I came up for a meeting of Killing Roads and a few other things, and now this.'

'Killing Roads?' That was what she had forgotten. Leo had founded a protest group some time ago, to heighten awareness of the dangerous state of Irish roads. And he was known to belong to other protest groups; he was a professional crank. But he was nice anyway. Solid.

'That's what we call it for short. The Enemies of the Killing Roads is its full, official, ridiculous title!' Leo said, in a deadpan voice. 'If you can think of a better one, let me know.'

'Hm, I will indeed,' said Anna.

But he wasn't listening to her. He was staring at Kate. She was looking very attractive tonight, Anna thought – she wore her hair in a strange, distracting style, most of it pulled across her forehead in a sort of coracle-shaped arc, which gave her a childish, gamine look. And she was lucky with her eyes: they were big saucers, enhanced by plenty of dark eye shadow and mascara.

But Kate was not returning Leo's gaze. She was much more interested in Vincy Erikson, who, with his fair hair, his slightly exotic accent, and a sort of energy he exuded, had a definite edge. Leo was, you had to acknowledge, a tiny bit dull. And then, he lived down there in the back of beyond and would be inaccessible most of the time. Kate might feel he was not worth taking an interest in. Anna felt sorry for him, as she observed this little unspoken drama. She was about to distract the unfortunate Leo, to ask him what it was like, living in the country in the winter, not because she cared but in order to pull him back into the conversation. But just then the speeches started.

They lasted for almost an hour: the President, resplendent in a lilac suit, the publisher, the chairman of the bank, a professor of Anglo-Irish literature, and Seamus Heaney, all went through their paces. Anna listened patiently for a while, trying to enjoy their words, their ideas. But soon her mind wandered. She tried to concentrate by comparing the different ways in which the speakers each pronounced basic words, like 'book' or 'poem'.

Buck, bewk; puem, powem, pom, pome … It was intriguing that someone who came from Belfast, like the President, could sound so different from someone who came from County Derry, like Seamus Heaney. It was intriguing that they both sounded so completely different from someone who came from Dublin, like the chairman of the bank, and from the publisher, who came from London, although they all spoke the same language and lived in the same place – right here, in Dublin.

Her mind wandered more. She looked around the vast room, at the sea of faces assembled under the elaborately plastered ceiling, to see how other people were responding. Most of them looked fascinated, and happy, to her surprise. She felt a stab of guilt. Was she the only person who got bored by worthy speeches? Suddenly she caught sight of Vincy Erikson. He was standing with his back to a pale yellow pillar. His eyes were closed and he seemed to be asleep. But as she stared, amused at the sight, he opened his eyes and looked back at her. They exchanged an understanding smile.

At that moment the last syllables of the last speech were uttered and the chamber exploded with an avalanche of grateful applause. Having slipped through the excited crowd, like a silent shadow, Alex appeared abruptly at her side. 'Let's go,' he said, under cover of the claps. 'As soon as she leaves.' He nodded impatiently in the direction of the President.

All around them, already, the crowd was breaking up into new formations, like cream breaking on the top of milk; some people used the opportunity of the speech end to move away from the company they were with and seek more congenial companions; many made a beeline for the door; the profligates settled in for an evening's chatter and drinking as close to the bar as they could be.

John Marvell and Carl Thompson were on their way out, together, no doubt going on to somewhere more exclusive and exciting. Katherine Molyneux was slipping around the walls, furtively, also making an exit. The successful people always left early. These were not even waiting for the President to go first.

'OK.' Anna would have liked to stay longer because so far nothing had really happened. She was still young enough to hope that a party, even a book launch, could offer something new and exciting. She had no idea what that could be. A laugh, a friend, an insight. A surprise.

'Hi, are you still here?' It was Anita the brash.

'We're just waiting for the President to leave,' said Anna.

'Oh is that protocol?' Anita asked. 'Well, it doesn't seem to bother some folks!' She looked around with a laugh. 'There's your brother over there. He's not one of the ones who's in a hurry to sneak out before the President, though, is he?' She made the gesture that mimics drinking.

Anna smiled uneasily and Alex snorted. 'You know my brother?' She blushed. Her brother was a part-time painter of portraits, but not as successful as she would have wished a brother of hers to be. He had a reputation for being a drinker, so he would be close to the drinks table, sucking up the wine.

'Yeah, I've known him for yonks. We had a good chat. He told me he was thinking of moving into town.'

'Let's go, Anna,' said Alex, paying no attention to Anita. His good manners wore thin very quickly when people impeded his wishes.

Anita scowled at Alex, which disconcerted him. 'Well, it's none of my business,' she said. 'Sorry I spoke. You better ask him about it.'

'Who is that woman?' asked Alex crossly, as they moved through the throng towards the door.

'Nobody,' said Anna carelessly, looking around for Gerry.

'Let's go now,' said Alex. 'She's left.' He was referring to the President, whose lilac suit could no longer be seen.

'I should talk to Gerry,' she said anxiously.

'He'll be drunk. Leave it. Whatever he's doing is his affair, he's a grown man,' said Alex.

Anna knew immediately that he knew something she did not know. What on earth did he mean, 'Whatever he's doing is his affair'?

'OK,' she said, knowing she would find out what the problem was sooner rather than later. 'I'll telephone him when I get home.'

At the exit, they bumped into Vincy Erikson and Kate.

Kate was getting her coat from the cloakroom. Vincy was standing by a marble pillar that supported the doorway, completely at ease. When Anna passed close to him, he looked up.

It was as if he had suddenly awoken from a deep sleep. Again. His eyes met hers briefly. He had not seen Alex, but somehow she felt he had instinctively realised that Alex was with her and that she was not a hundred per cent happy about that. She nodded at him but did not smile.

Then she was on Foster Place, in the dark.

Three

Anna's brother Gerry had not moved into town. Anita had either made up the story or had embroidered a rumour. How people got hold of such rumours relating to the most intimate details of the lives of their acquaintances was anybody's guess. No smoke without a fire, of course, and it was true that Gerry had been discovered to be having something – a relationship, a flirtation, a sexual dalliance, an affair (it depended on who you talked to) – with their au pair, and that Olwen, his wife, was annoyed about it. Very. His leaving the family home had been considered, shouted about, threatened, and even written about in cold little notes. But it had not, as yet, happened.

So after the launch, Gerry went home to the only home he had, the house he shared with Olwen and their two children in Bray, County Wicklow. He was among the very last guests to stagger out of the House of Lords, towards the taxi rank that was conveniently located at the corner of Foster Place. Gerry, however, did not get a taxi. He was never too drunk to remember that a taxi to Bray cost as much as two or three nights' decent drinking, or a return airfare to Barcelona or Paris or Seville, and so he found his way down to College Green, where he caught the 145 bus. It sped out of town along a traffic-free N11 and he was home long before midnight.

Olwen was up, watching television. The BBC was doing an

adaptation of *Bleak House*; she must have taped it, since it was screened at peak viewing time, at about nine o'clock.

When he came in and said good night, she did not answer. She had not spoken a word to him in four days.

'Be like that,' he said under his breath, and went up to bed.

They lived in a semi-detached house on a long street of such houses, on the north side of Bray. It was not a house he would have selected, given a choice: small, built in the 1980s, it represented to him and to Olwen more or less the opposite to their dream of what a family home should be. And what was that? A rambling vicarage, with about six bedrooms and a big kitchen, many secret little rooms, long mysterious passages, plum trees and artichokes in the garden. A babbling stream at the bottom of the lawn and a relaxing drive along the Bray Road into Dublin for the commuters. Or else a three-storeyed terraced red-brick in Ranelagh, with a good extended conservatory out the back and the Luas around the corner. Artists should live in places full of charm and character. Olwen, indeed, had lived in such a place, before she married Gerry.

But here they were, on Hazelwood Crescent, a place with no character at all, not in the estate agents' sense of the word, which concurred with Gerry's. The house had double-glazed PVC windows, which at this juncture in time and place were the archetypal symbol of suburban mediocrity; that you could catch a glimpse of the sea from the front ones and see the top of Sugar Loaf from the back was no compensation for the wound those windows inflicted on the ego of the socially ambitious. Which Gerry was, although he was too lazy to do much about it. His sister Anna's windows had a conservation order on them. That's what Gerry wanted, windows that were so significant the planning authorities could order you not to mess with them. Nobody cared what happened to windows, or anything else, on Hazelwood Crescent. You could knock the house down and build a concrete bunker in its place and the planning authorities would not bat an eyelid.

It was not, though, an address you had to be actively ashamed of. He knew many people who blushed to give their addresses, who lived in smaller houses than this in worse suburbs, where nice people, civil servants, schoolteachers, resided side by side with scobies and knackers, whose proximity lowered the value of everything except the groceries in the local rip-off Spar. Bray had banks and Tesco, Superquinn, mansions, leafy squares, as well as Hazelwood Crescent. It had a cinema and a theatre. At Christmas the local choir did the *Messiah* in the church on Main Street. Bray *had* a Main Street.

So it was OK. Perfectly OK. But very far from the cultural circles of Dublin, the circles to which Gerry belonged. Gerry seldom met people he knew here. He seldom met people it would be useful to know, who would boost his ego and promote his career. His failure to be a successful artist could be blamed partly on this – the suburban milieu in which he had been forced to reside. Real artists lived in old streets in the city centre, not out here in the sticks. Even the College of Art decreed that it was so: you could not have a college of art in a barren suburb; art belongs to colourful old urban milieux, where there are fruit and flower stalls on the street and interesting old gimcracks in the shop windows. There was nothing in the windows of Hazelwood Crescent except the backs of three-piece suites and the glow of plasma television screens.

Gerry's life had taken off on a course he had never planned or anticipated. Everything about it was almost the opposite of what he would have vaguely desired as a young man – but perhaps not desired strongly enough. He was not sure how that had happened – a series of unfortunate choices had led him in the wrong direction.

He was lost.

And that was probably why the unfortunate business with Ulla had happened.

Ulla from Karlstad, their au pair, now living somewhere in the midlands of Sweden.

He undressed rapidly and got into bed in the boxroom that served as a study and a spare room, and had been Ulla's until she left a fortnight ago, leaving the Kelly family in a state of chaos: Olwen sulking, while she gradually devised the most tortuous punishment possible for him, the children without anybody to mind them when they came home from playgroup and school. The difficulty of organising minders was complicated by Olwen's refusal to communicate orally with him. She left notes, brisk orders, written in block capitals in case he could use the excuse of not being able to decipher her handwriting, or in case her handwriting would be taken as a sign of intimacy: 'PICK UP JONATHAN 1.30'; 'EMILY DENTIST 11.00 AM'. No room for discussion. He had to obey the dispatches or he would be out – court-martialled, possibly, shot at dawn, on the patio.

Ulla had arrived just a year ago, in September last year, when Olwen went back to school after the summer holidays. Emily was five this year and in school until two; Jonathan had graduated from kindergarten to playgroup and finished at twelve. They no longer needed a full-time crèche, all they wanted was someone to mind them from noon until four, when Olwen usually got home from her secondary school, unless there was a meeting or an excursion. There hardly ever was – Olwen insisted that she was paid for teaching, not for going on excursions. Olwen, who was very practical, had decided that the cheapest form of childcare they could get now was an au pair.

'You only have to pay them about a hundred euro a week, and give them room and board,' she said. 'We'll be saving three hundred euro, every week! More, if she is anorexic.' The crèche had charged two hundred and fifty per child and had been a huge drain on the family budget – such a drain that Olwen had forced Gerry to have a vasectomy, since another child would have driven them onto the streets.

Gerry – ironic, ironic – had been completely against the au pair idea to begin with.

'We'll have someone here all the time!' he said, looking at the clematis that bloomed valiantly on the pergola Olwen had erected at the edge of their deck. The washing line was attached to the pergola, a touch he considered original and picturesque. Dangling from it were a few bright T-shirts, towels and tiny underpants, the universal flags of family occupancy. 'There'll be no privacy. And what if we don't get on with her?'

'We'll find a solution to that,' said Olwen. 'You're always so negative. She'll probably be fine, they usually are. And we won't even have to pay baby-sitters. We'll be able to go out again on Saturday nights, we can go to plays and things if we want to without remortgaging the house.'

They collected Ulla from the airport at midday on the Saturday before Olwen started back after the holidays. Olwen had been right: Ulla was fine. She didn't talk very much and her

English was weaker than the agency had promised. Something about her immediately reminded Gerry of an air hostess – though maybe that was the context in which they met her. Anyway, she was not the sort of girl who would end up in the A & E on Saturday nights, if demeanour was anything to go by (although he knew it was not; he did not look like the sort of person who would end up in A & E either, but he had, on two occasions, which Olwen did not know about).

'Hello, I am Ulla,' were her first words, pronounced with a big smile and a nod at the piece of cardboard bearing the slogan 'Welcome Ulla', which Olwen had forced Gerry to hold up in front of him.

She was just perfect, really. Neat-casual, in jeans and a nice little leather jacket, not too fat, not anorexic-looking either. Pretty enough but not stunning, which was exactly what you needed in an au pair. She was the sort of girl who would blend into anything, a school or a party or an office. Or a semi-detached house on Hazelwood Crescent.

Gerry felt cheated in one respect. Ulla did not look in the least bit Swedish. Her hair was not even blond; it was dark brown, black almost. And she was not tall and willowy, just an ordinary sort of height. She could have been from Blackrock, or even Bray. In fact, a lot of the girls he saw every day on the DART looked a lot more Scandinavian than she did.

Olwen had possibly selected her for just that reason. It was not that Gerry had ever strayed before but she would have played safe. Gerry had not been shown application forms or passport photos, but now he realised that these had been part of the process. Olwen had known what Ulla looked like months ago. The silly placard with the 'Welcome Ulla' sign had been quite unnecessary, designed to deceive him, probably.

The children were with them, appropriately, which meant that they had a noisy trip back from the airport, during which Emily quizzed Ulla.

'What age are you? ... Do you have any children? ... What's your favourite colour? ... What do you eat in Sweden? ... Are there Polar bears there?' And a thousand more such questions. 'How much money do you earn for looking after me and my brother?' Emily was always curious and unafraid to ask questions. She was a very clever child, in Gerry's opinion.

28

They were in the Volvo – his favourite material object in his whole life. Or, rather, his favourite object, animal, vegetable, mineral, or spiritual, in his whole life. The M50 was not busy at this time on Saturday, and he sped along at a steady 120. How he loved this road, especially now that it extended the whole way to Bray! Particularly now that he had the Volvo. He loved it especially as it moved southwards, savouring the view of the hills you got as you passed Exit 12, the great slices of granite at Exit 13 and the old-fashioned farm, a big bungalow and a barn with bales of hay in it, which you could see stretching right down to the edge of the motorway at Exit 16.

He loved having exits. He loved it that places with names like Rathfarnham and Dundrum had now been translated to short numbers, like 13. It was like moving from a Thomas Hardy sort of landscape into a modern American one, where a number – Route 3 – could evoke all sorts of memories and feelings. N11, which used to be the Bray Road, N7 instead of the Limerick Road, these were the brave new symbols of modern Ireland. Already Gerry got a nostalgic feeling in his gut when he thought about Exit 16, their exit. Exit 16 to Dublin 18 and then on a few yards over the border to the Garden of Ireland, County Wicklow. (They hadn't numbered the counties yet.)

'This is our ring road, the M50,' he explained in slow English to Ulla. Is that what you called it, a ring road? What's this they called the one around London?

She was sitting beside him in the passenger seat, since the children had insisted that Olwen sit in the back. 'Oh yes,' she said, without much enthusiasm.

The Orbital. Nice name. Suggestive of space ships rather than of traffic jams. He glanced at Ulla out of the corner of his eye and decided not to share this thought with her. 'Orbital' was not a word for your first hour speaking English.

'This road is brand new.' 'Brand new' was idiomatic and easy at the same time. Of course, calling the M50, nearly twenty years old and now riddled with roadworks, brand new was a bit of a simplification but you had to simplify for foreigners. 'The last stretch, which goes as far as where we live, Bray, opened only a few months ago. Before that we had to go to the airport, say, through the city centre.' He could sense how meaningless it all was as he said it but he couldn't stop himself once he'd got going.

'That was interesting,' she said, in the tone she might use to say, 'Please keep your seat belt fastened until the captain turns off the Fasten Seat Belt sign'. Odd that she did not know the present tense. Everything in its own good time.

'It used to take about two hours to get to the airport from Bray' – couldn't she realise what a hassle life had been, at least, even if she didn't notice the mountains, or the cows in that field at Exit 16? – 'now it takes about half an hour.'

'Mmm,' was what she said this time.

But neither did she express surprise or dismay when shown her tiny room, and the small bathroom she would share with the whole family, since the house had been built in that sad period between fireplaces in every room and en suites in every room – it belonged to the nothing-in-any-room school of architecture. Ulla settled in anyway. That is, she played with Jonathan and Emily, she answered questions when spoken to by Olwen and him, and she was as unobtrusive as a full-grown adult could be in a house containing one reception room, a kitchen, and four tiny bedrooms, of which hers was the tiniest. To suggestions that she should walk on the seafront or find the park or go to the cinema, she was positive and receptive. When she started to go to English classes in the town, she soon made friends with other Swedes – there seemed to be thousands of them in Bray – and could be seen sending text messages to them on her mobile phone.

'Aloof is how I would describe her,' Olwen said, as they lay in bed about a week after her arrival.

That was so like Olwen. Gerry could see that she was changing her mind already. However, he had discovered several years ago that saying 'I told you so' was not a wise option.

'She's a nice girl,' he said. 'Reliable and …' He considered. What else could you say about her? 'And decent,' he added lamely. 'The kids love her.'

'Yeah.' Olwen sounded sceptical. 'I wish she'd open up a bit more, that's all.'

'Ah,' said Gerry, yawning. 'She's not the type.'

How did he fall in love with her? How do you fall in love with a boring girl who happens to be an au pair in your house?

She grew on him, like a quiet picture that hangs on your wall unobtrusively for years and which you suddenly realise you could not live without.

The first move, towards the state in which he eventually – and now – found himself, had occurred during a dinner table discussion. They were all gathered around the table in the sunroom, as they called the little lean-to conservatory Olwen had had built at the back to extend the kitchen and create a family room of sorts. It was dark outside; December. The glass walls were black, reflecting the lamp, the candles on the table, creating a rather eerie, cavernlike atmosphere that he liked on the whole, although it made a lie of the epithet 'sunroom'. It was more of a moonroom.

For once, the discussion was not child-centred. Instead, it was focused on the kind of issue Irish people were obsessed with, it seemed to Ulla: namely, public transport. That and property values. In Sweden, property was there, and so was public transport, like the electricity or the water supply or the bank. It functioned, everyone used it, there were occasional breakdowns and failures, which were complained about, but on the whole nobody had an interest in it. Somebody looked after it – the commune, or the government, or somebody. Improvements were made periodically, without anyone caring much.

Here it was all very different. Gerry and Olwen talked about house prices, and about trains, buses and trams, at least three times a week. They were full of vehement opinions about all these things and expressed them trenchantly whenever they got a chance. A new bus lane was being created along a road in Bray. Trees would have to be cut down to make room for it and the residents of the road objected to this. A campaign against the cutting of the trees had been organised. Ulla had seen one of its projects: the protesters had tied yellow ribbons around the trees. She did not really know what the significance of ribbons, or the colour yellow, was in this context, but the ribbons looked quite pretty.

'We *need* an efficient bus service,' said Gerry. This was always his tack: practicality.

'Those trees are two hundred years old,' Olwen said. This was one of the ridiculous myths that was circulating in the town, along with others, some more outlandish. The trees were indigenous Irish oak. Some people were saying they were a thousand years old and the Fianna had hunted in them. The roots of

31

the trees underlay the houses and if you cut them down, the foundations would implode. If the trees were cut down, there would be no songbirds in Bray ever again. Or oxygen.

'I doubt it,' said Gerry. 'Those houses are only about eighty years old and the trees were planted then.'

'Are you saying we should just cut down everything to make room for roads and buses?' Olwen always deflected his logic with anger, which he hated. 'That the N3 should be allowed to destroy Tara, like the N11 played havoc with the ancient Irish wood in the Glen of the Downs.'

'It takes us hours to get to work in the morning,' said Gerry. 'We need more buses from Bray to town. If we have to cut down a few trees, well … They're just trees, not curly headed children.'

And Ulla laughed.

She caught his eye and actually laughed.

Olwen, who had been about to get really angry (she had her manic premenstrual look in her eye), got up and put on the kettle for tea; peace descended into the moonroom.

From such a simple seed a great emotion grew and thrived.

Gerry had felt a stab of gratitude that day at the table. It took him unawares. Just because she laughed at a bad joke – a cliché, but she wouldn't know that, her English was still bad. Just because her eyes caught his for a second of understanding.

He'd fielded sharper cupid's darts than that, sent them hurtling back right where they came from, in the office and elsewhere. Of course, the women in the office and elsewhere were not in his house, all the time. You did not meet them as you stumbled along the landing in your pyjamas, or as you groped on the doorstep for the milk cartons before the sun was up.

But Ulla was always popping up in the most unlikely situations.

She had seemed nondescript, but gradually her small figure and her pale face got a grip on his imagination. Her eyes, which he had never paid any attention to, began to intensify in colour and tantalise in expression. Before, they had seemed un-remarkable, light blue eyes. Now he noticed details: they were veined with green. When she sat facing the kitchen window in the afternoon, when the sun flooded the back of the house, they changed colour and became entirely green. Her other features, small and neat, appeared to him exquisitely moulded, like that of some porcelain ornament. One day at breakfast he found himself gazing at her ear, small and shapely, whorled like a beautiful shell. He compared it to Olwen's ears. They were hidden behind her hair, because they were too big. Ulla's ears were smaller even than Emily's. That nature could create such tiny intricate things suddenly astonished him. What a miracle she was!

Her straight, dark hair shone mysteriously. Oh dim dark waves, he thought, knowing he had read that phrase somewhere long ago. In school. Or maybe he had heard it at one of the poetry readings he went to, to satisfy Olwen's sister, Kate. Ulla's dullness, her lack of opinions, her air-hostessyness, stopped being dull and started being appealing. Whereas she had been boring, now she seemed simply, delightfully, sane. She did not have rigid views, crazy views, like Olwen, who seemed more and more bossy, opinionated, silly as time went on. Ulla was a rock of common sense and calmness.

Obviously he was not going to do anything about his feelings. She was a young woman, living in his house and he was in a position of trust. He was a responsible adult, a father, a married man.

For months – until May, to be precise, i.e. six months – he nurtured his growing affection for her in secret, enjoying it like a precious little jewel, a little pearly ear, he carried around in his pocket and could take out and look at from time to time, and fondle. But he soon understood that his feelings were reciprocated. Without a word being said, Ulla made it clear. On joyous days, her eyes met his and spoke to him; they were red-letter days. On B days, she would indicate her affection in some more indirect fashion, by avoiding him on the stairs, or going out when he came into the house. Those gestures were not so cheering, but he interpreted them in a positive way.

She continued to be a good au pair. The children continued to love her and Olwen to appreciate, if not like, her: she was completely reliable, but she had not become a friend, which was something Olwen had hoped for, unconsciously – to acquire a female ally. Ulla was never exactly cold, never impolite, but she kept her distance. 'Reserved' was the adjective Olwen used to describe her when she was talking about her to friends, as she frequently was. They chatted endlessly about their au pairs, complaining about them mostly, when they weren't complaining about their colleagues at work. That is why woman are so much healthier, mentally, than men: they spend most of their spare time castigating their enemies behind their backs, so they don't bottle up pain; they try to spread it around, like manure.

Olwen had wanted a miracle, someone who would transform the house with a glow of warmth and humanity and understanding, who would be always there to do her bidding when required and would conveniently vanish at other times. A treasure. Ulla was not a treasure; she was just a reliable au pair doing her job.

And having an affair with the man of the house.

Although Olwen did not know that. Not yet.

On the 5th of May Gerry and Ulla went to bed together. Olwen was at school, supervising end-of-term exams and trying to prevent the sixth years from committing suicide at least until after they had completed the Leaving Certificate and left school. It was the busiest month of the year for her.

Ulla's contract was up on the 6th of June, the day before the Leaving Cert would begin and the day Olwen would get her holidays. Probably the imminence of her departure had precipitated the consummation of the affair. But Olwen, miraculously as it seemed to both of them, suddenly asked Ulla to stay until the 1st of July, because she wanted to go away on a short trip with her book club as soon as school broke up. Someone had got a wonderful offer of a week in a five star hotel, with spa and beauty treatment, in Croatia. The chance of a week partly in the sun, partly in the spa, partly in a bar drinking wine or whatever it was they drank in Croatia, the chance of an entire week's gossip was too good to miss.

Did Gerry agree?

Certainly. Most certainly. Off you go, my dear. It will crown you. You deserve a treat after working so hard all year.

Ulla and Gerry had a whole week to themselves.

This cemented the relationship so much that Ulla could not bear the idea of parting from him on the 1st of July. Or ever. She got a job in a lunchtime café owned by a consortium of fellow Swedes, and a room in a shared house in Ballyfermot.

'I can stay in Ireland for as long as I like,' she told Gerry blissfully. 'Forever, if that is what we want.'

That was the first time Gerry felt another kind of stab. A stab of fear.

And very soon after this conversation, and after Ulla had moved into the house in Ballyfermot, a quality of hers that he had ignored, although he had known it existed, began to intrude more and more uncomfortably, then dangerously, into his life. The quality in question was her honesty, which came in a bulky package, accompanied by honesty's boon companions: integrity and foolhardiness. With a large dash of obstinacy thrown into the pernicious mix.

Ulla was as honest as the day and as stubborn as a mule.

These qualities began to detract from the seductiveness of her shell-shaped ears.

What she wanted was expressed in a variety of complicated ways but essentially it boiled down to this: Gerry was to confess everything to Olwen and then move in with her.

This all emerged gradually, over a period of about a month, the month after she left the house and moved in with the Swedish sandwich girls. By the end of the month, her emotions had changed from tenderness and passion to resentment and passion, and Gerry's had changed from love and lust to a very strong desire to escape from what had recently been Ulla's delicate baby hands and now were her hawk-like little clutches.

'I am sorry, I abused my position as your boss,' he said, in what he hoped, forlornly, was his farewell speech. 'You are very young and you should go back to Sweden and to college, as you had planned. I love you but I can't look after you.'

'Why the fuck not?' she asked angrily. Her command of idiom had improved since moving to Ballyfermot.

He shrugged. 'Because I have responsibilities to my children,' he said.

'I don't see what that has to do with it,' she said. 'Lots of people are divorced. In Sweden it is very common. The children don't have to suffer.'

And so on. She had plenty of arguments, and no lack of good English in which to articulate them. It seemed that the lessons at the ESOL place had been of a high standard.

He declared he could not see her again, and walked away.

35

Her next move was more vindictive than honest. She began to telephone the house and ask to speak to him, even when Olwen answered the phone. It took Olwen less than two days to smell a rat. When she next got an opportunity, she walked into the sandwich bar on Leeson Street where Ulla chopped onions and sliced ham for eight hours a day, and asked her to have a chat.

True to form, Ulla told her everything immediately. She never told a lie. Even to save her lover's skin. What had been one of her great advantages as an au pair, her relentless honesty, was now Gerry's nemesis.

That had been at the end of August.

Since then, Olwen had not spoken one word to Gerry. Ulla had also disappeared from his life, and from the sandwich bar and, he sincerely hoped, from the country. With any luck she was back where she came from, in that godforsaken town in the middle of Sweden. He missed her but had no intention of contacting her again.

The immediate problem for him was where he would be sleeping tomorrow night, or next week. Would Olwen, when her period of contemplative sulking was over, forgive him, stay on track, resume the journey to their nuptially agreed shared destination (i.e. death)? Or would she decide on a radical change and send him off in some other direction, down yet another byroad to God know's where?

Not for the first time, Gerry was lost in the forest of his own life.

Four

Anna's mornings were usually spent writing in her study, while over the rest of the house her cleaner, Ludmilla, roamed at will, tidying up and making the house ready for the afternoon. Anna often joined Ludmilla for a cup of coffee and a sandwich at lunchtime, but her mornings until then were her own. Her eleven o'clock coffee she took in solitude, or in the company of the family cat, Chekhov – so-named by Alex, who said he knew at least ten cats called Pushkin. There was an electric kettle conveniently placed close to her desk, to ensure that she avoided distractions while engaged in the important task of working at her books.

The study was at the front of the house, which overlooked Killiney Bay, and there she spent two or three hours every day writing novels for young people, as she liked to call them. So far, three had been published. All were historical, one set during the 1798, one during the Great Famine, and one during 1916. But now she was working on a contemporary fantasy story, in which supernatural beings played no small part. Her work was, she knew, highly original in execution, but its genesis had not been uninfluenced by the success of *Harry Potter* and its plot owed a certain amount to the books in which he features as the eponymous hero.

There were good sales for historical fiction for children, at least in Ireland. Teachers liked it, and children, the most tolerant of all readerships, did not mind, even if their first preference was for cheap humour and contrived nonsense literature. Competing with books called *The Unfortunate Adventures of the Goosebump Grundies* and authors with unlikely names like Snivelly Crickets, Anna Kelly Sweeney's historical novels for young people had done not too badly. Her third novel had sold twenty thousand copies, which, her publisher assured her, was very good for Ireland. But her royalties on the twenty thousand copies had amounted to just over six thousand euro, not a lot for a year's work. True, she did not need money, since Alex made so much of it, but like many children's writers she looked at the *Harry Potter* phenomenon with a rush of competitiveness. She would like to know that her books, too, were *worth* millions of euros. It was not just about the money: the money, she believed, would be no more than a token of the success of her work, of its ultimate value as literature, or entertainment, or whatever – Anna was not entirely sure what, exactly, she was writing, just as she had never really asked herself why she was doing it. So how else could its value, or her value, be assessed, except in terms of the market? It was the only objective criterion of literary success, any success, when it came right down to it. That was the point. Of course, she would not mind being a multimillionaire in her own right as a little bonus. If J.K. Rowling could do it, why not Anna Kelly Sweeney?

Thus reasoned Anna, and no doubt hundreds or thousands of other writers for children all over the world.

Fantasy was the way to go.

The children liked it.

The market demanded it.

Anna had never written fantasy before, but so what? She *had* fantasy. You couldn't write anything, even history, without at least a modicum of that.

What she was finding, though, was that you needed an awful lot of the commodity to write this fantasy stuff. It was easy at the start, but after about chapter two she began to understand that it was much harder than the historical novels. You had to make the whole thing up and go on making it up right to the end, whereas with historical fiction you could pick and choose: invent a bit, copy a bit, steal a bit. If invention failed, research – on the net as often as not, what could be handier? – would fill the gaps.

But there was no website for 'Great ideas for *Harry Potter*-style novels'. She had checked, and under other similar sounding words as well. (There were plenty of other ideas, and even programmes you could buy with your credit card, which would give you a template for a novel. All you had to do was fill in the names, the places, the descriptions, the dialogue … Easy-peasy. She had added some of those sites to her 'Favorites', for a rainy day.)

Oh well, she was enjoying the challenge of flogging her imagination as if it were a sluggish galley slave, and trying to get some work out of it. So she encouraged herself. And her imagination was becoming more active, as it got more exercise. It was learning to stand on its own two feet. Looking out at the ever-changing sea, opening her window to sniff the salt air, ideas came to Anna – most of the time anyway. She was working diligently, busily making a vast plan – this was what J.K.R. had done, she had made a plan – with chapter headings and content descriptions, character biographies, maps of locations, before moving on to write anything. It was like being an architect, something which she had often thought she might have been had she not gone the literary way. (She had also thought she might have been a doctor, or a teacher, or a journalist, or an organic farmer – the trouble with life was that the choices became more and more limited as soon as you reached the age of about twenty-five.)

At one o'clock she stopped to have lunch with Ludmilla, and to give her her instructions for the next day. Ludmilla was a treasure; she cost very little and worked like a trooper. But there was something about her that Anna didn't like – like Ulla in Bray, Ludmilla was aloof, and, unlike Ulla, Anna sensed, disapproving. But she felt this about almost everyone who came into the house to work for her. They all seemed to see through Anna, and reach the same conclusion: namely, that she was not up to scratch.

Ludmilla seldom revealed anything to Anna about her own life. She was Lithuanian and had let it be known that she came from a village fifty kilometres from Klaipeda and that she had been a teacher once, but that was about all. Anna did not know where she lived in Dublin, or what she did when she was not cleaning the Kelly Sweeney homestead, still less whether she had a boyfriend, or any friend at all.

After these uneasy, largely silent, lunch breaks, Anna usually drove around the Vico Road to the multidenominational school where Rory was a pupil. Then she gave Rory a snack and handed him over to Luz Mar, the Spanish au pair, who supervised his homework or brought him to his riding, music, swimming, football or karate lesson. Meanwhile, Anna spent her afternoons shopping, or going to art exhibitions in town, or meeting someone for coffee.

Today, the day after the launch in the House of Lords, she had planned to go to the Dundrum Shopping Centre to buy an evening dress, which she needed for a do they were invited to in three weeks' time – a dinner at Áras an Uachtaráin. Alex had been invited by the President. Spouses had been included in the invitations, and since Anna had not been to the Áras before, she was happy to accompany her husband on this occasion.

She changed her clothes, from the tracksuit in which she wrote her books to something smart – jeans and a new jacket – and put on her make-up. Normally she would not have bothered changing clothes to go shopping, but after one unpleasant occasion when she had dropped in to the Dundrum Centre in an old anorak and baggy trousers, she realised one had to dress up for this particular consumer experience. Her toilet complete, she hopped into her Land Rover and drove to Exit 15 and onto the M50. In a miraculous ten minutes she was swinging into the Green car park deep under the village of Dundrum. Guides in yellow jackets waved her to a free spot. Then she followed various colour-coded arrows to a lift that elevated her into the shopping centre – a modern apotheosis.

She emerged from the dim underground into a brilliantly lit palace of glass and mirrors. Everything was shining, reflective or transparent: the lifts were made of glass, so were the sides of the stairs; everywhere she went she caught sight of herself, reflected in some bright surface, rubbing shoulders with well-dressed people. Even in the early afternoon there were no old people here, hobbling around with their trolleys, or flabby women with streaky orange hair and plastic bags, the kind of people you found shopping in the afternoon in ordinary places. And there were no men. Not one. Only young women with good coiffures and elegant bags bearing the logos of the most fashionable shops and smiling brightly at one another as they made ironic comments. Most of them hunted in pairs, which was convenient for the coffee breaks.

Anna still found the place seductive but bewildering. She stood at the edge of the mall, sniffing the aroma of confectionery and coffee that floated up from the many cafés, gazing at the bright vista, and tried to get her bearings. She had no idea where she was, in relation to anything that lay outside the walls; the points of the compass were meaningless in here; she did not even know which floor she was on, or how many there were – there was a confusing arrangement of storeys and mezzanines, which meant that one always felt lost, but lost pleasantly, as in a dream of wonderland, a paradise of pleasures.

The newest and most prestigious shop was the one she wanted to visit first. With luck she would find what she needed there, and then get out of the place. But there was no indication as to where it was located. Bracing herself, she set off along the gleaming concourse.

Distractions abounded. Almost all the shops were dedicated to women's clothing, and so there was reason to pause at each and every window, and to pop inside on most occasions, even though she had a firm design and purpose. An hour passed, as she fondled textiles and riffled through rails of dresses and wraps, and also suits and trousers and shoes and bags, things she was not intending to buy today. She found herself with a new pink handbag and a short tweed skirt, and still not in the shop she had intended to visit first, when her phone rang.

'Hi, it's Gerry,' said her brother.

Anna was taken aback. Gerry never telephoned her.

'Hello Gerry,' she said. She wondered if her mother had had a heart attack. Usually if Gerry phoned it was with some bad news connected with her mother, whom Anna neglected guiltily. The light in the shopping centre seemed to grow dim.

'It's not Mam,' he said quickly. 'Can I come to see you?' he asked, in a voice that sounded vulnerable.

'Sure, of course,' she said. What had she on this evening? A poetry book launch, but she could pass it up, if necessary. 'What's wrong?'

'Everything is upset at home,' he said. 'I'll explain when I see you.'

'OK then. I'm out right now but come around in ... whenever. When would you like to drop in?'

'After work,' he said. 'About six? Is that OK?'

'Great. We'd love to see you,' she said. And she added, 'Will Olwen come too?'

There was a pause.

'No,' he said. 'I'll explain when I see you. OK? Thanks, Anna, you're a star. See you later.'

So that was it. Suddenly the whole shopping centre changed. Like fairy gold, it was transformed to a heap of dry leaves before her eyes. Its lights no longer dazzled, but irritated. Its heaps of sparkling things no longer charmed, but took on the quality of ephemeral rubbish. The sounds, human voices, ringing registers, clattering crockery, buzzing machines, were a cacophony of misery – the voices of the damned.

'She's thrown me out,' Gerry said. He paused, then repeated a sentence he had used on the phone. 'Everything is upset at home.'

He was sitting at the kitchen table drinking red wine, while Anna stirred chopped-up chicken in the pan. Rory was watching television in the den and Alex was at a meeting of one of his boards. A lot of them met at dinner time.

'Oh dear,' said Anna. 'I'd no idea all this was going on.' She looked into the pan to ensure he would not notice that she was not telling the whole truth.

'It's my own stupid fault,' he said. 'I deserve it. I don't blame her in the least.'

'No,' said Anna thoughtfully, looking over at him.

'Though I worry about the kids. Not that I'm the world's best dad ... still ...'

'You're a good dad,' Anna said.

She believed he was exemplary, or would have been if he didn't drink too much and carry on with the au pair. He played with his children, though, and brought them to football matches and events they enjoyed. The ice rink at Christmas, the beach in the summer. Alex loved Rory better than his life but became bored if he played with him for longer than five minutes. Alex felt any time spent away from his work was time wasted. Gerry, on the other hand, carried on like a ten-year-old child. It was curious how men differed from one another in these respects, when in so many others they were alike.

'Anyway, I'll have to find somewhere, a flat, I suppose, a bedsitter.'

'Yes. You shouldn't have a problem. They say it's easy to find rented accommodation in Dublin right now,' she said. Alex owned six apartments in the docklands area – much too expensive for Gerry – and had mentioned that letting was not as easy as it had been when the pool of flats was smaller.

'Mm.' Gerry considered his financial situation. Well, at least Olwen worked. But together they managed to pay the mortgage and live a reasonable lifestyle. Would she expect him to go on footing the mortgage and paying for his own place? Would he be able to stop his standing order without her consent?

'You're welcome to stay here for a week or so, until you find a place,' Anna offered, knowing Alex would not be best pleased. They had two spare bedrooms, however, so he would just have to put up with it.

Gerry looked around the kitchen, appreciating the size of his sister's accommodation. This room was five times as big as his kitchen in Bray. It had a beamed ceiling and one wall made entirely of glass, which looked out on a marble patio and large terracotta urns overflowing with trailing plants; in the distance, down the garden, large beech trees and small birches spread graceful branches, their leaves a deep, luscious yellow that glowed in the autumn twilight.

'Thanks, you are an angel.' He gave her a slightly cold kiss. He'd been hoping she would offer him one of Alex's apartments. 'I won't impose. I'll get somewhere as fast as I can.' Mean, they were. That's how they had it. An apartment would have solved all his problems.

'You'll have to,' she laughed, as she carried the pot of rice to the sink and poured it into the silver colander. You know what Alex is like, she might have added, but did not. She watched the water draining into the sink, forming a gelatinous grey puddle on the porcelain, faintly disgusting, as the rice became dry and pure and snowy. She gave it a few smart shakes and rinsed it for a second under the tap. She always enjoyed straining rice. It was the child in her that took pleasure in the simple task, she mused, as she turned back to Gerry and his problems.

'He's found a place in Sheriff Street,' she said to Olwen.

Anna was at another kitchen table, Olwen's, in the house in Bray. Two weeks had passed.

'I know,' said Olwen. 'It feels very strange. But what can I do?'

Anna looked around Olwen's kitchen, reading it as a symbol of her sister-in-law's life, as Gerry had looked around hers a few weeks ago. They had made every attempt to make it attractive, with terracotta tiles on the floor and fitted beech presses all around, but nothing could compensate for its cramped dimensions. It was full of furniture, and cluttered up with all kinds of things: on the counter top there was a packet of cornflakes, a bottle of ketchup, several jars of coffee, a slice of toast, cups, jugs, a little pile of pills, letters, a few newspapers, and other items. The place smelt strongly of cat pee, which Olwen did not seem to notice. She had no help now. No au pair, no cleaner, and now not even a husband who might occasionally throw out the cat. Olwen, who had been brought up in a comfortable house in Foxrock where there had always been hired help, was reduced to this, thanks to having married Gerry. Anna suppressed a shudder, seeing Pushkin, crouched on top of the cooker, staring malevolently at her. You too could have ended up like this, his hard green eyes seemed to tell her. But Anna had eluded Olwen's fate, quite unconsciously, so it seemed, by the simple expedient of falling in love with Alex. Alex, rich and dutiful, and kind as well. Alex who would not in his wildest dreams consider being unfaithful to her. Anna got Alex, and Olwen got Gerry. That was the luck of the draw.

'I'm partisan, no doubt, but I wonder if you couldn't try to patch it up and start again?'

Olwen was stony-faced. Stubbornness was her staunchest characteristic and she would not capitulate easily. Still, the lines in her skin and the mess in the kitchen told their own story.

Anna realised she would have to employ a more indirect strategy to persuade Olwen to do the sensible thing. She hugged Olwen warmly. 'He's been a complete eejit,' she said. 'You're doing the right thing and you are very brave.'

She let this sink in and was rewarded with a minuscule but perceptible lightening of expression in Olwen's sad eyes.

'You seem to be doing fine.' She smelt the cat pee again and suppressed another shudder. 'And Gerry is grand too, in his little flat. It's quite nice. I visited him a few days ago.'

'Actually it's very tough, being here alone with the children,' Olwen said crossly.

Anna feigned a look of surprise. 'Is it?'

'Of course it is. There's nobody to do anything ... At least he used to bring them to football, and mind them on Saturdays. And he did the washing up. Apart from anything else, I've got all that to do myself. I'm a wreck.'

'Mm.' Anna looked at her carefully. She was indeed a wreck. Her hair needed cutting, and colouring too – could some of her hair have turned in just a fortnight? 'Probably the thing to do is to get another au pair, or at least a cleaner.' And an appointment with a good hairdresser.

'Yeah right,' said Olwen, shaking her head. 'I need that, but I haven't got the energy to look for them. And I can't afford it either.'

Exactly.

That was what would save the marriage, eventually, Anna knew. People like Olwen and Gerry could not afford to separate. Divorce was available in Ireland these days, but it had arrived, strangely enough, at the same time as the big increase in house prices. When people could afford to divorce, it wasn't available, and then when it became available, it became unaffordable. Almost overnight. The free market economy was doing what the Church had done for centuries: reinforcing the institution Joyce had dubbed 'the Irish marriage': couples who stayed together even though they couldn't stand the sight of one another.

Anna did not really consider this a very bad arrangement. Life was easier for everyone if couples stayed together and made the best of it. It made for a cohesive society. So they said.

'You might consider it in the short term?' Anna suggested. 'It would make life so much more manageable for you, I think. I mean, I don't know what I'd do without Ludmilla.'

'And you don't even work,' said Olwen.

Anna coloured and felt an angry retort rising. It was astonishing how many people believed that writing, especially writing for children, was not really work, but something that happened by some sort of magic and did not require time or effort. You switched on your computer and the book appeared on the screen, was what they seemed to believe. They insisted on regarding Anna's work, Anna's *job*, as one of the more undemanding hobbies, like flower-arranging or embroidery, just because she did it at home and was not paid by the hour or the week, or whatever way they operated. And this was one more reason to finish her *Harry Potter*-style bestseller and show the blighters. They only believed writers who made masses of money and became household names counted as real workers. On a par with themselves in their nine-to-five slavery. Or, in Olwen's case, nine to half past two, seven and a half months of the year.

But for the sake of her brother, she suppressed these thoughts and smiled sweetly at Olwen. 'No,' she said. 'I don't.' It was very hard to utter those words. 'And I only have one child. But even so ... think about it. I'll ask Ludmilla if she knows anyone.'

Fat chance.

'OK,' said Olwen, in a voice that was flat and despairing.

Five

Leo Kavanagh, the publisher from Dingle whom Anna had immediately summed up as dull and boring when she had met him at the Seamus Heaney event, spent the day after the book launch engaged in the dull and boring activities that largely constituted his life.

His morning was spent at a meeting with the Arts Council and his afternoon at a lengthy meeting of one of the Irish language organisations that grant-aided his publications. For his evening entertainment he had convened a meeting – likely to be the longest of the lot – of the organisation he himself had founded about a year ago, The Enemies of the Killing Roads, or, as he had observed to Anna the night before, Killing Roads, as it was usually referred to by those who were aware of its existence. Not many.

The prospect of that particular meeting hung over Leo all day, casting a dark shadow on the others. Dull as they were, they would, he knew, be far superseded in dullness by the meeting in the evening. And the vision of an alternative meeting taunted him. A meeting with Kate Murphy. That the same word could be applied to that encounter and the event he was about to endure was curious. Dinner with Kate Murphy, in a candle-lit restaurant, the mellow light dappling her childish face, the atmosphere warm with the promise of love … He could see it, in his mind's eye, perfectly vividly, as if it were a reality. And at the same time he knew it was far from real. He was both enchanted and tortured by it. If only his dream could come true … it could so easily, so easily, it seemed to him. It depended only on her, on Kate saying yes.

How did she actually feel about him? That was the question. She was difficult to read. She had been very friendly last night. And on the other hand, he suspected she liked that other fellow, that Swedish fellow who looked like a mean and hungry wolf. Still she had given him, Leo, her card without hesitation, which looked promising. And then she had said she wasn't free to meet him today or tonight, which didn't. He could be sensible. He could just take her excuse at face value, interpret it literally. She was genuinely busy; there was no personal slight intended. But there were other ways to read her ambivalence. If she liked him as much as he liked her, wouldn't she have changed her plans, made an effort to meet him if only for a cup of coffee? Would that have been so difficult to fit in? How busy could an administrator at Poetry Plus actually be?

These thoughts were not uplifting. On the whole, he inclined towards the more negative reading.

He had a miserable day.

And then there was Killing Roads.

Killing Roads: a group, an organisation, a committee – it was hard to know what it was – had been established to solve a problem, but, like a lot of such organisations, it had quickly become a problem itself. There were several difficulties with this group, apart from its name – try as he might Leo had been unable to find a better one, and the members of the group were either so unimaginative or so lazy that they had not even tried at all. That was another problem: the general laziness, apathy and lack of imagination of all the members. And the third was that there were hardly any members anyway. Although he had tried to make this group large, busy and important on a national scale, his efforts to do so had been completely in vain. Hardly anyone joined. Hardly anyone even knew of its existence. Hardly anyone, it seemed to Leo, cared that the death toll on Irish roads was the highest in the Western world. In Kerry – where the road carnage was very bad – there was absolutely no interest in it, and so its extremely intermittent meetings were now confined to Dublin.

Leo usually managed to set one up when he had to be in the capital for business reasons as well, killing a few birds with one stone.

Tonight's meeting was to take place in the house of John Perry, the most committed member of the committee – indeed, apart from Leo, its only committed member. The meetings were usually held in members' houses to save money. A room in a hotel or a pub would have been preferable but nowadays even the most appalling room cost a hundred euro and the coffers of Killing Roads were completely empty. Members were supposed to pay an annual fee but they never did. Leo had considered expelling those who did not pay up but the difficulty with that strategy was that if he applied it, there would be no members at all – with the exception of John Perry. He was the only one who had ever paid the fifty euro required by the statutes.

John Perry lived in Rathcormac, miles away from where any of the other members lived. That was not the only reason for Leo's expectation that the attendance tonight would be small, but it was one of them. He was only coming from the city centre but it took him almost two hours to get to John's house – for some unaccountable reason, for much of its journey through the outskirts of Dublin the Luas, Red Line, stopped at various places in the middle of nowhere; it seemed to have been designed to cause maximum inconvenience to commuters. Instead of going into the village of Rathcormac, for instance, the nearest stop to that vast conglomeration of houses was situated out on the motorway on the side the Red Cow roundabout, about a mile and a half from the closest habitation. A bus was supposed to be available from there, but Leo knew from bitter experience that it was extremely unreliable, so he walked the rest of the way, along the motorway, then along a bleak slip road past some factories before finally hitting places where people actually lived, after about half an hour.

Rathcormac village, when he finally reached it, came as a pleasant surprise, as it always did on these treks out to John's house – the frustration of public transport tended to make him forget that he was heading for what had been an ecclesiastical settlement in the Middle Ages. Once, the suburbs of Dublin had been a land of saints and scholars and Rathcormac had been as saintly and scholarly as the best of them. Even still it possessed a round tower and a general aura of ancientness, which had been superseded in his, and the media and public imagination, by its reputation for bad housing estates. The beautiful melodious name was often heard on the news in connection with drug seizures and drug-related shootings, accompanied by images of small white houses with unkempt lawns surrounded by white plastic police cordons, or, if there had been a murder, a white marquee in which the chief state coroner would carry out a post-mortem examination of the latest victim of gangland crime.

In reality, though, Rathcormac was a pretty village; it had some nice clothes shops, and a pub. Even the houses in the much maligned estate had flowering shrubs and dahlias in their gardens, and looked much like suburban houses anywhere else. None that Leo passed was surrounded by policemen, or marred by shattered windows, or any other evidence of recent murderous exchanges. The only people he saw were three quite ordinary-looking boys playing football on a green, and a few dauntless, but well-dressed, small children extracting the last minutes of playtime from the dying autumn day. None of these people offered him heroin, or any kind of drug, or tried to shoot him.

John's house looked like a neglected version of any of the other houses. Every estate has one or two of these. The grass in his patch of lawn was cut in that haphazard way that suggests its owner resented nature's insistence that grass grow even in his garden, where anyone could see that it was not welcome. He hadn't bothered to pull up the weeds around the edges; there was not a single dahlia or even a common shrub in sight, but dandelion clocks, and thistles, very tall and very spiky, and the anonymous weeds that thrive in neglected gardens, abounded. The curtains on his windows had that limp, yellowed sadness of curtains that had never been washed since the day they were hung up; in this case a day that had apparently occurred about thirty years ago.

Inside was even worse. The smell of neglect accosted you as soon as you entered the dim hall. It wasn't exactly a smell of dirt but more an absence of anything pleasant – no chicken had been roasted in this house in a long, long time, or apple pies baked.

There had never been a vase of fragrant roses in the little dark hall, or even a chemical air-freshener.

In other words, it was a bachelor's house of the old-fashioned variety.

Bachelors' houses of the old-fashioned variety terrified Leo. They reminded him that he lived in a bachelor's house himself. The indisputable fact of his bachelordom was one which he didn't like to reflect upon very often – he was too busy working through his days to sit back and consider the larger issues affecting his own existence, although he spent a great deal of time worrying about the larger issues affecting everyone else's. When this aspect of his own life was suddenly brought to his attention, it shocked him, and filled him with dread. Could it be that this state in which he found himself, what he thought of as a purely temporary state, was in fact going to be permanent? Like most people, he believed his conditions were transitory, that he was merely on a journey to his real life, the life he desired. But when he saw John's garden and smelt John's hall, the dreadful realisation that perhaps the life he was living was the only life he was going to get dawned on him.

However, it was perfectly clear to anybody entering that hall that nobody could possibly have chosen the life it represented and accepted it as defining and permanent. John obviously thought that he was still in rehearsal. He hadn't even got as far as the dress rehearsal. He was still in the rented room in a disused warehouse, going over his lines, assuming that his real life would start on opening night.

And John was fifty years old.

All these uncomfortable insights flashed through Leo's mind in the seconds it took for John to usher him from the dark hall into the sitting room, a room in which the air seemed to be foggy, as if a depressing weather front had somehow managed to get in through the window and establish itself, permanently, inside.

John left to make a cup of tea. Leo sat down on a huge armchair covered with a fabric that had the colour and texture of rat's fur. Now he understood why he had been filled with foreboding all day. His latent memory of the effect John Perry's house had on his mood had been trying to assert itself, trying to prevent him for going back to the danger. Thinking about

51

the strange way his mind worked helped to dispel his fear. He sat in the rat-coloured room and watched his gloom float away through the dusty window and out, out into the darkening night.

'Don't think we'll have many tonight,' Leo managed cheerily enough, when John came back carrying one green mug of tea in his hand, with the tea bag bobbing around its surface like a shark's fin in a little mud pond.

John looked peeved. 'Well, it's not quite eight o'clock,' he said anxiously.

This was one of the problems with meetings in people's houses. The hosts took it as a personal slight when people didn't turn up.

'Look, I've started this scrapbook.' Leo tried to distract him. With a scrapbook. He pulled it from his backpack.

It was a child's scrapbook, made of coloured card. Leo opened it. A small clipping was glued in on the first page, which was a bright pink.

FIVE DIE IN KERRY COLLISION
Mary Lynch

Five people died after a two-car collision early yesterday in Co. Kerry. A sixth person is in intensive care in Tralee General Hospital following the accident, which took place at a blackspot on the road between Castleisland and Killarney at around 2.30 a.m.

This is the fourth multiple-death crash in this area in the past two years.

All six people in yesterday's crash are believed to be eastern Europeans living in the area.

Leo opened the next page, which was a dark, gloomy purple.

MORE THAN ONE A DAY ARE NOW DYING
Angela Moriarty

One person has died on Irish roads every twenty hours since the beginning of 2005.

The article, a full spread, carried statistics and photographs, images of wrecked cars, pictures of people who had been killed, and a large photograph of a young woman and her three-year-old daughter.

> Siobhán Murphy, of Castleknock, pictured here with her daughter Jane, was killed with her friend Ciara O'Connell when the car in which they were travelling was involved in a three-car collision on the M50 near the Red Cow roundabout last Friday.

John leafed through the thick pages, while Leo sipped his tea. Both activities were undertaken with similar degrees of trepidation. 'Pedestrian killed by a lorry in Ballinasloe'; 'Cyclist dies after accident involving a truck on Eden Quay'. There were photographs of lorries, broken-up cars, smiling faces (the victims before the accident) and weeping faces (their relations, after the accident).

Leo had begun keeping this scrapbook, his Killing Roads Collection, three months ago. Already one bumper-size book was full of brief reports of deaths on the road – he had tried to restrict himself to factual accounts, which on the whole was all that was available, although occasionally, after some particularly horrendous spate of carnage, the Sunday newspapers commissioned opinion pieces and articles based on what usually seemed to be about an hour's research by some heavyweight journalist. The statistics were in his scrapbook, Leo believed. The statistics, the story, the tragedy, the farce, all glued in on purple, pink, yellow and orange stiff paper, between two covers depicting a multicoloured roller coaster in which laughing children tumbled around against an azure sky.

He waited for a response from John. His hope – one of his many strange hopes – was that all the members of Killing Roads would start to keep scrapbooks. There would be overlap in contents of course, but probably not too much. He was always missing things, forgetting to glue in articles or too lazy to do so. And they would buy different newspapers, so the angle on the deaths would vary slightly. If they accumulated ten scrapbooks – there were ten members – and sent them to the Minister, or organised an exhibition somewhere, a library say, they would be sensational. So he believed. Graphics, touch-screens with statistics – the whole thing could be sensational. It would attract attention. It would shock, when people saw all the deaths gathered together in this way. Spread over the newspapers, drip fed, three a week, five a week, the news of carnage had lost its power to impress. The reports came as regularly and as predictably as the news from the stock exchange, or the weather forecast. Every week, six more deaths. Boring, predictable, and accumulating. Four thousand between 1996 and 2005. A statistic Leo often thought of, often quoted.

John looked up. 'Yeah,' he said, in his tired voice, apparently suppressing a yawn. He often sounded like that. At other times he became angry and irritated. 'But what's the point of this? Where will it lead?'

Leo concealed his impatience. John was one of those people who see the snags in everything. Indeed some members of Killing Roads had suggested, once when he was not at a meeting, that they ask him to resign. They felt he was a destructive force. But how could they throw him out when he had only missed one meeting in his life – when he had been sick, with Malta fever, whatever that was. It was typical of John Perry to have an illness nobody had ever heard of.

'I thought we could decide that at the end of the year,' Leo said. 'We could have an exhibition.'

'An exhibition?' John was genuinely flabbergasted.

'Yes. If we all keep a scrapbook with any regularity at all, we'll have dozens by the end of the year. I think they'd make a powerful impact displayed in some public place.'

'Like where?' said John in his querulous, annoying voice.

'I don't know yet. The National Library maybe. They have a lot of exhibitions.'

'The National Library? They'd never do an exhibition of scrapbooks about car crashes. They do exhibitions on dead writers ... who died in their beds, rich and famous, for the most part.'

'Well, some other library, or somewhere else ... that's a mere detail.'

'Not really,' said John. He began to tell Leo what was wrong with his idea.

He went on doing this for about an hour.

At that stage, since nobody else had come, Leo decided it was appropriate to call off the meeting. 'We don't have a quorum,' he said, although he did not know what they would want a quorum for, or even what a quorum was. But it must be more than him and John Perry.

The following morning Leo took the 10.45 train from Heuston Station to Tralee. He used public transport for a variety of reasons, the most pressing of which was that he could not drive. But he also used the train as a protest against the supremacy of the killing car in Ireland, and as a matter of environmental principle, and to give a good example to his neighbours in Kerry, almost all of whom drove SUVs. Upholding these principles did not mean that he found the train trip enjoyable. On the contrary, it irritated the life out of him.

Often on this journey he had to do special exercises, trans-cendental meditation, discreet yoga manoeuvres, to keep com-parisons with train journeys enjoyed in other European countries at bay. He had told himself time and time again that he should stop comparing Irish things to things on the Continent. But as he settled into a seat by a window that had not been cleaned in months, irritating memories of train journeys he had undertaken in other countries kept popping into his head. The TGV from Paris to Bordeaux: two and a half hours. Seville to Madrid: two and a half hours. Stockholm to Gothenburg: three hours. Dublin to Tralee: four hours and forty minutes.

Comparisons are odious. At least there still was a train to Tralee. It was not like going to Donegal, where the tracks had been closed down by de Valera long ago, to prevent people from going through the Six Counties and seeing what they were like, probably. Or to prevent people in Donegal from ever going anywhere.

This morning he experienced no anger management issues, even though the dining car was closed and the trolley service had been cancelled for some unexplained reason – apologies for any inconvenience caused were proffered on the fuzzy intercom, implying that such inconvenience was merely a distant possi-bility and that most people would have sensibly brought their own sandwiches with them. Leo hadn't. But he did not care. He sat in his plastic seat, ignoring the loud conversation of a couple of travellers who were a few seats away, and stared through the dusty window at the flat fields, not reading, not sleeping, not bored at the monotony of the vista – green grass for two hundred miles, occasionally relieved by a small, exquisite, cut-stone station where a few old age pensioners waited patiently on the platform with their trolleys, for who knew what?

The train to Ballybrophy, maybe, or the death coach, which-ever came first.

Leo was thinking about Kate.

Whatever her feelings about that wolfish Norwegian, or what-ever he claimed to be, she had talked to him for at least half an hour at the book launch, and afterwards had agreed to visit him in Kerry, handing over her mobile number without the slightest reservation, even though she had been unable to go on with him to the pub or meet him the following day.

He had come across her on a few previous occasions, at literary events, and had always liked her. She was bright but not in the least bit brash. Her eyes sparkled with insight and sympathy. She appeared to understand perfectly why he had chosen to live in the country, to get away from the rat race of Dublin, and, although he knew she had a successful career in public relations, he was quite sure that she would love to escape from urban life if she possibly could.

When he had first met her, he had not considered her espe-cially beautiful, but last night she had impressed him as being the most attractive woman by far in that large gathering. He tried to bring up her image to his mind. It was difficult. He couldn't remember what colour eyes she had – but they were very big, he remembered that, he could see them, laughing happily at something he had said. Her hair … it was not blond, some dark colour, brown, and she wore it in an unusual way. But what way? France was what she reminded him of, when it came to the crunch; slim, feminine, French women climbing stairs in Les Halles. She was as chic as that, very slim and dressed in some simple, tasteful style.

He was sure that she liked him. Her big eyes had met his on about four occasions, and hers, he believed, were full of empathy. That was what he had read in them, at the time, and when he was feeling happy, that was the reading he remembered. He would call her in a week and arrange for a meeting. If she did not want to come to Kerry, he would find an excuse to go to Dublin himself. He should go there soon again in any case, to hold another, proper, meeting of Killing Roads, where they could discuss their falling membership and the question of their future. Thus, his future with Kate and his future with Killing Roads could be dealt with in one fateful visit.

At Portlaoise his reveries, which were just becoming enjoyable, were disrupted and he was dragged from his daydreams. A woman sat opposite him, not the type he wanted to talk to. He pulled out a book, anxious to avoid conversation, hoping to find a way back into his head while pretending to read. On a commuter train such a problem would never have arisen. But on these intercity trains the rules were different. Many passengers believed it was quite normal to engage strangers in conversation, as if they had bought a right to entertainment with their return ticket. This woman was one of those passengers.

'An bhféadfainn breathnú i do nuachtán?' she asked. His copy of the *Irish Times* was on the table.

His eyes widened in surprise. 'Fáilte romhat,' he replied.

She took the paper.

How did she know he was an Irish speaker too? Was there something in his appearance that revealed it to everyone? He stroked his eyebrows nervously. If some physical trait, or something else – his clothes, perhaps? – indicated that he was an Irish speaker, it would not be anything very attractive, he was sure. Nobody wants to be told they look Irish, still less that they look like an Irish speaker. Much better to look like a French speaker, or a Swedish speaker, or a Polish speaker. Or a Scots-Gaelic speaker. Or even Welsh … though that would be down the list. What does the stereotypical Irish speaker look like? A burly potato head wearing a scratchy sweater, that's what. And I'm not wearing a scratchy sweater, thought Leo.

He had forgotten that one of the poetry books he published was on the table.

The woman read a few lines on the front page of the newspaper. Or seemed to. He glanced at her over the rim of his book, gradually taking in her unusual, her weird, appearance. Her hair was long, black and dry, like burnt straw. She had exceptionally pink cheeks and a wide red mouth. She did not look like an Irish speaker. Or an English speaker. He could not put his finger on it, but something about her looked extraordinary, as if she had possibly come, not just from another country, but from another planet.

And at the same time she looked familiar, as if he had met her before somewhere, at a book launch or a party ... it must have been the latter; she did not look like a book launch type.

'I can't read,' she said simply, as if she had read his thoughts. She looked up at him with a wide smile.

He put down his book, taken aback. He did not ask her why she had asked for a newspaper, if she couldn't read. He knew why. She had asked for it in the first place to test her theory that he spoke Irish and, secondly, to trap him. She had asked for it expressly to provide a dramatic context for her sensational confession. He sighed. He was in for a tête-à-tête.

Wondering where she was bound, and hoping it was not the terminus, he prepared to hear her story. Like the newspaper request, this was not unusual. The train to Tralee was always full of people who were dying to tell him their most intimate secrets at the drop of a hat. He had long ago stopped wondering if this had something to do with him: did he look kind and understanding, the sort of person a stranger would instinctively trust? He knew now that the transaction was all one-sided, and these people would have talked to anybody at all, anybody equipped with two ears and trapped in the seat at the other side of the hard grey table.

'Oh?' He tried to be as discouraging as possible, although as a poet, publisher and socialist he should have been interested.

'I never learned. I used to miss school a lot when I was young and there were about sixty in the class anyways.'

'But you learned Irish?'

She smiled. 'I never had to learn it,' she said. 'It's what we spoke at home.'

He nodded. 'And you tried to learn to read since you left school?' he asked.

'Oh yeah, loads of times. I went to some of those classes, literacy classes. I had a tutor all to myself. And the funny thing is, sometimes I can read.' She pointed at the poetry book. 'I can read this,' she said. 'That's why I borrowed your paper. I thought I could read it too. But I can't.' She frowned.

'Hm,' said Leo, unable to think of anything to say.

58

'Sometimes when I had a lesson, I'd just open the book and read away for myself. And for that again, the next time, I could hardly make out a word.'

'Curious,' he said. She needed a psychologist, probably, but he didn't say that. It might sound tactless. Also, he couldn't recall the Irish for psychologist.

'I need a psychologist really,' she said. A *siceolaí*. 'That's what my husband says,' she added. 'My husband that was.'

And so it all came out. Between Portlaoise and Mallow he learned that she was separated, that her husband was taking her to court and attempting to prove that she was an incompetent mother, suing for access to their two children, that he gave her no financial support, that she had been beaten as a child by her teacher (that was why she couldn't read), that she had worked in a factory but when she had been promoted to the job of manager, she had had to resign, because her secret would have been revealed.

This sad, almost tragic, tale she told with utmost cheerfulness, laughing as she disclosed the dreary details, her rosy cheeks glowing. Her deeply depressing life had not depressed her in the slightest, it seemed. She was as happy as if all she had known since birth had been a bed of roses.

At Mallow station she got up. Was she leaving the train or just going to the loo? He waited with bated breath.

'Goodbye,' she said. 'I have to get out here.'

Leo sighed happily and took a good look at her. Now he could see that she was wearing a very short pink coat, and black lacy stockings with pink, high-heeled shoes. Everything about her looked dotty. On the one hand, she reminded him of a character from a television series he had liked as a child, all about scarecrows. On the other, he wondered if she were some sort of low-grade prostitute – not that he supposed it likely that there would be any other kind in Mallow. But you never knew, of course, these days, with the new affluence.

'Goodbye, nice to meet you too,' he said. She kissed him. And then he did a stupid thing: he gave her his card, saying, 'Here, phone me if you, you know, need help.' With what? The reading, or the violent husband, or the mental problems? And how could he help anyway, with anything?

This was the sort of thing he was always doing. He was a

sucker for hard-luck stories. As soon as he said goodbye to her and saw her climbing onto the platform, wobbling in her high heels, he regretted his impulse. The next thing, she'd be burgling his house, or her crazy husband, if there was a husband, would be turning up on his doorstep with a sawn-off shotgun in his grubby little fist.

Hours later, Leo was on that doorstep himself, fiddling with the long key in the lock that was always troublesome. Sometimes he believed rain made it temperamental, but it hadn't rained much at all this year, most remarkably, and still there was always a question mark hanging over entry to the house. Would he get in or not? He did on this occasion, as on all others, but still that moment of uncertainty arose every time.

Leo's life was difficult, largely owing to his general insistence on placing ideals over practicalities and refusing to compromise. His environmentalism, his devotion to Irish, his career as a publisher of poetry, made life difficult for him. But there was one lucky thing in Leo's life: his house.

He had bought it from an American, a lawyer from Manhattan whom he had never met in person. Dean Swift. Mr Swift's father had had the house built in the late 1960s and had holidayed there on and off until he died, leaving it to his son, who had no interest in the house or the area. It had not been expensive. Houses in this district were reputed to be wildly overpriced, but as far as Leo could see, this was a myth. Nobody wanted to buy a second-hand house anyway; both the natives, young people settling down in the area, and the outsiders who 'fell in love' with the place and decided to get a holiday house in it, preferred to build their own. Sites were sold all the time and new houses mushroomed, but old ones, especially houses like this one, which were not really old, were not in demand. Leo had been able to buy it for a fraction of what he had got for his semi-d. in Dundrum.

It was a beautiful house. Nestling in a niche that had been dug out of the side of a hill overlooking the Atlantic, its south wall was constructed almost entirely of glass, so that even when he was indoors, he felt he was in the green field outside. The living room had a red stone floor and an oak ceiling. Everyone who came to visit exclaimed in delight, and surprise, since nobody expected Leo to live in any style at all. They expected him to live in the sort of place John Perry lived in. Leo expected that himself. Every time he walked into his own living room he was filled with astonishment. He might be a nerdy, Irish-speaking poetry publisher with a scratchy sweater and a potato head but this good house was his home.

Kate would have to come and see it. Once she did, she would be truly impressed. She would be as surprised as anyone else, and this surprise would rapidly transform into lifelong love for the owner of the beautiful house, for Leo.

The next few days passed quickly. He had a deadline with the printer for the end of the week, and as usual at such times, he was occupied almost full-time in making sure everything was ready – it always took longer than he anticipated. He managed to get down to the pub twice, to hear the local gossip – three sheep had been savaged by an Alsatian dog, owned by the Italian woman who had moved in last year, was the main news. Five people told him the story, each with its own variations – two sheep, six sheep, two ewes, a ram. Some people said the woman came from Spain and one said she was a Romanian gypsy. The dog had not been put down, they were all agreed on that, although there was a division of views as to whether this was a good thing or a bad thing.

A night's entertainment was derived from this one story, twisted and turned and viewed from many angles: a story goes a long way in the country. That was one of the things Leo loved about it. This endless, original, witty conversation about nothing at all. Talk for its own sake, talk as rich as Restoration comedy, talk as a secret art form that the world did not know about. So much better than endless, jargon-filled meetings and launches and rushing for the bus.

For a while he was thoroughly happy, just to be back in the country, back in the local pub, back to his own routines. He liked getting up when he felt like it and coming down to the big kitchen in his thick red dressing gown. Looking out to the field, with its ragged grass and clutches of rusting rushes, to see what he could see. A hare, sometimes a pheasant, which had come to nest in a ditch full of fuchsia at the next house. Occasionally, if he was up early, a red fox. Then coffee and Raidió na Gaeltachta before moving to his desk and doing a bit of work. Here, his house blended in with the field, and the field melted into the sea and most of the time you could hardly tell the sea from the sky. His work blended with his leisure. He could edit in bed, or while he waited for the potatoes to boil. There were no sharp divisions, the kind of divisions the city demanded of everyone, artificial barriers that had no place in the life of good faith, which was Leo's aspiration.

But time wore on and the bliss of rural life wore off. He began to feel lonely, more lonely than usual.

Kate did not telephone. She did not telephone on Monday and she did not telephone on Tuesday. His anxiety grew. Wednesday came and she did not telephone on Wednesday. On Thursday he decided he could not recall whether she had said she would phone him, or whether he was supposed to phone her. Of course he remembered perfectly well.

She said she'd ring him. So why hadn't she? Why didn't she?

There was probably some perfectly natural reason. For instance, that she was sick, or had been suddenly called abroad on some urgent Poetry Plus business. (Such as what? Advising the Taoiseach on poetry policy during an important trade mission to Iran or Afghanistan or some such place, where the Vodafone network hadn't penetrated?) He should ring and ask. She was probably wondering why he didn't phone and deducing that he was a cad who didn't care about her.

But on the other hand, perhaps she had simply decided that she didn't care about him and never wanted to see him or even talk to him on the phone again. He was reluctant to let on how much he cared. He did not want to harass her.

He set a deadline for himself. After this deadline he would allow himself to bury his pride and his scruples. He would telephone. He would harass. The alternative was to go mad. This deadline he set, after much deliberation, as lunchtime on Friday – since this was obviously the last possible time at which she could decide to come down for the weekend.

At one fifteen on Friday, a quarter of an hour after the deadline – he had made himself wait, and had sat with the phone in his hand for fifteen minutes, in agony – he dialled her number.

She answered immediately. That was reassuring. But she seemed surprised, which was not.

'How are you?' he asked, trying to keep the terror out of his voice.

'Very well, thank you,' she said, 'and you?'

Very well. It was too formal. Fine, grand, the best, not bad. Terrible. Any of those would have been better than 'very well'. His heart sank. But he pulled it back up again. She hadn't actually hung up.

'Oh the best.' Be cheerful, encourage her into a similar mood. 'Busy, of course.' He looked out at the field, at the clumps of rushes struggling in the wind, like mankind pitted against the awful giants of fate. The angry charcoal mist was rolling in over the sea and the seagulls were wheeling inland, screeching their heads off, seeking shelter from the coming storm.

'Yes, yes,' she said, trying to think of something to say. And it was clear that this something was not going to be 'I'll be down there with you tonight. I'm just leaving to catch the train this minute'.

There was silence on the line for a long, sad half a minute. Leo broke it.

'Well, I wondered … we spoke about the possibility of your coming down for a weekend? I wondered if you would like to come this weekend?'

There was an even more dreadful silence, this time very short, and, somehow, bristling with lively emotion.

Which turned out to be amusement. Some scorn and disbelief – and a lot of amusement.

'This weekend?' she laughed heartily. 'Ohmygod, no, no! Not this weekend. I'm really sorry! There's no way I could … did I really create that impression?'

That impression. Really. Create.

The telephone call went on for another minute or two, during which Leo's feelings slid downhill from the slope of embarrassment to the pit of despair.

When he put down the phone, he banged his head against the table six times, something he had not done since he was fifteen. He felt even younger, and smaller, and crazier. But when his head began to hurt, he stopped banging and stared out the window at the Great Blasket, its moss green slopes rising with serene defiance from the dark foggy sea, just as it had done for millions of years before the telephone call and as it would do for many years to come. And what difference did that make? One way or the bloody other? To him at this moment? If they pollute

63

the planet to pieces, so be it. What do I care? I'd be just as glad to go down with it, Killing Roads, Blasket Islands, Celtic Tigers, the whole fucking lot. One big bang and start again, or not start again, or anything.

He went to bed and slept for fifteen hours.

When he woke up, he felt much better.

He was a morning person. At around four, before dawn broke, he emailed everyone on the Killing Roads committee and suggested that they meet in Dublin soon, to discuss the future of the society.

After sending the emails, he felt much better. His connection with Dublin had been re-established. Soon enough he would be back there.

He went back to bed and snoozed until the sun rose over Mount Eagle.

Six

Kate's official title was delightfully vague – she was simply called administrator, the kind of tag Poetry Plus went for, like all the other organisations sort of the same, the small cultural institutions that were not really part of the public service but were funded by grants from DAST and the AC and the ACNI, and last but not least, the EU. The thing was that as the cultural and heritage industry had expanded in Ireland, art, and artists, needed more and more administrative back-up and, as a response, the number of small cultural organisations grew. Every county, practically, had at least one arts officer now, and as well as that there were heaps of organisations dealing with books in Irish, books for children, books for people with limited reading ability, books in translation, artists in schools, artists in libraries, artists in prisons, artists in hospitals, public visual art, statues on roundabouts, pictures in shopping centres, murals at railway stations, and so on. The list was endless, it really was. They used to say that Ireland had a standing army of a thousand poets, but now it had an even bigger army of arts administrators whose job it was to give the poets and their fellow artists funding, to send them off, abroad or around the country, giving exhibitions or readings, and generally to organise their lives for them. The Celtic Tiger had really let it all take off, there was loads of dosh sloshing around now in the coffers of the state and they liked to toss a good lot of it at The Arts. The Arts were a good thing, somehow, and politicians liked to be associated with them. Loads of photo opportunities with classy backgrounds, that was what they liked.

Kate was one of those artistic bureaucrats. Once, she had hoped to be an actual artist. While a student, she had published poems in the college magazines and she collected a ton of reject slips. Dear Miss Murphy, I regret to tell you that your poem is absolute shite. After getting squillions of these nice little notes from little and big poetry magazines and attending innumerable poetry readings, lectures, launches, and other events, she saw the light: writing poetry was for losers.

Listening to an officer from the Arts Council of Northern Ireland make a speech somewhere, Kate realised that there was a way to get her own back. She stopped writing poetry and started administering it. It was so gloriously simple! Already she was one of those deciding which poets got which grant, and who went to which conference. It was just brilliant! She took her revenge on those fucking editors who sent her the reject slips as soon as she was in the door. They never knew what hit them.

Now she organised poetic events from a small office down a back lane off Gardiner Street, the headquarters of Poetry Plus; her pay was crap, but it was much more regular and about ten times higher than that of the poets she worked with. But they didn't need money in the same way, artists were different, she believed. They sort of liked the freedom being strapped for cash gave them, and it was great for them to sort of learn to make their own way. Kate, to be honest, was against the grant culture. Even though she was still participating in it – selecting poets for bursaries and so on – she didn't hold with it. It was past its sell-by date, it was last century really. But anyway, she liked it for the moment.

Did she like her job? She adored it. It was fabulous. Really really really hard work, twenty-four seven, it took everything you could give it and she gave it everything she could. But it was brilliant. You got to meet loads of really interesting people, there was a fantastic social life, receptions every night, too many but she enjoyed them, they were just what she loved.

And there was more. She really really really liked the challenge of it all. She'd figured out – actually, she figured it out after about two days! – that administration was an activity at least as creative as writing poems. Tell that to the Arts Council! Her ambition was to climb the very complicated career ladder of the arts administration universe, a career game that was more like snakes and ladders than most. She had a five-year plan for herself. She knew where she wanted to be when she was thirty … ohmygod! You had to. If you didn't have a plan, you were a loser.

It was a funny old world: of mysterious alliances, delicate negotiation, careful manipulation. The thing you needed to understand real fast was that the real rules weren't written down anywhere, and nobody was going to explain them to you even if they knew them. You had to figure them out as you went along, noticing who was in favour and who was out, who should be flattered and who ignored, when to talk and when to shut your gob. Kate had experience. She'd been in a school yard for about twelve years, for God's sake, and where better to learn a thing or two about intriguing? There was no point in moaning about things. None at all. She learned instead to enjoy figuring out the complex web of the arts world, with its circles within circles, its cunning civil servants, its publicity-ravenous politicians, its inquisitive journalists. The foxes, the wolves, the jackdaws, she thought of them as, although she'd like to find a better metaphor for the journalists. 'Jackdaw' was much too kind. She saw herself as a dove among them. A downy, innocent pigeon. But not a stupid one, one who could read the signs. She had, she thought, the skills and gifts of a meteorologist rather than of an explorer or cartographer.

She had picked up and honed all these skills by the sheer force of her own intuition. If she had waited for anyone to teach her, she would have still been waiting.

In addition, she realised, with her quick insight, that in the arts world there was always an element of the unpredictable. A joker in the pack.

Namely, the artist.

This was not a thing many of the administrators, especially the male ones, knew about.

Most of the time, in the world of administration, once you got a grasp of the ropes, learned the tricky skills, you lived in an intricate but eventually predictable world where the smart succeeded and the naive went to the wall. It was the artist who brought an additional element of gambling to arts administration. Kate knew, she had to, just which ones counted and which ones didn't – there were A lists, B lists, C lists, D lists, and more. But all of a sudden, all the lists could be skewed overnight. Out of the blue some rank outsider could leap into the picture and screw the whole bloody thing up! Someone who was an outcast, published by the lowest of the low or exhibited somewhere off the map, could, all of a sudden, produce some brilliant book, put on a great exhibition, win some big international prize. Then everything in the arts world had to go through a rapid process of readjustment; the players all had to be moved around and various strategies and values reassessed to take account of the new standard.

It didn't happen very often, though. But when it did, it just added to the pleasure of the game. So thought Kate, in her good periods.

Kate was twenty-five. She had been brought up in Foxrock but for the past year had lived in an apartment on Gardiner Street in the centre of the city.

Did she have a life outside the office? Twice in her life she had been in love, once when she was a schoolgirl and once when she was a college student. The second relationship started at the end of first year and lasted until just two years ago, when the young man, now a law graduate, went off to Belgium on a *stage* and never came back, at least not to Kate's life. She had been bored with him for about a year and a half before they finished, but as soon as he went to Bruges, she began to miss him. The main effect of this was to prevent her feeling attracted to anyone else. Not until she had bumped into Vincy Erikson at the House of Lords a few weeks ago had she felt anything for anyone, though she'd scored loads of chaps, in that meaningless way you do, after parties and things.

She'd bumped into Vincy again on two occasions in the meantime, although they hadn't gone out together as yet. Fingers crossed. On both occasions they'd talked together for almost an hour, a very very long time at a reception, where, if Kate stuck to her own rule, she would never, ever, converse with any individual for longer than five minutes before moving on to the next group. Networking was her lifeline, after all, and she owed it to her poets and to her future to make as many new contacts as she possibly could whenever she was out and about. Like, it was expected.

But Vincy hypnotised her. Most journalists just annoyed her. Got her goat. They would telephone her for information when they needed it, then at receptions they'd brush her aside like she was a piece of shit. She always smiled anyway, exchanged a few words with them, and kept her feelings to herself when their eyes scanned the room for somebody famous.

Vincy was different. Totally different. He was not a cultural affairs journalist, so he had no professional interest in Kate's world. What he had been doing at the Heaney launch she did not know. And he looked just great. Oh his crazy hair, down to his shoulders, electric hair. His long body, taut, toned like some animal's, she wasn't sure which, she didn't do zoology. Cool dresser he was too. He was not everyone's idea of a dish but he was definitely hers, her type. And the thing was, he was a real journalist, even in his personal relations. He could listen. Unlike most men, he asked real questions, and then shut up and listened while she answered them. He'd got it all, in a nutshell.

She knew, that evening, as she put on her make-up in the tiny toilet in the corner of the office, and prepared for another literary event, that she was falling for Vincy Erikson.

Not in love, she said to herself, combing her eyelashes with the black mascara brush, which was supposed to make them longer, thicker, and more tear proof than any of its competitors. In infatuation. I don't know him. I don't know anything about him – where he lives, who his parents are, what age he is even (she guessed thirty; it was a good age, for a man).

She outlined her lips with a red pencil and brushed a deep pink paint into the gaps. Then she pressed her mouth on a tissue covered in powder and brushed them one more time. She wished her lips were bigger, and regretted not having succumbed to the temptation to have a collagen injection last summer. Her mouth was definitely her worst feature.

Damn, she thought, surveying her body. She was wearing a perfectly fitting black suit, which she had bought in Paris for an enormous sum of money, and a tiny bodice-type top in bronze-coloured silk. Black suits were boring, but they worked. No getting away from it. She looked better in this than in any other garment she possessed (even than in her other five black suits).

Why had she said damn? Because she was worried about her appearance. The wonderful advantage of being in a long-term, steady relationship, then not caring about men, was that worries about her looks had vanished from her life during all that period. Well, you know. Almost. She just picked the clothes for the occasion and left it at that. And that worked just fine. Now she wanted more. She wanted to be not just smart and presentable, or casual and presentable, the two main categories to which she had aspired for the past four years. She was asking herself to be mysterious, intriguing, bewitching, unusual, as well. She was asking herself to be beautiful. And the difficulty was, she could never tell if she was or not.

She might have to go the bohemian way after all, much as she hated it, if she was to get that intriguing look she wanted. But it sure as hell wouldn't come her way tonight. Tomorrow and tomorrow and tomorrow and tonight it was the little black suit. Damn!

The reception was on over at the Writers' Centre, a great gaff really, very nice, especially since they did it up, but not on the map. Northside. Unfortunate, but there you go, nobody went there, but nobody. The big names had their launches on the other side of the river. Not their fault, had to, to attract the numbers. The A list wouldn't be at this gig, at this launch of a collection of poems by some unknown nobody, Marina Baxter.

If Vincy showed his face there tonight, she'd take it as a yes. Interested. Because otherwise there was no reason why he'd be at something like this. Better things to do with his time.

Kate arrived a little late. The buzz of conversation and the smell of plonk floated downstairs to greet her; she could tell already that a large crowd had assembled. Well, wonders would never cease. That was the thing, you never could tell. Of course, the more minor the writer, the larger the crowd, of relations, neighbours, fellow members of writers' groups, friends. The famous names sometimes made the mistake of ignoring the foot soldiers. Hadn't it been blazoned about that John Marvell, who had won the Booker, had sold only a few hundred copies of his novel prior to scooping the big prize? Marina would sell more copies than that tonight – in fact, not being bitchy, the book would sell more copies tonight than it would during the remainder of its shelf life. Probably not more than five hundred had been printed, though, so the publisher would be happy.

The back room, where the wine was being served, was crammed. Kate scanned it with an expert eye. No Vincy. She squeezed into the front room, a big lovely room, such a shame it was stuck over here, with long windows looking into the trees of the Garden of Remembrance, and lovely paintings on the blue walls. One of the nicest rooms in Dublin.

The book table was set up in one corner. Nobody there of course, just the hopeful publisher's assistant, twiddling her thumbs, rearranging the books in little piles. People, for some reason, left the book-buying until towards the end of the launch as a rule, postponing the evil moment for as long as possible, or until they were sufficiently sloshed not to resent parting with their cash for a book they didn't really want. In the other corner the podium waited, like a gallows, for the speakers – hopefully not too many. Kate sometimes felt she would rather watch people hang than listen to them make speeches. Hanging must be faster.

Vincy was not in this room either.

Kate shrugged and made her way back to the wine room, where she began to work. Already she'd marked the territory, identified those individuals worth talking to. At events like this, socialising for its own sake was a waste of time (the encounters with Vincy were an aberration). Alcohol, the lubricant of the launches, lightening the atmosphere, raising the volume of sound, encouraging goodwill and good sales, she always had to avoid completely. Like an athlete in training, she knew that even half a glass would affect her performance. The wine was usually plonk, but even so, abstaining was a sacrifice, since it made these things much more enjoyable. Occupational hazard. Sobriety.

Only three people of any importance were in attendance … that she knew of. (What she missed was the Lord Mayor of Belfast, a cousin of the author of the book, and the director of one of the big banks, the author's brother; both of their telephone numbers Kate would have been very pleased to add to her phone book. That was one of the disadvantages of her systematic method: it presumed that she recognised everyone

71

and did not allow for the chance encounter.) First Kate approached a man who held a fairly menial post with the Arts Council. At the moment his influence was nil, but people like him could get promoted. Kevin was his name. He was in his late twenties, dark-eyed, dressed in a black shirt, black tie, and a loose black jacket. The literary uniform. He pretended not to know Kate, although he did. He was getting arrogant already. Creep.

She introduced herself and he became all friendly. His eyes sparkled as he made obvious remarks about the room. Yeah yeah it was lovely and the centre was looking good. 'Take my card,' said Kate, excusing herself with her usual 'Oh look, there is someone I absolutely have to say hello to! Lovely to have met you. Take care!'

She had spotted a gap in the circle that surrounded Eamon McKeown, producer of the arts programmes on radio and television; miraculous that he should have been here. She guessed, correctly, that he had some personal connection with the author, something which made her make drastic revisions in her estimation of the book's chances of success: if it had any merit at all, it would now get the requisite kick-start.

Eamon was an older man, well into his fifties. He was bald, small, chubby, and always rather grubbily clad. His trademark was a stain – it looked like egg, prehistoric egg – on his tie. Another creep, but he was really really popular with men and women of all ages; they said he'd had it off with half the woman in Dublin – you knew the kind of woman. As usual, he was knocking back glasses of red wine and holding forth to the little group of sycophants that surrounded him.

Kate, who'd met him several times, sidled into the circle and said quietly, 'Hello, Eamon.'

He looked at her uncomprehendingly. His face was red and pudgy from overdrinking and overeating, and from being so fucking full of himself.

'Kate Murphy,' she said. 'Poetry Plus.'

'Oh yes, Kate, how are you today?' he said.

As she was answering he turned to a waiter and grabbed another glass of wine. 'I hear you are doing an interview with Harold Pinter tomorrow?' she said, just to make conversation. Kate was always hearing things like that.

Eamon looked really really annoyed. 'Who told you that?' he asked crossly.

'I forget,' she lied. 'I heard it on the grapevine. Is it a secret?'

'Obviously not,' Eamon snarled, and turned to speak to someone who had approached him from the rear.

Kate went to the drinks table and tried to get a glass of water. There were no glasses left, however – something that could happen at this sort of Mickey Mouse event, where the publisher had no real idea of how many people would turn up and no experience of ensuring reserve supplies. The wine bottles looked fatally empty too. Of course there'd been no grub to start with, not a crisp or a peanut. A waitress, who was about sixteen, probably the daughter of the publisher, offered her a bottle of Ballygowan without a glass, but Kate declined.

The speeches were about to start. Soon escape would be impossible.

She pressed from body to body, making for the door. Would she make it? Before they started and it was rude to go. She felt hot and angry. Being snubbed by these idiots should not have bothered her – it often happened, they were ignorant and often deaf, so they didn't hear what organisation she represented or hadn't heard of it.

The speeches started, and the publisher was bleating on, thanking everyone, from the woman who cleaned the toilets to the head of the Arts Council, for existing, and somehow by their existence supporting him in his Herculean task, publishing this slim volume of poetry. Anyone would have thought he had invented the art of poetry to listen to him, or built Notre Dame, or discovered America.

Kate managed to slip out the back door without too many people noticing her. She skipped downstairs, as silently as she could, hoping she would not bump into some employee of the centre en route.

She was in luck. She pulled open the heavy hall door and reached the steps outside without being caught.

The sun had not gone down yet, and it was quite a warm evening. Mild. She stopped for a few seconds at the top of the steps, breathed in the lead-laden air, and let her eyes rest on the golden autumn trees in the garden across the street. Above them, the sky was a bleached pale blue, streaks of white cloud stretched across it like rags on a thorn bush.

'Hello there!' His voice. She was lost in a daydream. She jumped.

Her face broke into a huge smile. Unprofessional. Deeply. Everything in her body and her heart and her soul lifted.

'Gosh, I didn't even see you coming,' she said. She didn't think before speaking now. From being on top of things, in control, she'd mutated into a flake – a spontaneous human being, if you prefer. He could do that to her.

'You were in a world of your own,' said the voice, and its owner kissed her lightly on the cheek. Vincy had had no intention of doing it, but she was so little, so cute in her black suit and tiny silk bodice, so lost-looking, on the top of the steps, that he couldn't help it.

She laughed at him and touched his sleeve. His baggy tweed sleeve.

'But are you leaving already?' He glanced at his watch.

'I had to ... I felt a little bit sick,' she said. 'The speeches have begun and they will go on for a while, I think it's safe to say.'

'Oh!' He was at a loss. 'Why don't I take you somewhere for a cup of tea? Would that help?'

She made some weak protestations, said he should go in and be seen even for a few minutes. But he brushed them aside and they walked off towards the east side of the old shabby square, where there were a few hotels in which you could get tea, or whatever else you wanted.

Seven

Gerry was back in Bray. He had not let Anna know, feeling rather sheepish about it, but she had contacted him and quizzed him.

'Yeah, well, it seems like I'm back home,' he said. 'We're going to give it another go.'

'I'm glad to hear that,' Anna said. 'I think it's the best thing, by far, for everyone.'

This was her true opinion. Gerry and Olwen's marriage was important to her, but not Gerry's or Olwen's individual happiness. She herself would like to achieve great personal happiness, but she seldom considered that other people might nurture similar ambitions. Contentment and routine were what ordinary people, people like Gerry and Olwen, wanted in life.

This is what she must have believed. But she didn't formulate it. Anna formulated no beliefs whatsoever. She was vaguely agnostic, vaguely socialist, vaguely capitalist, vaguely materialistic, vaguely spiritual. The only thing she really believed in was her ambition to be a successful writer, by which she meant some sort of mixture of famous, bestselling and good. But she had never considered why she wrote or why she wanted to write a 'good' book, or what good such a book could do for its readers. Such questions – questions regarding the meaning of literature, or of writing – were never discussed in her literary circles. Similarly, questions as to the meaning of life were never discussed in her social or family circles. You wanted to live a successful, best-selling sort of life, just as the writers wanted to produce a successful and bestselling book. While waiting for success, you made the best of what you had. Anna also believed that when she was a bestselling, successful author, she would also be perfectly happy. The two ambitions were intertwined, were, in fact, one and the same.

Anna took it for granted that Gerry would never be a suc-cessful painter, as she understood it, or a successful civil servant, for that matter; in fact, she took it for granted that he would never achieve a successful life. What he believed about these things she had no idea.

He was a lot less talkative than usual. She divined that he was in an ambivalent frame of mind. He had probably become accustomed to the flat in town in the few weeks he had spent there. He had always wanted to live in town, close to the hub of things. Not having to spend two hours commuting every day would have been a relief, too, for anyone.

'Yeah.' His voice was flat. 'See you around.'

'Goodbye, Gerry,' she said. Not a word of thanks for her help in saving his marriage. That's the fate of the peacemaker, as often as not.

Anna's work on the book was progressing favourably. Having a master plan was useful; the words flowed out to fill the structure she had built to contain them, like water filling a jug, and as far as she could judge she was writing well. Her judgement was based on the feeling of ease with which she wrote and the sense of achievement she experienced every day when she clocked up a thousand, sometimes two thousand, words by lunchtime. She did not reread, as yet, knowing that that might break the flow and discourage her.

There was one disheartening aspect of the work: time. The book would contain about two hundred thousand words, and would take ages to complete. Even if she wrote a thousand a day, that meant two hundred days – a year almost, if you took week-ends and holidays off – before a first draft appeared. Could

J.K.R. be so slow? She seemed to churn them out every year. Or perhaps it was every two years? And they were enormous volumes. That's what the kids wanted: fantasy by the ton.

> *Sally is walking on the beach one lovely morning. The sun sparkles like the points of sharp swords on the summer sea. Three white guillemots [check are they white?] fly overhead, leading Sally onwards, onwards.*
>
> *The beach grows longer and longer as she walks. It is completely deserted. Not a single other human being is on it although this is the hottest day of the year so far. The hottest day Sally remembers, and the brightest. She is not worried by the loneliness of the beach – the high cliffs seem friendly, the cries of the seabirds sound happy.*
>
> *She sees a seal nosing its way along the line of the tide, keeping pace with her as she walks. This makes her feel even happier.*
>
> *And then suddenly, on the horizon, a ship appears.*
>
> *It is not like any ship Sally has ever seen before – it is not a sailing ship, it is not a yacht, it is not a steamer, it is not a cruiser. It is not a Viking longboat, like the one down on the Liffey. But it is a white, bouncing, glorious tub, shaped like a balloon, not a ship. And it is rolling and bouncing, jumping in towards her …*

Sally is taken away on this strange ship. There are all kinds of magical fantasy people on board – this needed development. She had sketched them in without giving them much thought. A merry sea captain, based on the father of Pippi Longstocking. Indeed, Sally began to get Pippi Longstocking characteristics as soon as her father had been filched from the books of the great Swedish writer. Anna would have to go back and make sure some of those qualities were in place, or hinted at, earlier on. Also, there were a talking duck and a dolphin and a duchess.

They sailed on the seas and did strange things. Then Sally's tour of the world began. First she became attached to a family living in a mountain village somewhere in Norway. She was going to visit Lapland, then Russia, then other places. The novel was to be a tour of the world in about the year 1000, although Anna was careful not to be too specific about the year. In a later chapter Sally might move into another age, into the future, but Anna had not made up her mind about that. The future would be hard to imagine in any way that had not been imagined before. Even beginning to think about it gave Anna a headache.

Was it any good?

Anna did not like feedback on work in progress. Her membership of a writers' group was a joke, since she hated reading her work to her fellow members and told herself that she was not particularly interested in their opinion of it anyway. In fact, although she never admitted it to herself, she did not want to hear that her work was bad before it was even finished. Or to sense that they thought it was bad, because they seldom criticised anything openly. Even if the stuff were terrible, nobody ever said so, but let its author go right on labouring on it, ringing the changes on material that had no potential whatsoever for improvement, wasting their time. So you had to read their true opinion between the encouraging lines: in the body language, facial expressions, or, more often, in the silences. Someone would read a piece that was essentially useless. A small chorus of voices would whisper that this adjective was excellent, that there were too many adjectives there – the critique often focused on use of adjectives, probably because they were harmless; even the most sensitive soul would not be offended at the suggestion that they should consider removing the word 'innocent' or 'beautiful' – for these were the kind of adjectives most frowned upon – from their work. Often this advice about adjectives was given when the secret opinion of most people was that the entire work should be scrapped because no amount of fiddling with adjectives or adverbs or anything else would ever render it anything other than awful. No amount of fiddling would disguise the truth that the writer had nothing new to say. 'It is awful; stop doing it': this was the useful piece of criticism that you could simply not give. True, there would be one or two women who sat in utter silence: this was the most damning indictment any work could receive. But usually a kind soul would dash in to fill the dreadful silence with some mild comment: 'I'm not sure about the word "tender" in the last paragraph', or 'Do you think "sad" is right for that line?'

It wasn't, in Anna's opinion, the kind of critique that was very useful, so although she was a faithful attender of her writing group, she kept her novel to herself for the time being. When she was at the group, she read a poem. Most people in the group liked poems. They were short.

All of this meant that *Sally and the Ship of Dreams* had still not been seen by any eyes other than her own. With her other books, not showing them to people had not bothered her. But this one was going to be so exceptionally long and demanding that she would welcome a second opinion before going too far.

Just in case.

A second opinion from someone she trusted and whose opinion she valued.

Lilian.

And Lilian was pleased to be asked. 'Of course I'll read it,' she said. 'And I'll give you my honest opinion. You can email it to me.'

'I can send you a print-out,' Anna offered.

'Not at all,' said Lilian. 'Just pop it into an email. I'll print it out on Jack's printer in the office.'

Jack being her husband.

The weather was still unseasonably mild – as Anna opened the car door, on her way to collect Rory from school, she recalled saying these words to herself last year too, in October. The weather was often unseasonably mild these days. She looked out at the sea. It trundled in towards her, navy blue, the waves choppy like prancing puppies and trimmed with white foam. Down on the beach they would be roaring in, she could tell, pulling in heaps of seaweed and pebbles, pulling out clay from the cliffs, pulling out the land on which she lived. Global warming, coastal erosion: these were terms that had in the past while become commonplace, everyday concepts. But they were not taken seriously by anyone. Anna, living on a cliff-top, did not take them seriously. Even global warming was something, she felt, that was somebody else's problem. It was as if she did not really live on the globe. She had a good house in Killiney, which was utterly safe. The globe, with all its problems, was where other people lived.

The cars were parked thickly along the road on which Rory's

school was built. Anna found a place three or four roads away, got a parking ticket for half an hour, and walked briskly along the leafy roads, with their graceful old red-brick houses, to the school, a modern concrete block out of kilter with its surroundings. Mothers and fathers and grandparents, childminders, gathered at the gate or on the footpath. Anna saw someone she liked and stood beside her. Monica. Monica was the mother of a boy called Ultan the Artist, so called because he was good at drawing. He looked artistic, too, even at the age of eight, because he had a long thin plait of hair emerging from his short back and sides. He could have been teased for this unconventional hairstyle but he was not. The other children had a capacity for acceptance. They did not want to have a plait themselves, but they valued it as a part of Ultan. This, Anna felt, was as indicative as anything of the ethos you got in a school like this, a middle-class, liberal school in south Dublin – a tolerant, civilised place.

Monica was an artist herself, so Anna felt they had something in common, although Monica was a single mother who lived in a rented flat somewhere in the hinterland of Dún Laoghaire, and Anna was what she was. Monica painted, like her son, and was a more successful artist than Anna. Her name appeared in the pages of the newspapers fairly often; she exhibited in one of the most prestigious small galleries, Pink and Green, and did very well. That she could not afford to buy a house or a flat of her own was startling – Monica had not revealed that she owned a cottage in the Pyrenees, where she and Ultan went the second school was over, on the 1st of July every year.

'Amazing weather, isn't it?' was Anna's unoriginal opening gambit.

'I love it,' said Monica. 'If this is global warming, why complain?'

They looked at the bright blue sky and the dark blue sea.

'Oh yes,' Anna sighed. 'How's Ultan?'

'Seems to be grand!' said Monica. 'He doesn't like the new teacher much but he's getting used to her.'

'Oh?' Rory hadn't expressed any concerns about this year's teacher.

'She's very nice, I think. But she's a bit young and inexperienced. I don't think she knows what to make of Ultan.'

'I haven't talked to her at all,' Anna said. The new teacher smiled all the time with a big cheerful smile and wore black jeans and a black jumper, with silver hoop earrings. She had long wiry black hair tied up in a ponytail. A gypsy look. Anna assumed a teacher who looked like that would be excellent.

'She means well, but Ultan is mildly dyslexic, as you know, and she doesn't seem to really believe that, even though I've told her. She keeps marking his spellings as if he were not dyslexic – and she's a devil for spellings, they learn twenty new words a week and have these tests on Friday.'

'Oh yes,' said Anna. This was not news to her. Rory had won prizes for getting them all right, which had pleased him and his parents very much.

'She gives out prizes. Ultan hates it because he never gets one of the prizes. He's getting disgruntled … I don't know what to do about it.'

'You'll have to talk to her again,' said Anna. 'She mustn't have taken it in, the first time.'

Monica shuffled her foot on the pavement. She was wearing green shoes with polka dots on them, Anna noticed. Monica travelled a lot, in connection with her work, and collected clothes as if they were works of art, although today she was wearing the jeans and anorak that most of the mothers and minders and grandmothers wore.

'Yeah,' she said. 'It's all I can do.' She looked seriously worried. So worried that Anna patted her on the back, in a comradely way. This was one of the things that happened: someone was immersed in their own worries, and she could not get in there and do anything about it. Rory loved the new teacher and the spelling tests and the prizes (a bar of chocolate, always the same kind, plain Cadbury's Milk – the teacher believed in consistency). It was impossible for her to empathise with Monica. She was sorry for her and Ultan, but she would not want to change the system to suit him, when it suited Rory so well.

Monica changed the subject to something banal, a news story about a politician who had been killed in a car crash in Moscow. The change was pointed. The conversation continued awkwardly. Anna was relieved when the school door opened and the children poured out into the yard in a babbling stream of bright colours; there was no uniform at this school and they vied with one another for the clearest, lightest, most childlike colours. These were young children from the first classes, and their faces were mildly anxious as they surveyed the gathering of adults at the gate, until they located their own adult, whoever it happened to be. Rory found Anna easily. He always did. No matter where she stood, and even though she did not come every day to collect him, he could pinpoint her in the crowd within seconds. He ran towards her.

She had to suppress her very strong desire to pick him up and hug him. He would hate to be hugged here at the school gate, although he was still physically affectionate in private.

'Hi!' she said, turning to say goodbye to Monica. But Monica had already disappeared, somehow. Anna could not see where she had gone. 'How was your day?'

'OK,' he said.

They began to walk away. 'I'm parked down that way,' she pointed. 'It's a bit of a walk, I'm afraid. I couldn't find anywhere nearer.'

'Aw, Mom!' he said. 'Have you got any food?'

'No,' she said. 'Are you hungry?'

He nodded in the affirmative.

'Can you wait till we get home?'

'I'm starving. I couldn't eat my lunch.'

'Why?'

'Someone stole it.'

Anna looked at him sharply. 'Who?'

He shook his head. 'Someone. It wasn't there at lunch time.'

'You mean, someone took it out of your schoolbag?'

'Yes,' he said.

'We could go to the shop and get you something now if you like,' she said. He wasn't allowed sweets or crisps except on Saturdays, but she would make an exception if he were hungry.

'OK,' he said.

They walked away from the car and down another road to where a small shop, the Midway, was located. It was the kind of shop that hardly existed any more in Dublin, a little local place selling sweets and bread and milk, newspapers, fruit. A bell rang when you opened the white entrance door and a woman with glasses and a pink nylon overall looked up and smiled, as if aware that she represented a world that was past.

They bought crisps, a can of Coke, two bars of chocolate, all of Rory's choosing. He was slow and careful in his choices, spending a long time deliberating over the chocolate in particular. Finally he was satisfied and they left. He ate the crisps as they went back to the car.

'You're not being bullied, are you?' she asked.

Rory didn't reply.

'You can tell me,' she said. 'It's all right. I won't tell anyone else if you don't want me to.'

He took out one of the bars of chocolate and began to tear off the paper wrapper, and eat it. But he remained silent.

'We can talk about it some other time,' she said.

'OK,' he said, his mouth full.

They had reached the car at this stage and she drove home.

Rory did not eat when he got home. 'Too much chocolate!' said Anna, giving him a hug. He returned it warmly and grinned. Anna left him cuddling the cat, under Luz Mar's supervision. He did not look like a child who was being bullied, or disturbed in any way, she told herself, as she set off on a long walk. She preferred walking to going to the gym, although she occasionally did that too. The afternoon was lovely now, warm and sunny with a deep mellow light. Autumn leaves were heaped in drifts at the sides of the narrow footpaths. She crunched through them, along the winding roads, each one hemmed in with high grey stone walls that characterised her area. Behind the walls were houses but you would hardly realise that, as you walked along. It was a strange area, with all these grim walls, but that had come to symbolise not just home, but a precious home, a lovely area, to Anna, and she liked the greyness, especially now when the leaves added colour to it.

She did not walk to the sea today, one of her usual routes, but instead went inland and upwards, to the hill. It was not a high hill, but it was still a real hill, covered with furze and heather. At the top there was an obelisk, a monument to Queen Victoria, who had visited here in the nineteenth century, and a great view of the whole of Dublin, the Wicklow mountains, the bay, the Irish Sea, was to be had. She stood there surveying it all, smelling the salt water, the strange tang of brambles. Her earlier worry about Rory and his lunch was forgotten. Everything was forgotten, for this moment, when, exhilarated by the walk and climb, she absorbed the beauty of her surroundings. She would have loved to stay there for a long time and soak all that in, deeper and deeper. She would have loved to wallow in the silence, hardly broken by the murmur of the waves, the muted cry of the seagulls. But she knew she could not. It would not work. It made her happy to see it, but it would not make her happier to stay there for hours, basking in the beauty. Once, when she had been a teenager, she had believed that it must be so, that if a view impressed her deeply, that if she stayed with it for long enough, that impression would go deeper and deeper into her soul, that some extraordinary happiness would be hers, if only she persevered. What had she thought the world was? A place of infinite possibility, infinite mystery. But now she knew better. She knew happiness was something that one caught in small quantities, and often abruptly, when one was not expecting it. She knew it was to be enjoyed in moderation, like the pleasure of eating something delicious. Eating more and more of it would not increase the pleasure. And if she stood on top of the hill, now that she was so much older, staring and staring, she would get bored and cold and annoyed, not transported to some divine ecstasy.

That is what had happened to her, as she grew older. She had lost her capacity for losing herself in nothingness. So back she went, back to the world that she thought was real, winding down and down the hill and the castellated roads until she was right back in her own kitchen.

Luz Mar was going out, so Anna would mind Rory for the rest of the day and evening.

He said he had finished his homework, and wanted to watch television. Anna had once believed she would ban television, that she would not have a television in her house. But she had never managed to do that, and now Rory spent nearly all his free time in front of it. She worried that he would grow up uneducated, ordinary, his head full of junk. But she could do nothing to stop him. Besides, she watched quite a lot of television herself, although she did not like to admit it to her literary friends.

Alex came home at six, earlier than usual. He was elated, she could see as soon as he came into the house. His skin glowed, as if he had been out in the fresh air, and he walked with a bounce.

She kissed him briefly. 'Hi,' she said.

A few years ago she would have commented on how he looked, she would have asked him what had happened to make him so pleased with himself. But she had lost the habit of intimacy with him. They co-existed now, rather than shared a life. She was not sure how this had happened.

'How are you?' He sat down at the kitchen table.

This alarmed her slightly, since he never did that. Usually when he came in, he greeted her and then went to his study, emerging for the evening meal. It was not companionable but it saved her from having to make forced conversation with him. Now he was there, waiting for her to talk. She was chopping onions, preparing the curry they would have for dinner, a meal Rory would eat.

'Oh fine,' she said. 'Nothing much happened. Went for a walk. Picked up Rory.' She considered telling him about the stolen lunch and decided not to bother. It was not the sort of detail that interested him.

'I have very good news,' he said.

She smiled and looked at him expectantly. But not too expectantly. Sometimes he said things like that and the good news would turn out to be something fairly insignificant – he had got a letter from some important busybody, congratulating him on his performance at a meeting, or he had got a new secretary, or something that was of marginal interest to anybody other than himself.

'I sold the place in Cork for forty million,' he said.

'That sounds like a lot,' she said.

'It cost me five million six years ago. So it is a lot,' he said proudly.

'Congratulations!' She kissed him, thinking that she should feel more elation, or jubilation, or admiration. Forty million was a lot of money. Anna had had no money when she was growing up. But somehow the figure meant nothing to her, because they didn't need it. It was extra, that was all. 'That's fantastic.'

He appreciated it much more than she did, patting himself on the back for his own astuteness, although he knew luck had been involved, and good timing.

'We should celebrate.'

'Of course!' she said. 'What would you like to do?'

'It calls for a real celebration.' He looked at her meaningfully, and she tried not to look away. What did he mean? Opening a bottle of champagne would hardly count as a real celebration. Would he want to go out to eat? With just her or with other people, with Rory?

'Shall we go out to somewhere really nice?'

'I think we should go for a weekend to somewhere really nice … some good hotel. You pick.'

'OK,' she said. 'Next weekend?'

'We can't leave it for longer … otherwise the feeling will go stale. And tonight we should eat out.'

'OK,' she said flatly. She had been looking forward to spending a night in front of the television. 'I'll ring René's,' she said.

She gave Rory his dinner and phoned for a baby-sitter; Rory was not pleased, since he liked to be baby-sat by Luz Mar, if Anna had to go out. She pacified him by promising to take him to the zoo in a few days' time.

She bathed and dressed carefully, even though she felt tired and did not feel particularly elated. So Alex had made a good deal. He had often made good sales before, but nothing on this scale. About thirty million after tax. It was much more than the lottery, she told herself, trying to understand what it might mean. But she couldn't. Probably it would mean very little, apart from this dinner and the weekend, wherever it was. Alex would invest the money in some other property, hoping to make another huge profit in a few years' time. They had everything they needed, everything they wanted – what more could they want? The house was as fine as they could have, almost … there was always something better, needless to say. She would not have minded an old country manor. When a professional couple had bought Lissadell a few years back, a purchase that had attracted much publicity, Anna had thought that she would like to live in just such a house, huge, old, celebrated, a house with a history, a house that had been described in the poetry of the greatest Irish poet.

She would have liked dozens of rooms and acres of land,

horses, chickens, all that. It would have represented a change from this suburban lifestyle. It would bring her real life into the realm of the fairy tale, which was, perhaps, where she had always unconsciously sought. But she knew it would not work. Alex had to be in town, for work. Rory was happy in his school, and in his suburb, and so was she; she liked to be able to go to the literary events in town, the plays and exhibitions, and she liked to shop. If they had a big house in the country, they would have needed a town house too, just as the landed gentry always had. And that would be too much, somehow.

There was nothing to buy with Alex's wealth. After a certain level had been reached, no more was needed. She did not really understand why he continued to work and slave, accumulating more and more property, when he must have known it was un-necessary. Still, she enjoyed the security of knowing there was so much money in their bank accounts, that Rory would have his own apartment or house as soon as he was old enough to want it, that financial worries would never be theirs. She had been an ordinary lower middle-class child, living with just enough to get by, and so she appreciated the security, the luxury that Alex's money could buy for her and her child.

'Beautiful!' Alex said, when she came down, carefully made up, dressed in an old 1920s silken suit, which she had bought at a vintage shop. 'It's new, isn't it?' He wouldn't notice that it was vintage, that she had discovered it, as if it were a hidden treasure, buried in a rack of clothes in a little old street in the city centre.

She nodded, 'Yes, it's new.'

Alex was neat as always, in a dark blue suit and white shirt. He always wore almost exactly the same outfit, for work or prestigious social occasions, the only kind of social occasion he considered worthwhile devoting time to.

'You are so beautiful!' He kissed her as they left to step into the taxi. The high stone walls of their road, a winding lane of a road, seemed to move closer to the sides of the car, threaten-ingly. The radio was playing loud music. She was glad she did not have to talk.

The taxi dropped them at the end of the lane on which the restaurant was situated, discreetly tucked out of view of the crowds. The weather had changed. It was raining and Anna had forgotten to take an umbrella. She pulled up her coat collar as they ran along the dark lane. She tripped over a man who lay on the ground wrapped in a sleeping bag and almost lost her footing.

'God,' said Alex. 'Couldn't you sleep in a porch like everyone else?'

The man grunted. Anna felt unreasonably angry at Alex. To show that she did not share his intolerance she reached into her pocket but there was nothing there. She glanced at the man, trying to indicate that she was not his enemy. But he wasn't looking at either her or Alex. Instead, to her astonishment, he was reading a book; he wore round, wiry spectacles. Although every second doorway in Dublin was stuffed with a sleeping man in a sleeping bag, she had never before noticed one of them doing this ordinary thing that everyone who slept at home in a bed did: reading. She began to open her bag. Alex grabbed her elbow and said, 'Come on!' in a sharp voice. 'But ...' she began. Then she shrugged and allowed herself to be guided, or pushed, into the restaurant.

It was almost full when they got there. The lobby had that cluttered, cosy charm that the lobbies of these places always had. Anna longed to sink into the deep red sofa, set beside a roaring fire, where she could put her irritation at Alex out of her mind. The room smelt comfortably of pleasant things: a suggestion of burning turf, fresh carnations, and roasting meat. But a waiter in a black suit ushered them immediately into the dining room and brought them to a table in the middle of the floor, where everyone would see them. Anna took this as a compliment to her appearance, but the waiter had been instructed that Alex was a regular customer and a rich man, even though nobody ever recognised him. So there they sat in the midst of a cross-section of Dublin's wealthiest and most celebrated personalities. Without bothering to look very closely, Anna recognised two government Ministers, the presenter of one of the most popular television programmes, and the owner of a chain of supermarkets in the room. There were no writers, actors, artists – you would not expect them in a place like this, unless they were brought along as the guests of someone who was a success in a more lucrative walk of life than art.

The room buzzed with conversation, laughter, energy. In sharp contrast to the old-fashioned, rather oppressive decor of the place – white tablecloths, heavy silver, a restaurant in a dress suit – the atmosphere was light and relaxed, due to the utter confidence of its customers. They were enjoying themselves, secure in the knowledge that the food would be perfect and that only their peers shared the room with them. This restaurant was so exclusive that it did not even allow itself to be reviewed in the newspapers or magazines. Unless you were in the know, you would never have heard of it.

Anna loved it for its liveliness, as well as for its food, although she found the surroundings in other ways unpleasant. Particularly irritating was the 'silver service', which they insisted upon – perhaps it was some sort of rule for restaurants with two or three Michelin stars, or whatever it was they had. Two waiters carried their starters on huge silver-topped plates, whipped off the covers with a dramatic flourish at exactly the same moment, and deposited in front of them the big white plates with their little mounds of salad and prawn, two fat prawns to be exact, for her, and pâté de foie gras for him. It was more ceremonious than Mass.

'Mm, delicious,' she said, as she bit into her prawn.

She raised her glass of wine and said, 'Congratulations!' to Alex, for the third or fourth time.

He touched glasses with her and bowed his head slightly. He belonged to another age, she thought. It was a thought she had often had. Once, it had been one of the characteristics that had attracted her to him, his gentlemanly aura, his whiff of the early nineteenth century. All men still looked and dressed like Beau Brummell, up to a point, not having changed their style in any essential way for about two hundred years. But Alex looked as if that style had been created specially for him.

'How is your book coming along?' he asked. Her reward for paying a compliment to his work was this rare question.

'Well, it's coming along.' She knew he had very little interest in it, but she had to talk about something. 'It's going to be very long, so it's a bit disheartening knowing that I'm still only about fifteen per cent of the way through it after four months' work.'

'Why does it have to be so long?'

'It's the genre. It's a fantasy novel, with its own complex world, like the Narnia books, or Philip Pullman's.' She did not want to mention *Harry Potter*, the real inspiration for the book, for some reason.

Alex was perplexed. He had never heard of Philip Pullman, and he recalled that the Narnia books, which he had not much liked as a child, were not actually particularly long. 'Like the *Harry Potter* books?' he said. Alex liked them. He had read a few aloud to Rory. He had found them much less irritating than the Narnia stuff.

'Yes, that sort of thing. It's not that it's like the *Harry Potter* books.' Was this true? 'It's historical. It's about a modern child in Dublin who travels in time, to various eras in history.' Which was a bit like *Sophie's World*, it occurred to her. Strange. She knew that *Harry Potter* was an influence, but now, all of a sudden, she realised that *Sophie's World*, a book she had enjoyed very much, was an unconscious one. In fact, her book was much more like *Sophie's World* than it was like *Harry Potter*. The influences of which the author is unaware are much more pernicious than those of which she is fully conscious. Well, with luck nobody else would notice – it was years since *Sophie's World* had been published.

She finished her prawns, her second prawn. Alex had eaten his pâté in two bites and now the waiters came and carried off their empty plates.

'Sounds very interesting,' said Alex.

'So far the heroine has visited Dalkey Island, in the age of the Vikings, and travelled to Iceland and Norway,' Anna went on brightly. 'Next she is going to go to America, just at the time of Columbus's arrival there. And so on. And she will travel into the future as well.' She hoped. If she could think of anything interesting to write about the future. She should probably keep the future for a future volume – volume two or three maybe.

Alex wasn't listening. He nodded, but she could tell he had not heard anything she had said for a few minutes. This was one of his habits. No matter how hard he tried – and he had been trying tonight – he could not maintain interest in her, or in anyone, for more than a minute or two. Then he became bored and reverted to his own thoughts. More than most, he lived in a world of his own.

They both did this for the next five minutes or so, focusing on their food. Anna, mildly dismayed as she often was at Alex's tendency to become bored with small talk and switch off, even though he seldom replaced it with any other kind of talk, managed to become philosophical about this as she dealt with her risotto. The problem with Alex, she reasoned, was that he was just too masculine. Masculine men could not understand any point of view except their own. Single-minded, they had developed blinkered vision millions of years ago to sharpen their hunting skills. Alex was a hunter supreme, even if what he was hunting was money rather than elks or bears. Empathising with other human beings was simply not a skill he needed for his life's work, and try as he did to pretend he was interested in them, he was too honest to keep up the pretence for long – not even as long as it took to eat a celebratory dinner with his wife.

She had not expected Alex to be like that when she married him. Then, he had been in love with her. He adored her, he could not bear to spend an evening apart from her. It had been ridiculous, the extent to which he was in love with her. Then, she had been the object of the hunt, so he focused exclusively on her. But even though she knew the intensity could not last, she had not expected it to be replaced with near apathy.

And she had not been in love with him in the same mad way that he was with her. That hadn't bothered her much – she could see that his emotion was exceptional, over the top, and felt that hers was at the more normal end of the spectrum. She hadn't felt that she was capable of the obsessive, intense love Alex had had for her, at the beginning. Demeaning, it had been, too, that sort of love, like an addiction to some toxic substance – although it was shorter lived than most chemical addictions. That sort of love had seemed to her something she was as well off without. She loved Alex. She liked him and respected him, and they got on well in bed together too. Marrying him had been the right thing to do.

Now, ten years later, she still liked him, and he liked her. But they slept together more and more rarely, and they had nothing to talk about. Was that what marriage was like for everyone? How could you really know? People lied about these things as a matter of course, to themselves and to their friends. You knew it because many couples seemed to be perfectly content, living even an idyllic life together. Then, out of the blue, they were splitting up, and other people gossiped and said, yes, it had been coming for a long time.

There was one subject Alex and Anna could both talk about,

with almost equal interest: Rory. But she wanted to keep him for dessert, so she raised general topics: the new railway bridge in Killiney, which was spectacularly beautiful and which locals were dubbing Xanadu; the fate of the government's new master plan on Dublin transport, which promised the sun, moon and stars, and which nobody believed would ever be implemented – Anna said this quite loudly, noticing, suddenly, that the Minister was in the room. She talked about their next city break, the one they would go on to celebrate the sale of the property. Seville, they thought, would be right. They hadn't been there, and it was close enough to make a weekend trip feasible.

Anna cheered up, thinking of that. She and Alex got on better on their holidays than they did at home, because on holiday he tended to become interested in his surroundings, whereas at home they meant nothing to him.

The evening sped by quickly enough, the fuss over the serving of the various courses and the pleasure of eating helped the time to pass. They did not have a lively conversation, but neither did they lapse into a prolonged silence, like so many married couples eating celebratory dinners.

She was standing up to leave when she spotted Vincy Erikson. That journalist from the book launch. She recognised him immediately. He was at a table at the edge of the room, behind her chair, which was why she had not seen him before.

What was *he* doing in a place like this?

He waved and she smiled. Alex had gone to the cloakroom. Vincy came across the room and said hello, and quickly kissed Anna on the cheek. She was taken aback. Everyone kissed on the cheek these days, some of them once, some of them twice, some even three times, like people in Spain or somewhere. It was the new handshake. Still, she was not usually kissed by people who had met her only once before in their lives.

'This is a pleasant surprise,' he said.

'Yes,' she said, confused, for some reason.

They smiled uneasily at one another. His long hair was as wild as ever, and he had not put on a tie, even in deference to this restaurant. His jacket, though, gave him a dressed-up look. Velvet. She thought velvet on men was a bit fishy, but on him it looked fine.

'I am here with the owner of the newspaper,' he said, as if he knew an explanation of his presence in this restaurant was required. 'It's a sort of business meeting.'

'We're celebrating a success of Alex's,' Anna said, not wanting to go into the details.

It didn't matter what they said. The words were like wrapping paper, enclosing secret messages. Anna sensed she was learning a new language, a code of signs and tones. She had to read under the English words another text, a message for her eyes only.

'Yes,' he said, his eyes meeting hers, twinkling. 'That's wonderful. I will be at the opening of *Hamlet* in the Abbey on Wednesday night. Will you be there?'

'Maybe,' said Anna, looking at him questioningly. He did not take his eyes off her face. She did not have a ticket to the opening on Wednesday night but she knew she could get one.

Alex came back then, and she introduced them. Alex said hello briskly and paid no attention to Vincy. He was ready to go home. Anna would have liked to linger and chat, but there was no point in delaying Alex. Regretfully, she said goodnight to Vincy. He inclined his head slightly, and did not kiss her this time.

On the way up the lane to the taxi, which had been ordered, Anna stooped and put a note under the sleeping bag of the man with the book -- he was still there but now was tucked up in his bag, his head invisible, just like any of the other hundreds of sleepers all over Dublin. She gave him ten euro -- about five times the amount she usually gave, hiding the sum with her hand. Now she glowed with generosity, tucking under the edge of the sleeping bag the rusty-tinted note. The man -- the man without a name or a label, a man who defied classification, the hobo or the homeless man or the tramp or whatever he was -- seemed to be asleep. She could just as well have ignored him and saved herself ten euro, she thought, regretfully. But as she and Alex walked away a thin white hand emerged from the bag, took the note and slipped it into his book, and a pair of glasses peeped over the rim of the sleeping bag and watched her going up the shady alley to the bright light of the street.

Eight

The light in the valley in the early afternoon was as rich as molten butterscotch. The good autumn weather had continued well into October. One glorious day followed on the heels of another, until you'd think warm days would never cease. Everyone in the valley clung on to routines that made the most of the Indian summer – some called it St Martin's summer. They continued eating out of doors; the brave ones went for daily swims in the ocean: this was the best time for swimming, they declared, shivering, when the water was still warm and the visitors had gone home. The pub organised barbecues in the car park on Sundays, in an attempt to extend the season before the doldrums of winter, when there would be two or three at the bar on weeknights, set well and truly in. Some of the summer-house people were still coming to the valley for weekends, getting use out of their houses, before they, too, would be closed up, put to bed like tired animals for the long hibernation.

Leo, too, in spite of all his problems, enjoyed the autumn. At about two o'clock each day, after a lunch of bread and cheese, he went for a walk in the hills behind his house, or down to the harbour, or along the narrow lanes in the middle of the valley. The lanes were thickly overhung with wild flowers and bushes for most of the year – saxifrage, wild woodbine, fuchsia. Now the last of the summer flowers, the orange montbretia, had lost their brilliant blossom and all that remained of them was the bladelike foliage, a strange rusty colour, a bit like the colour of a ten euro bill. They were gone, and soon the roadsides would be bare, but now it was the turn of the brambles to dominate the hedgerow. The unpredictable hooking branches shot up and out all over the place, and were heavy with the weight of purple berries.

Leo stuffed a few plastic bags into his pockets when he went on his walk, and if the fancy struck him, he picked the berries, sometimes for hours, sometimes for minutes. Sometimes he didn't bother picking at all, and left the bags in the dark of his pockets, doing no more than popping a few of the sweet berries into his mouth. But using this unsystematic approach, by tricking himself into picking berries, he had managed to collect a lot. He put them in old plastic ice-cream boxes in the freezer. Blackberries freeze well. Already he had ten boxes, a kilo a box, tucked away. His plan was to make wine. Blackberry wine in autumn, elderflower wine in spring … that was his goal. Maybe in winter, when he could no longer go for walks, he would spend some hours in the afternoon fulfilling it: making wine. It sounded like a good thing to do, a nurturing way to spend winter afternoons. Already he could imagine it: the bubbling wine in the big glass flagons, the scent of must and fermenting fruit. And months later – when, he did not know – the taste of rich, sweet, home-made blackberry wine. He hoped. Autumn in a bottle. He had never tasted blackberry wine but knew it was bound to be delicious.

The blackberries were small this year, as a result of the un-usually dry summer, but one of his neighbours told him that was good; they didn't look as lovely as the big fat juicy berries you got sometimes, but they were sweeter and you could add the water yourself. He picked them in a place known as *an gleann mór*, 'the big glen'; it was really a narrow cleft that ran from the centre of the parish, where the old church sat in a little overgrown graveyard, right back into the mountainside. A stream ran down the mountain and through the middle of this place, widening with the valley; he could hear it babbling noisily as he reached into the brambles and plucked the blackberries. Before the Famine, it was said that a hundred families had lived in the big glen but for many years it had been uninhabited. Now people were beginning to build here again. First, a New Age family, who had moved from Dublin in the eighties had built their own house deep in the side of the mountain, a higgledy-piggledy eco-house, with sunrooms and sunroofs and balconies, chickens and ducks and rabbits, their dream home built with their own hands, hidden behind huge fuchsia bushes and separated from the road by the river – they had to drive or wade through water to get to their front door, something which Leo had envied them. He knew they would make wine from blackberries and elderflower, from sloes and cowslips, from anything. They were that kind of people, famous for having ten children and never buying shop bread but baking wholemeal loaves, six of them, every morning when they got up.

More recently, sites had been sold in the big glen and other types of people, not New Age at all, had moved in. A pop star had built a mansion in a high field overlooking the river: a huge grey stone house that looked like a church, and was surrounded by paddocks for the horses his children were to ride, and an electric fence. He had a bar bigger than the one in the pub in his sitting room, and, outside the gable, a hot tub you couldn't see, where he and his guests bathed, naked, under the stars, drinking champagne and looking at the island in the night-time ocean. But the pop star had only stayed in the big glen for a year. Then he moved back to the city, complaining that the people of the valley had been unfriendly; nobody would accept his invitation to come in for a drink at the bar – he had asked his neigbours, old widows who never had a drink in their lives; they had said, 'A thousand thanks, I'll drop in sometime, of course I will', but that was the Irish for no, he was to discover. Others, who had not been invited, sneaked up the driveway to snoop, burning with curiosity about the hot tub, the jumps for the horses, the fabled bar. Soon the 'For Sale' sign was up again and had stayed up for a year and a half. Now a rich family had bought the house, but they kept themselves to themselves. Nobody knew them, or even knew who they were. They were not pop stars or celebrities of any kind; they did not own some big chain of supermarkets. Some people in the valley said they were dot.com millionaires, some said they were property developers. It was assumed they would not stay long.

A few more family houses had been built on the banks of the

stream, their gardens running down to the dancing water and their front rooms looking out at the island, the view everyone in this valley wanted to have.

Leo looked at the island with mixed feelings. Always iconic, it was the subject of controversy. Some people wanted it turned into a national park, others claimed it was private property and the owners should profit from its tourist potential. The island sat basking in the sun, oblivious to the wars that raged in the pub, in the courtroom, in the Sunday newspapers, on its behalf. Leo had his opinions. Naturally he wanted the island to be nationalised; it was what he wanted for most things. His views made him unpopular, he felt, looking at the island, green as moss on this lovely day, peeping up over the rim of a clutch of vicious brambles, which scratched his face like the hands of supernatural monsters in some gothic forest.

Leo, the valley idealist. The valley crank.

After his walk, lasting two hours as usual, he made his way back to his house, climbing the steep road, which when he was in a bad mood made him weary and wish he had bought a house down in the valley, in the big glen for instance, somewhere where he would not have to pant and lose his breath every time he went out.

But when he had bought the house, thirteen years ago, after his parents had been killed in a car crash and he had spent a year having a nervous breakdown, before selling the family home in Dundrum and using the money to move, there hadn't been so many options. In those days the 'Sites for Sale' signs had not been sprouting everywhere like mushrooms in the valley. You had to seek out a farmer and ask him to sell you a field, and then go through the planning application process yourself, or else buy a ramshackle old cottage that had been lived in by some ancient bachelor and do it up from top to bottom. The house on the hill had been the very best the valley had to offer, then. Now houses like that were all over the place. Mini-villages sprang up every summer: holiday homes, built for rent by entrepreneurs, who had also sprung up like dragons' teeth in the valley.

When he was not collecting blackberries, thinking about Kate, and moping, Leo worked at his publishing. He was waiting for the latest poetry collection to come from the printers. This one had been written by a new young writer, Tristan, who had recently graduated from one of the MA courses in creative writing that all the universities were offering these days. Leo used to get invitations to talk at these courses; one of the things they all did was invite in writers and people connected with writing to give seminars. Leo had told them all about the life of a small publisher in Ireland. He had told them about the difficulties of getting published at all, about how little money there was in it, about how the big conglomerates had eaten up the small houses, about how limited the chance of making a living was. 'I get a hundred manuscripts a month,' he would say – a gross exaggeration, but he wanted to teach them a lesson. 'Of which point two five per cent can get published. They will sell five hundred to a thousand copies, if they are lucky. If you take into account the money the writer spends on computers, paper, and ink, the writer always loses money.'

At first the directors of the MAs had admired Leo's honesty and forthrightness. He always got a strong reaction from the students: they were riveted by his gloomy manner, his sad story, his terrifying statistics. But after a few years the invitations had fizzled out. Leo gained a reputation. Some students had abandoned their creative writing courses after hearing him speak. It was rumoured that his seminar had triggered at least one suicide attempt. He had not given a seminar on poetry publishing now in about five years, even though there were more MAs than ever.

But like most of the students Leo had done his best to turn against writing as a career, Tristan believed that he was the one who would buck the trend. He planned to be a full-time writer. In the meantime, he was working part-time as a security guard in a fashion store in Tralee, a job which, he said, he liked, because it did not take his mind off his poetry. And now at the age of twenty-three, the age W.B. Yeats had been when *The Wanderings of Oisin* was published, Tristan's first book was out – it was fresh and funny; he had a sense of humour, and he was able to express it in both Irish and English. In his lighter moments, even Leo thought that Tristan might be right. He might be the lucky one, the one to make it.

Although Tristan came from this parish, and would have his main launch here in the pub, Leo had decided to have a second launch in Dublin. This would take place during an Irish poetry festival that was held every year in November. A launch held during that time could be counted as a festival event and funded by the organisers. Even though Leo knew nobody would come to the launch of a first-time poet in Irish in Dublin, he decided to go ahead with it, at the certain risk of causing Tristan great disappointment. Tristan was delighted with the prospect of exposure in Dublin, and Leo's mild attempts to dispel his illusions came to nothing.

The real reason Leo was bothering with the launch was that it would be an excuse to see Kate. He would send her an invitation and see what would happen. And of course there would also be a meeting of Killing Roads, a meeting where he would, if he could, kill the society dead for once and for all.

The Dingle launch was a great success. Kerry launches usually were. It was held in the local pub, which meant there was no hiring fee for the venue. Leo provided five bottles of white and five bottles of red, less than one glass of wine per guest, and six plates of cheese sandwiches. The guests could buy more alcohol if they felt like it; that was the beauty of using a pub as a venue.

All Tristan's relatives, from far and near, all his friends – half of the county – were in attendance. They made countless speeches praising Tristan and Leo, they ate the sandwiches and drank the wine, and then headed for the bar for pints. They stayed in the pub, talking and singing and playing the fiddle, until one in the morning. Many of them bought several copies of the book. Sales on the night amounted to almost three hundred copies, more than half the print run. Since grants had covered the printing costs, money Leo took in on this single night was almost all profit, or salary for himself – apart from the small royalty he would pay Tristan; Tristan had already got an author's grant from Bord na Leabhar Gaeilge. In fact he had done quite well, for a poet, an Irish language writer, and someone who was twenty-three. He should be well pleased.

Leo knew the Dublin launch would be very, very different. Tristan, unfortunately, seemed to believe that his urban literary experience would be a mirror image of his rural one, that the city launch would be as lively and successful as the Gaeltacht one, or even better. How he could possibly imagine this, Leo did not know. Didn't they teach them anything on those MAs? It was a great pity he, Leo, was not still giving his depressing talk about the sad realities of literary life.

Tristan's launch took place in St Martin's Hall, an old church hall on Stephen's Green where many poetry book launches were occurring this winter. It was an excellent location, being almost right beside the Luas terminus. Very central. But while the hall had certain advantages, it was dim and gloomy, its low ceiling oppressively burdened with thick oak beams. The floor was concrete and the room so filled with rows of black plastic chairs that there was no space for people to circulate.

Tristan came along early and helped Leo set up tables in a corner of the big room, filling them with stacks of books and bottles of wine and wine glasses.

'My girlfriend will help with the wine,' Tristan said. 'She came up with me. She's out looking at the shops in Grafton Street.'

Leo nodded. He would have to sell the books himself – but he usually did this at launches. 'Did you ask a lot of friends to come?' Leo asked thoughtfully.

'I asked any friend I have. But that's not an awful lot, in Dublin,' Tristan laughed anxiously. He was cheerful and good-humoured, but, like most poets, rather nervous under the surface.

'It'll be enough,' said Leo, with much more confidence than he felt. He was getting nervous too, not about the number of guests, since he knew what it would be, but because he began to be afraid that Kate would not turn up. She had not replied to the invitation even though he had sent her one in the post and one by email, stopping short of telephoning her as well, lest he seem too pushy.

A couple of people straggled into the ecclesiastical hall ten minutes before the starting time of seven o'clock. Both were organisers of the Irish poetry festival, coming to check out the event and compare it to others. Of course they did not feel they should have to buy a book. Leo had to give them one each instead, something he hated doing.

At seven about ten people had arrived, and by a quarter past

100

two more had come in. That would be it, Leo thought. It was actually better than he had expected although he pretended to Tristan that he was expecting many more. 'We'll give them till seven thirty,' he said. 'The traffic is very heavy.' It was something that publishers comforted poets with all the time at launches: the heavy traffic. The bad evening. You could not say that tonight because the evening was very fine. It was dark of course. You could suggest that that had put them off: the dark. It was difficult to make it convincing in the context of this particular festival, based on the idea that the dark nights of Samhain were the ideal time for storytelling sessions, poetry readings, and all the rest, but it was as true as anything else. 'Once they go home after work they don't feel like coming out again.' To something like this anyway.

Those who were here, all twelve of them, were having a good time though. Leo watched with dismay as the wine disappeared with great rapidity.

When, at half past seven, Kate had not arrived, Leo put a start to the launch. He introduced Tristan, saying he was the most talented writer he had ever come across and predicting that he would go very far and that these books would become collectors' items. And who knew? That might be true.

Tristan then proceeded to read half a dozen poems.

And – this was the great thing about this poet – his reading was a real pleasure. Tristan had developed his own style, which was modelled on Afro-American rap. He chanted, he sang, he shouted, he cried. His body swayed and his arms waved and he opened his mouth and wailed. He even had a mouth organ – he had copied this from one of his heroes, Bob Dylan – and interspersed stanzas with short traditional tunes, cheerful or sad as the poem dictated.

The audience was surprised and delighted – the last thing they had expected was to be genuinely entertained. And Tristan was experienced enough as a listener not to read for longer than his audience could stand. He did that great thing: he finished leaving them wanting more – a rare enough occurrence at any poetry reading, still less at the launch of a first book.

The applause was enthusiastic and people flocked, all of them, to buy the book, even the two who had got free copies already. Twelve copies: this was Dublin, and an audience accustomed to going to launches. Everyone bought the regulation single copy. Not a single journalist or photographer had attended, which was also par for the course. Leo knew he would have his work cut out to get a review, even a few lines, in any of the national newspapers. But, as can happen, in spite of everything, this launch had been a great success.

It had been a great success because Tristan was such a good poet and a good performer. Leo began to believe his own hype. This young man would go far. He must tuck away a box of the books and put them down for future use, like wine that would mature and become more valuable with the years. Tristan was not home-made blackberry. He might turn out be a good Bordeaux. Nobody would be happier for him than Leo.

Finally everyone went home. Leo should have asked Tristan out to dinner, but he excused himself, saying he was too tired. Instead, he offered to pay for a dinner for Tristan and his girl-friend, saying he could get a tax rebate for it, which was not true. Tristan believed him, however, and took the hundred euro offered with a grateful smile. He and his girlfriend, who had been kept busy all night pouring wine, would have a better time without Leo anyway.

Leo went back to his B & B on Amiens Street – one of those establishments that appeared towards the bottom of the 'budget accommodation' lists on the tourist websites. He always stayed there when he was in Dublin but, coincidentally, it was not far, he remembered ruefully, from Kate's apartment. For some reason he waited until he was safely inside his bedroom, a reasonably large room that smelt slightly damp or mouldy, before telephoning Kate. He needed to be alone, and sitting down, and private, for this conversation.

But he needn't have worried.

She was warm and friendly.

'Oh hi!' she said. 'I was hoping you'd call. I couldn't make it to the launch, I was held up at work, and I felt so bad. How did it go?'

He told her, and then asked if she was free to meet him for a drink or a coffee. It was already nine thirty.

'Sure, love to,' she said.

They arranged to meet in the bar of a new hotel, which was

not too far from her apartment, or from his room, although she did not know that.

He waited in the foyer until she arrived. He watched from a position slightly shielded by a potted plant as she came in. Her skin was rosy – she had been rushing – and her hair untidy from the wind, which had blown up after nightfall. She was wearing a short, pale blue raincoat, jeans and some sort of low-cut, dark T-shirt. This was much more casual attire than her usual black work outfit. It suited her. It made her seem, on the whole, less like his idea of a Parisian mannequin and more like a real human being. Leo did not notice any of this, but he noticed that Kate looked as if she could, possibly, live down the country. In Kerry. With him.

She kissed him on the cheek. His heart lifted, forgetting momentarily that a kiss on the cheek meant absolutely nothing. He ushered her up the wide staircase to the bar, which was on the first floor. To his relief it was not very busy and there was no difficulty in finding a table in a nice secluded corner, with two deep comfortable chairs.

'Mm, I like it here,' she said, looking around appreciatively. They were sitting on a very big balcony that was wrapped around an atrium. Below, on the ground, was the foyer, with some greenery in evidence. Five storeys above was a glass roof: the entire hotel was built around a big empty space, a tower of air. The walls all around this looked like exterior walls – rendered, with long Georgian windows. The whole effect was designed to encourage you to feel you were outdoors, even though you were in an interior where the climate was as controlled as it might be in a museum.

'Right,' said Leo, who thought it fairly hideous, just because it tried to be something it was not. 'So, how are you?' He wanted the conversation to become less architectural and more personal, as soon as possible.

The waitress came just then to spoil the intimacy. Leo ordered his usual Guinness, and Kate a dry white wine. There was a little ceremony as the waitress explained which kinds of white wine were available, and insisted on bringing three little labelled bottles to show them.

'She's so nice!' Kate said, when they had finally got their drinks. 'To go to so much trouble! Isn't she?'

'Yes, must remember to leave a tip,' said Leo, irritated.

Everything was OK in one way, but in another, he felt it was not going right. After the elaborate negotiations with the waitress, he found it difficult to get the conversation back to where he wanted it to be. He was never skilled at steering a conversation; he envied those who had the knack of always swinging the talk around to precisely the point most useful to themselves.

'How is work?' he started again. Not a great opener. Kate had too much to say about it, not too little.

'Oh, hectic, as always.' She launched into a detailed, manic account of the projects she was engaged on: she was going abroad to two conferences over the next fortnight, she was organising press receptions for three different openings, she was applying for funding to UNESCO. Much of her work was similar to his, he realised. She would be a good business partner.

He expressed the first part of this thought.

'Do you like living down there in the country?' she asked. It was a genuine query.

He stared at her, his eyes wide open – he had read that looking straight in the eye was a key tactic in courtship in a self-help book (*How to be Irresistible to Women*) that he had bought in a Tralee bookshop years ago. He still dipped into it from time to time, to be reminded to wash himself before going on a date, that no meant no and that a neat appearance seldom repelled the female of the species.

'Yes,' he said. 'I love it. I love the surroundings. It's so different from a city.' How profound could you be? He struggled on. 'Everything is more elemental – you get closer to what life means, I think, down there.' He tried to find a better way of expressing what he meant. But what was that? What did he mean? What was so good about the country, or so different? Not the slower pace. He never knew what that meant, the pace seemed exactly the same to him; his was anyway. 'I like the blackberries,' he said. That was true. 'And the other things that grow – the primroses, the *felastrim*, the early purple orchids … there's a cycle of flowers, every year they come at the same time and go away again, right on cue. And the birds the same.' He glanced at her hopefully. 'And the animals,' he added weakly. 'And the way people talk, in the pub, at nights.'

Not the way he was talking now.

But how different could two pubs be, he thought, looking at

the drinkers seated at their little isolated polished tables and thinking of the pub in the valley, with the plasma screen television in the corner and the regulars perched on their bar stools, talking about the roadworks or the weather.

'Hm,' she said thoughtfully, and sipped her wine. She looked at the big tree that they had growing in the hall, that stretched high up towards the glass ceiling. 'I never thought of ... all that.'

All what?

'I think that's what I like about it.' That it has seasons? And a pub? That was what he was saying. 'The stars at night. When it's not raining. You can't see as many stars in a city.'

'We see a lot of stars in the garden in Foxrock,' she said. 'Where Mummy and Daddy live.'

Leo sipped his pint. Mummy and Daddy was good. Should he ask her for more details about her family? Girls liked talking about that sort of thing. But she pre-empted him by saying 'But don't you get *bored* in the country?' in a cheeky sort of voice.

'No,' he said, although he did sometimes. 'No, it's never boring. I'm very busy with my work. Well, you know what it's like. It's like your work, more or less, with the selection and editing and proofreading thrown in. And then I do a lot of domestic stuff that I probably wouldn't do here. There's always something. I pick berries.'

'Mm,' she said.

Picking berries. She probably didn't think much of that as a way of entertaining yourself in the evening.

'And it's not lonely,' he said, although this was precisely the problem, the reason he was here trying to get a wife. 'There are other people around.' Not many. 'There's a pub. I can go down any night and know I'll meet friends.' He did not specify that they were four men over the age of seventy. 'There are a lot of committees as well, to promote the area, to encourage new enterprises, and so on, and I sit on all of them. And people have parties, especially during the winter. Then in the summer it's very active with all the summer people and tourists and so on.' He stared at her again. 'You'd like it.'

She laughed, in a way that he could not interpret. She had finished her glass of wine.

'Would you like another?' he asked.

Kate shook her head. 'I should go,' she said. She yawned. 'Early start tomorrow!'

'OK,' said Leo, trying to disguise his disappointment. 'I suppose I should get the bill then.'

'Yes,' she said firmly.

The waitress had been perfect, as Kate had commented, but she was nowhere to be seen now. He scanned every inch of the wide, elegant space. Not a single waiter in sight.

'I often wonder if you got up and walked out without paying, would anyone even notice, in a place like this?' he said, shaking his head wonderingly.

Kate laughed uneasily and she too tried to spot one of the elusive staff. 'Maybe they're hidden behind the greenery,' she said. 'Everything is so totally discreet here, hiding things is the house style.'

She and Leo saw Vincy Erikson at the same moment. He was sitting in an alcove with a few other people. They were engaged in animated conversation but Vincy happened to look up and he caught Kate's eye.

'Look, isn't that the man who was at the launch with the President, the Heaney thing,' Leo turned and asked Kate.

She was smiling so broadly at Vincy that she hardly heard what Leo was saying. Her face was transformed, as if she had been touched by a magic wand. As if she'd had an instantaneous make-over, as she might have put it herself. Even Leo could not fail to notice it. She was, all of a sudden, totally alive.

'What's that?' She turned back to Leo.

He was now watching Vincy, who waved at both of them. Leo returned the wave, not knowing why he was doing it.

'Isn't that the man we talked to at the Heaney book launch a while ago?' Leo repeated.

'Yes, yes, that's him,' said Kate. Her manner changed. She was brighter than before, but the face she turned to him was closed, like a door that has been shut and locked.

'What's this his name is?' he continued.

'Vincy. Vincy Erikson,' she said.

'Do you know him well?' he quizzed her.

'Oh, not really,' she said. 'I see him in connection with work sometimes. He's a journalist.'

The waitress picked that moment to arrive at their table with the bill.

He knew there was little point in trying to force Kate to commit herself to coming to Kerry. It was obvious that she was more interested in that journalist than she was in him, in spite of what she said. His heart, his sinking heart, told him that, even while his head persisted in believing what was said, in making crazily logical deductions: she had come here to meet him; she had said that Vincy chap was some sort of colleague only. So he persisted in his pathetic ambition, even taking out his pocket diary to write in a date, the date of her visit. Kate blanched at the sight of it but he didn't notice, thumbing through the pages.

'Why don't we arrange it?' He was talking as if they were arranging a publishers' meeting, not a date.

Kate frowned and flushed. 'I'm just so terribly busy right now.' She looked around at the high beige walls, the palm trees, the dark tables with the shining glasses. 'I just couldn't make a commitment.' Something in his face made her add, in a kinder tone, 'Maybe later, maybe in the spring ...'

He had to bite his lip to stop himself from howling.

Maybe in the spring.

It was only the first week of November.

He had been planning the wedding, practically. He had visualised it in detail. In the tiny chapel in the old graveyard in the big glen on a summer's day. He had seen the resplendent fuchsia tossing its crimson head in celebration; he had heard the lark singing in the clear bright air and smelt the honeysuckle, headily sweet, dangling delicious, inexpressible promises.

Now he saw the romantic picture again – Kate walking up the tiny aisle in a snowy dress, and standing there, to meet her at the altar, that fellow hiding over behind the aspidistra in the brass pot. That Vincy Erikson.

Nine

A few nights later, Anna met Vincy, just minutes before the curtain went up on the new production of *Hamlet* at the Abbey. She had found someone who had tickets – Lilian. Lilian got a lot of invitations.

Lilian had had a chance to read the piece of *Sally and the Ship of Dreams* that Anna had sent her a few weeks earlier. One of her many good qualities was that she was efficient. You didn't have to wait for weeks for Lilian to answer an email; you always got the reply by return of post.

'I think it's wonderful,' she said of the novel, the novel for young people or those who are young at heart. When she said 'wonderful', the word did not sound tired and clichéd. It sounded like a genuine endorsement. 'It's really original and entertaining.'

This was what Anna wanted to hear. Who would not?

'I'll look at it more closely,' Lilian went on. They were walking down Lower Abbey Street in the cold dark November night, past the China Showrooms. Anna stole a look at its interesting, shiny window as she passed – she always hoped she would see some gem there, amidst the heaps of crockery, china tea-sets, crystal ware, towels, duvets, and sweatshirts, which it contained. The shop windows on the north side were always more mysterious, more miscellaneous, than those south of the river. 'But honestly,' Lilian was continuing, her mind on the topic in hand, as always, 'I don't think there is anything in it that I would change.'

Anna was in very good humour indeed as they walked into the theatre and upstairs past the big portraits of Lady Gregory and the Fay brothers, up to the bar. Their seats were on the balcony so they had to go there anyway.

There, just at the top of the stairs on the velvet seats that backed onto the banister, was Vincy, drinking a coffee with some friends – one male, one female, neither known to Anna. He saw Anna as soon as she came in but he was out of her line of vision as she entered the bar area and glanced ahead, trying to see who was there, in the large throng that had already gathered.

Vincy could not contain himself. He stood up for a second and called to her, to catch her attention.

Anna turned and saw him, lanky and loose-limbed, with his too-thin face surrounded by his untidy hair, like a bony little bird in a rough nest. He looked younger than he was, and vulnerable. He seemed to sense that she was looking at him, because he turned immediately and saw her. His eyes lit up and met hers. For a few seconds they held the gaze. Then they both smiled, amused rather than embarrassed.

Lilian, observing this interplay with some shock, and the woman at Vincy's table knew at once that Vincy and Anna were attracted to one another. Anna and Vincy knew it too – at that moment the muddled emotion he engendered in her, which had been confusing her for weeks, seemed to define itself. It was as if an electric wire had run across the Abbey bar and enlightened both of them.

Lilian and the woman with Vincy could sense this, and it made them uneasy.

The man at Vincy's table, however, noticed nothing. He did not even wonder why Vincy had stood up abruptly. All his attention was directed at his coffee cup, which he was trying to empty before the play began. He glanced at his watch and said, as Vincy sat down again, 'We better go in; it'll be starting soon.'

The woman at the table – it was Kate's colleague, Lauren – glanced knowingly at Vincy and wanted to laugh at her partner's insensitivity, which she found both touching and amusing. But of course she did not laugh. Both she and Vincy pretended that nothing at all had happened one second before, just as Anna and Lilian were doing, as they walked quite naturally through the room, to the other side, where the toilets were and where Anna wanted to fix up her hair.

In another part of the room, the little place at the window, Kate stood, her heart pounding, her stomach sinking. She had come in her official capacity to the opening, and it was she who had given Vincy a ticket and invited him. (She was chalking it up as another 'date', nevertheless.) Earlier in the evening she had sat at that table with Vincy and Lauren and her boyfriend, and then left them to talk to some other people with whom she was duty bound to network. But all the time she was making conversation with people who might be useful to her organisation, chatting about the producer and the play and productions of *Hamlet* she had seen previously, she was conscious of Vincy, drinking coffee at the table near the top of the stairs. She had placed herself in a position where she could see him, because observing him gave her pleasure. She loved the look of him. It also gave her pain. She was for some reason always anxious, worried that she would lose him, even though she had not, strictly speaking, gained him yet, so if she thought about it, she had nothing to lose. Lauren had a live-in partner – the man at the table. She would never steal a boyfriend from a friend and colleague and she didn't even think Vincy looked very attractive. Still, Vincy might be attracted to her. Kate kept an eye on them, just in case, as she chirped and chatted to the first-nighters.

She had seen Anna come in with Lilian, since she had half an eye on the top of the stairs, spotting whoever came up. Lilian was a writer who was somewhere in the middle of Kate's B list, as indeed Anna was. Lilian was the sort of person she said hello to at events like this, but with whom she would not normally engage in conversation. Anna, of course, was a different matter, since she was Gerry's sister. Kate was busy with Carl Thompson and Katherine Molyneux, who were posing for a photograph by one of the press photographers who were rushing around. Even as the photograph was being taken, and Carl was putting his arm around her, she was examining Anna, fairly idly. Anna was wearing a black velvet coat, which suited her perfectly. The coat was open and underneath was a blouse or some garment made of rich cream lace. Kate saw the clothes first, and saw how perfect they were, how unusual, how well they suited Anna's personality and style.

And then she saw the look that passed between Vincy and Anna and she too saw that they were connected and that there was nothing she could do about it, nothing.

The conversation with Katherine Molyneux and Carl Thompson lost all its sparkle. Even when the celebrated John Marvell joined them, Kate could hardly bring herself to talk to him. Luckily, the bell rang and the doorman began to shout in a voice that was both singsong and authoritative: 'Ladies and gentlemen please take your seats; the performance is about to commence', using the formula, and probably the same tone of voice, that the ushers in the Abbey had used since 1904.

Anna was already inside, tucked into her seat in the front row of the balcony, a seat she always liked. She looked down over the rows of heads to the big wide stage and tried to concentrate on the play.

It was an experimental production. The characters were dressed in modern clothes, and the ghost of Hamlet's father appeared on a television screen. All the actors screamed a lot and Hamlet was interpreted as a manic depressive.

This much she took in, but for most of the time she could not hear what the actors were saying, even though they spoke very loudly and it was easier to hear in the Abbey on the balcony than it was anywhere else in the theatre. But they might have been speaking a foreign language that she did not understand. All she could think of was Vincy. His image was foremost in her mind and blocked out everything, even what was right before her eyes. She was not considering what sort of a person he was, what his attributes were, what his history was, not even what he was doing just now. He was simply on her mind, a large image that would not be blotted out, even by the vision of a manic-depressive Hamlet shopping for skulls in a skull supermarket.

Occasionally his image was displaced, but only by worrying thoughts about what she would do during the interval, or after the play. There would be an interval; people would leave their seats and go out for a coffee or a drink in that big bar. Should she talk to him? Should she avoid him? If she talked to him, would she blush and stammer and give herself away? Would he do that? Would they embarrass one another?

She decided about halfway through the first half that she would not go out for the interval and so solve the problem.

But when the lights went up, just after the play-within-a-play scene, she immediately turned to Lilian and said, 'Let's go out.'

She sat at one of the little wooden tables while Lilian went to the bar and got two glasses of wine – the wine was free and the glasses were standing there, waiting for people to take them, since it was a first night.

After what seemed like ages, Vincy came up the stairs from the stalls, with Kate at this side. He saw Anna straight away and smiled at her. Everything was fine; Vincy was so experienced, he knew exactly how to deal with the situation, to calm everyone down. He smiled as a friend would smile, and then he and Kate came over and asked if they could join Anna and Lilian. Vincy ushered Kate forward with a warm proprietary gesture, his hand lightly placed on her waist, and she looked happy and relaxed.

They talked about the production, and about other productions of *Hamlet*, and about other productions of other plays by the same director, who was young and talented. The conversation was exactly the same, with minor variations, as that which was taking place all over the theatre, in the bar and on the stairs and downstairs in the foyer, out on the street under the awning where people went to have a cigarette. Anna and Vincy preserved their dignity. No locking of eyes occurred. And still, in spite of all their good management, something buzzed around the table; everyone sensed that something strange was happening, as if there were a strange ghost hovering in the room. This spirit animated Vincy and Anna, so their conversation sparkled, while on Kate and even on Lilian it had the opposite effect. What they said, what they heard, seemed flat and dull to them. They gulped their wine. They were relieved when the ushers started shouting, 'Ladies and gentlemen please take your seats; the performance is about to recommence.' Up they jumped, at the first word, although Anna had not touched her wine and wondered where the time had gone. Kate would have liked simply to go home and sleep.

When the play was over, Anna wrapped her velvet coat tight

around her, hurried out and down the stairs as soon as she could, saying goodbye to Lilian, who wanted to stay and enjoy the reception. Lilian shrugged, annoyed and puzzled, as she watched Anna darting out onto the street, where she was going to take a taxi all the way home.

Ten

Hamlet had opened on a Wednesday night, a good night to open a play, since the reviews on Thursday, if they were good, would ensure packed houses for the weekend, a weekend that Anna was going to spend with her husband in Seville. They were flying down to Spain on the Friday night and returning early on the Monday morning. Rory was not coming with them. Luz Mar would mind him most of the time, and his Aunt Olwen was going to take him out to Bray to visit his cousins on Sunday afternoon.

Although these short breaks were supposed to require very little advance planning, Anna found, as she always did, that it took two days to prepare for Seville. It wasn't packing to go away that took so much time, it was preparing the house for every eventuality that might befall it in her absence. She had to ensure there was enough food for everyone while she was away; she had to provide spare cash in case it was needed; she had to talk to Ludmilla and to Luz Mar, and go over all the arrangements with them. That was before getting clothes from the dry-cleaners, packing, checking the passports and tickets, or any of that. It took two days, there was no way out of it, ever. On the Thursday and Friday, she did not write her novel at all, but devoted herself totally to these preparations.

Ludmilla was the first to be talked to. She did not usually

come to the house at weekends, but Anna wanted her to come in on both Saturday and Sunday, to make sure than Rory and Luz Mar had a proper meal. You could not trust Luz Mar to cook dinner, and she was quite sure she would not dream of tidying up, since she never even tidied her own room.

Ludmilla seemed happy to oblige. 'OK,' she said. 'It is not a problem. I will come on Saturday at twelve and on Sunday at eleven.'

'Thanks so much, Ludmilla,' said Anna. She showed her the frozen Bolognese sauce in the freezer, for Saturday, and the sausages and rashers in the fridge for lunch, and the fish fingers and pizzas and frozen lasagne in case Rory wanted them at any time, and the envelope full of money for spare supplies and emergencies, and her mobile phone number and her hotel phone number.

Ludmilla assured her everything would be fine. 'Do you want me to do anything else, apart from cook?' she asked.

'No, I think that's it,' said Anna. 'Three hours on Saturday and two hours on Sunday ... or could you stay for three hours on Sunday as well?'

She was calculating. She paid Ludmilla eight euro an hour, so that would be forty-eight for the weekend work – maybe she should give her a bit extra since it was the weekend? Some people got double for Sundays. But that would be ridiculous. People like Ludmilla would not expect it. In Lithuania a rocket scientist – or whatever they had, a doctor – would get less than forty-eight euro a month. Ludmilla seemed to be prepared to work for practically nothing.

'Yes,' said Ludmilla, who needed all the money she could get.

'OK, then, three hours on Sunday. You could vacuum around a bit, maybe ... I'll pay you now in advance,' said Anna. She opened her bag and decided on sixty euro. That was about one euro fifty extra per hour.

Ludmilla did not look very pleased, however. 'Thanks very much,' she said icily, picking up the notes as if they were something the cat had done under the sofa. Maybe she had expected double pay? When she had started, six months ago, she had been grateful for little but by now she knew something about working conditions, and living expenses, in Ireland. She was always polite, and a wonderful worker, but she had become colder towards Anna.

'All right, I really appreciate your doing this, Ludmilla,' said Anna. She wished she had paid her double. Rory was in her hands for the next two and a half days. He was worth more than sixty euro. He was priceless. But it was too late to think of that now.

'You are welcome,' said Ludmilla, going to get her anorak. 'Have a nice holiday!' She left, slamming the door behind her.

Anna went to the window and watched her cycling down the drive and out onto the road. Ludmilla went everywhere on a bicycle, for exercise, Anna supposed, although Ludmilla got a lot of exercise anyway, cleaning houses. She was probably going to clean somebody else's house right now. Although she told Anna very little about herself, she had revealed that she worked for four other families, and that she lived in the next surburb, which had a big working-class housing estate in it. Anna assumed that she had somehow managed to get accommodation there from the county council, although if she had thought about it she would have known that that was very unlikely, since single people very seldom got accommodation from the county council, especially not young immigrants like Ludmilla. (In fact, Ludmilla rented a small room in a tiny ex-corporation house in an older estate, where most of the houses had moved from council to private ownership. The house was shared by five people. The room, a boxroom, cost two hundred euro a month, before electricity or heat – they used as little of that as possible and wrapped up in blankets and jumpers when it was cold.)

Ludmilla had never told Anna anything about this, mainly because Anna, although she would have liked to know, had been too polite to ask. Ludmilla knew English, but she did not know how Irish people conducted conversations, zigzagging towards their goal, seldom asking a direct question, and Anna had never understood that the rules of conversation might be different in other cultures.

Anna decided to forget about Vincy after the Abbey encounter. How could he be of any interest to her? If he had been flirting – he had been, that night at the restaurant, of course he had – that was disgusting, really. Who did he think she was? Last night at the Abbey she had enjoyed his company. That was it. He was, undoubtedly, very good company, the sort of person who put everyone at ease, and who brought out the best in them. Everyone felt better when he was around. Not just her.

Still, as she went about the house, and to the shops, and to collect Rory from school, she found that Vincy's image popped into her head. She saw him standing there in the theatre bar, close to the picture of W.B. Yeats, his tweed jacket hanging off his shoulders. You could see a resemblance between the two men, the one dark, the other fair, but both sharing the same compelling eyes and emaciated good looks.

Why am I wasting my time daydreaming like this? She shook herself and made a firm decision to block him out of her mind, but in fact as the day wore on she was thinking about him all the time. And she allowed herself the liberty. His image hovered in her mind, his voice hovered in her ear. It became familiar, like a picture that has been hanging there for years. In fact, although she had never heard of him until about six weeks ago, he did seem familiar, as if she had known him before.

She had felt bright, energised, happy, all day. Sometimes during the morning she had found herself smiling inanely, and once she had laughed aloud, because she was happy. But as the afternoon wore on that energy was draining out of her and she was sinking. In no time at all she would be leaving the house and driving to the airport ... she should go early, the traffic on the M50 on Friday was always appalling. The flight was at six and she needed to be there by five, at the very latest, meaning she should be leaving the house ... at three, probably, or even earlier. This was the problem with the city breaks. The flight time looked short – two and a half hours and you were in Spain. But the Dublin traffic, the queues at the airport, meant that you could add three or four more hours to that, which meant that in fact you were travelling for more than half the day.

She kissed Rory and hugged him. 'I have to go,' she said tearfully.

She hated leaving him, always, and always wondered why she was not taking him with her. It would have all been much more enjoyable with Rory ... but he would not enjoy the travelling, and would not want to see old beautiful things once they got there, or go out to eat long dinners in cosy restaurants, so it was probably just as well that he did not have to endure all that torture.

They arrived at the airport in Seville on schedule, at an hour before midnight, and took a taxi to the hotel. She felt tired and grubby and was glad to be able to check in quickly and go immediately to their room. Alex was even more tired, so there was no question of romance this evening. He was content with a modest celebration – champagne from the mini-bar. Anna did not want any but took it to keep him company. They sat at the window, which looked out over the cathedral, floodlit, golden-coloured against the black sky, and drank their champagne silently. Then they went to bed and fell asleep almost immediately.

Anna slept soundly and woke up to sunshine streaming in the window. Alex was still asleep. She looked out the window again, as you were supposed to, no doubt, in this room with a view. The cathedral gleamed in the sunshine now, a huge golden edifice.

The day slid by slowly. Obedient to the dictates of the travel book, they went to see the things they were told to go and see: the cathedral, with its innumerable gilt altars; the Alcazar, blue and gold tiles, gardens that must be amazing in summer. The winding, narrow streets of the old part of town. The orange trees in little cobbled squares.

Then came the night.

Alex wanted to make love. Naturally enough.

In the gracious old room with its view of the cathedral their bodies came together, practised, efficiently. Anna experienced pleasure, but passionless pleasure. Alex fell asleep immediately afterwards and she lay for hours, her eyes open, watching the dappled reflections of the lights outside flicker on the wall. Was this all there was to it? She had let herself forget about this before and had let herself believe that perhaps other women, perhaps many, were like her. Now she began to doubt that. She began to feel that she was a coward and a fool and that she deserved more. Not deserved. Wanted.

This was the first time she had questioned her marriage in ten years.

She was thirty-five.

She honestly believed that time was running out.

* * *

The next day Alex wanted to go to Córdoba to see its famous site: the mosque.

The mosque was like a cathedral outside and inside it was like a forest: hundreds of pillars held up the roof, and were arranged in some clever way, which meant you always saw a lot of them simultaneously, their rounded arches overlapping. Anna wandered around, trying to get a sense of the history of the place – of Islamic Spain, of the reconquest, of the changes that can end a great civilization and replace it with another. Could the builders of this mosque, those Mehemets and Ahmeds, and their legions of wives, have imagined that one day a huge golden Christian altar would be inserted into the middle of their calm, perfect church? That their way of life would disappear, and their power, their houses, their prayers? No, they could not. Great civilizations are built on a sense of their own invulnerability, their permanence. But they all topple in the end. They never see it coming until it is too late.

It was unimaginable, unconscionable, that the civilization to which Anna and Alex belonged could disappear. What could replace it? How could they imagine anything other than what there was now, planes and city breaks, computers, four-wheel drives, new books every week, concerts and operas and a constant stream of easy entertainment on the television, the DVD, the cinema? Was that what the future would be like? The future to which she should, really, transport that heroine of hers, Sally. Would it be an absence of things, rather than a change or a development, a failure rather than a progression?

She had this thought in the middle of the Mezquita, close to the Renaissance cathedral, and it alarmed her, not so much because she feared such a future – she did not, since she could not comprehend it – as that it reminded her that she needed to be working on that novel. She didn't even have a notebook in her bag in which to jot down these useful thoughts about the future; that was her main concern, rather than the future itself.

She was standing there in the middle of the forest of columns, wondering if she could buy a notebook in one of the shops near the mosque to capitalise on the philosophical thoughts it had engendered, when her mobile rang.

The place was so vast that nobody appeared to mind, but she withdrew to a dark cranny, of which there were plenty.

'It's Vincy,' said the phone.

'Hi,' she said softly. She had, she knew now that she heard his voice, been expecting this call for days. She felt suddenly as calm as a lake after rain. 'How are you?'

'I'd like to see you.' He didn't answer the question.

'Yes,' she said. She did not need to deliberate. 'Me too.'

'Can you meet me today?' he asked.

She looked at the sea of arches and pillars, at their reddish stripes on terracotta stone. They reminded her of bees, buzzing in summer, buzzing with joy.

'Not today,' she said. 'Or tomorrow. The day after tomorrow?'

'That's all right,' he said, sounding disappointed.

Why didn't she tell him where she was? There was no reason to keep that a secret. But she did keep it a secret. She did not want to tell him she was on holiday, on a city break, with Alex. She did not want to remind him that she was married, just now.

'No, no. I'd like to,' she said, her eyes scanning the mosque. Where *was* Alex? 'But I can't. I'm busy, today and tomorrow. Busy. I could meet you on Tuesday, for lunch?'

Eleven

Being busy was what saved Kate's life for the next week. It saved her. Absolutely. If it hadn't been for work, she was – dead.

After *Hamlet*, which she hardly even saw, she had fled from the theatre, just fled, not even staying for the reception, insisting on getting home as fast as she possibly could (a taxi would have been comforting but, unfortunately, walking was quicker to where she lived, and even in the very worst extremities of distress Kate's pragmatism did not abandon her). She had to, absolutely had to, get away from Vincy. Not to mention Anna. What she did not know was that Anna was also rushing out of the Abbey, walking briskly to Eden Quay to flag down a cab and dash off home to hers. They might have met as they escaped, both running away from the same man, ohmygod, and would something, anything, everything, then have taken another turn? But they did not meet, so everything took the turn it took.

Being busy saved Kate.

As always in the office there was loads to do. Dozens of phone calls to make and emails to respond to and many many complicated arrangements to be made, unmade, remade, patched up. That was her work, an infinity of communications with an infinity of individuals, like herself, a universe of people who arranged things. Her job demanded two hundred per cent twenty-four seven and that was what saved her. She couldn't mope while doing this. Nobody could. Absolutely no way. Cheerfulness was essential. She was an expert at pasting cheerfulness onto her face in the mornings, along with her make-up. Whatever was going on underneath, inside her body or her mind, had to take care of itself while she chirped and chatted, always sounding as if life were a happy game, one long party where everyone enjoyed themselves and nobody mis-behaved or suffered any disappointment of any kind. The merry-go-round went round and round, and Kate was one of the people who led it. She was masked like a clown in the circus – and a clown's mask is not a bad thing to have, if your heart is broken. For some people it is enough to see them through the healing time, to the other side, when their heart is whole again. Kate was not one of those people, but she didn't know that. Not on the day after the play. Not for several days in fact.

Lauren was, not that it matters, since she was peripheral to everything – although perhaps that is not entirely true. Perhaps if she had been different, things would have taken another course. But she was not different and things took the turn they took.

Lauren always wore a mask. If one were cruel, one might say that she *was* a fucking mask. But that would be not just cruel. It would be glib. It would be, undoubtedly, inaccurate. Nobody *is* a mask. There is always something underneath. However little.

So. She wore a mask. All the time. Twenty-four seven.

So she did not mention the night at the theatre, or Vincy, at all. At all. Not a word. The night at the theatre had never happened in the world according to Lauren.

This was the ethos of the business: unpleasantness was dis-missed as if it had never happened; uncomfortable situations were not supposed to occur and if they did, they were erased, forgotten immediately, in case they would clog the smooth running of the business in which cheerfulness was essential, just as petrol is essential to a car. Kate hated all this silence, all this refusal to bring up the subject, although she would have behaved in exactly the same way herself had the shoe been on the other foot, although she recognised that Lauren was doing the right thing, the easiest thing – the right thing was the easiest thing, usually, she had found out in her career – once you found that out, life was so much easier. Usually, but not this time. Not when her life was in total chaos, not when the worst thing that could happen to a girl had happened to her. Ohmygod, this was worse than if she had got … smallpox. Than if she had woken up and found she had transmogrified into a bowler overnight, than if she weighed fourteen stone.

How could Lauren just act as if it had never happened?

And as the week wore on to its conclusion Kate became more and more resentful instead of less. It was just awful. She would have liked to talk about the whole thing to someone. To Lauren, obviously, since she had been there, a witness, since she was supposed to be a friend as well as a colleague. But as time wore on talking became less and less possible. The masks got tougher and the underneath got weaker.

And the thing was, of course, that the person she would really have liked to talk to was Vincy. But he was incommunicado too; he didn't contact her. She knew the relationship was over; it was not that she expected him to ask to see her again or anything like that. (Her dearest wish; it was not that she expected her dream to come true. Not after what happened at *Hamlet*.) But couldn't he have called just to see how she was? He must have noticed how upset she had been. And she could not believe that he, like Lauren, would be the sort of person who would brush everything awkward under the carpet and move swiftly on, like a robot pretending to be human. He was, she knew, what she called a caring person. That was why she had fallen in love with him. That he was a caring person, as well as being all the other things that he was.

But he wasn't all that caring, apparently. Not caring enough to ring up and ask 'Well, how are you? Are you OK?' Not even to email and say '?'.

The week moved on. Kate moved on with it, or on it, as if she were a little seabird floating on a wave. She got busier and busier, chirpier and chirpier, as day followed day. She filled the time with talk and emails and work, every minute. She had barely time to sleep seven hours a night, then she was up and into the bathroom, washing her hair, drying it, straightening it, doing her skin and her clothes and her make-up and then off, at a rush, trotting like a pony, to the office. Feeling lurked beneath the surface but she kept it there, in its place.

Then came the weekend.

You could come into the office at the weekend – she had a key – but there was no point. Nobody would answer the telephone, nobody would answer the emails. The urgency that affected every single thing you did during the week would have vanished, and if you came in at the weekend you might suspect, fatally, that none of it mattered all that much. All the perpetrators of the urgency were at home in bed, or even abroad in bed, or sitting in cafés, or walking around, as if nothing in the world of work was all that important, as if everything could be put on hold. Until Monday. It wasn't twenty-four seven when it came right down to it; it was twenty-four five, and for twenty-four two you were on your own. All those people who needed you so desperately all week vanished into thin air and forgot that you existed.

Going in to work would solve nothing.

So she did not go in.

So she had to stay at hers.

Hers. A dangerous place when you had forty-eight hours to call your own, forty-eight hours to get through on your own.

Especially if you had no friends.

Like Kate.

Kate had no friends.

Colleagues, whom she called friends, like Lauren, or Vincy, she had, but no real friends, because there was no time in her life for them. It wasn't her fault. She had had friends, of course she had, when she was at school and college. She'd been popular, well, not unpopular anyway. But none of them had meant that much to her. She'd never had a close friend, someone special, like other girls had, and the three or four she used to go for a drink with or whatever hadn't really been her type. It's not that she was using them, she'd never use anybody, that's so disgusting, but when they went their separate ways, she wasn't all that sorry. It's not that they weren't very nice people in their own ways. It was just that they weren't for her. In time she'd find replacements, meet people she really … felt she'd something in common with.

It hadn't happened yet, though.

Most of the time that was just fine. Her job demanded two hundred per cent and that was fine by her. And like all people who are in a very challenging, interesting job, her weekends were also very challenging. She had to use the time to do all the things she hadn't had time to do during the week. Domestic stuff and shopping and going to the cleaners and going to see her family (she had a family, quite a complicated one too, don't go there ... but she did go there, as a rule, on Sundays, for lunch – the dutiful daughter).

On Saturday morning when she could have slept in, or out, some people say, when she could have slept off her disappointment at losing something she had never had anyway, or at half losing the man she had half had, Kate had set her alarm for 7 a.m. and got up to give her apartment a really thorough going over. Not that it was not very clean and neat already. But she had high standards and the apartment was worth it. I mean to say, it was her biggest investment, it was her only investment. It was only right that she should take care of it.

God, she was lucky to have the bloody apartment; and it wasn't that she had got in before the prices went up. Before the prices went up she had been ten years old and unluckily her parents had not foreseen the property boom, had not bought when the prices were low, for their two daughters. But then, look on the bright side, they had helped out when the prices were high. Gave Olwen a deposit, and, Kate suspected, helped her out with the mortgage repayments more than occasionally too, when that ne'er-do-well husband of hers squandered his salary on booze and flooze. They'd paid Kate's deposit too. All she had to do was pay the mortgage repayments. Yeah, all! Oh well. The mortgage for the one-bedroom apartment on Gardiner Street, a street that had been a no-go area for decades, a street that had passed into urban mythology as the location for unknown legends about muggings and car theft, cost seventy per cent of her salary at the moment. Leaving thirty per cent for everything else. No point in complaining, grin and bear it, that's life, and she was damned lucky to have it. Most girls of her age were renting. Lauren, who had a wardrobe to die for, would probably never own her own place. A lovely girl, she really was. Bright. But ... she didn't own her own apartment and she couldn't save to save her life.

Cleaning this costly little apartment took Kate the better part of the morning. It was not possible to spend more than half an hour hoovering and dusting the two rooms, but she did much more than that. She cleaned out the kitchen cupboards, scrutinising cartons and tins to make sure they were not past their sell-by date, a job most people never did or hated but one that Kate enjoyed. She went through the contents of her wardrobe and weeded out a few blouses that she had not worn in a year. They went into a plastic bag for the Oxfam shop on Henry Street.

When all this was done, it was still not lunchtime.

On Saturday afternoons, Kate often drifted into town and wandered about, getting ideas for interior decor and clothes, rather than actually buying anything. Today she could not face that. Her interest in clothes and furniture had vanished and she did not want to see her reflection in a thousand mirrors and plate-glass windows. But staying in the apartment was equally unbearable.

A walk. She felt bloated from being indoors – her lunch had been toast and scrambled egg, not a lot of food, but it made her feel thick and uncomfortable. A walk was what she needed to walk off that horrible feeling.

Going for a walk from Gardiner Street was not so easy, especially if you wanted to avoid shops. Almost every way you went led either to a city-centre shopping street or to some complex of old, menacing corporation flats, where the washing hung on balconies and the streets were littered with broken glass, and where you expected gangs of scangers to pounce on you at every turn. People who lived in places like Kate's apartment block said that it was all very safe, that these old slum areas had lost their teeth, that the rough stuff had all grown up and mellowed years and years ago. But the balconies, where old women with sharp, mean tongues stared contemptuously at the likes of Kate, and the broken glass, told a story of some sort of anger that had not been assuaged overnight by the expedient of building expensive apartments next door to the old slums. Kate was afraid of most places outside her front door. She could not walk east, for fear of those dangerous territories, and she could not walk west, for fear of shops and mirrors, and she could not walk north, because there was a mixture of the two, of the shops and the outlaws.

She walked south, down to the river, and then along the banks on the boardwalks as far as they stretched, and up the whole way to Heuston Bridge and down the other side. A walk lasting almost two hours.

She followed that with a visit to the gym; her gym was on her own street, one of its new concessions to its new inhabitants.

It was only six o'clock when all that was over. What to do? A film in the Savoy, alone. Not a good idea, because the Savoy was a cinema that was full of couples on a Saturday night and where you felt weird if you were on your own. The film was crap too; she stuck it out to the bitter end and then struggled home down the dark little streets that were so empty, once you left O'Connell Street, so menacing, on a Saturday night.

Totally knackered.

When she got home, she took out a little tin of cocaine she had stored away in a bottom drawer for special occasions.

Kate didn't do drugs socially. If she was at something and the lines came out, she usually just shook her head – there were always a few refusals, it was never an issue. But she kept some, for her own use, when she needed it.

Like now.

She spread a thin white line on top of the tin and rolled a one hundred euro note – she always used a one hundred euro note for this ritual, the same note, which she kept with the tin – and sniffed it.

Then she went to bed.

Didn't get up till Monday really. Normally she visited the gaff in Foxrock for lunch, but she couldn't face her folks. In fact, she couldn't face anyone, even the man who sold newspapers in the little old shop that had survived against all the odds in an old tenement house next to the apartments.

There had not been much going on between her and Vincy. Admit it. Zilch really. But they had had three formal 'dates' over the past fortnight, not including the Abbey debacle. Two in a fortnight wouldn't have meant a huge amount – two in a fortnight might mean he was testing the water. But three was significant. Doubly significant, triply significant, when you took into account his busy twenty-four-seven schedule, not to mention her busy twenty-four-seven schedule. Yes, on balance, and without prejudice, and looking at the issue in a cool calm and collected manner, three in a fortnight meant something. Three in a fortnight meant he was more than casually interested.

He had seemed genuinely delighted to accept her invitation to the opening of *Hamlet*. And he had definitely been pleased to see her. From the minute they all met in the bar upstairs she had been absolutely certain that the relationship would be firmed up in some way that night. Until Anna Kelly Sweeney had walked into the bar and in one moment shattered all her dreams. As soon as she appeared, dressed in that dark velvet and exuding something mysterious, which retrospectively Kate decided was raw sexual energy, what did they call them, that sweat some women exuded like cats in heat, pheromones or something. Gross, although at the time it had seemed like some magical quality, some otherworldly beauty that had been as painful to see as it had been resistant to description. In that moment the mood of the evening had changed from one of joy to the complete opposite. Oh yes, she and Vincy had exchanged a few friendly words and he had gone through the motions of being warm and friendly. But a barrier had gone down between them. After that, even though he smiled and talked, his eyes did not meet hers and when she drew too close, as she did, in one of those stupid acts of desperation people who know they are losing someone practise, he pulled away from her as if she were dangerous, or repulsive, although earlier in the evening he had been drawing closer to her. When they were seated in their row, he made sure their arms never touched.

Not once.

By the time the long Sunday was over her speculation was taking yet another turn. Maybe she had been wrong about Anna and Vincy? Maybe he was attracted to her, but she was a married woman, after all. Her husband was important; his place on the invitation lists was much much higher up than Vincy's; it was always considered a coup if he turned up at a social event; he had a reputation for making himself scarce, which added to his lustre. As well as having a significant position, everyone knew he was wealthy and that his wealth was well-gotten, there was no rumour of corruption tarnishing it, although of course he had his ear to the ground and was close to those who knew about money, and property, and so on. Kate, ensconced in the small world of 'the arts', obsessed with its machinations, was barely aware of the other social groups that constituted Irish society, most of them more powerful and influential than the circle she considered so crucial to the flow of life. That there were circles which even the brightest stars in the artistic firmament would never penetrate was something she vaguely suspected, but she had little idea of how those other groups functioned, where they assembled, who belonged to them. But anyone could observe that the group to which she belonged included very few rich people. A handful of writers and artists in Ireland had broken into the international Anglophone literary world, where real money could be made by books or pictures. And those artists were the ones who kept themselves to themselves, rarely attending the innumerable events Kate organised. In general, in Ireland money was owned by others who did not come to the opening nights and the launches. But Alex was an exception. He had a foot in both camps, the public camp of the well-known and the more exclusive and hidden camp of the well-off. And Anna, by extension, belonged to both those worlds too.

She was not likely to want to give that up for Vincy, who was promising, likely to be very successful, but poor. He might do well but he would always be poor by comparison with Alex Sweeney.

On Monday Kate dragged herself out of bed and went right back to work. And back there in the office it was all so normal, so calming in its frenetic busyness, that she began to wonder if there were not hope for her relationship with Vincy, after all. The strong feelings of the night at *Hamlet* receded. That look across the foyer? Had it been in her imagination? Possibly she had also imagined his distancing himself from her, his pulling back, the uneasy looks in his eyes? What was not fantasy, what was a fact, was her crazy flight from the Abbey. She had almost run out with hardly a goodbye. Anyone would have taken offence. Anyone would have thought she was strange, slightly touched.

Of course he would not phone her. He was probably waiting for her to contact him and offer an apology. He was probably really really worried, not knowing what he should do. The ball was not in his court at all, as she had been deluding herself, but firmly in hers, waiting for her to do something with it.

Late on Monday afternoon she sent him an email.

Emailing was so great when you thought about it. It was so much easier than telephoning and actually talking to someone. If he didn't want to reply, there would be no harm done. In the etiquette of emails, not responding was one way of indicating your lack of interest in whatever had been proposed – it was a method Kate frequently employed herself in the course of her duties, briskly deleting queries or communications that were awkward or unwanted. She did not consider this unmannerly, whereas not responding to a telephone message, or a letter sent in the post, was something she would never do. Email etiquette was different, not subject to the rules of the older ways of corresponding. There was an ambiguity involved in communication by email that gave both sides of the correspondence a certain amount of leeway. You were never absolutely certain if your addressee had actually received your email – some got blocked, some were not opened for one reason or another. If a person did not reply, you could decide that some such accident had occurred, while simultaneously knowing, deep down, that they had not replied because they were not interested in you or your message. Emotions engendered by emails, however, were as shallow and swift as the technology itself. Within minutes of receiving or not receiving one, all feeling connected with the transaction would have been deleted and sent to trash. You would move swiftly on to the next communication, or event, or crisis, or emotion of your life. As communications and their concomitant emotions speeded up, so did their quality dilute.

Understanding all this intuitively, rather than laboriously explaining it to herself – she did not indulge in laborious explanations of anything, it was not her way, there wasn't time – she sent a neutral email that did not even refer to the play. After all, it had happened four days ago and was by now consigned to history (especially since it had got a bad review – Kate was careful to eliminate failed events from her conversation lest they contaminate her and her organisation). She just asked Vincy if he would like to come to a party she was organising in a week's time, to announce the launch of a new poetry prize.

He replied by return, and said, just as neutrally, that he would be busy next week and regretted he could not come. He asked her how she was and signed off without a salutation. Which was normal, on emails. You didn't even have to worry about the possible implications of 'Love' or 'Luv' or 'Cheers' or 'All the best', as you did on letters or cards. If you didn't want to, all you had to do was type your name, or even just an initial, or even, if you were rushed or annoyed, nothing at all.

Nothing at all was what he sent to her.

Nothing nothing nothing at all.

Twelve

Tuesday. Vincy and Anna were meeting for lunch in the café of the National Gallery, where she knew she was almost certain to bump into some of her acquaintances. This, she felt, meant that the meeting was above board in every way. There was nothing covert about it. Everyone could see them. Friends of hers would be there. They would see them and realise that Vincy and Anna were acquaintances. Probably they might imagine that they were discussing something professional – media coverage of her next book, or something like that, although of course Vincy would have absolutely nothing to do with media coverage of hers or anyone's book, ever, and although her book was so far from completion that no coverage would be necessary for at least two years, even if all went well.

She did not bother mentioning to Alex that she was having lunch with Vincy. There was no special reason for that, she did not usually inform him of her arrangements during the day. He had more important things to think about.

As soon as she reached the restaurant she wished she had chosen another. It was not at all because she recognised a few people straight away, but because of the crowds, and because you had to join a queue and serve yourself. When she was with a woman friend, this didn't bother her at all. They queued and talked, examining the contents of the big trays of food with interest, and chatting about other things as animatedly as if they had been sitting down waiting for service. But with Vincy it might be harder, to stand in the queue for ten minutes, it might be awkward.

She was first, which she did not like. She did not join the end of the queue, as she would have done had she been meeting an ordinary friend, but stood in the vast white hall near the gallery shop. She pretended to look at the things in the window – books and reproductions of paintings that hung on the walls in the gallery – while keeping an eye on the doorway.

She had to wait for almost ten minutes. After five, she began to wonder if he had forgotten, or if he had decided not to keep the appointment, although rationally she knew that could not possibly be the case. She knew this, partly because she trusted him, partly because she trusted the sincerity of his feelings for her, and most of all because her social position vis-à-vis his was such that he could not possibly afford to be rude to her, in case it reverberated in some obscure way on his career or social standing.

Eventually he arrived, rushing in the door and up the wide steps to where she stood, dressed in a red coat that she had chosen because it would look well against the white background of the building.

'I'm really sorry,' he said breathlessly. His face was pink and he smelt of rain. There were drops of water in his hair, and the rain had frizzed it so it stood out like a bush. 'I got held up in traffic.'

As soon as he looked at her with his magical eyes all her annoyance vanished. She felt happy and excited. Something was happening to her. At last.

Nothing mattered.

The queuing was not a problem. The queuing was fine. She didn't notice it, one way or the other. Somehow she was focused only on what they were talking about.

He could do that. He could make a person focus, even a person who was usually as scattered, as fragmented, as Anna was.

He could make her focus on him, although she did not admit that, as yet.

Vincy wanted to know about what she had been doing – now

she told him about the weekend in Seville, once they were face to face it was easy to tell him. It was easy to talk about Alex. About Rory. About the novel. Vincy seemed to know about all these people and projects already, and to be intensely interested in them. He asked questions and listened to the answers, really listened, as they snaked along by the old brick wall, as she chose, quite randomly, from the big selection of dishes on offer. 'Which salads would you like?' asked the waitress, with a strong Mandarin intonation that made her words difficult to understand. It was always hard to pick them from the bewildering array and now the need to select three salads seemed ludicrous. What did it matter? Disbelieving, Anna pointed at green salad, potato salad, and beetroot. When she had pointed to it, she knew the beetroot was a mistake, it would discolour her teeth. But what did she care?

Vincy selected with more deliberation, as if the contents of his lunch still mattered to him. (Lamb meatballs provençale, he took, and flageolet beans, potato salad, Waldorf salad.) She took this in with amusement. How odd that he cared about flageolet beans, at a time like this.

Eventually they had procured their food and were seated at a table for two in a quiet corner of the enormous, high room, which, with its hard surfaces and clinical colours, was more like a large hall, perhaps in a rich convent, than a restaurant. A place where everyone was easily visible to everyone else. A lemon tree, which sprouted from a patch of pebbles near their table, created an illusion of shelter, but provided none. Many eyes seemed to glance at them, half-recognising Vincy, probably.

Most people glanced at them and looked away quickly, feeling intrusive, or annoyed. Lovers – maybe they looked like lovers? They did not look right, they did not belong in this lunchtime place, which was packed with women from civil service offices cheerfully analysing their colleagues, and with friends catching up on news of family illnesses, children's successes in school.

Anna did not notice what she was eating, although she did eat it, even the beetroot, and it did discolour her teeth. She hardly noticed what they talked about, although they did talk, effortlessly, constantly. She did not see her surroundings. She just saw Vincy, his bright, lively eyes; his expression, which managed to be both kind and sharp at the same time. She just talked to him.

Most of the conversation was about Anna. It was as if he were carrying out an interview, finding out as much as he could about her in the hour at his disposal. Where were you born? Where did you go to school? What did you parents do? Your childhood home, where did you go on holidays, your friends, your brothers and sisters ...

All these details, the story of Anna's life, were news to him, good news, interesting news. She had never told it. She had never been asked to. Alex picked it up as he went along – he knew her mother and father and where they lived now, he didn't need to know where she had lived when she was three, where she had been born. Holles Street. Her mother had brought her home to her father's house, in Monkstown, for some reason. They lived there for three years, with Anna's grandparents ...

He wanted to hear *her* story. Can anyone pay you a greater compliment?

Time flew by.

It seemed incredible to Anna that the hour was over, the plates empty, all the diners pushing back their chairs and leaving. That anything so miraculous could finish, just like any other hour or any other event, seemed more ludicrous than the beetroot salad or the queue for the cash register or the lemon tree growing from a plate of pebbles in the middle of a room.

But Vincy was standing up, glancing at his watch, pulling his raincoat from the back of his chair and shoving his arms into the sleeves, awkwardly, as if it had been an ordinary lunch, and now it was time to get back to work.

She wanted to cry. She felt like a child who has been called in when the play is at its most intense, when she wants the day to go on and on forever.

But he was saying he wanted to see her again.

Tomorrow.

Too soon, a voice warned her. Too ... soon.

But without checking her diary, she said yes. She had no idea how she could do it. Not here, they both thought, simultaneously. He would text her with a venue when he thought of somewhere suitable for both of them.

Outside the school gate she chatted with great animation to Ultan's mother about furniture: Monica had been buying chairs and wanted to discuss this interesting topic with someone.

'You'd think it would be simple until you start looking,' she said. 'But I've spent days wandering up and down Capel Street, into Temple Bar, around that bit of town behind the Gaiety where there are nice little shops ... and now I think I have to go out to Blanchardstown or somewhere far along the M50 before making up my mind.'

Anna, who had not bought chairs for at least seven years, had plenty to say on this subject. She laughed and joked; the excitement in her voice was apparent to herself, although she hardly paid any attention to what she was saying. She felt that she had been wound up like a clockwork doll, and was behaving in a way that was different from her usual pattern. Instead of being grave and reserved, she was extrovert and excessively, noisily, cheerful.

It surprised her that Monica did not seem to notice that there was a difference in her, accepting this transformed version of Anna for the normal one.

When Rory came out of school, he was downcast. He would not talk.

Anna's high spirits sank. She held his hand as they walked to the car. The sun had gone in and it had turned into a grey, cold day. The gardens smelt of winter, of damp rotted leaves, that morbid smell. Below the suburban roads, the sea swelled, dark and ominous.

'Won't you tell me what happened?' she asked desperately.

He shook his head.

'Did somebody steal your lunch again?' she asked.

He shook his head again. In fact the lunch-stealing episode had not been repeated after the first time and Anna wondered if he had imagined the whole thing.

'Would you like some chocolate?' she asked.

'Yes,' he said immediately, but in a gloomy little voice.

He ate the chocolate in silence. Anna drove down from the

small road where she had parked on to the main seafront road, wondering again at the volatility of moods. One moment she was full of joy. Then a small thing, like Rory's silence, had the power to bring her back to earth, down to the petty worries of everyday life.

He did not tell her until they were at home, sitting in the kitchen, eating his snack, what was wrong. And it was trivial. Not a case of school-yard bullying, nothing like that. The teacher had told him his spelling was bad. He had missed five out of ten on the list they had today. Usually he got them all correct.

'I didn't do them. Luz Mar didn't do them with me when you were away,' he said, making her feel guilty.

'Couldn't you do them yourself?' she asked exasperatedly.

'No.' He shook his head. 'I can't do them myself.'

Then he became silent again, and sulked for another half an hour.

Anna wrote the next morning. It was the first time in almost a week that she had got a chance to attend to her novel. She found it difficult to remember what was going on in it, and had to spend a long time re-reading what she had written, even though she had a rule that forbade her to re-read until her first draft was completed. But this morning she could barely remember the characters' names, much less what they had been doing, so it was necessary. The re-reading on this occasion had a positive effect, however. The written chapters seemed good to her. Lilian had been right. There was a rhythm in the work, Sally and the other characters were living, breathing people, even though they were engaged in adventures that were totally incredible.

That was the secret of good fantasy literature; if you put real people in impossible situations, readers could suspend disbelief and fall for the fantasy. Why they wanted to do that she did not quite know. But obviously they did, and had from time immemorial. Maybe it encouraged their faith in the limitless potential of human beings? Or of animals – Anna had introduced talking animals to her novel, with some trepidation, since she departed from her template when she put in the first anthropomorphised creature, a dog. Soon there were talking cats, rabbits, tigers, fish. There are no talking animals in *Harry Potter*, but once she started, there was no going back. If a dog can talk in a book, then all the other animals have to talk too, it seemed to her.

In spite of her misgivings about the animals – the draft she had sent to Lilian had not included them – she still felt confident that this novel would be a success, and was determined to finish it soon and get it out.

So she wrote assiduously. For about an hour.

At ten she stopped writing. Her morning's work was over; she had written about a hundred words, just a couple of lines. But she had to stop, because now it was time to get ready for lunch.

She proceeded to take off her clothes and to try on others. She found it very hard to make up her mind what to wear – some things would be too dressy or too deliberate, and would put him off. Others were just not attractive enough. Yesterday she had given little thought to what she was wearing, but today she was as worried about it as a teenage girl going on a date.

Time went by.

Anna returned to her computer. Vincy texted the name and address of a pub she had never heard of, in Rathcormac, a place she had never visited and which had for her only its bad reputation, a place name synonymous with drug barons and gangland crime. But although she was about to head off into unknown territory, dangerous territory, telling nobody around her where she was going, her euphoric mood did not change. Vincy was not going to murder her at lunchtime. He had chosen the place because it was secret, because it was as unlike the National Gallery as any place could be. And probably more romantic too. So Anna moved happily in and out of her wardrobe, looking at herself from a variety of angles in the long mirrors on the doors. Finally she ended up wearing exactly what she had had on to begin with, with the addition of a silver pendant, and black boots replacing the trainers. Her make-up she had to do in a hurry.

'Bye, Ludmilla,' she called, as she opened the door.

She could see Ludmilla standing at the front window, looking at her, probably wondering what was going on, as she reversed her jeep down the drive and out into the road, narrowly avoiding a collision with a Mercedes, which was speeding along at about seventy miles an hour.

Rathcormac was far away, but traffic was light on the M50 and she reached it in about half an hour. The village, once she located it, was surprisingly pleasant, not at all what the news bulletins would lead you to expect. No drug barons. No drug addicts even, that she could see. Not even anyone sleeping in a doorway. There was an old church and a round tower at one end of the street. Who could imagine that a suburb like this, in the wild west of Dublin, could boast medieval ruins?

The pub was called the Tower. Outside, it was covered with pink stucco and decorated with a huge, richly coloured picture of a round tower; inside was dark and cosy like a cave, plentifully supplied with little snugs, in one of which they could sit in privacy.

'What an interesting place!' she said.

Vincy looked surprised. 'I'm really sorry to drag you all the way out here,' he said. 'But I'm on a job – there was a murder down the road last night. I'm interviewing neighbours, snooping around.'

'Oh!' said Anna. So there were murders going on, just as she suspected. It was gratifying, in a way, to know that. 'I didn't listen to the news. I thought you had chosen it for some other reason.'

He looked at the dark red banquette, the shiny black wooden table, and sniffed the roast beef and chips that scented the air. 'Here?' He smiled. 'Do you think I'd bring you to a place like this by choice?'

'I like it,' she said.

He reached out and took her hand, as if he could not help himself. Like a woman who is drowning, she grasped it and held it for as long as she dared. It was warm and dry, large, enclosing hers completely. She did not gasp or smile or say anything. She held his hand.

Thirteen

Down there in the country the winter grabbed you in its relentless grip as soon as the clocks went back in October. From then on, the darkness never let go. Before you got used to them, the grey mists of day were swallowed by the cloudy nights. In the blanket of darkness the little houses tried to hold their own; they glowed with a plucky desperation, like space ships lost in a black infinity. But the atmosphere that surrounded them was earthy, solid: it was noisy with the howling wind, which reached levels of absurd fury almost every night, battering against the roofs and the windows like herds of some crazed animal, buffalo or elk or – it could be – elephants. And the rain accompanied the wind. The great clouds raced in from the Atlantic as fast as they could and they broke and lashed against the first place they saw: the valley.

Leo always felt snowed in at this time of the year, although there was never any snow. This year he felt more snowed in than usual. How could he leave the house? Only a fool would step out into that weather more often than was strictly necessary.

He wished, more than usually, that he had a car. He had to step out into gale force winds, driving rain, sweating in his waterproof suit and hardly able to walk in his squelching wellingtons, to catch the bus to go to the town for food. While almost everyone else stepped into their jeep, heated it up, and moved around the countryside with ease and comfort. He doubted if he could learn to drive now. He was so clumsy. But he promised himself that he would try; he would take lessons in the spring. This is what he promised himself every winter.

Not having a car meant he was lonely. In the summer he walked down to the pub at night and chatted to whoever was there. But now it was often too cold and wet to walk down, so he spent a great deal of time alone in the house, getting in on himself, as people in the valley would put it. Getting in on himself, while nobody got in on him. He hadn't formed good enough relations with most his neighbours to have a circle of friends who felt free to visit unannounced. In his less self-pitying moments he decided that people in Ireland did not drop in casually as much as they had when he was a child, even here in the country. They telephoned in advance. Or they telephoned for a chat and then did not bother calling in at all. And there were, around here, several people like him, artists and writers and such people, who were holed up in their houses for the winter, isolated, them as well as the old people, the widows and bachelors who had been left bereaved and lived alone. Not a soul dropped in on Leo, apart from one neighbour, an American woman, Stacey, who lived a few yards away and owned very good rain gear.

Why do I live here? was a question he asked, also more often than usual, at this time of the year. Sometimes he promised himself that he would sell up and move once the spring came.

Move where? Dublin was the obvious place. And the obvious problem would be property prices. That was why, after all, he was here in the first place, and it was why he would stay here, because the money he would get for this house would never be sufficient to buy a place in Dublin. Although he might get a mortgage ... for someone like me, Leo felt, a freelancer, that is the last thing I want hanging around my neck.

Life would have been so perfect if Kate would have considered ... marrying him. Or even if she had liked him enough to visit him, to come down for weekends on a regular basis, even if she did not want to go as far as moving down or getting married. But she had wanted nothing, not even to make one visit, to see what the place was like. He wanted her to love him and she didn't even like him. She probably laughed at him behind his back. Quite possibly the look of him made her feel physically sick. He didn't like it much himself, why should she? He was getting old.

All his life – or all his life since his parents' death, since he had moved to the country – he had devoted himself to the well-being of society, of the country, of the planet. He had had big ambitions for the world, and no ambitions for himself. He had focused on global happiness, and paid little attention to his own. Now it seemed that he was just as selfish and self-centred as anyone else.

His true wish was for love and happiness, for himself.

He did not think of passion, transcendence, sexual bliss. All he wanted was a girl he loved, marriage … a child. Or two. Ordinary stuff. Just what most people wanted.

But time was running out.

He was thirty-five.

He was a survivor. He did not give up. Instead he flung himself into his work, since the alternative, as he knew from experience, was to sink more deeply into misery. He had two books, one of which he hoped to get out in time for Christmas, one by a Dublin woman who wrote strange, surreal poems about child abuse in orphanages in the 1950s, and one ordinary collection by an ordinary poet. The poems about the orphanages could be a hit, if properly marketed. There was, of course, a slight chance that people were weary of the theme – they wearied so easily and so quickly, no matter how shocking the story, and the story of the orphanages had now been told several times in fiction and journalism, but – it was to this fact that his hopes were pinned – not so often in poetry and especially not in Irish language poetry.

That would have to be his unique selling point. An old shocking story in an old beautiful language (Irish) and a new beautiful medium (the poetry of this woman, which he would insist was beautiful). She was beautiful herself, which helped. And black. The first black Irish language woman poet, he was almost certain, in the world. She had a lot going for her. If he couldn't sell her work, he was worse than useless.

He beavered away, editing, talking to the authors, sending thousands of emails, commissioning covers. He could work for ten hours a day, easily, and still have plenty of time on his hands in these dark days, which hardly seemed like days at all when the clouds came down and swamped everything in grey fog so that you could see nothing, and his house on the hill seemed more like a submarine than a cottage with a view of the sea.

In the evenings he lit a great turf fire on the stone hearth to cheer himself up, and after his vegetarian dinner, he liked to sit there reading detective novels or watching television. Then he turned off all the lights and enjoyed the flickering of the firelight on the walls.

In short, he was reduced to watching his own shadow for amusement.

Or animal shadows.

Sometimes he made shadow puppets, something someone – his mother – had taught him to do as a child. He could do a fox, a rabbit, and an animal with horns, which he variously decided was a goat, a cow, or a sheep.

Some people would think this is pathetic, Leo said to himself, aloud, watching quite a well-shaped goat nod his head on the wall. But he liked doing this. He liked creating shadows on the wall.

Well, it was better for you than snorting cocaine, on your own, in a flat so small that there was no wall to make shadow animals on, and a city so bright that there were no shadows anywhere.

Country life.

Stacey called in. A red letter day. A visitor!

'Hi!' she called out, as she opened the door and let herself in. He didn't lock the door during the day.

Leo left what he was doing and came out to the kitchen.

'Hi Stacey,' he said. They spoke English together. As usual, she accepted a cup of herbal tea.

'I'm going to town to see the reflexologist,' she said. 'I wondered if you wanted anything. A lift maybe?'

'I'm OK,' he said, boiling the kettle. He hadn't lit the fire and although the kitchen felt warm enough, it looked cold. Outside the big windows dark grey cotton-wool fog swathed everything in misery, as usual.

The raspberry tea cheered him up, with its deep red colour and fruity taste.

'I'm trying African reflexology for my arthritis. Everything else has failed, so might as well give it a go,' she said, stretching out her legs, which were very short. Stacey was a tiny woman.

'It can't do any harm,' Leo said.

There were clinics in the town offering acupuncture, a Chinese herbal doctor, Indian head massage, African reflexology, and Reiki. And other such things. Also two GPs and a dentist. Leo had gone to one of the clinics to get a head massage once, out of curiosity more than anything, although he had been suffering from blocked sinuses. There were scented candles in the waiting room, and a statue of Buddha, an orchid. The masseuse cleared his sinuses, for about a day; then they got blocked again.

'Mainey told me her grandmother – you know, old Lane – had a great cure for arthritis but alas it's gone to the grave with her. She had a great cure for everything, according to Mainey, but what use is that to us if nobody learned what the heck the cures were from her before she kicked the bucket?'

'Probably spurious anyway,' said Leo. 'Mainey says more than her prayers.' Mainey was one of the oldest women in the valley, a sort of mother figure to the entire parish, who sat in state at her fireside every night in her charmingly cluttered old kitchen and entertained callers with anecdotes about the old times. She was one of the few people you could drop in on unannounced. Leo reminded himself that it was time for him to pay her a visit.

'I know what you mean but this time she's right. I've heard it from other people too. Old Lane knew a lot about herbs. She had some funny ideas, such as eating a ferret's leavings for whooping cough and untying all the knots in the house when a woman was in labour, but she knew her stuff,' said Stacey. 'Where to find the selfheal and the eyebright.'

'Sure you know that yourself.'

Stacey could identify all the wild flowers in the locality, having helped some professor from the Botanic Gardens in Dublin to collect them one summer ages ago. She it was who had taught Leo the names of most of them. Before he had got to know her, he had known buttercups and primroses, cowslips, but now he could name almost every flower that grew in his own field, and on his wall, that endless, reliable, relentless cycle of plants, starting with the primroses and violets in March and ending with the montbretia in October. In between, thirty different flowers came and went in the patch of grass in front of his house, as they had grown and withered and seeded, grown and withered and seeded, for thousands and thousands of years in that very place – although there were newcomers. The fuchsia, which had come from South America, and the montbretia from South Africa, and the terrible Japanese knot, which threatened to oust everything else, including the houses, if the worst predictions were to be believed.

'I do, but I lack the magic touch. Somehow I know that if I make some concoction with eyebright, it won't do any good … and my cataracts prove it!'

Stacey had trouble with her eyes as well as with her limbs. She was always very cheerful when talking about her complaints, referring to them in an ironic, wry tone, the kind of tone other people used to talk complainingly but proudly about the antics of their clever children. Her attitude was very different from that of other sick people he had known – his father, before his death, for instance, had suffered incessantly from headaches and stomachaches and mysterious pains, and talked about them as if they were unassailable enemies. He had always frightened Leo into believing he was going to die. And then he did die, but not of any of his ailments.

'You're never sick, Leo?' Stacey had mentioned this before.

'I'm lucky,' he said. 'Or else it's the easy life.'

But it was his father. Watching his father, he had decided he would never complain about being sick. And so far he had never had to.

'Micheál is dying,' Stacey added cheerfully.

'Is he?' Micheál was a farmer down the road, one of the old men of the parish. Somebody was always dying here, especially in the winter. It was as if they looked out at the rain and the fog and the dark and gave up.

'They took him to Dingle the day before yesterday. He won't come home, they say. Stroke.'

'Poor man.' Leo had known him to nod to as he passed up and down on his tractor, his dog in the trailer.

'He was a nice man. Didn't have a lot to say but there was no

145

harm in him.' Stacey got up slowly. 'Well I'd best be off,' she said. 'You're quite sure you don't need anything?'

'I am,' said Leo. 'And drive carefully, you. Look at that fog!'

'Sure amn't I used to it by now?' said Stacey. She moved towards the door. 'You know what you should get? You should get yourself a nice girlfriend,' she said, looking back over her shoulder. 'But unfortunately I can't buy one for you in the supermarket.'

Even Stacey, who lived alone, who was a model of happy independence, could see that Leo was sinking and needed a helpmeet, to get him through – through life in the valley, through life in general. Everyone saw it. Lots of people had begun to hint that it was time Leo got himself a partner, or a girlfriend, or a boyfriend – some people thought he was gay, since he lived alone and published poetry. It was as if his single status had begun to upset the community, or as if they, like him, had realised the danger he was now in, the danger of a life of lonely bachelordom. Down here in the country, life was easier if you had company in the house, especially in the winter.

As if to make an effort, although there would be nobody down there, male or female, who would fit the bill, Leo went to a meeting in the community centre. That was one of the pastimes winter offered: you could go on a committee or two – as if he was not on enough already – and attend meetings and talk about problems.

Down he went, in the wind and the rain, togged out in a bulky, grey, waterproof suit and wellingtons, to a meeting of the local heritage committee, which they had put him on because he had attended the AGM and anyone who attended it got invited to sit on the committee. A group of ten, seven men and three women. They sat in the front row of the theatre in the heritage centre, along the tip-up plush seats, and talked about planning permission, and who would get the franchise on the ferry to the island, which had been the main topic of conversation in the valley for about three years.

Leo didn't have any view on the ferry franchise and he was sick of the issue. He could see that it would never be sorted out unless a ruling came from some Minister or other – democracy

146

wasn't going to provide a solution. Even a ruling from a Minister would probably not be obeyed. It was one of those problems that would run on and on forever.

The planning permissions he always had a stance on. He battled on the side of the environment, ranting on – as his opponents put it – about polluted ground water, destruction of habitats, unsustainable development. Most people on the committee, like most people around here, were all in favour of unsustainable development. They said they wanted planning permission for their children. Everyone said this, even people who were eighty years old, even people who had no children. But they also wanted to sell sites for high prices to anyone who would buy them.

Leo spoke out bravely against self-interest and defended Mother Earth against her residents. They saw him as an idealistic blow in, with his city perspective on the country – one of the urban know-alls who came to the country to tell the natives what was wrong with them. They tolerated him because it was their custom to tolerate everything and everyone, including their worst enemies. Like the bogs that surrounded it, the community absorbed whatever was tossed into it, sucking it down into its secret depths and thus rendering it harmless.

Leo by now was one of their beloved cranks. The committee, the valley, needed him to voice the alternative point of view and would have been disappointed had he failed to turn up with his predictable arguments at all their meetings. They listened, they argued a bit with him, they shook their heads at his persistence, and then adjourned to the pub, where they drank convivially together for hours, those who had opposed each other strenuously at the meeting buying one another pints now.

This is the great thing about here, Leo thought. People do not fall out, not for long. The place was too small to allow long-term animosity. You would meet your enemy, if you had one, every time you went to the shop, the church or the pub. Falling out openly was not a real option. So a sort of friendly duplicity prevailed.

News had broken about the torture of American prisoners in east European prisons. Extraordinary rendition. The ten o'clock news, in the corner of the bar, showed the little spaniel face of Condoleezza Rice, looking sad and serious. 'Mistakes happen,'

147

she said. Or errors. That is the word Condoleezza used, not 'mistakes'. 'Error' sounded better, less serious. Mistakes could be blamed on someone but errors simply happened. Had this something to do with the very sound of the word, all those soft and gentle *r*s, as opposed to the hard consonantal clusters in 'mistakes'? The Anglo-Saxon directness of it. 'The United States government does not condone the torture or inhumane treatment of prisoners.' Torturer Condoleezza, thought Leo, getting angry after a few pints. Torturer Bush. Torturer Taoiseach for allowing the planes to land at Shannon. Planes with prisoners, on their way to Poland or Romania, to be interrogated there, off the campus, had landed at Shannon for refuelling. Condoleezza said they hadn't and the Minister for Foreign Affairs had believed her, had asked no more questions. He was satisfied to know as little as possible. He was not going to interrogate Condoleezza, or interrogate the crews, or search the planes, in case he found what he did not want to find, because money was being made out of those planes at Shannon. The newscaster added, without comment but with a faint sinking of tone, that the landings were worth twenty thousand euro a day to the Irish economy, or was it a week, or a month or a year? She didn't actually specify or he had missed that. That was the price of sending men to the torture chambers of Poland, Ireland's Catholic neighbour in the north of Europe, thought Leo.

This is it, Leo got more and more angry, watching the doll face of Anne Doyle tell this terrible story, not a hair out of place as she described the train to Auschwitz, as it might be. He had often wondered what the next European holocaust would be and here it was. Iraq. Afghanistan. The knock on the door in the early morning, in Milan or Copenhagen or Paris. Come with us. Take nothing. We will fly you to the torture chamber as long as your captors pay the toll.

It is happening at this minute before my nose, thought Leo, and I'm drinking a pint of Guinness. While I know, or half know, just as people half knew about the concentration camps long, long before the war ended, and just like them, I am saying maybe it is not true, we don't have the evidence, and anyway what can I do about it?

He got up and left the noisy cosy pub, just as Daniel O'Shea was striking up on the accordion. The news was over, the television volume lowered. (They never turned it off, even when singers were performing, just lowered the volume. It was as if the television were a customer in the pub, and, like the regulars clustered around the bar, had a right to be there no matter who else came in.)

Outside it was cold and dark but for the first time in weeks the rain had stopped. The dark blue sky was full of white stars – like moths, Yeats got it right, or almost right, the way the stars flickered was like the twitching, mysterious movement of hardly visible insects, although they would have to be luminescent, glow-in-the-dark insects to make the metaphor exact. There were so many stars to be seen that the sky was crowded; you could always see more of them here than elsewhere; the Milky Way looked really milky, a smudge of white like a stain on a black coat across the sky; the Plough he could easily pick out, the Pleiades, and others.

Ranged over him and the absurdity of all his efforts to change the world, they had looked down for millions of years. Even here in this very spot human beings had been gazing up at these stars several thousand years ago. From the minuscule perspective enormous changes had taken place in the ant hill of human evolution, but *sub specie aeternitatis*, what did that matter? The valley had looked the same from the perspective of the stars for aeons. And vice versa.

For thirteen whole years of his tiny span on earth he, Leo Kavanagh, had been living here in the almost eternal valley, fighting for an eclectic mixture of good causes. The Irish language and vegetarianism. Road safety. The environment. The future of the globe – as if it mattered in the really broad scheme of things. The burdens of the world, big and little, global and national and parochial, had found a resting place on his broad and weary shoulders. Although he had tried to limit himself, the number of causes he was involved with was always growing. At least half his time was taken up with some society work or other. And had anything changed as a result of his efforts?

The answer the stars gave was: not really.

No, said the Plough, and No, said Sirius, and No, said Venus, and No No No No No, said all the splash of mothlike planets in the Milky Way.

No more people spoke Irish, or read Irish, in spite of his best

149

efforts. The environment, even in the immediate locality, the parochial environment, continued to be destroyed. Every week, it seemed, new houses sprang up in the fields, new septic tanks were dug to pollute still further the ground water, new SUVs appeared to churn up the surface of the boreens. Every month some young man or woman, or some old-age pensioner, was mowed down on the roads.

Before you even talk about animal rights, and vegetarianism.

He had tried, for thirteen years. He had tried to make a difference. What else could anyone serious do? Your allotted time was short enough; if you didn't use it to make some contribution, how would you feel when your time was up? Guilty, he supposed. But he felt guilty anyway. And stupid. He was just deluding himself that he could change something, or make a contribution. History rolled on inexorably in spite of what he, or anyone else, did to change its course. Killing Roads had not stopped a single car killing a single victim and it probably never would. His efforts to keep the Irish language alive were energetic and solid but the Irish language would continue to fade away in spite of all of them. That he ate vegetables did not prevent the butchery of innocent animals continuing and expanding. That he used public transport made no difference to the appalling record of Ireland as a car-dependent nation.

He could not stop the killing roads, he could not stop a rich man evading the planning laws, he could not stop the Taoiseach allowing Bush to land his prisoners at Shannon. Just as he could not stop Kate from running away with that Vincy fellow.

His life was passing him by and he was failing, at every single thing he did.

The stars twinkled and laughed their heads off at him, as he trudged sadly up the hill to his house. The world you are so busy saving is a moth, they laughed. We are moths to you and from our point of view you are also a mothlike star, flickering out, out, out.

Fourteen

Anna was stepping into a warm pub, as she did almost every day now, every lunchtime. It was not the Tower, but an ordinary pub in the city centre, whose claim to fame was that it had not been renovated or redecorated, not even painted, in about fifty years. Never mind. Before, she had never set foot inside such places and now she loved them. In these pubs, old and shabby or new and brash or picturesque and lovely, she was experiencing every day a very rare treat.

Happiness.

At last it had arrived.

There it was, in this grotty pub, waiting on a bar stool.

Happiness. Of a kind she had given up hope for years ago. Happiness, she had decided, was going to come from success. One day she would write that bestselling book, and then she would be completely happy. In the meantime, she had the satisfaction of her nice husband and her lovely son and her big house, of her friends and the parties and writing groups, of shopping and holidays and restaurants, to keep her going.

But happiness of this kind, she had stopped thinking about. Or had decided was a fairy tale, or so rare that most people would never experience it.

Now, every day it was given to her. In very small parcels, she had to admit, measured temporarily, sometimes in hours, sometimes merely minutes. But those times had a crystalline quality. They gleamed like diamonds stuck in quartz – their setting a smelly pub, usually, or a crowded café.

Talking to him – she was the one who did the talking, mainly – is what the happiness consisted in. Being with him, breathing the same air, feeling the warmth of his body not far from hers, was what she loved.

They hadn't had sex.

They had kissed.

What a funny thing a kiss is. Everyone was always kissing Anna. Rory, Alex, her friends, her enemies. The cat. And Anna was always kissing them back, human, animal, mineral. She kissed flowers in her garden, she kissed books and letters and photographs.

Kissing Vincy was not, of course, like any of that.

He kissed her in the underground car park at the Blackrock Shopping Centre, beside her Land Rover at the end of a line of parked cars. Nobody could see them. He believed. He kissed her and held her in his arms for a minute. The earth moved. The *car park* moved. All the cars slid along down to the end of the dark basement and then slid back again. Time stood still. A shopping centre eclipse.

Love.

Lust.

Passion.

Yes. Yes. Yes.

It was time to do more about it.

Vincy asked her to go away for the weekend, to London. He sometimes had to go there for work purposes. But she demurred. It was one thing to have lunch, another to spend the weekend with him. If they went to bed, that would be it. An unabashed admission of adultery. The end of her marriage.

Chaos.

He understood. He did not put her under any pressure. 'OK,' he said. 'When you want to go away for a weekend, we will. Not until then.'

That had made her feel unhappy, briefly. Maybe she wanted to be persuaded?

But once he made up his mind about anything, that was that. He was a very decisive man – a quality he shared with Alex.

Once a plan was made, he didn't like changing it. He did not see the point.

He decided that they would go here or go there, that they would meet every day or every second day. He even named the venues. He was the first man she had ever known who could think of the names of restaurants. Most men, even most women, hesitated as soon as a date was arranged. Where will we go? Usually nobody could remember anywhere, even though they ate out several times a month. Only after much dithering, attempts to recall names, would a venue be selected. But Vincy said, 'I'll see you tomorrow in the Blue Corner', or 'I'll be in Doheny & Nesbit's at one o'clock, is that OK for you?'

Yes, it was OK. All she had to do was acquiesce. None of this was in her control.

And now he never said, 'I'm going to London on Friday evening. Can you meet me at the check-in desk at five thirty?' or anything like that. Sex was off the agenda, and it would stay off it, it seemed, until she decided to put it back on.

This should have made Anna perfectly happy. But, curiously, it was one of the aspects of the relationship that kept it from perfection. While the sense of cheating, which should have marred it, had the opposite effect.

After the first few meetings, out in the open, they began to go to secluded venues, where they would be unlikely to bump into acquaintances. Vincy didn't put it so bluntly, but he suggested the new secret places, and she was much happier in them. Sneaking off to dark venues gave her a sense of security, on the one hand, and heightened her sense of risk-taking and subterfuge, on the other. It was like a game of hide-and-seek for grown-ups. Would they be caught? Or would they reach *den* – is that what the children called it? – safely?

The Tower, in far-off Rathcormac, with its dark red cushions and hidden snugs, was her favourite spot, but they could not go there every day. So they selected other similar pubs in unlikely suburbs, Ringsend or Sutton, or, as they became more advent-urous, Ballymun and Tallaght or Coolock. Into these wild regions they drove, to explore the concrete jungles on the outskirts of the city. The danger they faced from the natives was compensated for by their conviction that they would never be spotted. Nobody they knew would ever go to Ballymun for lunch, or for anything else (unless they were giving a creative writing workshop, or covering a murder for the news).

Anna gradually came to love these places for their own sake. To her they were more exotic than Seville or Stockholm or Barcelona or any of the other cities she was used to popping into for a weekend break; in many respects the great cities of Europe had a lot in common with one another, she told herself. You quickly became familiar with the type of thing on offer: an old town with narrow streets, a new town with wide streets, a cathedral and an art gallery and a bewildering multitude of picturesque restaurants. How much stranger and more exciting were Exit 9, to the Square, or Exit 4, to Ballymun! The little unknown roads that led from these exits to the big social housing estates were little roads to the unknown. The streets of houses, with their carefully tended gardens full of ponds and statues, were, she realised, more full of character, more creative and energetic, than the rich suburb in which she lived, where everyone copied everyone else, and in general where good taste decreed that you could never paint a wall unless you commissioned an interior decorator first, to tell you which shade of white was suitable. These places became much more than that. (She turned a blind eye to the odd neglected garden, to the houses with boarded up windows and broken windows that cropped up on every street.)

The pubs were different from the ones she knew, in the south suburbs of Dublin or the old town centres of Europe. The size of them was in direct contrast to the size of the houses that surrounded them: if the houses were tiny, the pubs were vast. And numerous. In her suburb, exactly the opposite situation prevailed. There was only one pub in the whole district, and it was small and poky, as if the owners accepted that the locals would not be dropping in for a jar in any numbers. Here there was a choice of venues and menus and places to sit. She liked the enormous carvery lunches or thin, toasted sandwiches, the comfortable banquettes, the plucky efforts at individuality – shelves of second-hand books in one, Chinese lanterns in another. She would sink into one of the soft seats and nibble her sandwich, melted cheddar cheese with strong mustard, or a 'boagie', a sort of sandwich that seemed to be native to this area; anyway she had never come across one in Killiney, or anywhere in the constituency of Dún Laoghaire–Rathdown. Sinking into the plush banquette, sinking into the boagie, she would gaze happily around the vast room.

'I had thought I was happy before,' she said to Vincy. 'But this is different from anything. Do you know what I mean?'

He did. He felt what she felt, precisely. So he said. They were totally united in their experience. And that was another new experience for Anna. How seldom did you share your feelings with another person! Usually you were at odds with them – if it was a man, he was talking, you were half-listening, even if you were interested in one another, even if you half-loved him, you were conscious of difference all the time, conscious that he might be bored, that his thoughts might be elsewhere – much as your own were. There was no dovetailing. Even when she and Alex had sex there was no dovetailing. Far from it.

But with Vincy, in these big, warm, seedy pubs, they were like two halves of an apple fitted together and made whole – a metaphor that would recur to her as the affair progressed.

'This is the best there is,' she said to him. They were at either side of a small bistro table out in the middle of the pub. That there was a real danger of discovery lent a frisson to their meeting. Sometimes she was overwhelmed by lust. She felt her face must reveal this to everyone. She felt it must be flushed, bloated even.

'Don't look at me like that,' he said, smiling warningly, touching her knees with his and holding the position. 'With those eyes. It drives me crazy.'

She slipped off her shoe and rubbed the inside of his calf with her stockinged foot.

They stared at one another in a mixture of amusement and desire.

Passion is so serious, Anna was about to say, but with you it's funny.

But she didn't. Because passion can't be serious if it expresses itself only under a table in a pub.

Vincy withdrew his leg abruptly. This was a habit of his: coming close, then withdrawing. She didn't understand why he did it but it did not bother her. Becoming familiar with his traits, especially those that seemed to be unique to him, was a pleasure in itself. She was still researching him, exploring his character, finding out: learning to read him. Everything that taught her something new about him delighted her.

Chicken tikka panini on her plate. Three white chrysanthemums on the table. A bright green plate. The sun might have been shining outside but there was artificial light here. A smell of beer and fried food. Many people gobbled their lunch, some gossiping, some silent and alone, reading newspapers. Most people were eating some kind of chunky sandwich, with crisps and coleslaw, and drinking coffee or tea. A lot of them took dessert; she gazed at them, tucking into thick wedges of apple pie with whipped cream, spooning up sweet gobbets of banoffee. Anna had not eaten dessert since she was sixteen.

As she left the pub, she noticed the inevitable beggar close to the doorway, and gave him five euro. Her eyes were on Vincy and she did not look at the man wrapped up in a blue sleeping bag. If she had, she would have seen he was wearing glasses, and reading a thick book. Over the rim of the book he peered with his bespectacled eyes and smiled when he recognised Anna, the woman who gave him such good tips that she was almost worth following around. Although that was not what he was doing. His encounters with her happened quite by chance. Without willing it, he was keeping track of her, though.

Unlike Alex.

He noticed nothing.

Her life was changed utterly and she was changed utterly, but their life together went on exactly as before.

Why? Maybe it was because he worked all the time; even his social life, limited as it was, was an extension of his work. Everything fed into that work – although Anna, and he himself, would have been hard set to describe exactly what that work consisted in. Whatever it was, it was all absorbing, and as a result, he was the most unobservant person Anna had ever known.

But some people in her immediate circle were, like the beggar with the book, more observant.

One of these was Ludmilla.

Ludmilla could have hardly helped noticing that Anna left the house now every second day at about eleven thirty in the morning, whereas previously she had usually stayed in her room until one o'clock. They never had lunch together these days. And even in the large house, where privacy was easily available, it was not hard to observe that before she left, Anna spent a long time preparing herself, washing and making up and selecting her clothes. It was also clear that Anna was both happier and better-looking than ever before.

It did not take Ludmilla long to reach the right conclusion. But it was none of her business and she said nothing, doing her work in exactly the same way as usual and, if anything, making an effort to pretend that everything was just as it had been before.

Luz Mar was less observant. Her main concern was that these days she was asked to collect Rory from school much more frequently than had been the case hitherto, which she found very annoying. She did not notice that Anna was better dressed, or more carefully dressed, than before, or that her complexion was clearer and her eyes brighter. She was nineteen. It would not have occurred to her that her employer could be having a relationship with a man not her husband. All she really noticed was that Anna was more demanding than before. What Anna's reasons were did not concern Luz Mar and in so far as she gave them any thought, she put it down to work.

Anna still wrote in the mornings. But instead of writing for four hours or more she wrote for one, at the most. The progress of the novel slowed up and the prospect of getting a first draft completed by Christmas receded. The fortunes of Sally inter-ested her less and less as her own life interested her more and more. Most of the time she couldn't care less about Sally and her adventures. All this work, which had seemed so essential for her, was on the brink of becoming pointless and trivial. By com-parison with what she was experiencing, writing about a non-existent, roughly conceived character journeying around an imaginary world seemed like one of life's more ridiculous activities. Soon she had to force herself to write even for half an hour a day. She would have preferred to go for a walk, or shop for ever more attractive outfits, or do her face, or even talk to Ludmilla as she cleaned the kitchen. Most of all she would have preferred to daydream, to prolong her enjoyment of Vincy when he was not present, to savour every nuance of her love. Vincy, or her idea of Vincy, had taken over that inner part of herself in which Sally existed. He was pushing Sally, and all her other imagined things, to the side, blotting them out.

She forced herself to write out of some loyalty to her old routines. She was afraid that if she stopped she would never start again. The question, why do I do it? which she had never asked herself before, began to pop up in her consciousness more and more often, but as an excuse not to write rather than a question to be answered. By the skin of her teeth, by some miracle of habit, she clung to her unarticulated belief that writing was what identified her. That was a reason for doing it, even if it were not a very profound one. 'I write' was the only possible answer to the question 'And what is it you do?', an answer that resulted in a somewhat more positive response, usually, than the other one she could give ('I'm a housewife').

Neither label really identified her now. She was not a writer; she was not a housewife. She was barely, even, a mother. What she was now was the woman who was in love with Vincy. That was all she was and that was everything in the world. But – although she felt tempted once or twice – it was not something she could reveal when some rude man at a dinner party would ask in an off-hand tone, 'And what is it you do?' 'I am the woman who is in love with Vincent.'

That her true identity was unknown to anyone apart from herself and Vincy was thrilling. She felt like a spy in Russia, a woman with blond hair and a mackintosh living a life of complete falseness, nurturing her true self like a pearl deep inside her body, while living every minute of her days as another human being.

Anna was two distinct people at the same time.

She was a character in her own fiction, and she was also the author of the fiction.

All I think about is him. I go over the conversations we have had, and moments of delight – a kiss in the car one dark night, a close hug in a park, when nobody could see us, when time stood still. Nobody would believe it. Nobody would believe what I feel, it seems like sentimental rubbish, the stuff of the kind of book I couldn't bring myself to read – if those books are even written these days – and it is the most glorious transcendent thing there is. When they – who? – talk about heavenly bliss, this is what they are talking about – how they transferred the emotion attached to sexual love to a non-existent supernatural being, I cannot fathom, but now I know that that is exactly what they did. Even using the same word 'love'. Love of God. There is no other happiness.

Thou shalt not have false images before me.

I simply think of his image. His mystery of a face, his quizzical eyes. His picture in my head.

Twenty-four hours a day, she filled her mind with him.

Playing with Rory, eating dinner with Alex, going to things with him or without him, she filled her mind with him.

Writing the increasingly preposterous and boring adventures of Sally, she filled her mind with him.

Sleeping on her wide, four-poster bed, she filled her mind with him.

Dinner with the President.

She filled her mind with him.

It should have been a big day. But – this was the downside of love, then, one of them – it wasn't. The ordinary little triumphs, the petty pleasures, the minor snobbish thrills, were not to be enjoyed. By comparison with what she felt when she was with Vincy, they were revealed in all their tawdriness. Rubble. Rubbish.

A dark plum dress, velvet. A black cloak. Silver jewellery.

But when she saw her reflection, she recognised immediately that it lacked spirit. Her skin was opaque and dull, and no amount of light-reflecting make-up would disguise its heavy texture. Her eyes were tired and small. Even her stomach bulged. Everything was bloated, thick, swollen. A lead weight of dullness sat in her stomach and polluted her blood.

'You look gorgeous.' Alex kissed her on the cheek. The meaninglessness of his compliment irritated her. He was her husband; he should notice that she was bloated, and pasty-faced, that she looked like a potato in plum velvet. His compliments couldn't be trusted – he always said, possibly always perceived, that she looked the same. What big ears he has, she thought crossly, wondering why she had not cared about this ever before.

The President's house was pretty, although somehow not as splendid, or big, or special, as Anna would have liked. There was something predictable about it, which was not just a result of having seen parts of it a thousand times before in photographs or on television. It lacked character. Anna had heard or read of various presidents making various renovations, but the sense she

159

got in the house was of a building that had been designed and decorated by the Office of Public Works, in the most neutral and safe style.

In a reception room she had often seen on the television screen, covered in an elaborate, strange green carpet covered with harps and shamrocks, the President received the guests. They lined up and shook her hand, and said a few friendly words. Anna should have anticipated this and prepared something to say in advance, but she hadn't. Now, as she stood in the queue, she was too distracted by the surroundings to concentrate and come up with some suitable greeting. But she hoped she would be inspired to say something witty and charming and original, something that would make an impression and please the President. When the moment came, what she said was: 'Thank you very much for inviting us. I am pleased to meet you.' The only original thing she did was reverse the usual order of these sentences, and that had been done accidentally. To her surprise she felt quite nervous as she stood there, on the leprechaun carpet, shaking the hand of this person who was very familiar and yet a complete stranger. The President had just smiled blandly and stuck out her hand for the next person.

The conversation at dinner was similarly stilted all through the first course – selection of pâtés with Melba toast – and into the second – roast lamb. Alex sat beside her, which was a blessing – she hated dinners where they separated the spouses so that you sat among complete strangers. The conversation at their table sounded lively if you were not actually listening to the words, but hearing them from a distance. Everyone talked and looked animated and engaged, and the babble was continuous. But when you were there, hearing what was said, you knew it was dull and forced, that people were talking only because they felt obliged to, and that not a single person had the slightest interest in anything that was being said even by themselves.

The man opposite Anna was some sort of politician, a very young man who had run for the last county council election but failed to get in. Since he had run in Anna's constituency, she ought to have recognised him – he talked about the problem of putting up posters containing his photograph (the problem was, they cost three euro a poster, and also that the opposition took them down as soon as your back was turned). But she could not

160

remember having seen his face on a single one of those expensive posters, even though the election had taken place recently enough.

He talked incessantly about all kinds of political issues, himself and his experiences, and about Charlie McGreevy and the Irish representation in the EU and the European Parliament. Anna knew nothing at all about any of this. The woman next to him, dressed in red, a tall woman with very white skin and a mop of black hair, which she had tried to subdue into a sort of chignon but which escaped as time wore on, was able to take up the themes; she seemed conversant with the detail, knew the names of other European members of parliament, and the issues that were pressing just at the moment. Alex also made a few contributions. All the talkers were articulate and informed but the conversation was boring anyway, and Anna sensed that they all knew this but felt obliged to keep talking. Nobody even had the nerve to change the subject. It was as if they were afraid if they did not let the stream of talk, the source of which had been quite arbitrary, the source of which was that young failed politician and his particular interests, the stream would dry up and they would have nothing more to say. The very worst thing that could happen at a dinner like this was to fall into silence.

Which was what Anna did. She could not contribute. Her ignorance appalled her more and more as the sea of facts washed over her. She read the newspaper daily, and she listened to the news at nine o'clock, but she hardly knew the names of any European members of parliament, apart from a few Irish ones – was Dana still over there? She wasn't even sure. Still less did she know what speeches they had been making, which journalists wrote about them in the papers, or what the big issues for the EU were just at the moment – all that had always seemed indescribably dull to her.

She remembered something when the lamb was being taken away.

'Emma Jane McFadden,' she said. She was an MEP for Sinn Féin. She thought. 'She has lost some weight again, hasn't she?'

This was the only thing Anna could remember that related to the European Parliament. She offered her comment in desperation. But to her astonishment they were all ready to jump on it. The conversation livened up immediately. Everyone – except

161

the young, pudgy politician, who looked annoyed – had a genuine, sometimes passionate, opinion on Emma Jane's figure. And clothes.

'No I don't think so,' the knowledgeable woman with the black chignon said earnestly. 'She never managed to shake it off. She doesn't seem to know that you can exercise even if you are an MEP with a baby. Such a pity, she was quite pretty.'

'That's how she got her seat,' the failed county councillor said. Annoyed as he was, he could not refrain from taking part in any conversation. He was quite fat himself and not all that good-looking. 'They know what they are doing, Sinn Féin, putting up young, beautiful women. They keep doing it.'

The conversation then expanded to discuss the appearances of all the other female politicians. Their hair, figures, their suits, their blouses, their coats, even their shoes or boots were commented upon in detail, and with great delight by everyone. From shoes to relationships and love affairs was almost a natural transition. Inadvertently, the failed county councillor revealed that a particular Minister had recently separated from his wife. There had been an intimation that he had had a relationship with his PR consultant, which he had successfully quashed. Now the people at the table who knew everything let it be known that all the people in the know were well aware that he had been having this affair for years. They then began to talk about other politicians who had had illicit affairs and who had succeeded in keeping them secret from the media, and about others who had not had the luck to succeed.

The table buzzed with animated talk.

Anna found all this fascinating, but also both reassuring and terrifying at the same time.

It was reassuring to find out that having an affair was so commonplace. From the way these people spoke about it, you would get the impression that it was more normal than anything else. It sounded as if everyone who was anyone was having an affair, and that their affairs were common knowledge, if you were in the right circles. There were always secret layers of activity in any society, and it seemed to Anna that she was always one of those who didn't understand what was going on under the surface of any of them. In school, even, it had been like that. Girls in whose mouths butter would not melt, you would think, were taking drugs in the woods behind the school every afternoon, and indulging in other kinds of debauchery as a matter of course, while turning up to get their five hundred points in the Leaving with their blouses ironed and their stockings straight. Probably all those seemingly devoted couples she knew were devoted because they were maintaining illicit liaisons in their spare time.

On the other hand, it was terrifying to realise that what the participants no doubt believed to be secret and underground was so well known.

She wondered if the particular Minister, who had gone to such pains to deny his affair to the press, realised that a group of his associates would be openly gossiping about it within earshot of the President of Ireland, apparently happily devouring her roast lamb but no doubt keeping her own ear open for titbits such as this? The President probably knew all about everyone's carrying on, since she was hosting dinners like this every night of the week.

It was most unlikely, though, Anna thought, that the Minister, or any of the other people whose secret liaisons were now amusing twenty diners in Áras an Uachtaráin, were aware of this. He, and they, no doubt believed it was a secret from everyone but him and his lover.

Anna began to wonder if these people knew about her and Vincy. Was the woman in red giving her knowing glances? Scrutinising her to see what she was like? A lot of them would know Vincy, even though nobody knew Anna.

But she dismissed her suspicions quickly, believing she was much too unimportant to be worth their attention. When Alex told them she was a writer, they looked taken aback – the standard reaction. Naturally they had never heard of her. But their faces suggested that they were genuinely surprised to hear that she was not illiterate, since she did not seem to know what the Maastricht Treaty was or which member states had signed up to the European Constitution.

'Why should you know all about those things?' Vincy asked. They were in the Tower, so much more comfortable in every way than Áras an Uachtaráin. 'They don't know anything about children's literature, or about any literature. Most of them never read a book.'

'I'm not so sure about that,' said Anna.

'Believe me. They don't. Not in the sense you mean it. They work in the diplomatic service, or they are civil servants or politicians, and they think they have a God-given right to talk shop morning, noon and night. Ridiculous prats!' He patted her hand with a paternal gentleness.

'There are people who read books and who also have a good knowledge of politics,' said Anna. But who were they? Most of the writers she knew had strong stances on subjects such as George Bush. They hated him. Certain facts about him they knew: he had started a war in Iraq and was engaged in the torture of prisoners in secret locations in Poland and Romania, and in Guantánamo Bay. The rest of their feeling about him was based on opinions, the staunchest of which was that George Bush was stupid. But how much did they really know about any of this? Their conversation was general, not detailed. From one another they picked up particular points of view, or biases. Bush is bad. Blair is silly. Bertie is not so bad, in spite of his northside accent.

'Yes, maybe,' said Vincy. 'Like me. One should know certain things, like who is the Taoiseach, or the Minister for Finance, or the Minister for Foreign Affairs. Do you know that?'

'Yes,' said Anna. Though she had to think for a few seconds about the Minister for Foreign Affairs.

'And what new legislation of importance is being enacted here. And in Europe. But everyone finds out if it really is important – you find out about the euro, about the Common Agricultural Policy, about sanctions to the Third World. Don't you?'

'I suppose so.' The Common Agricultural Policy. Was that what gave rise to sugar mountains and wine lakes? She was far from sure. 'It is just that at the sort of party I was at last night I never seem to know enough.' She paused. 'Actually, I never seem to know anything.'

He smiled and squeezed her hand again – in the Tower, they could hold hands over the table, whereas in the city centre all contact had to be under it. Anna longed to snuggle up in his arms and be kissed and comforted. He was listening to her in a way Alex would never, ever do. This conversation was not one she could have with Alex, because he would consider it so trivial that he could not bring himself to pay attention to it for more than one second, much less listen to all the little details, analyse them, and comment sensibly on them. Vincy was handsome and masculine and authoritative but talking to him was more like talking to a woman than to a man.

'That's their fault,' he said. 'They are ignorant. I bet they became more respectful when they found out you were a writer, even if they hadn't heard of you?'

'No,' she said rather forlornly. 'They just looked taken aback at first and then sceptical, like everyone does when they hear that.'

'You should be more confident,' he said.

'I don't write that much now anyway,' she said. 'It is as if I had been writing to attract attention ... from you.'

'What do you mean?'

'Not from you personally. But I have heard some writer say that he writes to make people love him. Now that you love me there seems to be less reason for writing.'

'I'll be very very very upset if you stop writing because of me,' Vincy said, frowning at her. 'You better promise me right now that you'll do no such thing.'

She smiled and shrugged.

'Anyway, it doesn't make any sense. What that fellow said. You write to make people love you. That's just one of those silly things writers say when they're being interviewed. They have to say something. Most of it is crap.' He took her hand and squeezed it firmly.

Then he had to get back to work.

'Is it that time already?' Anna asked. It shocked her, how swiftly the lunchtimes sped by. The allotted time was cruelly short. She felt as if she had been bitten by some snarling animal, some sharp-fanged watchdog, when she looked at the clock and realised, once again, that they had to part.

She did not know if Vincy felt the same, and suspected not. He loved being with her but he loved working just as much. That was the difference between them; what that writer had said was not crap, as far as she was concerned. She would rather sit with Vincy, doing nothing more than drinking coffee or watching the folk life in any village pub, than writing her book or doing anything else at all. But Vincy wanted to get back to his desk, to his projects, to his other life.

He knew that she saw things differently. He pressed his knees against hers, for a few seconds, in sympathy, to comfort her. Then they stood up and walked slowly towards the door.

Just as they reached it, Leo Kavanagh walked in. He looked at Anna in recognition and nodded.

'Oh hello,' said Anna, alarmed. She knew she had met this small man, with his curly hair and beard, with the tweedy clothes, somewhere before. Glancing at his shoes – big brown walking shoes – his name came to her. 'Leo!' The one from the country, who had been interested in Kate.

'Hello, Mrs Sweeney.' Leo stared at her and Vincy with undisguised curiosity.

'So what brings you to these parts?' Anna asked, as she recalled more about him.

'Oh, you know,' said Leo, looking inquisitively at Vincy. 'I come to Dublin fairly regularly. I'm organising a meeting of my lobby group among other things.'

'Yes, I'd heard something about that,' Vincy said. 'Have you sent out a press release lately?'

'We do it from time to time,' Leo said, although they hadn't this time, so Vincy could not possibly have heard about the meeting. 'The press doesn't pay much attention, unfortunately.'

Vincy smiled and nodded. 'Maybe I can jog some of them. Let me know when you're doing something, OK?'

At that moment John Perry followed Leo into the pub.

'I'll certainly do that,' Leo said.

'Great to have met you!' Vincy said. 'Take care so.' And he ushered Anna out the door.

'Do you think he suspected anything?' she asked, as they walked across the car park over to Vincy's car.

'No, why should he?' Vincy said carelessly. 'Get in for a minute, can you?'

At that moment he looked appallingly lonely, as she had never seen him before. Anna got into the car immediately, although not before glancing at the doorway of the pub to make sure Leo wasn't looking.

Vincy leaned across the handbrake and hugged her tightly, with desperation. They kissed as if their lives depended on it.

166

Now – she did not know why – his need for her was greater than hers for him. He kissed with a recklessness that was out of character. Something – the encounter with Leo? – had transformed him from an urbane sophisticate to a wild, vulnerable thing.

He opened her jacket and blouse, and began to touch her breasts.

'Not here.' Anna pulled away. 'Stop, let's go somewhere else.' She looked out at the rows of cars in the grey yard. Is there anything as ugly as a car park? she found herself thinking. It was so bleak, its surfaces so hard and cold, that it offended her.

Vincy settled into his own side of the car, into the driver's seat.

'Sorry,' he said, smoothing his own jacket. 'I don't know what came over me. I'm really sorry.'

'Don't be sorry,' said Anna. 'I mean … not at all. It's just a sort of public place. We could go somewhere else.' She looked out again. Two middle-aged women were walking past, their eyes judiciously averted. 'Almost anywhere else would be better than this.'

'I wish,' said Vincy. He glanced at his watch. 'But … Rory will be home from school, won't he?'

Luz Mar can look after him, Anna thought.

'And I need to be getting back. God, I've an appointment in fifteen minutes, I'll have to ring and tell them I'll be late.' He pulled his mobile out of his pocket.

'OK,' said Anna. 'So … we'll go home?'

He looked up from his mobile, puzzled. 'What? Oh yeah, bye. See you tomorrow?' He kissed her quickly on the cheek.

She left his car.

All of this Leo and John Perry observed with interest from the window of the pub.

Fifteen

After lunch with John Perry, Leo came back into the city and went to Rathmines to visit the poet who had written about child abuse.

The first black woman Irish-language poet. She had everything, the potential to be a star, Leo's first real star! Even though her Irish was not one hundred per cent. But then whose was? Nobody, hardly anybody, wrote correct and accurate Irish. Leo corrected the woman's poetry, corrected the grammatical errors, while leaving the thinness, the flatness, the anglicised syntax, since that was the woman's style.

Kambele Ngole.

Harder to say than an Irish name, even. But less offensive to the ears of the general populace.

She was round and beautiful, and dressed in flamboyant clothes – lime green and gold seemed to be the predominant colours. Great! Most of his women authors wore nothing but black. Their launches looked like funerals – which in a sense they were, unfortunately. Kambele's launch, he hoped, would be more like a wedding, fertile with sales and reprints.

A launch. He would have to have a launch, but he would also have to get the book into the shops before Christmas. There was very little time to spare – everything was running late. Could he possibly organise a launch for a week's time? Yes, of course he could, if he put his mind down to it. And employed a good person to help him.

Kate.

He had never employed anyone to help him before, but this time there were extenuating circumstances. Christmas was coming, and he had a potential success on his hands. The right book at the right time – it didn't happen often, in his publishing life. He had been lucky with Tristan. A second success in a season would be a real treat, a good Christmas present to himself. A resounding national success would be spectacular – and just what he needed right now.

Kate would be ideal. She would understand. She would know that his interest was purely professional.

He decided that as soon as he got back to his room he would phone her, and then he could run around to her office very quickly, since it was close to where he was staying. Now that he knew Vincy Erikson was having an affair with Anna Kelly Sweeney (Leo always remembered names, even difficult ones – it was a publisher's knack), telephoning Kate would be much easier. Presumably she knew about this carry-on? Everyone must. They were obviously not very concerned about keeping it a secret.

But he encountered problems. Getting to the B & B took considerably longer than it should have. He took a taxi from Rathmines into town, but it could not get further than Stephen's Green.

'De march,' said the taxi driver, who had been taciturn since Leo had made it clear he was not interested in talking. 'De SIPTU march about de ferries; it's huge. They could've waited till Saturday. Woulda caused less disruption to everyone.'

'Oh yes,' said Leo, remembering. Irish Ferries, the shipping line, had been in dispute with the unions for months. They had offered redundancy packages to their Irish workers to make way for east Europeans and others who would take a quarter of the wages. Because they sailed the high seas – or even the Irish Sea – the Irish legislature had no control over them, and neither had any other legislature, it seemed. Leo had not quite understood how this worked – you could not buy duty free goods in the air or on sea any more, because everything was in the EU. You could no longer buy a cheap bottle of whiskey on the Irish Sea but you could use slave labour on its waters with impunity. Odd. He should look into it. But at the moment he had more pressing concerns.

'Dey'll march from Liberty Hall to de Dáil,' said the taxi driver. 'You'd be as well off walking de rest of the way.'

Leo took his advice, paid him, and set off.

It was about one thirty. The streets close to the Green were crowded; lots of people were shopping, it seemed, march or no march. Walking down Grafton Street, he felt himself to be swimming against a tide of humanity. Waves of faces, every kind of face, met him, an endless swarm. But as long as he kept going forwards there was no difficulty in making progress. The bodies, which looked as if they would have to block him, parted, spontaneously, easily, as if in a patterned dance that everyone simply knew. There should have been collisions but there were not – only people trying to traverse the crowd, move from side to side, were bumped into, and glared at. There were no crossings for those who wanted to cross the flow of walkers; they had to do their best to weave through the flow, and usually trod on somebody's toes. Strange, he thought, that nobody had ever considered putting in pedestrian lights, never realised that walkers constituted a kind of traffic.

The protest march became visible at the bottom of the street. It was snaking around Trinity College, moving along Nassau Street towards Kildare Street and the Dáil. The line stretched as far as he could see in both directions. All the unions and many other groups were represented: seamen's unions from Wales and France had joined in. There were groups of Polish workers, students, Labour Party groups, community groups. 'No Slave Labour' the banners declared.

He continued on his way, which he was able to do. Even when he had to cross the street, the crowd politely made way for him, unlike the Grafton Street shoppers, although one man tried to corner him, shouting cheerfully, 'Come on, join us!' All the way down to O'Connell Street and down Eden Quay the line of marchers stretched, singing and shouting in the wintry sunshine. Leo had never seen such a long march in Dublin.

In Kerry this issue had seemed remote and he had hardly registered that it was happening. That Filipino workers on ships on the Irish Sea were being underpaid seemed irrelevant, down

170

there in the country, where the problem of how to get down to the bus without being blown away into the raging Atlantic took precedence over most things at this time of year. Dublin ... Dublin seemed far away and pointless, spineless, weak, down there.

It surprised him that the workers of Dublin possessed sufficient idealism and energy to mount such a spectacular protest. Of course, their own futures were at stake, so it wasn't entirely altruistic. Even so, one had to acknowledge that the trade-union movement seemed to be alive and well. It lifted his heart to see the long march, a line of humanity a mile long taking over the shopping streets in the interests of workers' rights. Modern people were not as apathetic as he usually believed they were. It was a good omen, the march, he decided.

He had to walk to his B & B, but he walked with an optimistic tread.

Kate was not at the office. He was not answered by a taped recording of her voice, however, but by an actual human voice – Lauren's.

'Oh, no,' she said. Her tone was neutral. 'She isn't here at the moment. Maybe I can help you?'

'It's ... thank you,' he said sadly. 'I am a friend of hers.'

Professionalism indeed.

There was a pause. Leo lifted his eyes and looked out his window at the grey railway station. For some reason it looked unaccountably sad and he began to wonder when it had been built. Connolly Station. He did not see James Connolly, strapped into a chair to be executed in front of another grey wall in the stone breakers' yard or whatever they called the execution ground in Kilmainham (was he mixing it up with Calvary? People did). He saw crowds of soldiers on their way to the Great War. There in front of his eyes he could see them, lines of marching men in their khaki uniforms, heading to Flanders and the Somme. And among the ranks someone odd marched, a woman who looked like a scarecrow, with black straw for hair and a wide red smile. On her head was a black straw hat with a red rose in the brim, a hat only a scarecrow would wear. I had not thought death had undone so many, said Leo to himself, and this scarecrow waved at him, cheerily.

'Is there something wrong?' he asked, knowing there was.

'Kate is on leave,' Lauren said cautiously but with more warmth. 'You should contact her family if you are a friend.'

'All right,' said Leo. The next question was going to be awkward. 'Can you give me her parents' telephone number? We went out together for a while, recently, Kate and I, but I don't know her family as such.'

There was another pause, quite a long one, but when she spoke again, she gave him the number.

'Two – eight – seven – six – five – double four.'

'Oh thanks,' said Leo.

'Take care!' she said, even more warmly.

If Leo had read her voice, its tone would have told him that something bad was about to happen. But he was too distracted to pay attention to Lauren's tone, to what she was saying between the lines.

Leo took the bus out to the psychiatric hospital in Stillorgan, or the looney bin, as he would have referred to it before this afternoon. He would have preferred to take a taxi but he was too embarrassed to get into one and say 'John of God's', lest the taxi driver think he was crazy. The name, John of God, bristled with unsavoury connotations. John of God he saw as a skeletal, demented creature, a figure painted in dark oils by El Greco, most unsavoury. For Leo, mental illness was one of the most frightening phrases in the English language – he had lived in the shadow of the mental asylum, as it had been known then, in his childhood. His mother used to frighten him with stories about the mad inmates, and warn him to stay away from the high stone walls.

And now he was going to a similar place to visit a woman he was in love with. Or had been in love with until an hour ago, because ever since he telephoned Kate's family home and her mother had told him, calmly, that she was a patient in this place, in the looney bin, his feelings had been in turmoil.

He waited sadly for the 46A and trundled slowly out the N11.

172

The evening had turned dark and gloomy, after the sunshine of midday and the glory of the protest march. Night was closing in as he got off the bus and made his way across the motorway to the hospital. It was a big, dark, old building, with wide gardens between it and the motorway. It was not, however, surrounded by the high grey walls, walls like those of a prison or a fortress that surrounded the place in Dundrum, keeping the mad monsters inside and the sane human race out. From here, the mad monsters, the lunatics, would be able to escape quite easily.

Some modern extensions, built mainly of glass, gave the building a rather up-to-date and harmless look. Signs indicating 'Stress Clinic' augmented this effect. If Kate were in the Stress Clinic, it would be all right, he thought, clutching at a straw. It was so much nicer to be in a stress clinic than in a mental hospital. Most people had stress in some form or other, if they were alive at all. He had it himself. Right now.

The rather harmless atmosphere, the sense of normality, suggested by this sign prevailed also inside the doors of the hospital. It was more pleasant than most hospitals. Of course, nobody was actually sick here, in the accepted meaning of the word. Just off the rails. So there were no smells of formaldehyde or whatever it was that gave regular hospitals their typical intimidating stink. A tree grew in the lobby, in front of a giant abstract mural, rather colourful. Behind a desk an elderly woman sat, with the unmistakable look of a nun, even though she wore what nuns apparently considered to be ordinary clothes, which were the sort of clothes old schoolteachers wore in the 1950s. Did they have a special shop for them, specialising in old schoolteachers' grey skirts and blue cardigans, like those shops that sold school uniforms? Or had they kept them in mothballs for fifty years in the attics of convents?

'I am looking for St Paul's Ward,' he said.

'Which patient?' she asked, in a neutral rather than a kind voice.

He resented this. 'Kate Murphy,' he said, however.

She answered immediately, without checking anything. 'Room six. Down the corridor, take the lift to the second floor and then turn left.'

He found his way to St Paul's: not a ward so much as a wide

area in which armchairs were clustered here and there around coffee tables. It was decorated with potted plants and reproductions of popular Impressionist pictures with nature motifs. *Sunflowers. Starry Night. Water Lilies.* Obviously they were attempting to create a welcoming, cheerful environment for the inmates – something they didn't bother to do in normal hospitals, where by the time you got to the ward you were too sick to care that the corridors were hung with pictures of the crucifixion interspersed with portraits of former surgeons.

Number six was one of several doors along the inside wall of this space, which was fronted with glass on the other side.

He knocked and was admitted.

Kate was not in bed, but sitting in a chair, looking at the television.

He kissed her quickly, eyes averted.

'Kate!' He moved away from her and forced himself to look. Clad all in black, she sat in the red plastic chair looking like an insect sleeping in a tomato. She was thinner than before. Even thinner. 'Kate!'

She did not seem surprised to see him. He assumed that somehow, although he could not think how, she had found out that he was coming.

'Hello, Leo.' She smiled and spoke in a perfectly normal tone of voice. 'How are you?'

She still hadn't turned off the television. A quiz show was on, very loudly.

He was confused and she seemed very poised – as usual.

'Fine thanks,' he said. 'And you?'

'Well …' she shrugged. 'I suppose I should be telling you what I am doing here!'

'Only if you feel like it,' he said.

'Oh, it's not a problem.' She smiled very brightly. 'I got depressed. And anorexic, a tendency I have.'

'Yes?' He had a momentary impulse to take her hand, but he resisted it. 'I say,' he said, embarrassed. 'Could you lower the sound on the television? Slightly hard of hearing.' He touched his ear apologetically.

'Oh, sorry, I forgot!' She zapped it off with the remote control. 'There!' She smiled brightly again. 'Do you watch television much?'

'Eh, no. Not too much,' he said. 'I have a set all right, but mostly I prefer to read.'

'Me too. I don't ever watch it at home. But here I can't read and there's nothing else to do.'

He looked around the room. It was an ordinary, basic room, pink walls and a large window looking out on bare trees and rooftops. He could see the orange glow of the lights along the Bray Road.

'I've been here for two weeks,' she said. She smiled, in a rather strange, glassy, way. 'I'm getting bored.'

'Is that a good sign?' he asked.

'Not really. It just *is* a very boring place,' she said. She twisted her hands. Her hair was unkempt and she did not look very clean. No make-up.

'What do you do all day?' he asked perfunctorily. They were not going to have an intimate conversation. She was not going to confide in him the reason for her breakdown, whether it had something to do with that Vincy fellow or not. And he was not going to confide in her about his feelings, which were suddenly very ambivalent.

'I watch television,' she said. 'There's nothing else to do.'

'Hm.' He looked around the room again. There were no books, not even one, that he could see. 'Do you read?' he asked.

'I *can* read,' she said quickly. He was about to retort but thought better of it. It dawned on him that the medication had affected her responses. 'But I can't read in here.' Tears filled her eyes, to his alarm. He couldn't cope if she started to cry. 'I can't concentrate, because of all the drugs.'

He nodded. 'You're on a lot of drugs?' He sounded as if he were on a lot of drugs himself, it occurred to him.

'Yes, a lot. Do you read?'

They'd already discussed this.

'Yes, yes, I do. I read all the time, at home.'

'Where do you live?' she asked.

'What? You know perfectly well ...' he started to say. But then he just answered the question. 'Down the country. In Kerry.'

'Kerry is beautiful,' she said. 'I'd like to go there sometime. I went on a holiday once when I was a child.' She paused. 'I think it was there. Or Derry. There's a place called Derry?'

'You must come down to Kerry,' he said slowly. 'When you're

better.' He didn't mean that she must come down to visit him. 'When are you getting out?' he asked.

'When they decide I'm OK. They come around and talk to me once a week and weigh me. Then make up their minds.'

She looked sad again. She twisted her hands. There was a silence that sat heavily in the little pink room.

'It's nice of you to come.'

'I was in Dublin. I was going to ask you out to dinner.'

She laughed. 'Dinner!' she repeated.

He smiled uneasily. 'Yes.'

'They spend their whole time trying to get me to eat.'

Leo patted her hand, without moving closer to her. She smelt slightly of bodily smells, sweat, maybe even a faint trace of urine.

'I haven't eaten a dinner in months.' She laughed. Now she was alert and logical. 'But on Monday they'll let me down for coffee.'

Leo didn't know what to make of this. 'Down for coffee?' he asked.

'There's a café. It's a treat, and a test. The first step to getting out of here is getting down the stairs for coffee. Then after a week or so, they let you walk in the grounds. And then they let you home on Sunday and so on. That's their little system.'

'Hm.' He thought quickly. Or did not think at all. 'Well, OK, can I buy you coffee on Monday?'

'That would be lovely.' She smiled graciously, like an ordinary woman accepting an invitation to an ordinary date, not like someone who was drugged out of her senses in a lunatic asylum.

The hospital café had a cheerful aspect – it was large with dark tables and chairs, and palm trees in brass pots, like Bewley's used to be. One glass wall looked out on a terrace thick with potted palms, against a backdrop of bare black trees. In a corner, someone played the piano. The music, which might have been something by Debussy, provided a gentle soothing accompaniment to the hum of voices and the clatter of cups and saucers: that comforting tune. People sat around drinking coffee and eating cakes.

Kate seemed to accept Leo's presence without question. It was

176

as if they were friends of long standing. There was something odd about the way she queried nothing, but today she was less forgetful than she had been during their first meeting. Already he could read the signs; she was probably on a lower dose, or a different dose, of medication. But although she was much more normal, her conversation was all about the present and focused on life in the hospital. And her health. She didn't even ask how he was, even though she seemed to know exactly who he was this time.

'The food is quite good really, but of course I don't want to eat it. They give me special meals, small portions, and not heavy, but it is very difficult for me to eat.'

She sipped her coffee, which was black. She had gone to some trouble with her appearance. Her hair had been washed and brushed and she was well dressed, in jeans and a long-sleeved shirt. In these clothes he could see how thin she had become.

'I weigh just under six stone,' she said cheerfully, noticing that he was examining her.

Leo had no idea what a woman like Kate would normally weigh. He knew that he himself weighed thirteen stone and a bit, though, so could grasp that less than half that weight seemed unnatural, even for a woman.

'They'd like me to be seven before they let me go home, and then I should try to increase to eight or eight and a half. Or nine.' She shuddered.

He looked at her carefully. He found it hard to understand these details, but she was fascinated by them. 'Is that what you normally weigh in at?' he asked.

She shook her head and widened her eyes in mock alarm. 'I never weigh more than seven and a half stone,' she said. 'At least I haven't for years. I was a fatty when I was fifteen, about ten stone, it was horrific. That's of course where the whole problem started.'

Debussy, definitely. He couldn't name it, some lovely inter-lude. He listened to the clink of spoons on saucers; he looked at the waving palm trees, at the trees' black limbs stretched like supplicated arms against the evening sky.

'But as a rule, you're fine?'

'Yes.' She closed her eyes for a second. 'I am always fine. I like being thin and I can get by, at seven and a half. That's within my

BMI range. I'm small anyway.'

'And this time …'

'It was brought on by a crisis.' She didn't want to talk about Vincy, so he didn't bring it up. 'It's very relaxing here, but there is nothing to do. They don't do any therapy at all. You just take the medication, lots of different kinds of medication. Or if you get too bad, they give you ECT.'

He started. *One Flew over the Cuckoo's Nest. A Beautiful Mind,* John Nash thrashing around in his bed. He hadn't known they still used ECT. 'Have they given you ECT?' he asked.

'Yes,' she said. 'Just once.'

'God,' he said, shaking his head.

'It's great,' she said. 'It makes a huge difference. It means I'll be better soon. And when I get out, I will see a therapist who will do cognitive therapy with me, and teach me to be … not to be anorexic.'

Leo came across Anna Kelly Sweeney and Vincy Erikson a few nights later.

He had planned to go back home after meeting Kate for the second time, but, without questioning his decision, he lingered on. He had the excuse of organising the book launch for Kambele Ngole – he was doing it on his own after all. With the help of his laptop he was able to do that easily enough from the B & B. When not visiting Kate, he was busy emailing invitations to people, making phone calls, arranging a caterer. Luckily the place on the Green, or off the Green, where he had held his last launch, was available – it had been decorated for Christmas and looked more cheerful than it had in November.

It was an emailed invitation to another book event that brought him into contact with Anna and Vincy. A novel by Marcus Browne, a young novelist who was highly thought of by everyone, was being launched. The event was being held in the Westbury Hotel, an unusually glamorous venue, testimony to the publishers' faith in their new boy. He was in fact, Leo thought, one of the few Irish writers under the age of forty who had achieved any recognition, so he could understand the publishers' optimism. If things went well, a long, successful career could be starting this very night – just as Leo hoped a successful career would start in a few days' time in St Martin's Hall.

The whole mezzanine area of the hotel, a vast space full of elegant Louis Quatorze chairs, with crystal chandeliers, a grand piano, palms in brass pots, was in use for the launch. Champagne was served and many of the important literati were present, chattering at the tops of their voices. It could not have been more different from Leo's launches. The surprising thing was that there could be so much variation in an event that went by the same name. Instead of a handful of embarrassed or proud relations of the writer, here were hordes of people, who, like himself, would not have recognised the writer if they met him on the street, but whose own faces were well known. Leo saw features he knew from the pages of the weekend newspapers, voices he heard on the arts show, names from the spines of paperbacks published by Penguin and Picador and Faber & Faber. John McGann himself, who never came to anything, and was rumoured to be ill, was sitting on one of those gold brocade chairs, a glass of champagne in hand, listening to Deirdre O'Dea, her chestnut hair flowing over her porcelain shoulders. Leo slid across the room to eavesdrop. He had never seen these two people at a book launch before. This was an opportunity not to be missed.

'I stay in the Shelbourne usually, John,' Ireland's leading woman novelist was saying to Ireland's leading man novelist, in her famously mellifluous tones. 'But it's closed for renovations so I'm putting up here for tonight and then I'll go to my little place down the country for a few days. I love it in the country. I'm a country person, just like you, darling, although I never write a thing while I'm there.' She drew out the words 'down the counth-ree', rolling the consonants around in her mouth and filling the simple phrase with the mixture of poetry and irony that was her hallmark.

'It's funny, the places where you can write and where you can't,' said the other great Irish novelist in a flat voice.

'Isn't it? I write in London. I can write in other places … I do when I go to France sometimes and rent a villa, but in my own little cottage in the country I just can't. It's because I am so distracted. I am always needing to get a plumber or a painter or someone to fix the light. There is always something wrong with the house. Is it like that in Tipperary, John, is it?' She leaned over, unconsciously it seemed, so that he would hear her better.

'I can fix the light myself,' said John McGann.

Deirdre O'Dea smiled appreciatively and kissed him, being so close anyway. His face was raw, as if his skin had become very thin, and he looked tired. Leo thought that the rumours of illness were probably correct.

'That's what it means to be a man, a real countryman. You can turn your hand to anything.' She said these things in a dramatic, sensuous, deeply sonorous voice, as if uttering statements of the utmost profundity.

Leo would have liked to eavesdrop for longer, but Deirdre O'Dea glanced up and saw him standing there, his ear cocked. So he looked away hurriedly, pretending not to see her, and scanned the room studiously for other famous people, or for a friendly face. There were plenty of the former but not so many of the latter. None of the Irish language crowd would be here, they weren't important enough to merit an invitation to a launch like this.

Then someone tapped him on the shoulder.

'Gerry.' Leo smiled. 'How nice to see you.' Meaning, he would have been pleased to see anyone who would talk to him.

'What brings you to Dublin?' Gerry asked.

Leo hesitated. He did not know if it would be tactful to mention Kate. Her parents had been quite open about her mental illness but Gerry might find it embarrassing to have the subject broached. Leo would be embarrassed to be related to someone in a mental hospital. Or he would have been, before now, before he had become accustomed to Kate's illness, and to the hospital.

'Oh you know, work mostly,' he said. 'A few people to see, the usual. How is life treating you these days?'

'Great!' said Gerry, who had already had four glasses of champagne, more than anyone else attending this launch. 'I'm having an exhibition in the new year, I've finally got my show on the road. I'll send you a card.'

'You're still working in the civil service?' Leo asked.

'Oh yes, yes,' Gerry said dismissively. 'It pays the bills. But I've taken a bit of time off. Enough to get this exhibition finished.'

'Well that's great. Send me an invite, I'll come if I can at all.' said Leo. 'So how is everyone? Anna?'

Leo looked as sly as Leo ever would.

'Anna? My sister?'

Leo nodded slowly.

Gerry looked less cheerful all of a sudden. 'Oh, I haven't seen her for a while,' he said.

'That's about to be remedied,' said Leo. 'She's just come up the stairs. And that's Vincy, the big fellow with the Swedish surname, with her, I think.'

Gerry turned to look. Then he said abruptly, 'I've got to talk to someone about a ... Look, good to have met you.' He went to the other end of the room.

Leo smiled to himself, feeling powerful all of a sudden. He had seldom been so nasty, in, as he considered it, a subtle way, although he had often been at the receiving end of such unpleasantness. Although it was contrary to his main moral principle, namely that people should be kind to one another, his dig at Gerry did not make him feel morally defective. It did not make him feel mean. Buoyed up by a new confidence, he made his way towards Anna and Vincy. He would say hello. He would mention Kate's name just to see how they reacted. Just to annoy them. But when he came close to the head of the stairs, where they had been standing, they had disappeared. He looked around. The crowd had thickened. There were hundreds of people in the room. Anna and Vincy must have got lost in the mêlée very quickly after arriving.

Disconsolately he began to shove back into the crowd. Contrary to his initial impression, he now saw that the room contained dozens of people he knew well enough to talk to. Now, when he didn't want them, they emerged from the amorphous mass, and greeted him and kept him engaged in trivial conversation.

He found himself pulled into a group of writers whom he hardly knew, although he recognised their faces. 'Houseman got a huge advance from Secker and Warburg for his latest,' one of the company said. 'So they say. He wouldn't give it to them unless they upped their usual by twenty-five per cent. It's not that he cares about the money, it's his way of measuring his literary worth, he says.'

They laughed.

'Secker and Warburg must have been pissed off. How many did he sell?'

'I reckon not more than twenty-five thousand. They would have been hoping for a hundred. Thanks to you going and writing a book on the same subject.' He poked someone – that was Jonathan Bewley, Leo knew him to see – in the chest.

Leo felt so jealous that he had to move off.

How much were those advances? The exact figure was something you never got to know, except in reports in the newspaper, which were undoubtedly inaccurate. A huge advance. Twenty-five per cent more. Did the lucky writer get a million or two million? Or five hundred thousand?

He gave lucky writers an advance of two thousand euro. Some of the really lucky ones got commissions from Bord na Leabhar Gaeilge, but the best of them would get about ten thousand. That there was another literary world, in which literature was big business, was something he had known of but preferred not to think about too much. He had seldom heard a frank discussion where actual figures were named, as he had just this minute. Writers were notoriously coy about revealing how much they earned, probably because, like the writer they were discussing, they knew their literary value would be assessed by a lot of people according to the money they got for their books. Leo had always assumed that there was plenty of exaggeration in the figures occasionally splashed about the newspapers and that writers were happy to allow the people to believe they earned much more than was actually the case. But here were two Irishmen obviously involved in fiction as big business, while the writers he knew were involved in fiction and poetry as … pastime. Amateurs, lucky to get a small publisher, lucky to get even Leo, to take them on.

A woman who had been eavesdropping on the rim of the rich circle raised her eyebrows. 'Makes you sick,' she said to Leo. 'My biggest advance ever was six thousand pounds, and I got that after I was short-listed for a major prize.' She did not mention what this major prize was, however.

'Oh?' Leo looked at her, a tall woman in a sparkling black dress. He had seen her at something. Of course, he had seen everyone here at something. He thought quickly. 'You must be

Lilian Meaney?' His memory for names, as always, never let him down.

'Yes, that's me.'

'Nice to meet you. I'm Leo Kavanagh. I publish poetry books, in Irish, so the world of the big advance is to me unknown as well.'

'Oh well' – she raised her glass to him – 'we shouldn't get disheartened. The best writers were poor in their own lifetime.'

That wasn't strictly true, but Leo knew unsuccessful writers liked to comfort themselves with this belief, which he called the Emily Dickinson Bullshit.

'What are you working on at the moment?' Leo asked.

'A book for young people.'

'That's a new departure for you, or am I wrong?'

'No, you're right, usually I write for adults.' Lilian, who had a warm voice and was very appealing in most ways, looked across the room. 'Listen, there is someone I must say hello to. Lovely to have met you, Leo! Take care.'

'Goodbye, Lilian,' he said. 'By the way, have you seen Anna Kelly Sweeney here?'

'She's over there talking to J.K. Rowling. Imagine, they got J.K. Rowling to come to this. I've never seen her at anything in Dublin before, have you?'

'No,' said Leo impatiently. Like most small publishers, he hated *Harry Potter* and everything he stood for in the literary world.

He moved towards the small group surrounding the famous writer.

'Meet J.K. Rowling,' Anna said, after the greetings were exchanged. She obviously had no idea that Leo had witnessed her passionate exchange with Vincy in the car park of the Tower, and was as cool and poised as ever. Vincy was not in the immediate vicinity.

'Hello, it's a pleasure to meet you,' Leo said politely, to the woman famed for being a book multimillionaire, in the first place, and the creator of Hogwarts, in the second. 'Do you do magic tricks?'

'I wish,' she said. Her hair was long and breezy and she wore a simple mini-dress. She was altogether natural looking and charming.

'Sorry, people probably say that all the time,' he said. 'To you, I mean.'

'Yes, as a matter of fact they do,' she said, but without animosity. She looked past him, scanning the room.

'I suppose it's just that they feel overawed, meeting the creator of *Harry Potter*. You are the most famous author in the world, I don't know what to say. I feel I should bow or something.'

'Please don't do that,' she said. 'I'd be horribly embarrassed.'

'What brings you to Dublin?'

'You obviously didn't read the invitation very carefully. Or are you crashing the party?'

'Oh dear! No I am not crashing ... I didn't read it. You know, one doesn't always, although one should.'

'I know,' she said sweetly. 'You would have found out that I'm launching the book, if you'd bothered.'

'Well ... that explains everything.' It dawned on him. 'The crowds, I mean, and the cameras. Is it a book for chil ... for young people?'

'For young and old,' she said. 'It transcends genre and generation. Just like mine.'

'Oh yes,' said Leo; 'I mean, yes, of course, great!'

She smiled understandingly. 'And now I'm going to put on my cloak of invisibility and fly off,' she said. 'Lovely to have met you.' She smiled and was gone.

'J.K. Rowling!' said Leo. 'Phew!'

'You can't imagine how I feel,' said Anna wanly.

'No, how? Overwhelmed?'

'My children's book should be finished but it's hardly started. And here is that horrible Marcus whatever he is bringing one out, someone who has never written for children in his life, someone who has never talked to a child in his life.'

'It's probably terrible,' said Leo consolingly, forgetting that he no longer liked Anna.

'No, it's probably excellent,' said Anna. 'Obviously *she* wouldn't launch it if it weren't.'

'She must think it's not as excellent as her own, otherwise she wouldn't come near it,' said Leo.

'Well, maybe.' Anna's face lightened. 'Still, it's frustrating.'

'So why ... how is yours coming along?' He could guess, since she spent her days running out to grotty pubs with Vincy.

184

'It's not coming along. It's stuck.'

'Writer's block,' he said, wondering what multitude of sins that phrase had been used to cover. Affairs, nervous breakdowns, murders, no doubt, amongst others.

He could see Vincy coming towards them, then turning and talking to someone else.

'Oh there's Vincy,' said Leo. 'What a coincidence … and do you know I was just visiting your sister-in-law … is that what she is? Kate Murphy.'

Anna blushed deeply and opened her mouth, but no words came out.

She was saved from having to find some by the fairy god-mother figure of J.K. Rowling, who at that moment began her speech. There was no opportunity to pursue the conversation and by the time the speeches were over, Anna had disappeared. Cloaks of invisibility were in fashion, at this launch.

Sixteen

Anna was on the Luas. It swerved down from the new glass bridge that spanned the inscrutable waters of the Grand Canal into Peter's Place – very, very slowly. As it swung into Harcourt Street it was crawling along in a weary way, like Thomas the Tank Engine going up a hill. I know I can I know I can I know I can, Anna found herself saying inanely; she had read the sentence aloud to Rory a hundred times, and her mother had read it to her a hundred times when she was a child. I know I can.

So the Luas wasn't perfect, after all. These days the newspapers were full of reports about problems with the tracks; they had been laid in the wrong way and were now starting to crack. It was dismaying to read these things, although in practice the cracks did not seem to make any difference to anything.

Anna was on her way to town, to meet her editor, Elizabeth, and explain that she was delayed and that her book would not be ready for another six months, and to get her reaction to the extract she had sent her – so-called extract, because she had sent Elizabeth every word she had written. She was not looking forward to the encounter much. On top of that, this morning Ludmilla had been more than usually cheeky. When Anna had said she was going out early, Ludmilla had tossed her head and said nothing. She suspected, Anna knew. She suspects and she's treating me accordingly.

There is definitely a way to let your cleaner know that cheekiness is not acceptable. But what is it? To some women such a skill would be second nature. But Anna was not a bossy person and – like most women – had not been brought up in a household with staff; she found it difficult enough to ask Ludmilla to wash the floor or clear out the fridge, much less how to let her know that it was not her place to make moral judgements on her employer's behaviour. Not that Ludmilla had made any overt comments. Her indignation was expressed in silences, in the set of her shoulders, and in a madly irritating superior way of walking, a gait every step of which said, 'I know just what you're up to'. It is hard to find a suitable reprimand for that sort of thing. Anna, knowing this strategy was yet another mistake, responded in kind. She sulked back. She and Ludmilla hardly spoke to one another these days. The house was full of heavy silence, punctuated with the occasional shrug or grunt – these from Ludmilla, who was an expert grunter.

Anna left the house earlier than usual. On this occasion her business was legitimate, but how was Ludmilla to know that? She did not say goodbye when Anna took her leave, just muttered something inaudible, probably in Lithuanian, from her place by the dishwasher, where she was removing the clean delft with much more rattling and banging than was necessary. Interesting, Anna thought, as she opened the door of the jeep and climbed up, that as soon as speech was withheld in a household, other kinds of sound immediately rushed in to fill the vacuum: slams, rattles, crashes. Sighs, grunts, screams. Not that Ludmilla would ever scream. Or break anything. Her repertoire of annoying noises was limited to grunts, rattling cutlery, and controlled slow slams, the artillery of the restrained angry person.

McCarthy's, the publishers, had an office on the sixth floor of a large glass and concrete building. This was the Irish branch of a big international publishing house, which had opened a few years back to deal with the Irish authors who were now very important to them, it was said – although it was not very clear what they meant by that. Maybe they had discovered that more people in Ireland read books than in England?

She had an appointment for midday, and the clock stood at

twelve noon exactly as she arrived at the McCarthy building. In a covered walkway leading from an underground car park to the main entrance, a beggar wrapped in a blue sleeping bag sat reading the *Metro*, one of the free tabloids. He looked up as Anna passed, staring at her through his round spectacles. He recognised her but she did not even see him, so concentrated or anxious was she. As she swept past, oblivious of his existence, he laughed quietly and returned to his newspaper.

Anna climbed the stairs to the office. The door was on the latch but when she went inside there was nobody in the reception room. A side table was stacked with a high pile of Jiffy bags, about fifty of them: the day's rejected manuscripts. Elizabeth had told her they received a hundred unsolicited manuscripts every week, of which ninety-nine point five per cent were returned to the writers. This information was intended to make Anna feel lucky and important, and it did, but it also bewildered her in an unpleasant way. She tried to imagine the accumulated disappointment of ninety-nine and a half writers, to comprehend the time they had spent writing their two to three hundred novels – two to three hundred years, cumulatively, all for nothing except the cold, abandoned feeling rejection must engender, no matter how justified. What a lot of pain and time wasting! Would those writers have been better off going for a swim, or watching movies, or doing whatever it is people who don't write do in those long hours when the others are at their PCs? Perhaps not. At least they had their manuscripts at the end of their efforts. Products. Made by their own hands, minds, hearts, lives. Home-made books. Did they derive some satisfaction from that, a satisfaction that was greater than the pleasure of having had a good time enjoying someone else's creation? Could creative work be an end in itself, even if the product never reached an audience? She didn't know. Every writer she had ever known wanted to be published. Every writer she had ever known dreamed of fame and fortune, the way people long ago dreamed of marble halls and fairy-tale marriages. Every writer wanted to be the new Emily Dickinson, or Anton Chekhov, or James Joyce. (Not to mention J.K. Rowling.) Quite a few believed they were. No writer wanted to hear their own manuscript dropping onto the hall floor in a Jiffy bag – a precious gift generously sent to the world and sent back by return of post.

This was not a very welcoming office. There were no bells to press to attract attention. There was not even a chair to sit down on, unless you went behind the desk and sat in the orange swivel chair used by the receptionist. So Anna stood, tapping her foot against the wooden floor and getting increasingly anxious. A quarter of an hour passed, very slowly. Then Linda, the receptionist, bounced busily into the room, sat down with a sprightly motion, as if she had springs in her bottom as well as her feet, and said, in the cheery tones she would have used greeting anyone, from the Revenue Commissioner's bailiff to their bestselling chick-lit writer, 'Oh Anna! How *are* you? What a lovely coat!'

Anna was wearing a pink coat she had bought the day before in Brown Thomas to impress Vincy.

'Thanks,' said Anna. Linda, she suddenly remembered, irritated her at the best of times. Anna refrained from adding some warm and friendly comment. She had learned some tricks from Ludmilla. She said nothing.

This had the gratifying effect of embarrassing Linda, if only slightly. She had retained some dregs of human vulnerability, in spite of her job as guard dog for the publisher, which entailed dealing with annoyed authors several times a day. Most of them never came near the place, contenting themselves with sighs on the phone, but among every heap of rejects one or two would have the sort of owner who would come storming up in the lift, letting Linda know exactly how they felt. She had an alarm button under her desk, which she had been forced to use only once in her life when the writer of a post-modernist work of fiction about Irish politicians had pulled a sawn-off shotgun out of his backpack. He had calmed down when he heard the sirens and scuttled off before the gardaí arrived on the scene, forgetting his terrible manuscript in the process. (Linda had not known what to do with it: if she sent it back, it might elicit another angry response; on the other hand, she was afraid to shred it, lest that too have dire consequences. So she kept it. She still had it. It had been sitting in the reject pile on the table for two and a half years. The paper was yellowing at the edges.)

'Well, em, what can I do for you?' she asked.

'I had an appointment with Elizabeth for twelve o'clock,' said Anna stonily.

'Oh!' Linda looked surprised. 'She hasn't mentioned it to me.'

She fiddled with her computer. 'She's at a meeting,' she said flatly, after a moment's pause.

Anna felt her stomach sink. 'Well, tell her I'm here, please,' she said.

'The meeting is in London,' said Linda. She looked Anna in the eye. 'Some mix up. I'm very sorry ... you didn't come in specially, did you?'

As if I were in the habit of dropping in for a cup of tea, thought Anna. Again she was silent.

'Look, I'll phone her and tell her.' Linda took pity on her.

Anna waited while she dialled. Impatience was now beginning to etch itself on Linda's face. The office was very neat, and still not impersonal. It was a nice place to be, if you were being looked after, but if you were not, its orderly, pleasant atmosphere emphasised your sense of abandonment. It was like being very ill on a lovely summer's day in the country.

Linda got an answering machine, as Anna had known she would. She left a message asking Elizabeth to ring Anna as soon as she could.

'That's all I can do, I'm afraid,' said Linda, looking apologetic but impatient. 'She won't be back until tomorrow, she's staying over for a launch, so she'll ring you in the meantime.'

'Can't be helped,' said Anna. 'Goodbye.'

In two weeks it would be Christmas. Her novel should have been finished by the 31st of December, but it was so far from completion that at this rate it would be next Christmas before she'd have anything to show. And it looked as if Elizabeth had not been impressed by the chapters she had seen. No wonder, thought Anna. They were wooden. They were so wooden that they were dead, deader than wood. In a way, she thought, wooden characters, talking stiffly in a wooden fashion and moving stiffly like sticks, could be interesting, in a post-modernist, stylised way. But not, probably, in a book aimed at a juvenile mass market. Not in a book that, like a million other books being written all over the world at this very moment, was aiming to be the next *Harry Potter*. To succeed in becoming the pre-eminently successful children's author of worldwide repute, she would have to come up with a better strategy than writing a wooden book about wooden characters, with a predictable but at the same time totally unbelievable plot.

Lilian had said it was good. But she was probably lying. Indeed, since sending her chapters to Lilian, Anna had hardly heard a word from her. At the J.K. Rowling thing the other night Lilian had seemed to be avoiding her, although in that huge press of bodies it was hard to tell. At any rate, they had not even exchanged a greeting, whereas usually they got together and gossiped long and hard at these events, of which that had been one of the most glittering all year. Of course Anna had been with Vincy. Lilian probably had her suspicions about them. Perhaps she disapproved?

Anna was now walking aimlessly around the streets near O'Connell Street, walking off her annoyance with Elizabeth.

The streets were decorated and the choirs of carol singers were belting out the songs and rattling the boxes. The shop windows were crammed with shiny clothes and tinsel. All this delighted her usually, but today she felt mixed up. She could take no interest in the preparations for the festival, just as she could take no interest in writing her book. Her plan had been to do some of the Christmas shopping after her meeting, but now she did not have the heart for it.

The writing was on the wall. It was her own fault. She had a good publisher, something a lot of her friends would die for, and she had failed to come up with the goods.

Against her better judgement, she telephoned Vincy, who had made it clear that he didn't like being phoned during the day.

His mobile is not accessible at the moment or it may be turned off, the voice told her.

Just when you most needed someone, the customer was out of range or inaccessible. He was in a meeting, no doubt. Like most people she knew, he spent a lot of his time in a meeting, inaccessible, out of range, protected by his turned-off mobile or a guard dog of a secretary.

She had a cup of coffee in a department store café and when she phoned again after the coffee, he was still out of range or had his mobile turned off.

It was then that she decided, why she could hardly say, to go and look at his apartment. She had never been there. It was

191

mainly out of bounds, because he shared it with a friend, another journalist, Joe McFale. Anna had never met Joe and had not come across his work. All she knew about him was that he seldom left the apartment, for which Anna had been grateful – it meant she was under no pressure to go there and sleep with Vincy. Now, however, what had once been a blessing was gradually evolving into a nuisance, at best. When Anna thought of Joe McFale, she usually added the phrase 'pain in the ass' to his name. She would be very pleased if he got a place on his own, or if he emigrated to some far-off land. Or died.

The affair had been going on for almost two months. Ludmilla knew about it. That greenhorn Leo suspected it – he'd caught them in the pub. Who else had spotted them, unbeknownst to Anna? Half of Dublin, probably.

The affair that was not an affair. The affair that lacked the single, essential ingredient of any proper affair: sex. Platonic, some people called such relationships. A nice word for a wishy-washy, half-hearted, excuse of a thing. A euphemism for sexual hypocrisy. Or something worse.

What was the point in being so abstemious? She was risking her reputation and that of her husband and child, but not experiencing the unbelievable pleasure a love affair was supposed to bring. Because of some stupid scruple, some innate cautiousness, that would not permit her to let herself go completely?

She was cheating on Alex anyway, although she didn't want to admit it. He would be devastated if he knew what was going on – that she was meeting Vincy Erikson almost every day, that she was in love with Vincy, not with him, Alex, her husband. Would Alex be any less disturbed if she explained, yes, yes, but we haven't had sex, so it doesn't count? No. Not in the least. Alex would not be consoled in the slightest by that; he was not a fool.

He would be much happier, probably, if she had sex discreetly with Vincy, and stopped meeting him in pubs and cafés, where anyone could see them and suspect the worst. He would care about appearances. Not because he was a hypocrite, or shallow. He was neither of those. Because he was human.

Alex did not deserve to be betrayed by his wife. But half

192

betraying him was not making it better – it was just alleviating her own feelings of guilt.

She rang Vincy's doorbell.

Somewhat to her shock, he opened the door almost immediately.

'This is a bit of a surprise,' he said, when he had admitted her to the gloomy hall. He half-smiled and she knew he was annoyed.

'I was upset. I phoned and you were out of range.'

'Well, it's nice to see you anyway.' He did not hug her as he ushered her up two flights of uncarpeted stairs and into his rooms. He was wearing an old green cardigan, and carpet slippers. He looked older than usual.

She sat down beside him on a rickety sofa.

The room was big, with a high ceiling and its original ornate plasterwork intact. A marble fireplace of enormous dimensions. It was immensely shabby, its wallpaper about a hundred years old, browny beige, dripping off the walls in places. The wooden floors were ancient, uneven. The furnishings were junk-shop antiques, mismatched, broken.

'It's lovely.' Anna gazed around her, awestruck. It was the sort of room hired out by film crews for arty documentaries, or advertisements for instant coffee or spaghetti sauce. 'You never told me you lived in a place like this.'

'No,' he said. 'I don't think about it as anything special. I take it for granted.'

'It's amazing,' she said.

'It isn't mine,' he looked at her, amused.

She was taken aback slightly.

'Who owns it?' she asked. 'Joe?'

'Yeah.'

'Lucky Joe.'

'Yes, lucky Joe.'

'I bet he lets it to film crews and things all the time? I think I've seen it on an ad.'

'It happens.' Vincy was not cross but he was still uneasy, as if he didn't know what to do next. This was not a situation he found himself in very often. 'Do you want something to eat? Coffee?'

She nodded.

There was no further mention of Joe.

Vincy made the coffee and got out some bread and cheese, heated some soup. He regained his composure. A phone call was made, and that changed his mood. He seemed certain that Joe would not come back to the flat.

After lunch, they made love.

He did not ask her if she had changed her mind. He just led her into his bedroom, paused for a few seconds – a parenthesis in which she could say anything, as they both knew. She unbuttoned his cardigan. Could there be a more unsexy garment to unbutton in the world than a man's cardigan? No. But even as she was thinking this she unbuttoned it, with a fine show of passion.

It was so simple.

All she had to do was come to his flat. Even though he had not planned any of this, once he had taken control of the situation, he knew exactly what was expected of him and carried it out.

It was not as momentous, as wonderful, as the kiss in the car park.

She loved him. But nobody had made love to her, ever, apart from Alex. Nobody apart from him – and a few doctors – had seen her naked body in ten years. She felt at home with Vincy's wiry hair, with his smell – grass, smoke. The fact was, she felt at home with his cardigan. And the body inside that cardigan did not seem strange to her, felt as familiar as a body she had slept with a thousand times. But she was shy about her own, about revealing it, in this weird room, with its peeling plaster, its cavernous proportions.

They made love, and it was successful, but not what she had hoped for.

And he didn't seem to notice.

'I love you,' she said, as they lay side by side. He smoked a cigarette. She loved that about him, that he smoked, although it made no sense. 'I adore you.'

'I'm flattered,' he said, laughing. His eyes twinkled mischievously and mysteriously.

She kissed him, got up and started to pull on her clothes. He lay against the pillow, blue smoke climbing in wreaths above his head. He gazed at her, appreciatively, silent and, it seemed to her, thoughtful. 'I love you,' she said again. He did not reciprocate with any declaration of his own, just continued to smoke his cigarette, and stare. Anna's mood was so buoyant that she ignored his silence, the distance he seemed to be placing between her and him, now that she had left his bed. The room, its walls the colour of putty and brown skin, was the perfect setting for sex. A candle or two, thick and dripping in ancient candlesticks, would have made it completely perfect – there were a few candles around, she noticed, but he didn't think of lighting them. As it was, the low slanting sun of December falling through the window, long and narrow, and dusty, cast rays of reddish light into the shadowy room. It could have been ... the past. Vermeer and Scarlett Johansson. Yeats and one of his lovers in Woburn Buildings, or some rented room in a Dublin hotel.

Anna felt changed. Too changed to take a taxi and go home, which was what she should have done. Instead she walked back towards the Luas stop at Stephen's Green, braving the *terra incognita* of Mountjoy Square and Upper O'Connell Street. Vincy was unconcerned for her safety. Like most people who live in bad areas, he did not subscribe to the belief that this was more dangerous than anywhere else. He *was* concerned that she would be very late in getting home. But in her brave new mood she dismissed these concerns, called Luz Mar to make sure she collected Rory from school and said she would be home in time for dinner.

She was halfway down O'Connell Street, when Elizabeth, her editor, phoned.

Anna had forgotten all about the morning's events. That is how happy she was: the world of books and editors and publishing did not matter. By comparison with what she had experienced, the writing of a book, the fortunes of a book, were trivial in the extreme. Books would come and go, but the joy in her heart would go on forever. So she believed, just then, in the cold crisp evening on O'Connell Street, with the giant pine tree from Norway glittering behind her and the decorated shop windows lighting her way.

Elizabeth was very apologetic. She asked Anna how she was, in her warm, caring tones, the tone that was the house style, and said she would ring and arrange for another meeting, in about a week's time. She hadn't had a chance to read everything as yet.

Everything about the conversation – which had lasted about two minutes – added to Anna's euphoria. It was quite clear to her now that Elizabeth liked whatever she had read, was on her side, and would publish *Sally and the Ship of Dreams*, as soon as it existed, and would spend heaps of money marketing it. All this she was able to deduce from the warmth of the 'How are you?'

Alex was already in, worried about where she was, when she arrived home laden with bags – Anna had slipped down Henry Street and shopped frantically for half an hour before coming home.

'Sorry!' she said, wondering why she had to apologise (after all, he did not know she had spent most of the afternoon committing adultery). 'I had to get a taxi, I had so much stuff, and of course the traffic was awful. Friday.'

'It's not Friday,' said Alex, in his most irritating neutral tone. 'It's Wednesday.'

'So it is,' said Anna lightly.

Rory came in to the kitchen.

'You're so late,' he said. He whined, 'Why are you always so late?'

'I'm not always so late,' said Anna cheerfully. 'I was doing the Christmas shopping for the big day. I have to do that, don't I?'

He ignored her and went to sit with his father, showing him a copybook. 'Look,' he said, pointing to something he had written or drawn. 'Read it.'

Alex read it, silently, probably to make sure Anna did not share the experience.

'Good stuff, Rory.' He patted him on the head, something Rory quite liked having him do. 'It's a ...' he paused, to find the right word. 'It's a very original story.'

'Can I see it?' Anna asked, genuinely curious. She put on a mock wheedling voice.

Rory closed the copy book and pressed it to his chest. 'No,' he said, and moved to the door.

'Please, Rory. I'd really love to read your story.'

Rory turned and looked at her. 'You can't. You're naughty,' he said.

'Oh,' she said, 'I'm not naughty.'

Rory had nothing to say to this. He looked knowingly at her and then went off clumping up the stairs.

Had Ludmilla been priming him?

Alex was looking at her.

'What was that about?' he asked.

Anna felt very anxious but she did not show it. 'I don't know,' she said. 'So what was the story like?'

'Great. Very symbolic, I thought, but what would I know?'

She opened the Aga oven, to see if he had put in something for dinner. He hadn't. He wouldn't, ever, even if he were to starve.

There were pizzas in the freezer, so she selected two, Tesco's Finest, tore them out of their elaborate packages and placed them directly on the grid of the top oven, the hottest one. Then she decided to make a decent salad, to compensate for the perfunctory main course.

She would have liked to have heard more about Rory's story, but was, stupidly, afraid to ask. Alex, unprompted, did not enlighten her any further.

'When will dinner be ready?' he asked.

Sometimes this question, put to her at a time like this, when she had just walked in the door, irritated her profoundly and provoked an angry rejoinder. Although she had been married to Alex for many years, she could still not understand why he could not cook, even to the extent of putting a pizza in the oven, or why he accepted it as normal that she should make all the decisions and execute or arrange for the execution of every single household task. Of course, she did not really know what other men were like, but she assumed they were mainly more active than Alex in the domestic sphere. Some of her friends had husbands who were good cooks. 'Fred does all the cooking!' some of them said. Anna had sometimes wondered if the wives of these Freds were making it up, but Vincy could cook. He had given her lunch today; without batting an eyelid, he had heated soup, home-made soup, which had been made by himself, he had said when asked. A hearty peasant soup, full of vegetables and chunks of chorizo and lentils. He had served it in big coloured bowls with brown bread and cheese, all of which he had, there, in his larder, ready for himself or anyone who called. Or the flatmate, maybe, the mysterious Joe. Who bought candles.

Maybe, if Alex could have made a soup like that, she would have loved him. But he couldn't. Not even that. It was one of a very long catalogue of things Alex could not do.

And the equally long catalogue of things he could do, such as make a lot of money, make a snap decision on an issue of immense importance and stick to it, win respect and influence people while being the quietest man in Ireland – he had a reputation for being clever, brilliant and honest, which his lack of sparkle seemed to enhance. His boringness was interpreted as intelligence, and often given a nice name: gravitas. Another word for dull as ditchwater, thought Anna, but there were plenty of lively, witty men in the boardrooms. Alex was well off and successful, and therefore it was universally acknowledged that under his quiet exterior there lurked a most superior intellect.

She chopped scallions and sliced tomatoes on a wooden board. He didn't suspect a thing. Even that was annoying, as if he did not have the imagination to be suspicious. Or as if he didn't care what she did, as long as she was around to prepare his dinner, to look after the house, and to accompany him to the events he had to go to.

Or because he loved her.

That was, in the end, the main problem with Alex.

They ate the pizzas at the big kitchen table. She had lit candles, as usual, and opened a bottle of wine, as she did most nights. Shadows flickered on the walls and floor of the big, warm space, so fluid in its design, with a glass wall on one side and open-sided on the other, that you could not call it a room. The glow that had been inside her since making love with Vincy was faint, but still there, like, she felt fancifully, a candle flame flickering deep inside.

Rory seemed to have forgotten about his earlier sulkiness. He liked pizza, and as a very special treat, to celebrate his mother's sexual liberation, he was allowed a Coke. He chatted about what he wanted for Christmas, and about his friends in school. Cuan was getting a new bicycle. Michael was getting a piano. Rory thought a piano was an odd sort of present for anyone to get. How could Santa bring it?

'He won't bring it down the chimney,' Anna said.

'I know that,' said Rory. 'I know he doesn't bring anything down the chimney. He doesn't exist.'

'Oh!' said Anna, shocked.

'I wish you'd stop pretending he does.'

Alex shrugged his shoulders and glanced questioningly at Anna, but she ignored the look.

'Well …' said Anna. She hadn't given any thought to this moment, the moment when Rory challenged the belief in Santa. And she certainly hadn't expected the moment to arrive this evening, the same day that she had, in a way, rediscovered her belief in Santa, or at least in superhuman gift-bringers. The way she was feeling was not normal, or human: like Santa, she was up there among the stars, dashing across the sparkling skies.

Rory's challenge brought her back to earth.

What was she supposed to do now?

It wasn't like telling him about babies, or AIDS, or even death – for all of those difficult challenges in her life as a parent, she had prepared by going to lectures and reading books. But Santa – she couldn't remember what the books had said about him, if anything. Actually, she had supposed Rory had given up on Santa ages ago and had been pretending to believe in him, just as she did, for years, when she was a child.

Her mother had never confirmed for her that Santa did not exist.

Old-fashioned ways.

But you didn't get away with that sort of evasion these days.

'You're right,' she said, looking him in the eye.

Alex looked alarmed.

'There really is no Santa?' He wanted even more.

Anna gave it.

'No. There isn't. Not literally. I suppose he represents something – people's love for one another, and for children.'

199

'Well …' Rory looked mildly disgusted.

She began to wonder if she had handled the situation optimally.

'We still give presents even when we stop believing in him.' She offered materialism as an alternative to superstition. It worked for most people.

But not for Rory. Not now.

He started to cry. 'I can't believe there is no Santa,' he whined.

Anna was taken aback. Alex continued to eat his pizza and paid no further attention to what was going on.

'Well, I said there was, in a way,' she said lamely. Had she said this? When?

'No you didn't. You said there really is no Santa.' He sobbed. 'There isn't a real person who drives a sleigh and comes from the North Pole with presents for us all.'

Pianos, computers, bicycles. Dolls' houses. How could anyone be naive enough to believe it, even a three-year-old child? But Rory had, apparently, until right now. In spite of moments of scepticism, in spite of teasing by more enlightened children, he had clung to the belief that the red-clothed gift-bringer came from the North Pole transporting millions of bicycles and computers and pianos in a *sleigh* and carried out a global delivery in one twelve-hour period every year on the 24th of December.

He usually got ninety-nine per cent of his spellings right, got one hundred per cent in his maths exams, and watched the Discovery Channel on a regular basis.

But he believed this.

What strange creatures human beings are, she thought, wondering how this applied to herself.

'No, there isn't a Santa,' was what she said sadly. Because there is no going back, no matter how much everyone wanted to.

Seventeen

All happy families are happy in different ways, and unhappy families are also unhappy in different ways, but at Christmas they are particularly unhappy, and mostly in the same way. Because the feast of the Holy Family gives them more opportunities than usual to compare themselves to the perfect family: Jesus, Mary and Joseph, surrounded by interesting and prestigious guests from far and near, by fabulous presents, and lovely cuddly animals. On top of this, Christmas forces every family, happy or unhappy, to spend more time together than any family, happy or unhappy, could possibly want.

That Christmas is a time for families was one of Alex's few domestic principles; it was, according to him, a time for shutting the door on the rest of the world and sinking into the deep, deep peace of your own home. After the run of social events in the weeks before the festival, he liked to take two weeks' holiday in the bosom of his family. This year, as every year, his plan was to spend the three Christmas days at home, the second three days visiting relations, and then to spend the final week skiing in Italy, at a small resort in the Alps that he had always favoured.

Anna persuaded him to abandon the skiing, since she could not bear the prospect of not seeing Vincy for more than three weeks. Luckily last year she had broken her arm coming down a black piste, so she had that as an excuse. 'You go, alone,' she said to Alex. But he refused. Christmas is a time for families. And so is a ski holiday. Nobody goes skiing on their own; it's a horrible thought. As bad as eating Christmas dinner on your own.

In the week before Christmas she had just one meeting with Vincy, a meeting not in his apartment but in the Tower. The pub had lost a lot of its charm for Anna after the encounter there with Leo Kavanagh, but it still seemed to be a safer place than most.

'I won't see you for more than a week,' she said. 'It will be … I can't imagine what it will be like.'

'Hell,' he said. They were holding hands. Around them the life of the pub continued, oblivious – they hoped – to them. The barmen handed out sandwiches and coffees, plates of lasagne and chips, turkey and roast potatoes and sprouts, which the pub offered for two weeks every day coming up the the holiday. Young women in black suits and men in grey suits wolfed their lunches, chatting blithely about nothing much. A big Christmas tree sparkled in one corner and there were little holly sprays dotted around the walls. Christmas music – Bing Crosby singing seasonal songs – played faintly in the background. It was a hot, noisy, cheerful setting. Everyone was getting more excited as Christmas approached; somehow the pace speeded up, there was a gaiety, an urgency, to things that appeared to have been induced entirely by commercial interests. You must be entertained, drink more, eat more, buy more, have more fun, the machine ordered, and everyone obeyed.

Outside this merry-go-round of activity Anna and Vincy sat, nursing the strange present that had been tossed to them by some generous but careless benefactor: true love. Today they were very much in love and very sad. Anna was definitely not feeling transcendent. It is hard to transcend Bing Crosby singing 'I'm Dreaming of a White Christmas' on an endless loop, and it is hard to transcend one's ridiculous misery at the thought of a long separation – a week at least.

'I wish I could be at your flat again,' she said. 'Just once more before it all starts. It would set us up.'

She would have liked to try again, to see if she could do better.

'Yeah,' he said, shrugging and frowning. 'But it's not possible. Joe is there today, and every day this week. Working at home.'

'We will do something after Christmas,' she said. The ordeal ahead she deleted from her mind, willing herself into that time after Christmas, when things would be back to normal and they could do something. By which she meant, go to bed again.

He stretched across the table and gave her a quick kiss, like a visitor kissing a prisoner when the guard's back is turned. He still believed there was a guard. He still believed his relationship with Anna was a secret from everyone, and that she would want it kept that way. 'It will be OK,' he said seriously.

She looked into his eyes, willing to believe him, although she had no real idea what he meant.

The only family Leo had ever possessed had been killed when he was a very young man. Now he was one of those who have either to spend the great feast of the family all alone, or find a family, any family, with which to get over it.

For Christmas he had a family though: he was always invited to spend the festival with a friend of his who lived in Clare. This year, however, he got a message from the friend, Paul, in which Paul apologised and said that this year he was going away for the holidays. Leo should have anticipated this and found an alternative Christmas family, because this year everyone who was anyone was going abroad. Only a year ago the St Stephen's Day tsunami had struck, but the memory of that had faded fast, and deterred nobody from getting out of Ireland for the holiday. The planes to Thailand and Madeira and Barbados, and what have you, must have been stuffed to the gills with people escaping to the sun.

Leo received Paul's message, a text, when he was already on the train going back down the country. 'Going to S Af for Xmas. C U Hap Xmas B good.'

He could have stayed in Dublin. For the Christmas days, Kate was going home to her family, like almost the entire population of the hospital was. No matter how depressed or crazy they were, if they had any family at all to go to, they were shipped out, with their bags of medication in their backpacks (mostly they had backpacks because most of them were men aged about twenty). As many staff members as possible would be given leave for the holiday, so it was essential to get rid of the patients. The ritual of the family Christmas had to be celebrated; it demanded sacrifices from everyone, including the psychiatrically ill.

Kate, whose medication had been decreased again and who was back to normal, as far as he could see, had invited him to Christmas dinner with her parents, but he had made an excuse and refused. Accepting that invitation to join that family would have meant much more than being a Christmas guest. He knew that if he set foot in that house of hers, it would be viewed as a token of his attachment to Kate. He might as well announce their engagement in the *Irish Times* and book a hotel for the reception. There would be no going back because only a real cad would dump a girl in her condition. It would be like running out on a girl who was pregnant. Worse than that, these days.

And he wasn't sure if he really wanted to marry someone who was a patient in a mental asylum. When it came to the crunch, that was his position. He still liked Kate. But ... there were limits.

So here he was, on his way back to Kerry, looking forward to spending Christmas all on his own.

Never mind. He would survive. He would work. He would watch television. He would cook a good nut roast. He would drink that bottle of Brunello, which he had been keeping for a special occasion. And he would consider his position. For the hundredth time.

When he arrived at the house, the front door opened more easily than usual. Well, that was his door, temperamental to the last. You would expect it to be stiff and awkward now in the midwinter, when it hadn't been used for weeks, but that was the very time it would function perfectly.

As soon as he stepped into the dark hall he sensed that something was wrong.

The television was on.

He could hear the sound of Eddie Hobbs, advising someone to stop buying cappuccinos twice a day and in that way save up to put a deposit on a house.

His heart pounded and he clutched his mobile phone for protection. Perhaps, he reasoned as he opened the door to the

204

living room, he had left the television on when he left some weeks ago?

He opened the kitchen door.

A big fire was blazing in the hearth. Above the back of his armchair, the back of a head could be seen. Dense black hair, like soot.

There was someone in his house.

The volume was so loud that that person had not heard Leo opening the door and coming in.

'Ahem,' said Leo loudly.

Now the person heard, jumped up with a start, and faced him. A strange woman with rosy cheeks, a wide mouth and black dry hair. She smiled uneasily at him – uneasily, and somewhat crazily. Her teeth looked very white in her rather dark face.

'Hello,' said Leo stupidly. 'Who on earth are you?' He tried to inject some authority or annoyance into his voice.

'Charlene,' she said, with a silly grin.

The name meant nothing. He had never heard it before. Never had he known a Charlene. Was it a real name? Or the sort of name characters in American soap operas had?

'What on earth are you doing here?' Two 'on earths' one after the other. Leo was shaking, which is what being in shock probably means.

'Don't you remember me?' Charlene said helpfully, her tone getting warmer, as if she expected him to be pleased to see her installed in his kitchen. 'I met you on the train a while back.' She pulled something out of her pocket. She was wearing a flowery apron. Now she switched to speaking Irish. 'You told me to call you if I needed help.'

It came back to him ... the *Irish Times*, the woman who looked like Aunt Poppy or something from that programme about scarecrows.

She handed him his own card.

He sat down and stared at the card in horror. Leo Kavanagh, Éan Dearg. Foilseathóir. And his address, telephone number and email address.

'I have nowhere to go.' Now she sounded woebegone.

Charlene told him her story. Her husband had maltreated her so much that she had had to go to hospital. They had sent her home for Christmas. But as soon as she had been home for a

205

day her husband was at it again. This time he had beat her up so badly that she had had to leave.

There was something about this story that seemed odd to Leo but he couldn't put his finger on what it was.

'Are you going back to the hospital after Christmas?' Leo clutched at straws.

'No.' Charlene shook her head emphatically and smiled in triumph. 'I'm discharged, I don't have to go back there again. They gave me pills and a prescription.' She began to delve into the pocket of her apron again and pulled out a medical prescription, which she insisted on showing him. 'What does it say? I can't read it,' she said.

'Neither can I,' said Leo impatiently, glancing at the illegible scrawl. *Nocte* was all he could make out. 'Look … I'm not even going to ask you how you got in here.'

'Oh it was easy!' she said. 'The door was open.'

He groaned. Had he really left the door open and gone to Dublin for an indefinite period? Could you believe anything this woman said? Anyway, she was in the house, however she had got in.

'I just walked in. There was nobody at home, so I thought I'd wait till you came back.'

He looked at the blazing fire.

'When was that?'

'I don't know. A while back.'

Not that long ago, hopefully, if she had been discharged for Christmas.

She sat down again and resumed her television watching.

He walked over, turned it off, and faced her. 'Look, Charlene,' he said. 'Of course I want to help you in any reasonable way I can. But that doesn't mean you can live here.'

She pouted and her skin became red. Her large brown eyes swam wistfully.

'Obviously,' he said, listening to the wind howling and hating himself for being such a soft touch, 'obviously you can stay here for a few days, until Christmas is past, but then you're really going to have to leave.'

'Where will I go, Leo?' she asked imploringly. Leo. The use of his name was somehow unnerving. She had appropriated him.

'I don't know.' He shrugged. 'Wherever you like.'

'I used to live with my husband in Mallow,' she said brightly.

'Good.' Leo relaxed slightly. 'I'll get in touch with him then.'

'He'd murder you as soon as look at you,' said Charlene, with a cheerful laugh.

Leo's tension returned. This he was inclined to believe. In case he didn't, Charlene furnished a few concrete examples of her husband's bloodthirstiness and quick temper – he'd shot a boy who had stolen his bike when he was sixteen, and was never caught for it; he had done time for robbing a post office and breaking the arms of the elderly postmistress. There was enough detail in her stories to convince Leo of their truth and he decided he would have to throw Charlene out on the road, alone, as soon as he had a rest and the energy to undertake that course of action.

After a sandwich and apple pie – she had actually baked a pie in his oven; it was quite good – he did what he always did at about nine thirty. He went down to the pub, not inviting Charlene.

The place was packed. Card games were going on, and raffles for hampers and turkeys and bottles of whiskey.

Leo did not feel like playing cards but he bought raffle tickets and won a box of Afternoon Tea biscuits. His pleasure at winning this was excessive, given that he didn't like shop biscuits and particularly disliked this kind, which came packed in rippled paper in big tins. But he guessed Charlene would like them, and planned to use them as a Christmas present for her. Before saying goodbye. She could bring them back to Mallow to her psychopathic husband.

He also picked up an invitation to Christmas lunch on his own behalf, which he accepted gratefully.

He was quite right about Charlene and the biscuits.

'How did you know they were my favourite kind?' she said, a question that he didn't answer. 'I always loved them ever since I was a tiny little girl.'

'They're all yours,' he said. This was the moment for kicking her out, with the full tin of biscuits in her hands. But looking at her face wreathed in smiles as she selected the chocolate biscuit with the red jelly on top – the one he hated more than all the others – he could not bring himself to say, 'Time's up, Charlene, tomorrow you've got to go'. Or the day after tomorrow. Or the day after that. Probably there were no buses on Stephen's Day.

He said nothing at all, just sighed and went into his office, slamming the door behind him. He slept there, on the spare bed he kept for guests, since he did not want to become too closely involved with Charlene's sleeping arrangements. (Later he discovered that she had appropriated the main bedroom for herself. His bedroom.)

She spent Christmas morning cleaning the kitchen, interspersing her housework with two tea breaks, at which she munched biscuits from the tin with great delight.

When he was about to set off to the lunch, a pang of guilt seized him. He could not just walk off and leave Charlene alone on Christmas Day.

'I'm invited out.' He made it sound as if it were an invitation of long standing rather than one that had been offered by a very drunk woman late last night. 'But look, I don't like leaving you here alone, on the day that's in it.'

'Don't worry your head about that,' said Charlene. 'Sure I like being alone. I'll watch television. *The King and I* is on; I'm really looking forward to it.'

The King and I. What was that?

'I could telephone them and ask if I could bring a friend.'

'No no, then I'd miss the film,' said Charlene animatedly. 'I'd hate that. I always wanted to see it. Jodie Foster is in it, and she's great.'

She was still wearing her flowery apron, and eating Afternoon Teas. Half the tin was gone.

He could understand that she might not enjoy being presented to a house of strangers, although 'shy' was hardly an adjective that could be applied with any accuracy to someone who had invited herself to read his *Irish Times* on the train, told him a graphic version of her life story, and then broken into his house and taken up residence there in his absence. And yet she did seem shy, in a way, like a wild animal, or a human being at some earlier stage of evolution. Her mad scarecrow eyes were not a bit frightening. On the contrary, they exuded an endearing quality, a hypnotic charm. They reminded him of the eyes of the hares that sometimes danced in his garden, or of the birds who pecked for worms after he had cut the grass.

The invitation to dinner had come from a woman called Caoilfhionn, a traditional singer who also acted occasionally in an Irish-language soap opera, and lived in a large cottage with her partner, Molly, who was a schoolteacher.

There were other guests: a man from a village in Poland who worked with a builder in Dingle, building holiday homes and apartments, and had been unable to go home for Christmas; a Latvian in a similar situation; a Nigerian woman who was in a legal limbo situation as her application for refugee status was being assessed by the Department of Justice; and an old man from the valley, Máirtín, wearing a *caipín*.

Caoilfhionn was a soft-hearted do-gooder who had gathered together this motley assortment of losers, Leo realised, people whom she pitied and who had no family of their own to go to on Christmas Day. He guessed she did this kind of thing every year – and he was right. Caoilfhionn was one of those who celebrated Christmas by making an ad hoc family for the day, perhaps subconsciously, to substitute for the large family she would have liked to have had but did not. (Though she had Molly, which was more than you could say for her guests.)

Charlene would have fitted into this company well enough.

Leo had hoped his was a special invitation. He had believed she had asked him because she admired and respected him, the well-known publisher of Irish poetry. He had even suspected that she was manipulating him, as people did, and the next thing would be that he would receive a thick envelope stuffed with poems in inaccurate Irish, and he would feel obliged to read them and, probably, unless they were truly atrocious – which they wouldn't be, because she was reasonably clued in – he would have to publish them.

But now he saw that there would be no manuscript in the post, and that she hadn't given a thought to him or who he was. In her eyes he was just one of a bunch of misfits who had gathered together so that she could do her charitable good deed for the year, and prevent several loners from jumping off the pier.

The only thing was, they did not seem all that lonely, or likely to jump off piers.

'The last Gaeltacht bachelor in Ireland,' Máirtín said, as soon as he was introduced, putting on his peaked cap to emphasise his status. 'I am the proud representative of a dying breed.'

They were all sitting around the living room, which was not as nice as Leo's room but was very cosy nonetheless. A huge turf fire blazed in the stone fireplace and the room was fragrant with the smell of it, and with other smells from the kitchen: roasting turkey, parsley and thyme and basil and cumin and garlic, and nut roast. The horrible smell of boiling sprouts had not kicked in as yet. Outside they could hear the stream gurgling like a happy baby.

They were speaking English, the lingua franca, although Leo was the only one of those present with English as a mother tongue.

'Do you have Gaeltacht-type bachelors in Latvia?' Caoilfhionn asked.

'I think that type of person is found everywhere in the world,' Josef replied. His measured phrases and flat foreign accent made him sound very intelligent. 'In my village there are old men too. There is one who says he is the last speaker of his language.'

'Sure isn't it the same here?' asked Máirtín. His quick humorous way of expressing himself gave the impression that he was flippant and untrustworthy, although he was neither.

'No.' Josef looked straight at him with his clear pale blue eyes. 'It is true. He really is the last speaker. In our village and in the world there is no other person who speaks this language. He is the only one. He speaks it into a tape recorder for someone from the city. The tape will be there forever. Perhaps. But nobody can speak this language when he dies.'

They were all curious, if disbelieving.

'What is this language?' asked Leo sceptically. There were always people claiming to be the last – the last of the tribe, the last of the name, the last of the language.

'Livonian.' That seemed to clinch it. A language with a name. Livonian. 'It is a little bit like Latvian but it is not the same.'

'Begob,' said Máirtín. 'Livonian. Do you know, I never heard of it. Isn't that a shame now. And do you know what? I bet that Livonian chap never heard of our language either. Irish.'

'Not your version of it anyhow,' Molly said, coming in from the kitchen.

She was a person whose appearance always lifted Leo's heart, because she looked so different from most women he knew, or from most women he had ever seen, even on television or in the movies. The main reason for this was that her hair had been allowed to go grey, unlike the hair of any other middle-aged women he had ever met. The only women with grey hair were aged about ninety, while all men had grey hair when they were in their mid-forties: browny grey, blacky grey, blondy grey. But grey. Molly's had been black and was now an iron grey. She had a lot of it, which had perhaps been part of the incentive to let nature take its course. She wore it in a thick mop of ringlets and looked like an aged Irish dancer. She wore a rainbow-striped jumper, which was unravelling slightly on one sleeve. Anything less like a schoolteacher would be hard to imagine.

'I was at a lecture about minority languages a few months ago,' she said. 'There are sixty languages right now – or when this guy was giving the lecture – sixty, spoken by just one person. He mentioned Livonian, actually. He showed us a video of that man in your village, Josef. He's a stoutish man with glasses, he was sitting in front of his television set. He said he was the last, there was no one for him to talk to in Livonian.'

'That is him,' said Josef. 'Of course he speaks Latvian too. And Russian. And now we are all speaking English in my village, too, all of us who are over here working.'

'Does it matter?' The Nigerian woman looked up. 'In my country there are dozens of languages. But we have to speak English too. We have to understand each other, and the world.'

'This lecturer said it was like species of animals dying out, Chimanda. Except the situation for languages is worse. In the last twenty years or so more and more of them have been disappearing. Lots of them have never even been recorded. Nobody cares.'

'We care,' said Leo.

'What can we do?' Hlavek, the Polish man, spoke. 'If they die, they die.'

'He thought we should at least try to get them recorded. It would cost about six hundred million dollars to do that, today.'

211

'Humph!' said Josef. 'That is a lot of money.'

'It's peanuts,' Molly said. 'OPEC makes that much profit in one day.'

'Peanuts?' Josef shrugged. 'If we had a little money at home, we could stay there and speak Latvian. I would learn Livonian if I could earn enough money to stay at home.'

The conversation was turning sour.

Caoilfhionn tried to distract them by pouring more wine but they could not be stopped.

'I suppose you're very homesick?' Máirtín said cheerfully, draining half his glass.

'Yes,' said Josef. 'It is good to be here,' he said politely. 'But everyone would like to be home for Christmas.'

'I would too,' said Hlavek. 'I could not get a flight. All the flights cost twice as much as usual but they were booked out in October. Even the bus to Warsaw was booked out.'

'There are a lot of Poles in Dublin,' said Leo.

'Yes. Not so many here,' he laughed. 'I do not know how I ended up here.'

'We're happy to have you,' said Caoilfhionn, sniffing the air for smells of burning food. 'We will teach you Irish and you can teach us Polish. There are as many Polish speakers as Irish speakers in Ireland now.'

'One hundred and sixty thousand, they say,' said Hlavek.

'It depends on how you define an Irish speaker,' said Molly. 'A million said they were Irish speakers in the last census and I'm happy with that.'

Leo expostulated. 'That's a crazy number. Most of those can't speak Irish.'

'Why would they say they could if they couldn't?' Molly asked.

'I don't know. But we know it's not accurate. Most of them … they speak broken Irish, incorrect Irish. Not even fluent Irish.'

'That was another thing that lecturer said. The greatest enemies to a minority language are the enemies within. People who say things like that, Leo!' She did not sound angry. She looked amused.

'We have to have some standards,' he said.

'Yes. But there are more ways than one to speak a language,' she said, going back to the kitchen, where something was boiling over. 'It's not just us, or professors, who can speak it. A million.'

'It's better than Livonian,' said Josef.

'How is it that we always end up talking about the Irish language? Even on Christmas Day?' said Caoilfhionn.

'We talked about Livonina and Latvian and Polish and ... what do you speak when you're at home, Chimanda?' Máirtín said.

'Ibu. It is spoken by millions of people.'

'Ibu.'

'Irish is just a shorthand for all of them. Ibu and Livonian and those aboriginal languages spoken only by a man with red hair or a woman with one leg,' said Máirtín. 'Just like I am shorthand for all lonely old men.'

Leo was stunned. How surprising that Máirtín would use a word like 'shorthand' in that metaphorical way. He expected him to borrow all his metaphors from the world of agriculture or fishing, not from the world of commerce, however outdated.

On Hazelwood Crescent, the Kelly children woke up at three in the morning to see what Santa had brought them. Theirs was an under-the-Christmas-tree family, rather than an end-of-the-bed one. Olwen, who had not fallen asleep – she slept badly ever since Gerry had come back home – heard Emily getting up first and waking Jonathan, because she would be afraid to go downstairs on her own in the middle of the night, even on Christmas Eve. The landing light went on, and a slight bar of light, irritating to Olwen, appeared under her bedroom door. Then there was silence for almost five minutes. They were unwrapping – Olwen liked every single item, even the tiny stocking fillers like pencil cases and socks, to be carefully gift-wrapped. She smiled, envisaging the scene downstairs – the darkness of the window, the glittering tree, the children in their pyjamas on the floor, deeply engrossed in unwrapping their presents. A fairy tale scene, enacted in millions and millions of households all over the world, at this moment or at various moments over the next hours – she began to calculate the time in New York, in San Francisco, in Moscow, in Sydney ... in Sydney this had

213

happened already, twelve hours ago. In Sydney they were well into Christmas afternoon, on the beach of course …

Her musings were interrupted by a scream from downstairs. Emily.

Olwen shuddered and waited for a few seconds to see if she would stop.

The screaming stopped, but changed to sobs. Then Emily left the room – she could hear the door slamming – and started coming upstairs.

Olwen shook Gerry, who had been sleeping heavily.

'Go down to them,' she said simply. 'I can't face them at this time of the night.'

Gerry, who had been dreaming about scarecrows on an island off the west coast, an island of green fields and white cottages (he dreamed pictures), felt his limbs heavy as iron. Reluctance to wake up, to get up, flooded him like poison.

But he got up.

Bleary-eyed, he met Emily on the stairs.

She started to punch his stomach, with painfully hard thumps. 'I asked for an Xbox,' she yelled.

'Didn't he bring you one?' Gerry was awake enough to remember having paid two hundred euro for an Xbox for Emily.

'It's the wrong one. I wanted an Xbox 360 …' She sobbed as if her heart were broken.

Gerry remembered. Everyone wanted an Xbox 360. But an Xbox 360 hadn't been available in Dublin since early November.

He hugged Emily. 'Poor you!' he said. 'Maybe Santa ran out of them.'

'He promised,' said Emily, which was a lie.

'I'm sure he meant well,' said Gerry, leading her back to her room, where he planned to put her to bed.

'It's not good enough,' said Emily. 'People should keep their promises.'

'Yes,' said Gerry. 'But sometimes it's impossible.'

She suddenly realised what he was trying to do. 'I'm not going to bed,' she said, in a tone of outraged contempt.

'Well, maybe you'd feel better after a little sleep.' Gerry looked at his watch. Ten past three. 'It's still the middle of the night, love.'

'It's Christmas Day,' said Emily firmly. 'I'd like my breakfast.'

Gerry sighed.

The heating was not even on. The house was freezing.

'What would you like to eat?' he asked wearily.

'Orange juice and sausages and rashers,' she said firmly. 'And toast.'

Gerry went to the fridge.

Rory Kelly Sweeney did not get up until about five o'clock and opened all his presents quietly in his bedroom – the Sweeneys were a presents-at-the-end-of-the-bed family. He had recovered from the shock of finding out that there was no Santa and was happy with what he had got. Anna had remembered to buy every single thing on the long list, and had added several extra things as well. He smiled happily. His presents had cost more than three thousand euro, not that he knew or cared whether they had cost a million euro or ten euro, as long as his every wish was satisfied.

Although he did not believe in Santa, he ran in to Anna and Alex to tell them the good news. But then he went back to his room, played, and fell asleep. They did not have to get up until after the sun rose over the sea, in a bright red ball, at about half past eight.

Anna tried to make everything special for Christmas. So it had been at home when she was a child. They had had a special breakfast, with lots of sausages and rashers and mushrooms and tomatoes, and fried bread, and orange juice. Her mother would be up lighting fires in all the rooms and spreading the tablecloth on the kitchen table, making it a really unusual, festive day.

But then it had been easy to make it special and unusual, because on most days they had a very small breakfast, and even on Sunday one sausage and rasher and piece of pudding per person. Orange juice was a rare treat, so even that, in its blue carton, had been special. Everything about Christmas had been great then because everything about it was different from everyday life. You stayed in your house; you spent Christmas in the rooms where all other days were spent. But it was transformed utterly. For a day the locus of your life was transformed to perfection.

Nowadays it was harder to make it different because in the Kelly Sweeney household everything was perfect all the time. It was always warm, so there was no big deal about that. They always had exactly what they wanted to eat. Chocolate, juice, fruit, cake, all those things were constantly available. Anything anyone wanted to eat was bought immediately. Considerations of health and weight imposed certain limits and so the licentiousness of Christmas could be enjoyable. But considerations of health and weight were not the same as financial restrictions. For the Kelly Sweeneys, as for a lot people, it wasn't easy to make Christmas special because every day was Christmas.

That was probably why so many people went away these days. There was nothing they could do to make their home in Ireland better than it already was. So to experience the change that Christmas was intended to bring, to experience the sense of Saturnalia, they had to fly ever further afield. In Anna's childhood, fires in the bedrooms had generated Christmas warmth and cheer. Now you had to go to Thailand to achieve the same effect.

Perhaps they should have gone away? Alex had suggested it, when she had rejected the skiing option, and she had hummed a neutral response, and not bothered to book anything. (Alex never booked holidays; he considered it her job.) She had not wanted to go away because of Vincy, even though she was separated from Vincy anyway. Still, while she was here there was hope. Maybe she would manage to slip away on one of the between days? Being in Dublin felt safer than being in Thailand or India. (Where was he? In that apartment? He had a family; they had a farm in Offaly and minded his horse for him. But he hadn't said he was going to see them.)

On Christmas Day, she made every effort to create a festive atmosphere, to create a festive day. The weather was lovely. Bright sun bathed the garden, the hillside, the sea. She asked Alex and Rory to go for a walk with her and they spent almost an hour promenading on the pebbly beach, strolling all the way from the old tea house past the station to the river. Cormorants sunned themselves on the rocks; dozens of other people were out walking; there was even a large group swimming in ordinary summer swimsuits, for charity, halfway down the beach. They ran in and swam a few strokes and then ran out again. Anna put her hands in the water. It was cold, as it always was here on this beach, but not much colder than it would be in summer, it seemed. The sun was beaming down brilliantly on the sand and the air temperature felt high.

Swimming in winter was not a thing she had ever tried. She could do it. The time was available, and she was in the right location. Probably she would feel very healthy, very invigorated, purified, if she dipped in every day, the way some people did – she often saw them, little bunches of them, some club or other, or solitary swimmers, fat and old as often as not, walking up the beach after their freezing swim, their skin bluish, goose-pimpled.

'Maybe I'll try it, just once, to see what it's like,' she said to Alex. They were holding hands. She was huddled into her red duffle coat, which made her feel childish and safe.

'I don't see the point,' he said. He looked dismissively at the swimmers, who were wrapped in towels and jumpers, drinking coffee and smiling at passers-by, conscious of their achievement. They annoyed Alex. Anyone who diminished him, even in the remotest way, annoyed him. He was envious, although he would never admit that.

A shadow passed across Anna's mind, or it would have, had she not been in love with Vincy. Now Alex's flaws pleased her. Every time he revealed one of them she was able to use it as justification for what was happening. How could anyone love someone as flawed as Alex?

At four o'clock in the afternoon, just as they were sitting down to the turkey, the telephone rang four times.

Anna's heart lifted. Her whole body was flooded with warmth and she became so energised she could hardly continue with the mundane task of serving up sprouts and roast potatoes. That was Vincy ringing, ringing to signal his love, she felt sure.

But when she answered the telephone, a child's voice said, 'Do you like to be fucked under the mistletoe?'

Leo, who had enjoyed the party at Caoilfhionn's, excused himself soon after dinner and went home. They were surprised. Everyone else was going to stay until midnight at least. He felt rude, but he couldn't prevent himself. He wanted to see how

217

Charlene was. It even struck him that she might have left as abruptly as she had arrived, and he wasn't sure how he would feel about that.

He walked home in the cold, clear night. The sky was awash with stars, it was a milk and silver wonderland. But he paid little attention, shining his little flashlight on the dark road, trotting along as fast as he could.

Charlene had not disappeared. She was sitting by the blazing fire, watching the Christmas *Late Late Show*. The house was filled with a pleasant smell, the smell of baking.

'Did you bake something?' Leo asked, sniffing appreciatively.

'Brown bread,' she said unapologetically, nodding at the table. A large round loaf with a cross on it was standing on a rack, cooling, on the table.

'Hm.' He sat down and sighed.

'Was it a good party?' she asked. She was knitting something.

'It was OK,' he said. 'How was your own day?'

'Lovely,' she said. 'Lovely. I went for a walk before lunch. It was a nice day for a walk. I saw a pheasant in the field down there, a big pheasant with gorgeous feathers, all the colours under the sun. Then I came back and had a bit of lunch and then I watched *The King and I*. I cried my eyes out …'

She went on and on.

Listening to her soothed him. He forgot about Kate, and Máirtín the bachelor, and his uneasy worries about his own looming bachelordom. Or, if he were honest, his own present bachelordom. Charlene's meaningless meandering narrative, with its splashes of colourful description, its inaccuracies, its enthusiasm about nothing, was strangely comforting.

Quite soon he felt relaxed enough to go to bed, where he slept soundly and had a rich dream about a voyage to Africa.

Eighteen

Anna and Alex went to see *Brokeback Mountain* in an old fleapit in a town in County Wicklow. The cinema was half-full of women, crying their eyes out.

Afterwards Anna was too moved to talk.

Alex didn't have much to say either, but for a different reason.

'It's sentimental crap,' he said finally, when Anna had overcome her tears and they were in the car driving home. 'It's *Love Story* for gays.'

Even the actors had looked a bit like the boy and girl in *Love Story*. The blond Nordic man, the dark emotional woman.

But he was not a dark emotional woman, he was a dark emotional man. And the lovemaking looked much more physical, more elemental, than heterosexual love could ever be. By contrast with the highly explicit sexual scenes in homosexual movies, heterosexual coupling looked tame and unexciting. Maybe because women hadn't got all those muscles. Because women were not men. The movie made you feel that the best love was love between men.

Is that why Alex didn't like it? Probably not. The women in the cinema should not have liked it, because the implication of everything in the film was that they were second best. If you wanted the real thing, it had to be with a man, a tough, deeply emotional, muscular man, a cowboy with poetry in his soul, was the subliminal message of this film. Anna should have been the one not to like it. But she did, because it extolled the virtue of true love, true thwarted love, the kind she was experiencing now in her affair with Vincy – she fancied that he looked ever so slightly like the blond macho one in the film, the one all the women had a soft spot for.

Love like that is exactly what I feel for Vincy, Anna thought.

But was it what Vincy felt for her?

For some reason, the image of him, sitting up in his big tossed bed, smoking a cigarette and eyeing her with an emotion that she could not put a name on, but which now, with the benefit of a Hollywood version of modern true love for purposes of comparison, could not be described as being anywhere on passion's spectrum. That was her reading of the scene, right now.

Insecure, uneasy, worried, she telephoned him, contrary to what she had been asked, on the fourth day of Christmas, the day after she had seen the movie. The picture of those two men unable to restrain their passion had moved her deeply and aroused her own love so that she too was unable to resist her desire – to telephone.

But the course of passion was thwarted, as it so often is, by technical failure. She got the voice, that smug, dismayingly firm, mobile phone voice, saying the mobile phone user was out of range or had their mobile switched off.

Over the next week she rang Vincy's number ten times, and always got the same message.

Leo, in spite of his best judgement, found that living with Charlene was the most natural thing in the world. He had fully intended to throw her out on the 27th of December, the minute the buses started running with some semblance of normality. But when the time came he was … hung over, for one thing. She made him a prairie oyster, which she claimed was the best cure for a hangover ever invented. She had learned how to do it from *Cabaret*, where Liza Minnelli makes one for Michael York. Her flowery apron was in place, a loaf of bread was in the oven, the fire was roaring in the grate. She had no intention whatsoever of leaving.

'Do you know what I was thinking?' she asked, having administered the prairie oyster.

He guessed she was not going to say 'I was thinking it was high time I got the hell out of here and back to my hospital', or 'husband', or 'children'. And he was right.

'I was thinking you could give me a hand with the reading.'

'Were you now?' What next?

'Yes I was. You read a lot yourself.' He had given no evidence of this since she had joined his household. She must have been basing her idea on the books she saw all over the house. 'What better person to teach me?'

He laughed despairingly.

Minutes later they were seated at the big table, a jotter and pens at the ready, and a copy of *Noddy and Tessie Bear*, the first book Leo had ever read himself (he read it when he was six – he had taught himself to read), open in front of them. He had kept his childhood copy. He anticipated that this was a book that would appeal to Charlene, and in that he was perfectly correct.

And so lessons began. Every afternoon, after his walk, they sat at the kitchen table and he taught her how to read.

A routine established itself. Charlene cooked and did all the housework. The kitchen always smelt of baking bread, or slowly cooking vegetable curries. The fire was always blazing in the stone fireplace and the tiles were always cleanly swept. The house came to life under Charlene's care and Leo quickly came to appreciate the comforts she provided.

She could not stay for long, that was obvious, but it was all turning out better than he had expected it would.

Kate was on his mind, however.

He had made no promises about going back to Dublin and she understood that he had his work to do here – although, actually, he was not doing much work at the moment. When he phoned, which he did only on Christmas Day, he indicated that he was snowed under and would probably not go back to see her for at least a month.

'Oh, that's OK,' she said, apparently unsurprised. Nothing seemed to surprise her: that was an effect of the medication. 'I know how it is.'

After New Year's Day she was going back to hospital. It struck him as odd that she had been out, at home, for about ten days and would now return to sit in a room in a hospital, but he had stopped expressing scepticism about the benefits of her psychiatric care. She found his questions upsetting and seemed to need to believe that she was in good hands. The whole thing depended on that, he presumed. It was some kind of faith healing, even if it also involved what seemed to him unhealthily high doses of drugs.

'I'll go to see you when I get back to town,' he said. 'Phone me any time.'

'All right,' she said, in that bland way of hers, which was disconcerting. 'Are you having a nice time?'

'It's fine.' He told her about the party on Christmas Day, but not about Charlene. That was a mistake. He knew it, as he gave a report on his days, omitting the most sensational news. But having to explain Charlene over the phone would be too difficult. He hadn't mentioned her to anyone ... soon he would have to. If he knew anything, everyone down in the pub would already have noticed that he had a stranger staying in his house. Charlene went for walks sometimes, and she must have visited the local grocer's van, the one that did the rounds of the old folk twice a week, at one of its halting points. There was no other explanation for the constant supply of brown bread, and bacon and egg and sausage, which he never bought himself, being a vegetarian.

The days and nights after Christmas were glorious. A cloudless sky presented the valley with bright sunny days, the green of the fields and the blue of the sea was scintillating; at night the dark blue sky was crowded with silver stars. It was exhilarating weather.

Replete with Charlene's good bread, delicious porridge (she always added cream and berries, wherever she got those from), and nut roasts, and a general sense of well-being, Leo took longer and longer afternoon walks. He felt healthier and stronger than he had ever in his life before. He walked for five or six miles, up into the hills where the sheep dotted the hummocky turf like big white flowers, and their bleats sang like a strange winter symphony, the essential music of Ireland, it seemed to him. He wished he could replicate it, that lonely, ethereal sound, like messages from another world.

He began to play around with poems – not a thing he had

done since he was young, and in Dublin, and his parents were still alive.

On New Year's Eve when he returned from his afternoon walk, Charlene said: 'There was a phone call for you.'

He was taken aback. 'I told you not to answer the phone,' he said.

Charlene smiled her dotty smile and said, 'Ah yeah, but I forgot.'

'Who was it?'

'Kate Murphy.'

'Oh my God,' said Leo, using an exclamatory expression he hated. 'Well ... didn't she ask who you were?'

'No she didn't,' said Charlene nonchalantly. Nothing moved this woman. She was incorrigible. She was lifting an apple pie out of the oven. It had a golden crust and at the crescent of the pie were three leaves shaped from pastry. The edges had been pricked with a fork so that it looked as if it was surrounded by a pastry frill. She pricked it with a fork and a divine smell of apples, sugar and cloves wafted across the kitchen.

Suddenly Leo saw another face and another body carrying the pie from the oven to the counter, and he smelt another room, a room in which he had spent years and years, long ago. But he did not get a chance to pursue this memory because Charlene began to talk and by the time she had finished he had forgotten what it was he had been about to recall. Like a wonderful dream, the details of which vanish as soon as you become conscious, it evaporated.

'I asked her how she knew you,' she said.

Leo was so flabbergasted that he couldn't reply.

'She sounds like a lovely girl,' said Charlene. 'And she is wondering why you're not up there with her.'

'Charlene!' Leo began.

'I know it's none of my business but it's high time you settled down,' Charlene said, in a firm maternal tone.

'I am settled down.' Leo sounded like a teenager defending the indefensible.

Charlene ignored his comment completely. 'You don't want

to end up a lonely old bachelor like that Máirtín at the party.'

He didn't remember telling her about Máirtín, but he didn't remember much of what had happened on Christmas night. He and Charlene, he vaguely recalled, had chatted quite a lot, and he had drunk a great deal of wine before that chattering occurred. In his cups, he knew from bitter experience, he often revealed much more than was wise.

'Charlene, you're quite right. This is none of your business,' he said, taking off his coat and preparing to go into his study.

'Kate told me she was in the mental hospital.'

He stopped at the door of the study. 'She told you *what*?'

'It's nothing to be ashamed of. I was in one myself once.'

'Yes,' said Leo wearily. 'I'm not surprised.'

Charlene always ignored all negative remarks. 'You should go up to Dublin and ask that girl to marry you.'

Leo went into the study and slammed the door.

There were no trains on New Year's Day, but there was a limited bus service. Leo managed to catch one of the few on offer at ten o'clock. It was able to travel swiftly across Ireland – there was very little traffic. There were only three people on the bus, although the towns they passed through were busy: some shops were open, and festivities were taking place here and there. In Toomevara, there was a rubber duck race in the stream, and in Mountrath a small carnival was being held on the main street, complete with swingboats and a small ferris wheel.

Night had fallen by the time he reached Kate's parents' house, a big mansion of a place in its own grounds. The taxi – there were a few taxis about – dropped him at the gate. He walked down the gravelled avenue between bare winter trees. On the lawn in front of the house two birches were lit with bluish fairy lights. Behind them, the mock Tudor windows of the house, which was one of those pretty late Victorian houses, all gables and mullioned windows, like Samuel Beckett's childhood home, Cooldrinagh – the Beckett house must be just down the road, in fact.

He rang the bell and Kate answered. He had been just mildly apprehensive. The journey was so long and tiring. Maybe he had made a mistake. She was mental. Was she beautiful or was she plain? But when he saw her, dressed in a simple black polo neck jumper and a red skirt, her eyes enormous, her hair newly cut and washed, his heart filled. Beautiful, was the answer. Unambiguously beautiful. And she looked so healthy, and so happy, and so glad to see him.

They kissed for some time without exchanging a word.

She brought him from the hall, which had a marble floor and a chandelier, into a huge living room. Shaded floor-lamps cast pools of golden light on the rich wooden floor. A great bouquet of roses and lilies gleamed in a corner, and their scent drifted in the warm air. On an old-fashioned velvet sofa, in front of a blazing log fire, Kate's parents sat and watched the flat screen television, which had been put into a gilt frame on the wall so that it looked like an old master – a slightly weird effect, Leo thought, as he took it all in and realised that Kate came from a much richer background than he would have anticipated from her stories. It seemed that a lot of people he met came from such backgrounds these days, while there were also a lot like Charlene, who had no home at all, or like the people in Kerry, who lived in little bungalows or cottages.

Her parents were not intimidating, and appeared to feel that their surroundings were perfectly ordinary and nothing to be proud of. Her mother was blond, slightly overweight, with a big mouth and a chirpy, rather comical face. Leo did not notice what she was wearing. Her father had a large head of snow white hair and a wrinkled, distinguished face, a face, in fact, that was curiously reminiscent of Samuel Beckett's. He was dressed in a very old-looking Aran jumper and cord pants, obviously some sort of old favourite clothes to relax in. Like Kate, they seemed almost impervious to shock, although it could be assumed that the reasons for this imperturbability were natural, not chemical. When Kate told them that this complete stranger was going to be her husband, they expressed no surprise. In fact, they seemed delighted. That was not said but it was clear. Probably, Leo thought, not cynically, the illness had something to do with their attitude. They had been through so much that nothing fazed them. That could happen to people. In a way it had happened to him. The issue of her illness was not hidden. He would have almost preferred if it had been. But they talked about it openly, as if it were a touch of flu … which was what it amounted to now, it seemed. She would go back to hospital to see the consultant, who would probably discharge her straight away.

'We can get married then, as soon as you come out,' Leo said. Suddenly he did not want to wait. He wanted her down in Kerry in his house, their life to begin there, without any more delay.

There was a surprised silence.

Kate's mother broke it. 'You can't do that!' she said, laughing. 'It all takes time.'

'Does it?' Leo realised he knew nothing about these things.

'Well, apart from the legalities, which entail giving three months' notice, or maybe even six, there is a lot of preparation.'

'We don't want any fuss,' said Leo, looking at Kate. 'Do we?'

She hesitated. Her mother looked carefully at her. Kate said, 'No', in an unconvinced tone.

'A quiet wedding!' said Kate's father, laughing. 'Do you believe that for one second?'

Kate, as she had anticipated, was discharged from hospital a few days after going back in. Leo collected her from the ward. She had her bag packed and was going around hugging patients and telling them she would phone, she would call in to see them. Everyone was kissing, waving, saying goodbye. It was as if she were leaving a place where she had been on holiday. There was a sort of gala atmosphere about it. She smiled triumphantly at the nun in the hall and waved, but did not shake hands with her, which the nun did not expect.

'It's a funny place,' Leo said, as they walked along the gravelled path to the car park.

'It is the funny farm,' said Kate.

'It sort of grows on you,' he said, looking back at the big grey building. A few weeks ago it had seemed like an alien place, somewhere he would rather not think about, somewhere danger-ous, which he never wanted to go near. And now it seemed ordinary and friendly. The mentally ill seemed not like a sub-human group to be avoided, but like everyone else. The funny thing was that they did not seem mentally ill, they seemed exactly like the mentally healthy, at least while they were in the hospital. He wondered if there really was a difference? But if not, why were they there, locked up?

'It hasn't grown on me,' said Kate. 'I'm glad to be getting out of it.'

'So … back home to Mammy? And then home to Leo?' he asked, giving her a friendly dig.

'Let's think about it all,' she said. 'I mean, of course we are getting married and everything …' He had looked frightened. 'But would it be more fun to postpone going to Kerry until we actually are married?'

'You want to be strictly conventional all of a sudden?'

'It's nothing to do with that. I just think it would be more … exciting. In every way.' She looked at him meaningfully. 'You know?'

'Mm,' he said dubiously.

Nineteen

New Year's Day, that unnerving feast of abandoned hopes and cold promises, had dawned and passed. The Christmas break was well and truly over. January set in.

'Where were you?' Anna asked Vincy brightly.

They were having lunch in the Tower. She was smiling. It was as if nothing had happened, as if she had not spent the past five days twisting her hands and feeling as depressed as she ever had been in her life. She arrived at the pub full of anger, full of fear, full of anxiety. As soon as she saw him all that emotion vanished, to be replaced by joy – or was it a form of intense relief? He was like a magician.

'In Grenoble,' he said, as if he were saying, 'I was caught up in the office'. He added, 'I went there skiing with Joe. A spare ticket became available at the last minute.'

Jealousy jumped into her like an angry animal, claws bared.

'So … and you turned off your mobile phone?'

'No.' He shrugged. 'There was no coverage in the mountains. Were you trying to call?'

Were you trying to call? What sort of a question was that?

'Yes.' She looked bleakly at the brown panelling of the pub. Suddenly its dark decor and greasy smells seemed sordid rather than comforting.

'I'm so sorry.' He took her hand and patted it as if she were a child. 'You look beautiful. I missed you.' He kissed her quickly on the forehead. 'A lot.'

She believed him when he said it. And yet if he'd missed her as much as she missed him, wouldn't he have phoned? There must have been landlines in Grenoble that worked. Ski resorts were not the back of beyond. Thousands of people who would want to be on the phone all the time frequented ski resorts.

But he was back. She couldn't waste the precious hour quibbling. So they talked about other things.

She wanted to meet him in his apartment again. To make love. Not like they had. Like the guys in *Brokeback Mountain*.

'Joe!' he said, throwing up his hands.

In the movie the cowboys had made love in the porch, with the wife and child inside the door, watching. It was not that they were cruel or thoughtless; no, it was that their passion could simply not be restrained.

'Joe must go out sometimes,' she said.

'Yes,' Vincy said. 'But I never know when. He's very erratic in his habits.'

Anna suddenly remembered Jack in *The Importance of Being Earnest*. Or was it Earnest? The one who Bunberryed.

'You could come to my house,' she said, although she had not wanted this before. Ludmilla and Luz Mar were not back yet, though, so it was safer than usual. The only problem would be Rory, but she could get rid of him for an afternoon easily enough.

To her astonishment he said yes. 'I'd like to see the house anyway.'

It wasn't a *Brokeback Mountain* response but it was better than Bunberrying.

Vincy had seen her house before, something he seemed to have forgotten. He had driven out and looked at it, from the outside, a few weeks after their friendship began. When he told her this, she was very upset. The thought of him, sitting on her road in his car, examining her house from the outside, like a spy or a burglar, disturbed her for more reasons than one. But he explained that he had just wanted to know everything about her. She let it pass.

He came just before lunch the next day.

'Mm,' he said, and looked, rather too inquisitively and

critically, at everything, stopping to check out a picture, picking up an alabaster vase, one she had bought on a holiday in Egypt, and fondling its smooth, warm surface. 'It's a nice house,' he said.

'Different from yours,' she said.

Somehow his tone of voice disparaged her house and made her feel his was superior. That derelict couple of rooms in a rented house in Mountjoy Square. She loved him but increasingly, already, he seemed to be wrong-footing her, ever so subtly, in tiny, sly ways. Maybe she was imagining it.

She fed him a simple lunch of soup, sandwiches – what they always ate. This was the first time she had ever prepared food for him. Why should she like doing that for him, since she resented doing it for Alex and even Rory? One of her main complaints about Alex was that he never cooked anything, or even made her a cup of tea. Now here she was, delighted to be waiting on Vincy. What bliss it would be to cook him a real dinner, she thought. To sweep his floor. Until now she had not consciously considered anything like this; she had not considered sharing a real life with him. He belonged to the realm of imagination, or of play. But now, after the pain of the Christmas separation, she began to realise that she wanted him in her everyday life – as a partner, not a lover.

He ate the sandwiches and soup without comment, taking them for granted, exactly as Alex and Rory would have done, Anna noted: to that extent he was already behaving like a partner.

They were uneasy in this house, however. Anna knew that nobody would come home. Alex was at work, Rory had gone to a matinée pantomime with a friend from school, Luz Mar was in Spain. The coast would be clear for several hours. But they both felt nervous anyway. Vincy sat upright, his muscles tense and his expression alert. He sniffed nervously, like a dog investigating strange territory. His stone-coloured eyes darted around the room, examining corners and crevices.

When lunch was over, Anna kissed him quietly, aware of his anxiety. Vincy, she was realising, looked like a wolf or some wild thing, but at heart he was a mild, careful, modern man, with the instincts of a civil servant. Like herself. He was the product of generations of mild bureaucratic ancestors. He had a horse at his family's home in the country, but it was a tame old trekking horse, not an unbroken stallion. Vincy was not a cowboy; he had never ridden bareback at a rodeo. He had never lived for months in a tent at the top of a mountain, herding sheep.

Sadly she led him upstairs. The best room to use would have been hers and Alex's, where the bed was big and the huge window looked directly out on the sky and the sea. But some instinct prevented her from bringing him there, and instead they went to the spare room at the back of the house, which for some reason she had decked out with sky blue, flowery wallpaper and snowy lace, in some indulgence of a schoolgirl fantasy. In this room they made love, quickly and nervously, with their clothes on, on the princess bed. It was not like *Brokeback Mountain* at all.

Anna felt anxious all the time, although there was no reason for it. She felt as if gangs of fundamentalists wearing Ku Klux Klan outfits were at that moment assembling at the end of the drive, preparing to ride up waving torches, and planning some unspeakable end for both herself and Vincy.

She was glad when it was all over and Vincy was out of the house, driving down the hill and back to where he had come from.

He did not telephone her the next day, or the next.

The first day she was not unduly alarmed. She presumed that some practical problem had arisen. Work. The second day she was anxious. When he did not telephone on the third day, she felt distraught and abandoned.

He was tiring of her. This was her punishment, for drawing too close to him. For pressurising him to go to bed with her here, with the Ku Klux Klan at the gate. It was not coming to the house that had upset him. He had wanted that, more than her. His curiosity about her house had been enormous. It was making love to her in her own house that had upset him, as it had upset her, at the time, although probably not for the same reason.

They had been in love for several months, and made love twice, and already he was falling out of love, and preparing to leave her.

Could this be happening, already?

She blamed herself. She had done something wrong and she knew what it was. Anyone could see that she had overdone it. She was a woman who loved too much. Never give all the heart,

Yeats had said, and he knew what he was talking about. If you care, don't let them know. Literature was full of warnings, instructions on how to be successful in love. Popular parlance too. Make yourself scarce, some people said. Never phone! was a maxim her own mother had taught her in her youth. 'They know your number.'

That seemed old-fashioned, non-assertive, anti-feminist.

But wise.

She didn't phone.

Instead she sank into misery, into a kind of paralysis. She went through the motions of her life. Most of the time she felt physically wounded. The image of an apple sliced in two hovered in her imagination, its sliced centre unbearably raw and sore. She felt she had been skinned alive.

Alex noticed none of this, as usual. Rory did not either. He did not even notice that she was at home more than usual. Nobody paid the slightest attention to the fact that she was not going out, that she was hardly talking, or that she was not writing a word of her book. But then, they never noticed that.

Her editor, who had promised to get in touch before Christmas, had not contacted her as yet. Anna did not care. If they didn't like her novel, it as all the same to her. They could lump it. What did it matter, by comparison with this abandonment by Vincy?

A week passed.

She had not capitulated. She had not telephoned.

That should have made her feel strong and victorious, but it didn't. The strategy had had no effect at all on Vincy. He had not phoned her either.

The 13th of January. An article in the newspaper said it was the most depressing day of the year.

On the 13th of January, Anna realised that she might have something new to worry about.

Pregnancy.

Anna first did a home test, and then went to a doctor for a confirmation, which took a few days to come through. She didn't contact Vincy. As soon as she had suspected she was pregnant, her need to talk to him vanished. Now she could wait.

He would contact her, soon – suddenly what she could not believe before became self-evident.

And then she would tell him the news.

It was his.

Almost certainly.

She and Alex had hardly had sex at all in months. The last time had been two months ago. She knew the baby was not his. But Alex would not remember when they had last had sex – that was not the sort of thing he noticed much. So he would assume it was, unless she told him the truth.

It seemed to her, for a few days, that suddenly all the strings were in her hands and she could manipulate the situation whatever way suited her. Vincy was a modern man. He would want to do the right thing. He would want to be father to his child.

If she wanted him now she would have him.

She did not put it as crudely as this.

She told nobody about the pregnancy. But she felt calm and almost happy, as she went about her work.

The writing recommenced. She read the novel so far from beginning to end, and saw that there were some good things in it, as well as some bad. Over two days she wrote a new chapter, the first new chapter she had written in months.

Luz Mar and Ludmilla both came back.

Ludmilla had enjoyed her holiday, she said. It had been good to see her family again, and her friends. She was friendlier than before – the visit home had softened her.

'What is it like?' Anna asked. She thought it might be like a village in Russia, wooden houses, some apartment blocks in an Eastern bloc style. A bare, boring place with a duck pond or a lake nearby, maybe, a grocery store, a garage.

'I can't describe it,' said Ludmilla. 'It is just home.'

She showed Anna photographs of people who looked like Ludmilla: good-looking, fair, with what seemed to be hard expressions, as if they would not tolerate any weakness or nonsense. Ludmilla was like that, as well as looking like that. In fact, rather like Vincy, she managed to convey that she was always slightly superior to everyone. Probably that was as a result of fearing that they believed otherwise. She was defensive.

The photographs were all of interiors, which looked OK, rather drab, but with furniture that was surprisingly smart and modern, out of place in the surroundings – but then, the people them-selves looked as if they belonged in a more modern, smart setting than that which they possessed. They looked like tourists in their own country.

'Would you like to go back to live there?' Anna asked.

'Oh yes,' said Ludmilla, with the first expression of emotion Anna had ever seen in her. 'I would love to.' Her eyes were wist-ful, but then she smiled. 'I will go back.'

Some days passed. Anna worked with deep concentration on the book. Ludmilla spring-cleaned the house. Rory was busy at school, and Luz Mar settled back into her English classes and baby-sitting with a spurt of energy.

Harmony and order reigned in the house. Energy and work filled it like a sweet perfume.

Finally Vincy telephoned.

Anna spoke nonchalantly to him, as he did to her, although she detected a guilty tone under the surface. He had been away, of course, in Iraq, doing a story. Hadn't she watched the news? She would have seen him reporting from Basra, where there had been renewed upsurges of violence.

'Why did you go there?' she asked. Until now he had always covered home stories – non-news about the government, usually.

'I got an opportunity,' he said. 'I always wanted to go there, to report from a war zone.'

Anna did not know what to make of this.

He wanted to meet for lunch.

'OK,' said Anna, not feeling the need to get involved in an argument or recriminations.

He suggested meeting at his flat, to her surprise. This time she would have preferred the Tower, or any of the pubs they usually frequented.

He had prepared some lunch, with care; there was a premeditated air to the encounter. Anna decided to wait until after the lunch to tell him the news.

But as soon as they had eaten he drew her into the bedroom. The wide, comfortable bed was covered with what looked like a very new white spread, and the pillows and sheets were fresh.

He had lit a fire in the big old black grate, so that the room was warm. The flames danced in the grate, the old browny walls with their charming stains and drips of wallpaper were bathed in soft sunlight, filtering in through the tall old window.

Her happiest fantasy had been realised.

He had prepared an elaborate scene of seduction.

Obviously he had missed her deeply, and realised how much he loved her.

Now was not the time to break the news.

They went to bed and stayed there for two hours. This time, everything worked very well. His smoke smell, his sweat smell, the fuzzy texture of his hair, his legs, his chest – hair was everywhere. She traced the line of his ribs, like the bent wood of a longship, with her fingers. She explored, she watched her skin against his – and their bodies joined, then, finally, neatly, like two pieces of a jigsaw, finding the right mate.

Today it happened.

Now was not the time to tell.

Twenty

Regarding the wedding, there was now a change of plan: Kate and her mother wanted it to take place in Dingle instead of Dublin. It was such a pretty town with such a pretty church. (They assumed this; neither of them had ever been there.) Dingle, however, had become one of the most fashionable places for weddings in Ireland. Brides flocked there, and almost every day in summer a wedding party splashed across the streets like birds of paradise who had migrated from some tropical hemisphere to the little town. This they did know, somehow – they had an-tennae for such details that Leo found bewildering. He had been in Dingle thousands of times but had never noticed that it got more than its fair share of weddings. Now the arrangements for his own fell on his shoulders. He was to go to the parish priest, discuss the ceremony and report back to Kate, and her mother.

He had only been to the church in the valley for funerals, of which there were about four or five a year, as the old people died off. He wondered if the priest would know that? But he only wondered for about five seconds. Of course he would know. Down here they knew everything.

And the priest did know. Leo had never paid much attention to him, but he knew all about Leo. Like everyone else, he had been to launches of the poetry collections Leo published; his nephew had been one of Leo's authors. That Leo was coming to make the arrangements for a wedding didn't seem to surprise him in the least. Nor was he concerned that Leo was not a practising Catholic. The majority of those who married in his picturesque church were not. It was not something he was glad about, but he was a philosophical old man and did not ask too many awkward questions.

'It's great news! Congratulations!' he said.

They spoke Irish. It suddenly struck Leo that Kate and her mother had not thought about this aspect of a Dingle wedding, that it might be conducted in Irish. Like most people, they didn't believe that Irish was a real language, spoken by real, ordinary people on a daily basis, a language that you could have a Mass or a funeral or a wedding in. They looked on it as something that had been invented by schoolteachers for the sole purpose of annoying children.

But the parish priest was accommodating. He was wise and knew the general attitude. The wedding would be conducted mainly in English. 'Sure that's the way it is, here in this town. I often have to do some of the ceremonies in English. Does your wife-to-be know any Irish at all?'

'Not much,' said Leo.

'Well, she can learn, I suppose, if she comes to live here in the Gaeltacht?'

'I'm sure she will,' said Leo, although this, too, was a matter to which he hadn't given much thought. It had occurred to him that if they had children, which he hoped they would, that they would be brought up speaking Irish. That would be normal in this surrounding, and it would please him to contribute to saving Irish by passing it on to his children – the simplest and most efficient way of saving any minority language, he realised, much simpler and more useful than writing or publishing books in it. Where Kate fitted into this project, apart from giving birth to these Irish-speaking children, he had not considered in depth, still less discussed with her.

There was more to this business of marrying and settling down than met the eye.

At least he was able to arrange a date for the wedding. The priest told him, as Kate had warned, that he and Kate would be obliged to undertake a marriage guidance course, consisting of six talks by a trained counsellor. They could do the course here or in Dublin, but he would not marry them unless they produced a certificate proving they had taken the course.

'It's a bit of a nuisance for people like yourself, who are not teenagers,' he said sympathetically. 'It was designed long ago for young innocent people who knew nothing about what they were letting themselves in for. But it's a rule now and you have to do it. Here's the information – just get it over with and send me the cert. a month before the wedding, that's all I need.'

Leo telephoned Kate even before going home, from his mobile, as he walked down the hilly street from the church to the supermarket.

'Would you come up here?' she asked.

'Well ...' He was annoyed. She seemed very reluctant to come to Kerry under any circumstances – she wanted to get married here, and then live here for the rest of her life, but in the mean-time she had not visited even for a weekend.

'Maybe I can find a course that happens on Saturdays,' she said. 'You'd just have to come up for the six weekends ... you would be anyway.'

'Except that you were going to come here for half those weekends,' he said, as evenly as he could.

'I want to,' she said. 'But there is so much to do here. We will come down next weekend to look at the hotel and the church and so on, but after that ... you have no idea how much stuff there is to do.'

'We were going to keep it simple,' he said.

'We are, we are,' she said.

He was almost at the foot of the hill, and decided to go into a coffee shop on the corner, where he could wait until the bus came.

Even a simple wedding required a great deal of preparation and money and time, she was saying, not for the first time.

As always, he capitulated. He would go to Dublin and do this marriage training course.

And then in July they would finally be here, for good, and Kate would just have to stay put.

Leo raised the issue of Irish when he was next in Dublin to attend the pre-marriage course.

Kate was taken aback. 'I never think of you as a Gaeilgeoir,' she said.

Leo said, 'But you know I write poetry and publish books in Irish.'

She frowned as if this had nothing to do with the issue. 'Well, sure. But I always get the impression that's something you do for a living, to make money.' She opened her eyes wide and clapped her hand over her mouth in mock dismay.

'To make *money*?' Leo was so flabbergasted he could not help repeating these words.

'Yeah, well, you know, all those grants and things Irish-language people get,' she said. 'Sorry, that sounds cynical,' she added.

Yes, Leo thought. And stupid. But it's probably what a lot of people believe.

'It's my fault. I don't make it clear that I speak Irish when I'm at home. I'm not a fanatic or anything,' he felt compelled to add.

'Well, thank goodness for that. There's nothing worse than a fanatic,' she said stoutly, as if she had declared some important truth.

And when did you ever meet a fanatic? he thought. The problem was the opposite. No fanatics. Most Irish speakers were like Leo: so polite or so craven or so indifferent that they never insisted on speaking the language. They whispered instead of shouting. Laws were passed giving them all kinds of rights but the laws, just like the laws about driving, were never implemented.

'I'm not a fanatic, of course.' He had to make some things clear. 'But I have beliefs about the importance of minority languages,' he said, sounding pompous. Her eyes glazed over. 'Irish is the language of the valley, just like French is the language of Paris.'

Nobody outside the Gaeltacht ever believed this, so he should have been prepared for her next comment.

'Well, how could I know that?' she said.

His heart sank. What did she think the word 'Gaeltacht' meant? A holiday place by the sea or something?

'I mean, I thought the valley was full of people from America and Germany and all over the place.'

'It is that, as well,' he said.

'Well surely they can't speak Irish?' She was getting seriously annoyed. She shared the common Irish belief that it was impossible for anyone who was non-Irish to learn the language.

'A lot of them can,' he said, exaggerating wildly. 'They pick it up.' This was not strictly speaking true. Irish is not the sort of language you can 'pick up'. 'They learn it.'

'How?' she laughed. 'I could never learn it! I got an F in the Leaving.' She spoke with pride. She wore this failure like a badge of honour, although she would never have admitted that she failed maths, for instance, or geography.

'You weren't taught properly,' he said wearily, falling back on the accepted excuse. 'It's just a language, with nouns and verbs and adjectives. And grammar. Once you learn them, you know them.'

She smiled in disbelief. She knew otherwise.

'Never mind, let's talk about something else.' He gave her a hug. He loved Irish, but he was not going to risk his marriage to Kate because of it.

By the end of the day, which soon became dominated by the marriage preparation course, they were happy again.

Leo, listening to Kate snoring softly, like a cat, beside him in her bed in Gardiner Street, wondered what would happen, in the end, in relation to the language. If it came to a choice between Kate and Irish, there was no competition. She had clearly won it long ago. If they had a child or children, and who knows, they hadn't even got as far as talking about that, he could always speak Irish to it or them, while she spoke English. Such arrangements could work. He would just have to compromise. Irish speakers did. That was the way of the world.

A meeting of Killing Roads was held on Sunday morning, in the Tower. They discussed the need to expand the organisation and find new members. Once again, Leo postponed telling the group of his strong desire to abolish it.

'Yes,' said Leo. 'But let's just focus on one other thing. What can we do to … achieve success?'

The sun shone into the room, dancing on the wooden floor.

Today Leo, didn't care about carnage on the roads. He had difficulty focusing on anything, let alone one of the issues relating to road safety.

'I don't know. There is a sense of heightened public awareness at the moment,' said Marcella. 'The figures are so bad that even the politicians are getting worried.'

Fifty people had been killed on the roads in January, the highest number for that month in years.

'Can we call for the resignation of the Minister?'

'We can call for it but we won't get it,' said someone else. 'That bastard will never resign. He's wrecked other portfolios before ... it's hard to understand why he is so successful in getting these good posts. Must have something on the Taoiseach.'

'It makes sense,' Leo said. 'But we're never going to find out what that is. If it is. I propose that we send a letter to the newspapers complaining about the lack of progress, about his abysmal record. We can blame him directly for the deaths on the road.'

'Let's come out and say it. Accuse the Taoiseach and the Minister of murder. Call for their resignation. Let's not be polite, let's call them what they are.'

Reservations were expressed. The papers would not publish anything that was too offensive. RTÉ would give them no hearing. Even some members of Killing Roads felt censored personally. They worked in the public service.

However, they agreed to write a call for the resignation of the Minister for Transport and the Taoiseach, accusing them of having colluded in the murder of a thousand people since taking office. The letter would be on their headed paper, The Enemies of the Killing Roads, and would be circulated to every newspaper, radio and television station on the country.

'We'll see what happens,' said Leo. 'If we get a response, we should call a mass rally outside Leinster House. That always shakes them up.'

'We'd probably get more members as well,' said Marcella. 'They always want to join anything they see on the telly.'

Leo would be in Dublin every weekend for weeks to attend the marriage course. He did not tell them this, or that he was getting married. Afterwards he felt silly for being so reserved. The news might have cheered them up – all of them apart from John Perry, anyway.

Twenty-one

Anna's news left Vincy dumbfounded. It was not a condition he experienced very often.

'You're what?' he said.

Anna laughed. 'That's a joke,' she said. 'How did the northsider propose to his girlfriend? "You're wha?"'

'Sorry.' He put his arm around her shoulder, in a demonstration of solicitude. But he did not call her 'darling' or 'Anna'.

They were in his apartment again. Joe was still away. Anna had visited the apartment three times during the past few weeks. Her wish had come true. All along, the problem had been simply, as Vincy had said, that Joe was in the way. Anna had been wrong to be so suspicious.

'When is he coming back?' she asked.

'I'm not sure,' Vincy said. 'Not for a while.'

Before she was pregnant, Anna would have found this answer unsatisfactory. She would have wanted to ask for a date and a time, but would not have. However, she would have worried. A while? What did that mean? A week, a month? A year? She would have accused him of evasiveness and felt frantic.

He was evasive, but she didn't care, since she was more than evasive herself. The time had come, however, to break the news. So she had.

She had told him almost casually, as she lay in bed, relaxed as a jellyfish. The fire was not lit today – he only bothered to make a fire on that one occasion, after he had come back from Basra. But the flat was warm enough anyway without one. He had a few electric heaters. The bed floated like a white ship in the big dark room.

'But Anna … are you sure about this?'

She nodded. 'Mm, quite sure. It happened that time in my house, I'm pretty sure.'

'And …' He looked embarrassed. 'You're sure …'

She nodded again. 'We can do a DNA test when it's born if you like. But I know.'

He looked as if he might cry. 'What are we going to do?' he asked.

She pulled the duvet up around her chin. She had not known exactly how he would react, but this was not what she had anticipated.

She shrugged. 'I don't know,' she said neutrally, looking at him. Although she knew exactly, and it astonished her that he could not read her mind on this issue, he who had understood her every thought and mood so well at the start of their courtship.

He set his mouth in a hard line and looked at her accusingly.

He got out of bed and started to dress. 'I've got a meeting,' he said. 'And I suppose you need to be getting home. We can talk about it tomorrow.'

'Sure,' she said.

'Look,' he said. 'I'm sorry. It's a shock. And there isn't time to deal with it now.'

'Oh, I understand,' she said. 'Work.'

'Yes, there is work. I've to meet this Leo Kavanagh in half an hour … you know him, the fellow from Kerry.'

'Him?' Anna could not place him immediately.

'You know. Leo Kavanagh. Kate's chap.'

Kate. Not a name Anna wanted to hear at this moment.

'His lobby group, Killing Roads or whatever it is he calls it, is calling for the resignation of the Taoiseach and the Minister for Transport. One's not enough for him!'

'What?'

'As you say, what? And so what? It'll never happen. The Taoiseach! It's mad. But the story might get bigger than it is … there might be something behind it.'

'Well that's obviously more important than my baby,' said Anna. 'That there might be something behind Leo Kavanagh's crank campaign.'

He winced. 'Anna. Don't. Come around tomorrow, can you, at noon? We'll have three hours. We'll have a good talk.'

Twenty-two

Leo was not looking forward to meeting Vincy Erikson again, the man who had dumped Kate to have an affair with a married woman, the man who had been the cause of Kate's nervous breakdown. But when the production assistant from Vincy's news programme had asked Leo if he would do an interview with Vincy, he could not refuse. The publicity for the campaign would be tremendous, if they broadcast the interview.

Leo met Vincy in the atrium of the hotel, where he had met Kate last autumn during the bad time when she had been infatuated with Vincy.

'Good to see you again.' Vincy shook his hand. 'How's life?'

'Great,' said Leo, feeling a spasm of hatred rise in his stomach.

'Still living in the depths of the country?' Vincy said.

'I've been up and down more than usual,' said Leo.

'With this campaign?'

'That, mainly,' lied Leo. He could not bring himself to mention Kate's name to Vincy.

'OK, so fill me in on it,' said Vincy. 'I'll be honest, I hadn't paid much attention to the organisation until yesterday, although of course I'd known of its existence.'

'Of course,' said Leo drily. But he filled him in.

'And why are you calling for the resignation of the Minister, and the Taoiseach?' asked Vincy. 'It's a drastic demand.' He stared at Leo as if he were doing the television interview already.

'We've been campaigning quietly for a long time,' said Leo. 'As you know, there is a fuss every time the death toll is shown to rise again. The Minister comes out and makes some fussy little speech in which he blames the drivers; if pressurised enough by the likes of yourselves, he promises a few more penalty points, better enforcement. But nothing actually happens.'

'He's not the only Minister who has a bad record on this issue,' said Vincy.

'No, he's not. But his predecessor was reasonably good. He changed things. He introduced the penalty points system, which was a huge achievement in itself. He reduced the rate of carnage by twenty per cent. Then he got pushed out of his job.'

'Why does Killing Roads think that happened?'

'Who knows? Probably because he represented some kind of challenge to the leadership. Showed up the Taoiseach. He was demoted soon afterwards. Success is more dangerous than failure in this government. Maybe in all governments. Any Minister to show innovation, leadership, whatever they like to call it, gets pushed to one side.'

'It's one way of looking at it,' said Vincy. He did not take notes. 'Do you or anyone in your organisation know of any other reason why this Minister should seem to enjoy the Taoiseach's favour?'

Leo shook his head. 'No. Some people think he may know something about the Taoiseach. Some scandal.'

'Like what? Financial? Personal?'

'Like that he took some sum of money from businessmen – they all did, back in the eighties. Or something about his marriage break-up.'

'Domestic violence? Did he beat his wife up?'

Leo shrugged. 'Not that I know of.'

'No?' Vincy waited expectantly.

'No.' Leo began to get impatient. 'How would I know if he did? Why should it matter anyway? Five hundred dead bodies is important enough. We don't need some back story about thirty thousand pounds changing hands to push some re-zoning deal, do we?'

'Maybe not,' said Vincy, with a smile. He decided to finish the interview. Leo had nothing to give him. 'Thanks for talking to me and good luck with everything.'

So he wasn't going to run with it.

'It's a worthy cause,' Vincy said.

Worthy cause. Faint praise. Fuck you, thought Leo.

'Nice to meet you too,' was what he said. 'By the way, I don't
know if you've heard. I'm getting married to Kate Murphy.'

Vincy was visibly taken aback, to Leo's gratification.

'Well, I hadn't heard.' He composed himself. 'Congratulations! When is the big day?'

Leo told him.

Vincy stood up. 'Give my very best to Kate.'

Leo did not reply.

'He lost interest when he found out we had no scandal on the
Taoiseach.' Leo drank his Guinness with a wry expression on
his face.

'Incredible!' said Kate.

'The carnage is not sensational enough. Dead pedestrians,
people wrecked by grief … who cares about them? Well, obviously it's not news. Bertie taking a few thousand quid in a
brown envelope twenty-five years ago would rock the country.
Bertie killing five hundred citizens every year – ah sure, that's
just the way life is.'

'It's hardly fair to say he kills them.'

'Sins of omission. Next thing, people will be suing for compensation. Like the army deafness or the blood tribunals. Due
care was not exercised by those in a position of responsibility.
They'll be bloody right too.'

Leo was red in the face. His eyes grew wild with emotion and
he clenched his fists. Kate had never seen him like this.

She kissed him. The bar was dark and cosy, the coloured glass
bottles twinkling like lamps. People glanced at the couple and
smiled. Kate was so small and childish-looking, her looped
crescent of hair dark as a chocolate Easter egg; and although Leo
never looked exactly handsome, there was something uncannily
appealing about him in this animated state. He looked whole-
some and vigorous, like a well-groomed pony.

'You're fantastic, Leo,' she said. 'Something will happen.

You'll make something happen. You and Killing Roads.'

'Me and Killing Roads.' He looked attractive, but he felt terrible. If only Vincy had done that interview! Five minutes on prime time television would be worth a hundred protests in front of the Dáil. He sighed deeply.

'I'll help,' she said. 'I don't feel as strongly as you do about this. But I'll help … as soon as I get my wedding behind me.'

Leo ordered more drinks. My wedding. She was referring to it as her own. It wasn't exactly democratic, but it did indicate a high level of commitment. And it meant he wasn't expected to do anything about it, beyond getting the priest and the church, which was fine, since he had no intention of playing any role other than hiring an ecologically acceptable morning suit and turning up to marry her.

Killing Roads had an emergency meeting in the upstairs room of the Tower. Leo told them about his unfortunate failure to interest the media in their campaign, at which the group, with an unusual spurt of energy, resolved to hold a protest march on Leinster House the very next week, the hope being that this would capitalise on the limited publicity their letter to the newspapers calling for the double resignation of the Taoiseach and Minister had acquired.

So Leo had to stay in Dublin for the whole week, leaving Charlene to her own devices – indeed, blocking her out of his memory. Preparations for the march dominated the agenda – Kate acted as project manager; she and Leo did all the work of advertising, getting posters printed, making placards. Predictably, although most of the other members promised to come along to the march, none of them had time to help with its organisation.

Leo and Kate had to take time off to go to the second of the pre-marriage course talks.

'This is romantic, in a way,' Kate said, as they made their way to the place where the classes were held, a church hall on Whitefriar Street.

'I need to take you somewhere really romantic,' said Leo. 'Venice, or Valparaíso.'

'I'm just as happy around here,' she said. 'This part of town.

I love it.'

They were walking up from South Great George's Street. Having once been a grand street, it had fallen on hard times and for as long as Kate could remember had been derelict, its windows boarded up, its high red-bricked buildings with their Dutch gables the surprised victims of a whim of fashion or commerce that dictated that nobody shopped here any more. Lately the trend had reversed. A few shops had opened, and about a hundred restaurants. The wheel had turned. What had once seemed sad and derelict was beginning to emerge in a new light.

As one moved upwards, through Aungier Street and Whitefriar Street, that dissipated. These were still down-at-heel streets. The shops were small and tacky, old furniture stores, chippers and kebab huts. The high buildings ensured that the streets were always dark and gloomy in atmosphere.

'It's sort of medieval,' she said.

'Is it?' Leo looked at the grey stone. He couldn't place the age of these streets. They didn't look medieval to him. They belonged to the same section, really, as Stephen's Green and Grafton Street. He thought they probably were eighteenth century. Odd to think that the fashionable hub of Dublin was a stone's throw away, and here you were almost in a slum. Dublin always surprised him by its abrupt changes. One minute you were on a street where you could buy an Armani handbag for several thousand euro, and the next minute in a place where an Armani bag would be snatched from you, at knife-point, as you passed by charity shops of the less salubrious kind.

'It's authentic, in its ... sort of ugliness,' she said.

'I love you when you say things like that.' He gave her a hug.

'I hope you love me at other times as well,' she said. 'No doubt we will be given a lecture on the importance of just that. Love each other when you are old and fat and worn out.'

But they were not.

In this second session, a rather worn-out woman lectured them instead on the need to use the rhythm method of contraception, pointing out the evils and dangers of the Pill and of condoms. She told them they would be happy if they had children and brought them up in the Catholic faith. She advised them not to marry until they had a home and an income that could support children, and added, cheerfully, that romance did not last.

Leo wanted to walk out after the advice on natural birth control.

Kate restrained him, clamping his foot to the floor with hers. All around the room, young people gritted their teeth.

The hall was small, painted a cheerful yellow. It contained only one statue of the Virgin Mary, but that was a very big one, life-size. It had in fact migrated from the church next door, which had replaced its old statues with new modern ones a few years earlier.

'How can they go on teaching this stuff?' Leo said, as they walked down Aungier Street in the dark. 'It's amazing that anyone goes ahead and gets married after they've finished dis-illusioning you. Romance doesn't last. Artificial contraception can give you cancer.' (The woman had not said that, precisely, but had hinted darkly at evil consequences, other than the fires of hell, for women who took the Pill.)

'What did you expect?' Kate asked.

'I don't know. They could just ignore all that side of things. They know everyone is going to use whatever form of con-traception they like.'

'That's Church teaching.'

'You forget about it most of the time and even imagine the Church has a role in the modern world.'

'That's because you never go near a church,' said Kate, uncritically.

'I do!' said Leo, pretending to be shocked. 'I go to funerals. I go to Midnight Mass at Christmas.' He added, 'If I can manage it.'

'And weddings!' She kissed him.

'It's salutary in a way.' He brought the subject back to the issue of the role of the Church. 'At least it reminds me of what's wrong with the Church and why we have rejected it. As you say, not going is dangerous. You might imagine you're missing something.'

'Maybe you are,' said Kate. 'The spiritual dimension.'

'Poetry will have to supply that for me,' said Leo. 'What that woman is talking about is not the spiritual dimension. She's as spiritual as a Muslim telling his wife the Prophet says she has to cover her face with a veil, or else he'll kill her.'

'Now you're getting racist,' she said. 'Talking of which, will we eat in one of the nice ethnic places along here? They look like fun.' They were on South Great George's Street.

'Let's,' he said. 'Sorry to be so upset. I don't know why I care about this stuff so much.'

'You care about all stuff so much,' she said. 'That's just you, Leo. Doesn't this Mexican place look good?'

She stopped outside a restaurant that was fairly full. It was painted red, orange, yellow and purple. In the context of the austere grey street, this looked better than it sounds.

Twenty-three

'You want to marry me?' said Vincy, dumbfounded once again. Every time he met Anna now she had some new shock for him.

'Why not? After the acceptable period of separation is over,' said Anna.

They were in a bar too, in the middle of the day, in Blessington, as far away as they could go at lunchtime. Their meetings in Vincy's apartment had been suspended again, ever since Anna had dropped her bombshell, two weeks earlier. Vincy had been kind, since then, but distant. She was now two and a half months gone and her sense of a slight swelling of the stomach was not imaginary. Her waist was going; her skin was clearing. She had very little sickness. It would be an easy, healthy pregnancy, just like her last one had been.

Vincy laughed a special, dry laugh that he reserved for moments of disbelief. 'That "acceptable" period of separation, as you call it, is four years,' he said. 'That's what the courts accept.'

'I thought it was five,' said Anna, with a toss of her head. 'So you're saying you don't want to marry me, in four, or five, years' time?'

'I'm not saying anything of the kind,' said Vincy, sighing. 'But … we have to think about this. You're married to Alex; you've got a child already.'

'That's my problem,' she said. 'I will get shared custody, at the very least. I might be able to make a case for complete custody.'

Vincy looked even more worried. Would he have to take in Rory as well? 'Could you?' he asked desperately.

'Alex is not much of a father. He's always at work. He hardly even sees Rory. And there are other mitigating factors.'

Vincy took her hand and squeezed it. He glanced at the clock, which took the form of a wrought-iron cartwheel on the wall over the bar.

'It sounds good,' he said, in a voice that made it sound like a prison sentence. 'But let's give it very serious thought. Don't do anything hasty.' He looked over his shoulder, at the window behind him. 'You haven't told Alex yet?'

'No,' said Anna. 'And soon I won't have to. He's not blind. Or stupid.'

Although she often said he was both of these things, now she believed what she was saying.

'There is still time,' said Vincy in a tense tone, looking over his shoulder again like a spy in a thriller.

'To have it aborted?' She looked at him coldly.

He withdrew his hand. 'Well, it is an option,' he said.

'Thank you for reminding me,' she said.

'Look, Anna.' He took her hand again and spoke warmly. 'I really do love you. You know that. But I think you are being a tiny bit unreasonable. And unrealistic.'

She shut her eyes.

'You didn't warn me that this might happen, you know. We were … having a wonderful time. We were so lucky, Anna. It was different. It was special.'

She saw herself in the snug of the Tower, clutching his hand when the barman wasn't looking. She smelt the roasting beef from the carvery. The beer. Her hand in his, under cover of the tablecloth, if there was one.

She saw herself on the big tossed bed in his shadowy room.

If she had an abortion, would he let her back into that bed again? Would he let her back into that room again?

Would he?

'We can go back there,' she said. 'The baby won't make any difference.' But babies always make a difference, she knew.

'I love you. I adore you.' She meant what she said.

'Oh darling!' He squeezed her hand again. 'Let's meet in a few days and talk about it again. We'll find a way.' He jumped up. 'Anyway, I've got to go. I've a meeting.'

Before she could say anything, he was kissing her on the forehead, he was loping across to the door, as quickly as a wolf. Her hand was still hovering over the red plush dent where until a second ago he had been sitting.

Ludmilla was the first at home to notice that Anna was pregnant.

She eyed her waistline meaningfully when Anna was handing over her money on Friday. 'Are you well?' she asked, in her foreign accent. Some foreign accents sound innocent and childish. Ludmilla had the kind that sounded like a scientist who does evil experiments in Batman movies. She always seemed to know more than she let on.

'Yes thank you,' said Anna. Ludmilla continued to smile insolently at her, even though she had got her packet and should be heading off down the hill on her rickety bicycle. Anna screwed up her eyes. 'Considering my condition.'

'Oh!' said Ludmilla, taken aback.

'Yes,' said Anna. 'You know what it is. So now, if you don't mind, I have work to do. Have a nice weekend!'

Ludmilla said 'Humph', or some version of it which required no translation, and swaggered off.

Before Anna could savour even a second of triumph, the telephone rang.

It was somebody called Sharon, who wanted to speak to the telephone account payer.

Anna said, 'I'm sorry, there is nobody of that profession here' – a formula she had evolved and one that left the unfortunate telesales assistant speechless, giving her a chance to replace the receiver. As always, she felt guilty for doing this – she knew the people who worked as telesales assistants were poor and underpaid and forced to do the worst job in the world, by all accounts. But she did not feel guilty enough to change her telephone company every two days, which was apparently what the employers of the telesales people believed people like her would do, if talked to persuasively enough.

As soon as she put the receiver down it rang again.

They usually did not ring twice, in the same half-hour, but perhaps there was a new tack? Telephone torture.

'Hello,' said Anna crossly.

'Anna,' said Elizabeth. Her very confident ringing voice was down a key. She did not expect authors to be cross.

'Gosh,' said Anna. 'Elizabeth! Hello. How are you?'

'That's better!' Elizabeth tended to be mildly patronising. 'First of all, I'm really sorry it's taken so long to get back to you. I have been so busy, you would not believe!'

'I understand,' said Anna neutrally.

'My mother has been ill,' she said.

'I'm sorry to hear that,' said Anna, thinking, it's none of my business. 'I hope she's all right.'

'She died,' said Elizabeth sadly.

'Oh dear, I'm very sorry,' said Anna guiltily. 'I hadn't heard.'

'I only got around to reading the chapters you sent me of *Sally and the Ship of Dreams* last week,' Elizabeth said in a colder tone, implying that Anna was a brute.

This is one of those liminal moments, Anna was thinking. Elizabeth could say something that will be either wonderful and make my day, make my year. Or she could do the very opposite. In a few seconds I could be ecstatic or in despair. Not *could*. Will be.

The strange thing was that she had no real way of predicting which it would be. You would think, at this point in her career, she should know. She had read and written enough books. She always knew very quickly what was wrong or right with everyone else's. Oddly, this power of judgement could not be transferred to her own work.

'Well!' There was a fateful pause, timed to let Anna's hopes drop slightly before anything had to be said. 'The narrative has a lot of good aspects.'

Anna allowed herself to hope, stupidly, since she knew what was coming. But there was still a moment between having the worst news confirmed and hoping for the best news. She was, just for another second or two, on the fence separating the great from the terrible.

'But I have to be honest.' Why? Why do you have to be

honest, you cluck? There were lots of awful books out there, the shops were full of them. Would one more do so much harm? 'I don't love it enough to take it on.'

Don't love it enough? For God's sake. Do they have to use this patronising chick-lit jargon all the time, even to writers, the people who are least likely to tolerate bullshit? I know the English language, Anna wanted to scream. Keep those dreadful clichés for the readers, or the press – although she doubted if anyone would be taken in by them, or even find it possible to hear them without wincing in pain.

'Why?' Anna asked, although she knew this was a word they hated.

Sure enough, Elizabeth paused again. This time the silence was more hostile than the first one. When she spoke, her tone had changed. All the warmth, insincere as it had been, had left it. She was brisk and businesslike.

'I could have sent you a letter, but I decided it would be more considerate to talk on the phone.'

Now I'm supposed to be grateful to her for this, Anna thought. For being so considerate as to actually make a phone call. 'Thank you,' she said sarcastically.

Elizabeth had a professional immunity to sarcasm. Like a mother who ignores her child's sulking, she moved right on. Eat up your cabbage.

'You are a wonderful writer, Anna, one of the best I know.' Exactly. 'But this does not do you justice. It's derivative. It's repetitive. It's … it's dull … need I go on?'

'Please do.'

In a mood even marginally better than that into which she had sunk, Anna might have liked to hear more reasons for this reaction to her work, or she might have liked to force Elizabeth to suffer the painful effort of coming up with a catalogue of synonyms for 'bad'.

'Listen, Anna,' said Elizabeth, in an intimate but firm tone, indicating her intention to finish the conversation. 'My advice is, abandon it. Throw it in the bin. Take a break and then start afresh on something else.'

'Will you be interested in that? Will you …?'

'Have to fly. I've a call waiting. Bye, Anna, bye, see you soon. Bye-ee!'

She hung up.

Call ended.

Anna put her phone back on the receiver, slowly slotting it into its cradle, as if attention to the minor routines would now save her from … screaming, crying, breaking the window.

Two years' work. Or was it one? She'd been doing it for ages anyway.

Throw it in the bin.

It was probably good advice. But she decided not to take it.

'So how is the novel going?' Anita asked brightly.

They were at a launch in a very small bookshop in Temple Bar. This was one of the few independently owned bookshops left in the city. It was the kind of shop that held launches for new poets, first-time short-story writers, or people who had written an imaginative pamphlet about saving the environment. It was the sort of shop that went as far as to stock Leo Kavanagh's publications; Kambele Ngole's new collection was on the shelves, and a small portrait of Kambele on the wall. They didn't charge for the use of the premises as long as they could sell the books at the launch. The hope of the owner of the shop, an idealistic woman with long black hair and pink cheeks, always dressed in a black T-shirt and purple skirt, was to develop a niche market, to make her bookshop a place of character and refinement, to supply discerning readers with the kind of shop they used to love before the international giants colonised the book trade. The shop had survived for two years and everyone hoped it was now secure.

Christine, fed up with rejection slips, had abandoned not just the conglomerates, but every commercial publisher and published her first collection of poetry herself. She had taken a desktop publishing course and here was the result: *The Witches of Walkinstown*. Bound in a plain yellow cover with the title and her name, and the title of the press she had 'founded' – Acorn Press – printed in Gothic lettering on it. The Gothic font was the only concession to decoration she had been able to afford. 'It looks great,' everyone said, thinking, did you ever see such a shoddy production? And it was not cheap. Fifteen euro, the price of any properly produced poetry collection. Christine hoped to cover her costs and romp home with a small profit.

That is how impractical she was.

The aisle of the little shop was crammed with women writers, and a few men (Christine's husband, brother, and two sons, all together in a corner and looking uncomfortable). For everyone else present this was a comfortable, a pleasant, occasion, where everyone knew everyone else and felt at ease. The women liked to be amongst women. Literary women. Women who loved to write and women who loved to read. Women who had published ten books, women who had published one, women who had been working on a collection of poems or short stories for the past ten years, or who had won a prize in Listowel in 1988, or who were members of a writing group and had long ago given up on their ambition to publish, stood around sipping red wine and chatting animatedly to one another, about the books they were reading, the illnesses they were suffering, and what their children were doing with their lives. They talked about poems and novels. They gave one another tips for losing weight – 'Don't eat bread' – or for storing fruit.

'You should never put bananas on top of a fruit bowl,' Anna had been told by a novelist, before she started talking to Anita. 'They make the other fruit rot.'

'I never knew that,' she said, troubled. She always put bananas on top of everything else in the fruit bowl.

'It's true,' the novelist nodded sagely. 'You should hang them up. Or' – noticing Anna's consternation, as she wondered where she could hang her bananas – 'put them in their own bowl.'

'I must remember that,' said Anna.

At another launch, this woman had told her that the best way to cook salmon was to put it in the dishwasher 'in loads and loads of tinfoil. Comes out perfect.'

'Have you read the Thomas Hardy biography?' the woman added, without pausing.

Now that woman was engaged in conversation elsewhere and Anna was being interrogated by Anita.

'Oh, my novel is doing fine,' said Anna. She had no intention of revealing the sad state of her literary affairs to anyone. She was at ease, but not a fool.

'When will it be published?' Anita was not one to give up easily. There was a mischievous glint in her dark eyes.

'Next year,' Anna lied.

Lilian, who had joined them, glanced at her quickly. 'That's great news,' she said. 'I thought it was very good, the bit of it I read. You must have written a lot more by now.'

'Yes,' said Anna. 'It's almost finished. I have to rewrite it and polish it off but it shouldn't take too long.'

'Good,' said Lilian, although a slight furrow appeared in her forehead. 'So it should be finished in a week or two?'

'Well, maybe a month or two.' Anna laughed. 'Or ten or eleven! You know yourself.'

'Oh yes,' said Lilian, the frown smoothing out as she smiled.

'So that's three books in a year from … *us*!' Anita said in an enigmatic tone, which could have been happy or irritated.

'Three?' asked Anna.

'Christine's, yours, and Lilian's,' said Anita.

'Oh?' Anna looked at Lilian questioningly. 'I didn't know you had one due!'

'I have,' Lilian said, in a somewhat apologetic tone of voice. She looked troubled, probably because she disliked revealing good news when others might not be so lucky. 'I didn't say much about it, I hadn't any real hope that anything would come of it. But now …'

'Something has,' finished Anna. 'That's fantastic,' she added. 'What is it?'

'Oh, just a little thing, a short novel. A sort of novella really.'

'And who is publishing it?' Anna asked. She could have asked a more pertinent question – the one which had passed through her mind, fleetingly, but which she had dismissed. That question was 'What is it about?'. Anna had a bad habit of hopping over the first question that came to mind, which was usually the most crucial one, and asking the next one, which was often un-important.

'I don't want to say that right now,' said Lilian. 'My agent is still negotiating, so it could be one of two. I'm sorry to be so mysterious but you know how it is.' She smiled conspiratorially.

'Of course,' said Anna. So Lilian had an agent and her book was being auctioned. 'It sounds as if you've hit the jackpot!'

Lilian smiled wanly. 'Fingers crossed. I've been through the mill. But, yes, things are looking good at the minute.'

'I *will* keep my fingers crossed,' said Anna warmly.

'I appreciate that, Anna,' said Lilian. She smiled and moved away to join another group.

Anna enjoyed herself at the launch, and afterwards joined a group of the women for an Italian meal in a restaurant on the quays, where they chatted on in the same vein as in the shop, about their books and their children and their houses and their illnesses.

Nobody asked if she were pregnant.

But everybody noticed that she was.

Twenty-four

Anna's house was such that some of its habitual residents rarely met. Rory and Alex, for instance, hardly ever encountered Ludmilla, who came after they had left for school and work and was gone by lunchtime. Luz Mar sometimes met Ludmilla, if she were not at class, but did not often meet Alex, since she was officially free most nights from six o'clock, and went off with her friends before he got home. Anna, and the cat, were the only members of the household who were in daily contact with all its other members.

She knew the chances of Ludmilla mentioning her pregnancy to Alex were very slight, not because Ludmilla would not like to mention such a thing, from feelings of delicacy or loyalty. She was neither delicate nor likely to be loyal to Anna. But she would never get an opportunity. She never talked to Alex because he was never there at the same time as her. And if she did encounter him, it was unlikely that she would immediately take the opportunity to discuss his wife's pregnancy with him.

Telling Ludmilla, then, had really put Anna under no particular pressure to reveal her condition to Alex. But nevertheless it was very soon after her disclosure to the house-cleaner that she decided to let him in on the secret.

Alex had been working even harder than usual since Christmas. He was finalising another important property deal;

261

Anna was uninterested in the finer details, but knew that he had sold off almost all his equity and was sinking everything into a new venture, an entire block of apartments in one of the new south Dublin suburbs, which, although not top of the market at present, were predicted to rise exponentially in value, since the area had been designated one of the new transport hubs of the city: close to the DART, the proposed Luas extension, and the M50. Around such hubs, the new satellite dormitory suburbs – even Alex would not abuse the language by calling them towns – were going to mushroom in the next phase of development. So they said in the property supplements.

Anna did not know why it took so long to sell some buildings and buy others. But it did. Alex was not lying. He worked sixteen hours a day, telephoning people and writing letters and signing forms and seeing lawyers. It was not the sort of work someone like Anna, who usually saw a product for her labours, could really appreciate. In the end, of course, Alex would see a product: money. (The apartments were not a product, in his view, they were a means to an end. They could have been anything, trucks or animals or works of art or shops or hotels. They were apartments not because he felt people should have new and better apartments, but merely because new apartments were now the most profitable investment for any businessman.) But for long stretches he lost money, gambled money, and saw nothing for his efforts except his own weariness.

He came home at about nine o'clock now, usually, an hour after Rory had gone, disappointed, to bed. The first thing Alex always did was to go upstairs and look in on Rory, and give him a kiss. Since Rory was asleep, it didn't register with him, at least not consciously, but it comforted Alex. He missed his son more than he missed Anna, and every night had to console himself with the thought that they would meet at breakfast and perhaps he would give Rory a lift to school – although in practice the latter part of the arrangement seldom materialised, since Alex always had to leave earlier than Rory needed to.

Anna had prepared a decent dinner, something she had not bothered doing since Christmas. They were having prawns Marie Rose, an old-fashioned starter that was Alex's favourite, and *coq au vin*, the sort of hearty French peasant dish Anna liked: cooking it, smelling it, eating it, made her feel she was in

Provence, not in Killiney. She had cooked it for six hours, so that it was a delicious, disintegrating mess by now. There was even a home-made dessert: fruit salad. As a rule, Anna was too lazy to chop up all the fruit but today she had made a special effort.

A chilled Chablis accompanied this meal. She allowed herself a glass, although she recalled that when she had been expecting Rory, she had never drunk any alcohol. She was not sure that she could force herself to be so abstemious this time round. It seemed to her that alcohol had become much more a part of everyday life than it had been even eight years ago. Now Alex would think it strange if they did not have wine with dinner every day, whereas then it had been a weekend treat, or something you had on a special occasion. This was how it was in the Kelly Sweeney house anyway, though, like sex, or quarrels with your spouse, you could never know for sure if your private customs were the same as most other people's, or if they were unique or unusual. And there were still questions you could not ask, even at the book clubs or the writers' groups.

She had placed a vase of white freesias on the table, and filled the house with daffodils. They were at their peak and her garden had thousands. Into vases she had crammed thirty or forty at a time, so the house had, she felt, a cheery, fertile air. Matching her condition.

She waited until they had almost finished the main course to tell him. She did not want to waste the *coq au vin* – she had had a craving for it for days. During the meal, they had talked about Rory and his progress. He had joined a local football club and was enthusiastic about the game. He was having some problems with spelling and Anna was wondering if, like Ultan, he had become a bit dyslexic. She thought perhaps they should see a specialist.

'But he used to be a champion speller,' Alex objected.

'Yes,' said Anna. 'He used to be. But that's changed in the last few months, for some reason.'

'I don't think he could have become dyslexic in the last few months,' said Alex. 'I don't think that can happen to anyone. There must be something else wrong. I don't know. I hardly ever see him these days.'

He sighed, thinking of all the work he had to do. He never

liked to talk much about what went on there but he told her something about the problems he was encountering: one of the banks was causing difficulties about loans because the project was delayed; he had had to apply elsewhere for a loan to replace the problematic one, and the interest rate was unacceptably high. But not to worry, everything would sort itself out soon, he said. There were always hiccups during a transition period like this.

He was always in transition, though, Anna thought. As soon as one project was finished, the money pocketed, he would move on to another one.

He was considering resigning from the two arts boards he was on, he said then, to her surprise. They were taking up too much of his time or else he was missing meetings, which made him feel guilty.

'But you enjoy those, so much,' Anna said, remembering how he had liked going to Áras an Uachtaráin.

'Yes, sometimes,' he admitted. 'But I take them seriously, which I know is a mistake. I hate to see the messing around that goes on. All the pointless bureaucracy.'

'Well, you probably help them to do less than they would otherwise.'

'Not really. Everything will all go on happening no matter what I say,' he said. 'I'm on those boards really to be a sort of financial adviser, I know it. But they never take my advice. They do their own thing no matter what.'

'There's always a bit of wastage, I suppose, everywhere,' she said.

'More in this country than most places,' he said. 'There's a culture of carelessness. But I'm not going to change it.'

'They admire you for trying,' she said.

He drank some wine. 'I'm not so sure.' But he looked pleased. She hardly ever complimented him on anything.

This was the moment she chose to deliver her bombshell.

'Alex, I have something to tell you,' she said.

He put down his glass. His face was set, implacable. He was still wearing his dark-grey work suit and snow-white shirt, which made him look invulnerable, as if he were dressed in a suit of armour, but strangely fragile as well.

'What is it?' he asked, in a thin voice.

She felt frightened and for a second wished she could

withdraw her statement. There was still time to have an abortion. But she could not think of anything to say now except the truth.

'I'm pregnant.'

She waited. She had no idea what would happen next.

He got up, came across to her side of the table, and kissed her. His face was relaxed, wreathed in smiles. 'That's fantastic,' he said.

'Em …' She patted his head.

'When is it due?' he asked.

'September,' she said. Would he be able to calculate?

'So you are three months gone,' he said. 'And I never noticed a thing. I'm so unobservant.'

'Yes,' she said. 'You are sometimes.'

Chekhov came to the glass door and she got up to let him in. But Alex forced her to stay seated and opened the door instead. He even got the cat food from the fridge and filled the cat dish.

'Stay where you are,' he said. 'You must feel tired. Are you … OK? Have you seen the doctor?'

So she carried on the conversation any couple would have about their latest pregnancy. Doctors, tests, gender, reaction of Rory, were all discussed lovingly by Alex, for whom this was the best news he could possibly have imagined.

Now she had two fathers for one baby.

Twenty-five

About three hundred people gathered outside the GPO, which was where the marchers gathered, on Saturday. Leo addressed them briefly, thanking them for coming and advising them of the route. He would talk again when they were handing in their petition at Leinster House.

The protesters, waving placards bearing slogans such as 'Stop the Carnage', 'Killer Taoiseach Resign!', 'STOP Minister!', made their way along the well-trodden route: over O'Connell Bridge, down D'Olier Street and around by Trinity up to Kildare Street. How many groups had marched this route before, since the foundation of the state? Leo remembered the enormous march against the dismissal of the Irish Ferries workers and the foreign workforce being paid low rates, which had taken place just a couple of months earlier. Tens of thousands had marched in protest. He could not understand why so few people had turned out for their march, which was about something much more important, a life and death issue if ever there was one.

'This won't set the world on fire!' he said glumly.

'It's not a bad response,' Kate said. She was so cheerful now that nothing could upset her. Snugly wrapped up in a red anorak and woolly hat, big fur mittens on her hands, she felt the event was a success. Three hundred people. A few weeks ago Leo would have been lucky to get three. 'The Irish Ferries thing was different. All the unions were involved, so it had a completely different structure. This is a success.'

Leo was not convinced. His heart was heavy, as he marched along, at the head of the little group. The air of 'Roddy McCorley' kept running through his mind, depressing him. Roddy McCorley is going to die on the bridge of Toome today.

Kate began to shout slogans, leading the troop.

'End the carnage now!' she roared through the loud-hailer.

They took it up.

'Stop the Killing Roads!'

The shouts echoed through the streets. It was a fine cold day and sound carried well on the clear air. The wind blew from the east, driving the river into a frenzy of electric blue ripples. Seagulls wheeled overhead. 'End the carnage,' they seemed to scream, as they circled and looked at the crowd. 'Stop the Killing Roads!'

On Westmoreland Street pedestrians halted to look at the marchers.

'End the killing!' shouted Kate. 'No more death!'

Some pedestrians drifted into the group of protesters.

'Join in!' shouted Kate. 'March on Leinster House! Tell them you want an end to the killing!'

A miracle happened.

More and more people moved from the footpath to the road, and joined the marchers. This continued to happen as they moved around College Green and along Nassau Street. By the time they were on Kildare Street, the group had grown from three hundred to three thousand. They milled around the gate of Leinster House, and flowed back all the length of Molesworth Street.

Gardaí appeared as if by magic and began to redirect traffic.

Cars hooted angrily, adding to the noise and attracting more people to the protest group.

Kate immediately telephoned the newspapers, RTÉ and BBC.

By the time Leo was on his box in front of the railings of Leinster House, the cameras had arrived.

'By Monday, three young men will be dead. Three other people, any age from one day to one hundred, will be in their coffins, cut down on Irish roads,' he started, in his low, intense voice. He went on, for six minutes, describing the history of

267

carnage, the lack of political will to change anything, and ended by calling for the resignation of the Minister for Transport.

'He is a killer. He does not go out and shoot people but he facilitates murder, every day of the week. He blames the motorists. He blames the cars. He blames the roads. He blames everything but the one person who is to blame: himself. One person has to have responsibility. One person has to be accountable. The Minister. He has reneged on this duty. He is presiding over a culture of death. We call for his resignation. We also call for the resignation of the Taoiseach, who as leader of the government is ultimately responsible for the institutionalised apathy on this issue. We beg the government to tackle this issue and to stop the death. It can be done. They have to do it.'

The roars of acclamation for Leo, the call for the resignation of the Taoiseach, could be heard everywhere within a radius of half a mile or more. Shoppers on Grafton Street heard them. Children feeding the ducks in the Green heard them. Lovers kissing in the shady corners of Merrion Square heard them. Students moving across Front Square in Trinity heard them.

But the Taoiseach did not hear them, because he was away at a conference in Europe, and the Minister did not hear them, because he was in his constituency far away in the country, where he topped the poll at every election. Even though he was a bad Minister for Transport, he was a very good local representative, and the people of his constituency had received large amounts of government funding for their roads, their industries, their schools, ever since he had got into office.

And thousands of young drivers drove happily, untested, unlicensed, in his constituency as in every other constituency all over Ireland. Thousands of publicans made money selling alcohol to drivers who would go out and drive home, secure in the knowledge that no policeman would ever check them. Millions of motorists speeded, broke red lights, didn't bother getting the National Car Test, knowing they were safe from inspection.

The government's ineffectualness was useful to a lot of people.

Which the Minister and the Taoiseach knew.

Which was why, when they opened the Sunday newspaper the next day, they were surprised, but not unduly worried.

One of the people who had joined the protest march was Gerry Kelly. He had been walking along Nassau Street towards the railway station when Leo and Kate and the parade came along. Recognising them, he moved over and said hello. Next thing, he was marching along too, shouting 'Stop the Killing Roads!' with the rest of the mob.

Afterwards he had a drink with Leo and Kate in a hotel on Molesworth Street. This was the first time he had met them since their engagement, so they drank champagne.

'Olwen is very chuffed about it,' he said.

'You'll both come to the wedding?' Kate asked.

'We will indeed,' said Gerry.

'Great!' Leo said.

'The two of you must come out to see us sometime,' Gerry said. 'Olwen would love to meet you, Leo. She's always going on about how good you've been for Kate.'

Kate and Leo froze perceptibly.

'I mean … well you know what I mean,' blundered Gerry. 'You were so ill and now you're so well. And happy. And looking like … like a ripe apple.'

'Hm,' said Leo, softening.

'We'll be sure to come and see you,' said Kate. 'It's great that you're back together again.'

It came as an unpleasant surprise to Gerry to know that Olwen had revealed to Kate they'd been apart. But he didn't let it show. 'Ah sure,' he said. 'We all have our ups and downs. That's married life. As you'll soon find out.'

Kate and Leo smiled at one another in amusement, perfectly confident that their married life would have no ups and downs. Theirs was going to be the perfect marriage of minds, bodies and lives. Of this they were absolutely certain.

Leo had a triumphant weekend.

The Killing Roads protest featured in all the Sunday newspapers. Photos of the march as it reached Leinster House were widely published, as were snaps of Leo on the soap box. His words were quoted and misquoted everywhere. He was not interviewed live, since most journalists were taking the weekend off and preferred news that happened on weekdays. But Kate assured him that he would be inundated with phone calls on Monday morning.

On Saturday night, four young men were killed in a two-car collision on the N11 near Wexford.

Another man was fatally injured when his car struck a wall at one in the morning just outside Tralee.

On Sunday evening, a seventy-year-old woman was struck by a lorry when crossing the road in Moate and killed instantly.

On Sunday night, two men and a woman were killed and one woman seriously injured when their car collided with a bus on the Dublin–Sligo road.

It was a normal weekend in the Irish countryside.

The corpses of badgers, foxes, cats and crows littered the motorways. They were never taken away; eventually they would become splats of blood and mashed-up bone on the concrete or tarmacadam, and later still would disappear entirely.

The human corpses were removed within hours of being killed; all that remained of them would be a few bunches of flowers, placed by sad relatives on the side of the road near the scene of the death. Those flowers would also wither and disappear, sooner than the animal carcasses. They would melt back into the timeless ditches of bramble and meadowsweet and alder, and leave as little trace as the human tragedy seemed to leave on the collective consciousness.

Nobody even raised an eyebrow, hearing that these nine people who had been alive when The Enemies of the Killing Roads were marching on Leinster House on Saturday afternoon were dead by Monday morning.

'The toll is worse than usual,' said Kate. 'Good news for Killing Roads!'

Leo said nothing. 'Too long a sacrifice may make a stone of the heart,' he was thinking. Not of his. Every time he heard of a new killing his hair stood on end. His body grew cold, he shivered uncontrollably. Every time. This was the one thing he could not inure himself to. That Kate was light-hearted about the latest accidents did not shock him, but he could never be light-hearted about them himself. Every killing reminded him. The knock on the door, the two guards standing there with solemn, embarrassed faces. The mangled remains of his parents in the mortuary in Portlaoise hospital – they had crashed on the N7.

For most people, human death on the roads was as non-consequential as the death of a rat, the withering of a buttercup, thought Leo. It was accepted as if it were as ordinary and natural as any fatality from natural causes. Death by car crash, people seemed to believe, was as outside human control as death from old age, or an incurable disease.

But he mourned for the dead, as he did every time he heard about these accidents. Angrily, he mourned, and sadly. He could see the wrecked cars. He could see the wrecked bodies, the torn-apart limbs, the blood streaming from the broken brains, the eyes tumbling onto the roadside. He could feel the agony of the last moments of those whom the newscasters said had been 'killed instantly'.

Hardly anybody was killed instantly. Most died in agony. Terrible agony.

His mother and father had.

First he had been told, by those poor policemen who knocked on his front door, that his parents had been killed instantly. But later he found out that this had not been the case at all. Someone had revealed the truth to him some time after the funeral. A nurse from the hospital, who had not known who he was. She told him his father had lived for two hours, and his mother for four. 'It is like a crucifixion,' she said. 'It's often like that.'

They didn't tell you that on the news.

The bloody weekend was indeed good news for Killing Roads, as Kate had anticipated. On Monday the phone was hopping. Leo was contacted by several reporters. He was interviewed briefly on *Morning Ireland* and on the one o'clock news on the radio, and asked to appear on the panel of *Questions and Answers* on Monday night. The Minister had been invited but had been unable to attend and was represented by a Junior Minister from some other government department. The question 'Should the Taoiseach and the Minister for Transport resign?' was asked from the audience. Leo was invited to respond first. He made his usual points: cited the dreadful statistics, noted that the Irish death toll was twice as high as any other northern European country; stated that the situation could be changed radically if some simple measures, based on easily available templates from

271

Sweden, Denmark, the UK, were introduced: proper driving training, lower speed limits on country roads, random breathalysing, and implementation by a Garda traffic corps.

'It's not rocket science!' he said with a smile. 'We don't even have to think about what needs to be done. All we need to do is copy the countries that are doing a better job than us, which is almost every country in the First World that you can think of. We just need to do it.'

The Junior Minister defended the government's reputation and, as usual, listed the various steps that had been taken and the changes that would be made very soon.

'You're always talking about changes that will be made very soon,' Leo interrupted, throwing up his hands in genuine annoyance.

'Wait a minute, I didn't interrupt you,' said the Junior Minister, looking righteously indignant.

They must get lessons in how to look aggrieved and put upon, thought Leo. They can all do it so well.

'As I was saying before I was interrupted,' the Junior Minister said smugly, 'the truth is that finally the responsibility rests with the individual motorist. If we all decide to slow down, to go five kilometres slower, never to drink and drive, the problem will be solved.'

The audience applauded and the Junior Minister smiled, pleased with himself.

'Are you saying,' John Bowman, the programme presenter, asked, his eyes twinkling disarmingly, 'that the government has no role to play in reducing deaths on the road?'

The Junior Minister looked horrified at this wilful misinterpretation of his point of view. He blustered. 'I'm not saying that at all. Of course the government has a role. Of course it has a role and it is playing that role well. But I am saying that all the laws in the world won't stop the deaths unless the individual motorist takes individual responsibility.'

'Especially if the laws are never enforced,' Leo butted in.

'I didn't interrupt you,' said the Junior Minister. 'I didn't interrupt you. We have introduced penalty points, a strategy is in place to speed up the driver testing process so that we won't in a year or two have so many learner drivers on the roads – '

'A hundred and forty thousand,' said Leo darkly.

John Bowman shot him a warning glance.

The Junior Minister did not deign to respond but went right on. 'We have banned the use of hand-held mobile phones in cars; we are introducing random breath testing.'

'So you're saying enough is being done?' said John Bowman. He turned to the panellist who was representing the opposition, a Labour Party TD. 'Do you agree? Enough is being done?'

The TD lowered her head as if preparing to head-butt somebody and then tossed it back and spoke in quick confident tones. 'I agree that a certain amount has been done but a lot more needs to be done. I agree with Leo and I'd like to take this opportunity of congratulating him and his organisation, The .... The ... The ...'

'Enemies of the Killing Roads,' said the presenter quickly, reading it from his script.

'Yes, Enemies of the Killing Roads,' repeated the TD, 'on doing such a great job in highlighting this problem, which has dogged us for so long and which has, I think we have to acknowledge, now reached a crisis point of kinds. We need to put strong policies in place and make sure they are implemented.'

'So you're satisfied that the government is doing all that is necessary?'

She seemed to take time to think.

'The government has been slow to respond to the crisis,' she said.

'So has your party,' said Leo.

She smiled and shook her head disapprovingly. 'The Labour Party has had a road safety policy in place for the past ten years,' she said. 'We advocate the abolishing of unaccompanied learner drivers, the introduction of random breath-testing, the enforcement of use of seat belts. It's nonsense to say that we have been slow to respond to the crisis.'

'Is it?' John Bowman turned to Leo.

'No opposition party has made any strong statement relating to the road carnage,' he said. 'It could easily be turned into a political issue but this has never happened. For some very strange reason the opposition has maintained an uncanny silence on this issue. They seem to accept, like the government, that it is completely outside their control, that ten dead bodies every Monday morning is a natural event, like death by old age.'

The Labour TD was looking very angry. 'That is absolute nonsense. We have had a road safety policy on our agenda for ten years. We have demanded the introduction of random breath-testing – '

'Yes, you said that before,' said John Bowman. He turned again to Leo. 'So you think the opposition is also at fault? Why are they so silent on this issue?'

Leo shrugged. 'Vested interests,' he said. 'I don't know what they are. Maybe all politicians are bad drivers themselves.'

'Maybe they're all learner drivers,' John Bowman laughed. 'Well there we'll have to leave it, I'm afraid, it's time for a commercial break. Don't go away. More questions after the break.'

Twenty-six

'Alex is happy about it,' said Anna.

She and Vincy were in an oriental art café in the centre of the city. These days, neither of them felt like trekking out of town to have lunch. It no longer mattered to Anna whether people saw them together or not – she wanted the relationship to be out in the open. There was, however, a tacit understanding between them that they were in some sort of transition – Anna assumed that the end of this period would find her and Vincy living together. Vincy did not know what he wanted.

They were sitting at the back of the restaurant area, which was reasonably private. It was a quiet day; not all that many people lunched out on Tuesdays.

'So he thinks …' Vincy looked up from his couscous.

'Yes,' said Anna. 'He insists on pretending to himself that the baby is his.'

'And you are really sure that that is impossible? I'm sorry …' Vincy said.

'Do you want a DNA test?' she asked, irritated. She knew the answer, since it was not the first time she had proposed the question. Vincy felt it would be ignoble to demand such a test.

'Of course not,' he said, just as she had expected. What he wanted was for it never to have happened. He wanted to go back to square one. He wanted what was impossible – to move back in time to a place before Anna, where he had never met her, where he would make another choice entirely.

Anna was drinking sparkling water and eating noodles; they did very good noodles in this little restaurant, which was oriental in the broadest sense: a bit of Chinese, a bit of Indian, a bit of the Middle East. The decor was soothing, soft blues and willow patterns. Perhaps she would call the child an oriental name? Ling or Lu or Li, one of those short, pretty names? Or some nature name, Snow or Rain or Peach, such as the Japanese often used. She was hoping for a girl. She knew, in her heart, that she was carrying a girl.

While she was thinking of names, Vincy was thinking about abortion. Anna could tell. His face was drawn. He had, abruptly, had his hair cut very short, and now he looked even younger, and more slight and vulnerable than ever before, without his wild mop of hair. His feelings showed more plainly on his newly exposed face. Anna felt a sudden pang of deep solicitude for him, as if he were a child who needed protection. But she said what she had planned to say.

'I'm going to tell Alex the truth,' she said. 'That it's yours.'

He started.

'Take your time,' he said. 'Think it all through before you do anything.'

'Vincy,' she said firmly. He looked nervously around the café. 'I am carrying your child. I am in love with you. Being with you has made me happier than I have ever been.' That bit was in the past tense. Since she had told him about the baby, being with him often made her miserable. She was miserable now. Nothing was developing as she had hoped it would. 'Being in love with you has been my taste of heaven on earth.' She looked at the mosaics on the walls, copied from the Alhambra and the Alcazar and Byzantine palaces. 'I don't expect more of human life, of my life. I don't expect to get that chance of happiness again, in my life.'

Vincy looked bewildered. He had been in love with Anna. He was still fond of her but the pregnancy had changed everything for him. It amazed him that she could not understand that. They had been so happy as they were. They had been playing, outside the restrictions of adult life. They had been liberated, they had been free. Now Anna had changed all that. It had not been enough for her. She had acted like a free spirit, but in fact she was deeply conventional and ordinary. That, and illogical.

Happiness was what she had been after. But when happiness came her way, she wasn't content with it. Something in her could not simply take it for what it was worth, play with the butterfly on the wing. Instead, she needed to pin it down in a glass case, imprison it in convention. She was in one unhappy marriage and now she wanted to exchange that for another one.

What was wrong with having an affair for your whole life if you felt like it? Like people in France. Or the aristocracy at any time in history. Ordinary Irish people were now aristocrats, in a sense, Vincy believed, and they should be learning to behave in kind. You could have true love without the nuisance of marriage, or living together. He was inclined to believe that that might be the only way to have true love in the long term.

He did not express any of these views to Anna.

'I don't know what to say,' he said neutrally. 'I love you too. I accept that you are going to have my baby. It just takes a bit of time to get used to the idea.'

'I want the baby. *And* I want you. Both of you,' Anna said. 'I don't want you for lunch, I want you all the time. Weekdays and nights and weekends and holidays.' Vincy paled. 'I want to live with you as your partner, or wife, whatever it can be. Commitment, is what I want.'

Commitment. It is such a cliché, Vincy thought. And being a man who does not want to commit is such a cliché too. Was he really such a man? The common villain of every popular romance, the man who wants to run away? Not really. He did not want to commit to marriage, to settling down into what seemed to him the essence of dullness and the end of romantic love. He had been committed to Anna, though. He had loved her and the relationship they had been having before she changed. Before the pregnancy. He had been committed to romance. That was what characterised him. Commitment to love, to life, to fun.

How odd that he had not formulated this important keystone to his moral and philosophical life until this moment, this moment when he had to accept that, willy-nilly, he was going to be a father in six months. That he already *was* a father. How could it have come to this? How could he not have known himself until now?

He never said, once, to Anna, 'You cheated me.'

He never thought it, for more than a split second. Cheated.

He would have liked to take comfort in thinking that Anna was unbalanced. Taking this outrageous step, abandoning her wealthy husband, her secure lifestyle, her son, for him, surely indicated a certain lack of common sense? But he knew she was not unbalanced. Not very.

'Well,' he said, taking her hand and looking at her with love of a kind in his eyes. He abandoned good sense. He plunged into recklessness, almost for the hell of it. 'We'll do it.' There was only one thing to say. 'Will you marry me?'

'Yes,' she said, smiling.

Vincy let go of her hand because a waitress was passing the table. 'That's settled then.'

'Yes,' she said, looking dreamily at the large refrigerator that stood at the back wall, filled with small bottles of juice and water and wine. She wondered why she was not feeling happy, now that she had got exactly what she had longed for. She looked at Vincy, at his face, fresh as an apple right now. He wore a white shirt in some soft cotton material: she had transformed a wolf into a lamb.

'Let's not say anything for a while,' Vincy said, wondering what the steps would be. 'Leave it with me and I'll think it through. We have to find a resolution that works for everyone, especially Rory.'

'Yes, of course,' said Anna. Peace flew across the room like a golden nightingale and landed in her lap.

She relaxed. She told herself that everything was perfect now. She was going to have Vincy's baby, and she and Vincy were going to live together openly, and get married at some stage. He was even thinking about Rory.

Twenty-seven

Iraq.

The war had been officially over for more than a year but the peace did not seem different from war. Every night the news reported bombings, burnings, shootings, and atrocities. Baghdad, Basra, Mosul were household names. Even Rory knew them, although he did not know exactly where they were. All together somewhere in that desert country called Iraq.

For as long as he could remember, Rory had been hearing about Iraq; 9/11 he did not remember. He had been three when it happened, and he had seen it on television, but it had made no impact on his memory. Iraq he did not associate with 9/11. He did not associate it with anything, but took it as a fact, like the suburb where he lived or the existence of his parents, or the fact that they had a four-wheel drive, a house with four bathrooms, and a lot of money in their family stocks and shares, money that was stashed away for his future. (Now he would be sharing it with Butterfly, or Peach, but he had not been told about the new arrival, as yet. For some reason, Anna found that it was much harder to break the news to Rory than it had been to tell Alex about it.)

Now Iraq was about to threaten his destiny in a way that nobody could have foreseen.

An Irish journalist was taken hostage.

Journalists and aid workers had been taken hostage many times before. A woman who had been born in Ireland and had held an Irish passport, although she was really English, everyone said, had been captured in Iraq some time ago – who could remember exactly when? 2003, or 2004? The Minister for Foreign Affairs had been over there talking, trying to get her released. But he had not succeeded. She was beheaded.

Rory had been six then. He could remember that woman's face. She had looked a bit like a much older version of Anna, that is why he had noticed it. The story of her death had terrified him, because he could see Anna's head, dripping blood, detached from her body.

Margaret was the woman's name. He remembered that too.

But now a real Irish person, a woman who was a freelance journalist and who reported for various international television channels, a young, and, it was said, immensely talented woman with an amazing future before her, had been taken hostage. There was some connection between the kidnapping and a furore that was sweeping the Muslim world after the publication of anti-Islamic cartoons in an obscure Danish newspaper. Sorcha Toomey was the kidnapped woman's name. She was twenty-seven; she had been in Iraq for a few months and her face was familiar to most people in Ireland, since she appeared frequently on the news, describing bombings and atrocities in a voice that was unusual – genuinely concerned and sad, as if she had never become accustomed to the tragedy of the situation.

Rory looked at pictures of Sorcha on television. She did not look like the other woman, Margaret. Sorcha had fair hair, long, to her shoulders, and looked more like Luz Mar, his au pair, than his mother. Rory wondered how they would deal with the hair when they were chopping off her head. Would they slice through it, or would they tie it up in a ponytail, or would they cut it first at the hairdressers and then decapitate her?

He hardly knew whether he hoped they would behead her or not. He knew that people hoped she would come home safe and sound, and he would in a way like that as well, although he did not know her and could not remember ever having seen her on television before now. But he would also like to know how they would deal with the hair and what her head would look like, separated from her body.

It had not been a clever move by the Iraqis to capture a woman like Sorcha, or anyone at all, given the mood of the Western world – it was bathed in abject guilt about the foolish Danes, for whom nobody seemed to have a good word to say, the right to freedom of expression having been completely forgotten, it seemed, in the rush to conciliate the offended world of Islam, who were quite understandably threatening to kill every Dane in sight, and who had already succeeded in banishing that absurd people from a dozen countries in the world, and moreover doing their best to wreck their economy. That should teach them to draw cartoons!

'It was different when Salman Rushdie wrote *The Satanic Verses*,' said Anna thoughtfully. 'Our President and the rest of the world weren't running to sympathise with the Islamic fundamentalists then. Everybody was on his side. But now it's the opposite.'

'It is different, isn't it?' Vincy was with her. They were having lunch. Their routines had not changed, although they were now planning to find a place and move in together. 'The Dane was not one of them, for a start, like Rushdie was. And the situation is more volatile now.'

'And the Dane wasn't a famous Booker prize-winner, just an unknown cartoonist,' said Anna. 'Freedom of artistic expression is different, if you're famous?'

'It's about the situation,' said Vincy. 'It's all different now, so values change.'

'Basically we are afraid to open our mouths in case a fundamentalist kills us if we offend them,' said Anna. 'That's the difference. Give in to the bullies.'

Vincy had something to tell Anna.

'I've to go out there,' he said. 'To report on Sorcha.'

Anna was dumbfounded.

It was May. She was more than halfway through her pregnancy. She had still not told Alex that he was not the father or that she was going to leave him and ask for a divorce. Vincy had decided they should move in together later in the summer. He was looking for a place to live, a place that would be suitable for them and a baby. A little house, somewhere. Anna had decided that she would tell everyone what was happening when this place had been acquired and they were about to move in.

Now he was going to Iraq.

'But why? You said the last time you'd never do it again.'

'They've specially requested that I do it.' He could not disguise his pride in himself. They wanted him to take on this key post. 'And' – he shrugged – 'I want to. It won't be for long, necessarily.'

'Not unless they kidnap you too,' said Anna flatly. Her voice began to break up. Tears filled her eyes.

'Anna!' He took her hand. 'What is this? I'll be back in a few weeks. Everything will be fine. I'll phone every night.'

'When are you going?'

'Tomorrow,' he said guiltily.

'Tomorrow?' she repeated stupidly. The dark walls of the pub they were in seemed to swim away from her and she thought she might faint.

'It's urgent,' he said, still guiltily. He had deliberately postponed telling her until the last minute; he had even flirted with the attractive notion of not telling her at all until he was actually over there.

'Don't go!' she said desperately. 'Tell them you're expecting a child. What happens if you don't get back before the birth?'

'I will. It's not due for months.'

'I'll feel terrified if you are not here.' She started to cry.

They were hidden behind a palm tree but in a place where voices carried easily.

Vincy patted her on the shoulder. 'Do you want to come back to the flat for a bit?'

Anna knew she was being humoured. He was offering her sex to shut her up. But she agreed, and went with him.

And the next day he went to Iraq.

The whole nation knew it. It was announced on the main evening news and Vincy was interviewed by a reporter who was probably delighted not to have to go out there himself.

Anna got up at six o'clock the following morning, the morning he was flying out. She walked over to the window. The sun was already well up over the horizon, about half an hour, maybe an hour up. It hung what looked like a yard or two over the rim of the sea, an impossibly bright disc, and cast onto the water a path of brilliant orange-golden light. How did it do that? A straight road about a yard wide dissected the sea from horizon to the shore – how long was that distance? Miles, twenty or thirty miles, half the Irish Sea, *mare nostra*, although we never call it that, was traversed by this miraculous golden road.

This was the sort of thing you saw if you got up early enough, the things that usually only the milkman got to see – she could hear his truck trundling around the corner, already leaving.

Then more roads appeared, in the pure, blemish-free blue of the sky, blemish-free until the white track of an airplane dissected it. She glanced at her watch. Five past six. Vincy could be on that plane, going across the sea, in a south-easterly direction. But less than a minute later another white track began to draw itself across the azure, a few feet, so it seemed from her viewpoint, under the first. And a minute or two later yet another. From five past six until six thirty, fifteen planes crossed the skyline, each one leaving a fluffy trail in its wake. Sometimes the trails seemed to intersect and Anna held her breath, waiting for an explosion, a conflagration, another ball of fire in the eastern sky. But her perspective gave her a false impression of what was going on, a sense that large distances were small. Nothing happened.

At about half past six the planes stopped coming.

The Saturday morning planes, charters more than likely, so probably he was not on one; he would leave later when the scheduled flights started. These were the charters bringing their passengers to Spain and Portugal, Greece and Turkey, down to the south, the land of holidays, where, Anna felt, she would not want to go this year, or any year for a long time to come.

By now her pregnancy was very obvious, and her friends were suspicious about the parentage of the baby. Like Alex, they pretended it was his. But unlike Alex, who had buried his head in the sand for months, assiduously ignoring every obvious sign that his wife was unfaithful, they knew she had a lover. The affair that Vincy and Anna had imagined was such a carefully cherished secret was common knowledge around town. They had been seen on innumerable occasions, even in the pubs and cafés they believed were so removed from the haunts of their social circle as to be invisible. The affair had been delighting gossips for months. And now that Anna was pregnant they had even more to speculate about. Would Anna leave Alex? Would Alex force her to leave? How did Vincy feel about all this?

He had gone to Iraq. Odd, the gossips said. Why had he done that? To get away from the situation at home, some suspected. He wanted out, and no wonder. He would never come back to Anna. She would be stuck with Alex and the life she had already. Or, another view went, Alex would find out what was going on – how could he not know? – and throw her out. Serve her right too.

Other people took a kinder view of Vincy and Anna. They believed that he had gone to the danger zone in order to make a lot of money, so he would be able to afford to get a house for Anna and the baby.

Some thought Alex would have to give Anna half his money and property and others believed that he would not have to give her anything, if they got divorced. Nobody was very sure how it worked, divorce was still so new. 'No fault divorce' was a phrase that was tossed around, at the launches and over lunches, but nobody was sure what it really meant.

'It means Anna gets half the loot, even though she's the one who dumped Alex,' Anita said, laughing.

'Mm,' murmured Lilian. 'It may work out differently. It's a complex law, I've been told.'

They all waited to see what would happen. It was not often that such a dramatic story occurred in real life, in Dublin's literary circles. It was not often that a tale of passion and betrayal, the stuff of soap opera, played itself out before their eyes, on the public stage.

The day after Vincy went to Iraq, Anna told Rory about the new baby.

'Did you notice I was pregnant?' she asked. They were at the Natural History Museum on Sunday afternoon.

'No, I didn't,' he said. He was examining a stuffed python in a glass case. 'Did they have them here once?' he asked, pointing at the snake.

Anna wasn't sure. 'Maybe,' she said. 'St Patrick is supposed to have banished the snakes from Ireland, so they must have been

284

here before that.' She read the caption. This snake had come from Africa.

'Who's St Patrick?' asked Rory.

'Hm,' said Anna. 'You must have heard of him. You know St Patrick's Day? When we go to the parade?'

Rory nodded.

'The saint we commemorate is St Patrick. He lived in the fifth century.' Didn't they teach them anything at that school? 'I'll get you a book about him,' she said. 'But feel this.' She returned to the original topic of conversation, took his hand and placed it on her belly. 'See how big I am.'

He felt hurriedly and pulled away his hand. 'Is it a boy or a girl?' he asked.

Anna didn't know. She explained that she could find out but had decided not to, which was something Rory could not understand.

'But you will find out in the end anyway,' he said.

'I know.' Anna wondered why she did not want to know, for sure, in advance, even though she felt she was carrying a girl. Maybe she wanted the satisfaction of being proved right, in her instinct, at the moment of birth? It would add an extra sense of achievement to the event. But waiting for the birth to discover the sex was childish – just a hankering after the past, when you just did not know, just as you would not have known if it had spina bifida or was retarded or whatever. Now you could discover all these aspects much much earlier – you could pop over to England and have an abortion if something awful was the matter. Heidi, a poet she knew, had done that two years ago. She had had no hesitation. 'I could just about manage a healthy child and work and write my poetry,' she said. 'There's no way I could handle a child with a serious handicap. How could I? How can anyone? Everyone knows the services are not there and nobody is going to come along and pay the mortgage.' She was a civil servant of some kind and her husband was a teacher. By Anna's standards they were poor. She was in a different boat. She could afford any kind of child or any number of children, as long as she was married to Alex.

'Do you see that elephant?' said Rory. He left the snake behind and they moved on to the mammoth. 'He's rusty on one side. See? All rusty?'

'So he is,' said Anna.

The stuffed elephant wasn't rusty, but something had happened to its skin. It had become mouldy on the side nearest the wall.

'Can I get an elephant on the way out?' he asked. 'They have them in that shop at the door.'

'Sure,' said Anna. She knew she should not give him absolutely everything he asked for but it was so much easier than having a fight.

They moved along, and looked at stoats, weasels and otters, tastefully arranged in a woodland setting.

Once he had found out that Anna did not know whether she was carrying a boy or a girl, he seemed to be completely uninterested in the prospect of his new sibling.

Vincy phoned every night for the first three nights. He reassured her that everything was fine, that he was safe and that he loved her. The phone calls were very short. The details of what he was doing professionally she could see on the news; every night he filed a report, and spoke to the camera, telling the nation what was happening.

In the middle of his first week out the phone calls stopped.

After four days, she phoned him.

'Are you OK?' she asked pointlessly. She knew quite well how he was, because she saw him on the news every night, looking great in khaki shorts and a T-shirt, his crew cut and clean-shaven face cool-looking, already nicely tanned. She did not nag him about not telephoning and he didn't offer any excuse. No doubt he had already forgotten his promise to call every night. 'I worry about you. How is it going?' she said.

'It's awful,' he said. 'You can see it yourself, on television. But you don't feel the heat. A lot of the time it's just a bore, sitting in the hotel room, trying to make contact, but at least there's air conditioning. As you know, there is stalemate on the Sorcha thing.'

'When are you coming back?' Anna asked, unable to conceal a catch in her voice.

'As soon as I can. I miss you. How are you?' His voice became soft and caring, an intimate, gentle voice that was completely different from the voice he used on television, a voice reserved for her.

She melted. She felt selfish and guilty, for not really caring about how he was, for not caring at all about poor Sorcha Toomey, imprisoned in some dark hot room, not knowing what was going to happen to her. She had been thinking only of herself and her own petty needs.

She told him she was fine, if his query referred to her physical well-being. Which it did.

Twenty-eight

Dingle Bay was a bright sapphire in its nest of green hills. The candy-coloured houses of the town revelled in the warm sunshine; they seemed to be singing. Tourists in summer glad clothes, sunhats and sunglasses, sauntered up and down the little lanes.

And in front of the church on the steep slope of Green Street the wedding guests were gathering. They spilled out from the footpath onto the road, in their pastel silks and flowery hats. Their chatter rose into the blue sky, and joined the voices of the rooks, the seagulls, the starlings who sailed like flocks of black cinders behind the spire of the church.

Anna and Alex were among the guests, as were Gerry and Olwen. Olwen was not matron of honour, however. Kate had chosen her partner at work, Lauren, as a bridesmaid. Leo didn't really have a close friend – Paul, the friend who usually invited him to spend Christmas with him at his cottage in Clare, was as close a friend as he'd got, oddly enough. But Paul, inspired by his Christmas visit to South Africa was at present doing a round-the-world trip, facilitated by a windfall inheritance from an aunt (that that kind of aunt still existed came as news to Leo). When Paul, texting from China, regretted that he could not do the job, Leo had wanted to ask John Perry, the *bête noire* of Killing Roads. He had thought it might do him good. But, like most people, Kate had taken a dislike to John, so Leo had ended up inviting the young poet from the valley, Tristan, to be his best man.

Olwen was dressed in a red linen dress and a black picture hat. She looked stunning until you noticed her face, which had a weary expression. Gerry was as cheerful and full of bonhomie as always.

'*You're* looking well anyhow!' said Olwen to Anna.

Gerry gave her a warning glance.

'Thank you,' said Anna politely. 'So are you!'

Olwen grimaced. She had not seen Anna in months, although Anna had had lunch with Gerry a few times. Anna suspected he was having a fling with another young woman, this time a girl in his office. He was incorrigible. Olwen seemed to have decided to put up with it all, for the sake of the children and the house. She was not averse to playing the role of martyr, either, or holding the superior moral ground.

'And how is Alex?' Olwen turned a pitying smile on him, a smile that told the world, this is the poor cuckold.

Even Alex, insensitive as he was to nuances, felt uncomfortable. '*Alex*,' he said with emphasis, 'is also very well. Will we go inside, dear?' He began to push Anna towards the door.

'Honestly, the cheek,' said Olwen, while they were in earshot.

'Shut up, Olwen,' said Gerry unceremoniously. 'She is my sister.'

'Don't I know it,' said Olwen. The wedding had not even started and she was on the verge of a nervous fit. 'I really can't believe that that whore would come here.'

'She got an invitation and probably didn't like to refuse. Kate always liked Anna.'

'Yeah right. That was before she cheated on her husband.' She was almost shouting, making sure everyone could hear.

'Olwen!' He was alarmed. 'You shut up right now or I am going to walk away from here and leave you on your own. Do you get it?'

'Oh for God's sake,' said Olwen, tossing her head so that her hat fell off.

Gerry kindly picked it up and placed it back on her head. 'You look a picture,' he said. 'Or you would if you could stop bitching. It's bad for your complexion. Let Alex and Anna sort out their own problems. Try to concentrate on Kate. It's her day. God knows she deserves it.'

'Just out of the looney bin,' said Olwen.

'With a sister like you, is it surprising?' said Gerry in a low voice to himself.

Leo was just arriving, driven by his best man, dressed in an almost black suit made of some homespun cloth of indeterminate description. Probably a mixture of wool, which was plentiful around here, and some other local product. Nettles, possibly, or straw. Feathers? It looked ecological and, in so far as such a thing could, suited Leo. He had a flower in his buttonhole, a red rose, which Charlene had given him from a bush she had managed to grow in the windswept garden. She would not come to the wedding, although it was partly thanks to her that it was taking place. Nor did she say what her more long-term plans were.

Leo had explained, tactfully, that Kate would come back with him to live in the house. Without handing her an eviction notice, he had given the strongest possible hint that it was time for Charlene to move on. But, as usual, she had seemed impervious to hints. She had just smiled her big, dotty smile, fiddled with the pink bow in her hair, and said she would make sure the place was nice and clean for Kate.

Leo, who had got so used to Charlene that he could hardly imagine life without her, was still waiting for the right moment to tell Kate about her. He imagined he would explain that she was a live-in housekeeper – and in a way she was. In the old days she would have been perfectly acceptable, the sort of ancient retainer who might have once been Leo's nanny and had stayed on, forever. A family slave. Today was probably not going to be the right day, he thought, as he stepped out of Tristan's battered old car: Kate had wanted him to come in a limousine, or at least a decent taxi, but Leo had refused. 'I hate that kind of thing,' he said. 'I'll be nervous enough anyway.'

But he wasn't nervous at all, now, just curious and delighted. He looked at the cheerfully coloured cluster of guests crowding the entrance to the grey chapel and smiled at them. On the other side of the street, just opposite, crowds of strangers had gathered, tourists and Saturday shoppers, to look at the wedding party. Leo had often stood there himself, with his shopping bag at his feet, in front of the bakery on a hot Saturday afternoon, to observe, sometimes wistfully, the wedding of an unknown couple. Weddings on sunny Saturdays had evolved into a form of public entertainment in the little town. Now he was the one putting on the show, one of the main performers in the afternoon's tableau. He looked across the street again, at the sea of happy faces: everyone liked a wedding. He smiled at his audience graciously, like a king. It would have been great to give them something – a blessing, or a shower of flowers. Suddenly he remembered hearing about an old custom, the grush, whereby a bridegroom threw a big handful of coins to the crowd in celebration of his good fortune. He shoved his hand into the pocket of his homespun suit but there were no coins there. Of course not. He had never worn this jacket before. In his breast pocket he could feel his wallet sitting snugly, flat as a pancake, containing his passport, two plane tickets, and his credit cards. He couldn't throw his credit cards at the crowd, so he contented himself with waving brightly at them. To his gratification they cheered loudly. The whole street resounded with hurrahs.

Then the bride arrived. Down the steep hill of the street she came, her father by her side, in a horse-drawn vehicle.

Leo stared in astonishment. The vehicle was a sort of caleche, black with enormous red wheels. It was pulled by a big docile chestnut bay, his coat groomed until it shone, and his traces decorated with white rosettes.

Olwen nudged Gerry. 'Tell him to go inside. He should be inside.'

Gerry ignored her. But Tristan, who knew the etiquette of weddings, reminded Leo that he should hurry up to the altar rails and be there to meet Kate when she came up the aisle.

'A horse and carriage!' Leo groaned. 'She didn't tell me. Will I have to go through the town in that?'

'Well, you don't like cars,' said Tristan, pushing him through the door. 'You should be grateful.'

'It must have been her mother's idea,' said Leo.

'You can be sure,' said Tristan soothingly. 'Mothers love things like that. Old age must have its fling.'

Olwen and Gerry followed Leo into the church. The big grey place, like the inside of an upside down ship, was almost full – clever guests had come in early, to take the best seats near the altar. The peculiar grey light with which almost all churches are

291

filled was brightened by the colourful dresses of the women, and the lingering smell of candle grease and incense mixed with the myriad rich perfumes they wore. It was an OK church, Gerry decided, not more than that. There were Harry Clarke windows nearby in the Convent of Mercy cloister, but nothing as classy here. Just a run of the mill, post-Famine, small town church, big enough to hold about four hundred people, plentifully stocked with late nineteenth-century plaster-cast statues – and why despise them? thought Gerry. They were getting old now, just like all religious art, and had a charm of their own. The church was also plentifully stocked with twenty-first-century wedding guests. In Ireland at this particular moment, that meant men in some sort of suit, any sort of suit, and women in very fine dresses made of silk or satin, pink and mint and lilac, and very large and very dramatic hats. Olwen, in her red linen and black straw, was understated by comparison with the other female guests.

'Lots of style here!' he whispered, to restore the relationship, to his wife.

'A national treasure assembled under one roof,' she said.

She was still staring at Anna. Six months gone now, Anna could hardly aspire to be stylish, but she was. Her dress was one of those hey-look-at-my-bump! styles, tight everywhere, designed to emphasise the pregnancy rather than disguise it. It was snow white and skintight. Around her shoulders she wore a small fur stole, and on her head an elephant. A small white elephant, clearly designed and made for her by Philip what's-his-name, the famous hat designer who had had an exhibition in the National Museum recently. Treacy, that's it. Philip Treacy. Brazenly on the arm of her husband, pregnant with the child of that chap who had dumped Kate and pushed her over the edge and had now gone off to Iraq to show off on the nine o'clock news to the nation. With any luck he'd be beheaded. Of course, they never got the ones you'd like to see tortured and murdered but probably only decent people who had done no harm to anyone in their lives.

Leo and Tristan took their places at the altar rails in the nick of time. Minutes later Kate and her father entered, and the organ erupted into a rousing rendition of the 'Wedding March', filling the church with its robust golden notes.

Kate and her father processed up the aisle.

'She looks tired,' Olwen said to Gerry.

'The dress drains her,' Anna whispered to Alex.

'She is not at her best,' someone else said. 'All the fuss before-hand can tire the bride out. It's a thing I've noticed.'

But to Leo she looked perfect. He kissed her quickly on the cheek when she arrived, smiling, beside him, at the top of the church.

'You are beautiful,' he said.

She was dressed in a simple white frock, which had cost four thousand euro and had been designed by one of the reigning fashion queens of the day. Her wreath of lily of the valley had been made by herself with flowers from her parents' garden, and she carried a small bunch of the same fragrant flowers in her hand. She thought Leo would appreciate these flowers and their scent, and that was true.

When Leo saw her little childish face, circled by the white flowers and her dark hair, his love for her overflowed. He longed more than anything for all this fuss to be over so they could be alone together, in his house, and their real life, his real life, could start at last.

But there was a great deal of fuss to be got through before that happened.

The hotel in which the reception was held was on the shore of Dingle Bay; its dining room opened onto smooth lawns running down to the water's edge. You could see the fishing boats and the boats bringing people out to look at the dolphin, and the big house where Lord Ventry had once lived and which was now a boarding school for girls nestling in spreading chestnut trees across the rippling water.

That is what Anna could see from the window of her bedroom when she woke up the next morning. Like most of the guests at the wedding, she and Alex had stayed in the hotel. Leo and Kate had remained there until midnight and then moved to another hotel in the town. Leo would have to spend almost three weeks in Italy before the real life he longed for would begin. Already when Anna got up, he and Kate were at the airport near Tralee, waiting for their plane.

Alex was not in the room. It was ten o'clock, so she assumed he had gone for a walk.

Olwen had continued to be unpleasant the night before. She had made it clear to Anna that she knew all about her affair with Vincy, and had treated her with a cold rudeness, staring at Anna's bump whenever she could with an insolent look. Kate had been kindness itself; she seemed genuinely delighted that Anna had come to the wedding and if she had once borne resentment towards her, she didn't show it. Even this made Anna feel uneasy. Kate pitied her, she could see that. Some instinct gave her an insight into Anna's situation that even Anna herself did not have. Kate could see clearly that now she was perfectly happy, and that Anna was very unhappy. Kate, who had seemed, and believed herself, to have lost everything, and who had envied Anna so much, was now triumphant. Anna, beautiful and stylish as ever, had lost the sparkle she used to have. She was not the centre of attention, the person everyone wanted to talk to and be with.

At the wedding, people had avoided her. Nobody was as rude as Olwen, but many gave her curious looks, and did not bother even saying hello to her. Without saying a word, they had let her know that they were aware of what was going on. And there was no sympathy for her. They knew Vincy was in Iraq, they saw she was pregnant, but they hated her. The adulteress: there was no place for her in their view of the world. Cheating men were laughed about but tolerated: the unfaithful man was an accepted type, well represented in soap operas, popular literature, the tabloid newspapers. Possibly well represented in every town and suburb of Ireland. Women were the unwilling victims, the heroic martyrs, of the adultery stories. That was the woman's role. Olwen was playing the right part. The women the philandering men cheated with were not in the stories or the tabloids – they were outsiders, incidental to the real action.

Anna had made the mistake of playing the wrong role. Alex should have been cheating on her; she should have been wringing her hands in righteous indignation, bemoaning the stupidity and shallowness of men. But here she was, as bad as any of them, as driven by selfish lust, putting her own happiness before her husband's or her child's. Flaunting it.

The guests at the wedding did not analyse what they felt about Anna. But they knew she was not someone they should be friendly with. There were few moral rules in the world they inhabited, but although they could not articulate it, they knew that Anna had broken one of them. She had stepped outside the woman's place. She had let the side down. She was behaving like a man. Like Gerry, her brother. They could forgive Gerry, because he conformed to type; but they could not forgive her, because she did the opposite, throwing everything into confusion.

Anna did not feel like going down for breakfast without Alex to protect her. The thought of sitting alone in the bright sunny dining room with its doors opening to the sea terrified her. But she forced herself to go down. She was not going to be bullied by these small-minded people, with their outmoded hypocritical morality. It was not a crime to fall in love. She had loved as none of them ever had, probably, as few people ever did. She had had a true passion and those cold shoulders were caused by envy, as much as by anything else. The group wanted her to conform to their own low standards – to live a humdrum life, where great love had no place. What did she care for that? It would have been a crime, a crime against herself, a crime against everything that was best and most transcendent in life, not to love Vincy. Her love had been courageous and noble. It had not been a low lust that overwhelmed her, but a deliberate choice. From the beginning she knew it would be difficult but she had decided to accept it, to live it.

She went down.

The dining room was full. Everyone had slept late, after the reception which, for most, had gone on until one in the morning. Now they were eating big breakfasts before going home, some by car, many flying back to Dublin from the local airport. They were all casually dressed today, in pale linen garments and fresh cottons. The room was full of summer colours and the sound of cheerfully chattering voices.

'I'm afraid it's full at the moment, madam,' said the waitress. 'Would you like to wait? Or would you like to share a table?'

Anna knew many of the people here only slightly, and did not particularly want to join any of them. She was about to say she would wait when she saw Alex, sitting by the window with Olwen and Gerry.

'I see my husband over there, actually,' she said, very glad to have done so. 'I'll join him.'

295

She walked across the room, treading carefully, her bump quite prominent in her close-fitting black T-shirt and white leggings. Gerry was making some joke and the three of them were laughing as she arrived.

'Good morning!' she said, smiling brightly at all of them. 'You should have woken me up, Alex!'

Gerry said good morning.

Olwen stood up. 'We're just finished and we have to get back to Dublin,' she said icily but loudly, so that many could hear. 'If you'll excuse us. Goodbye, Alex.'

She walked away, not saying a word to Anna.

Gerry shrugged. 'Don't mind her,' he said, kissing Anna. 'She's ... you know how she is. She gets like this.'

Anna could not speak. She motioned Gerry to go away. Dismayed, he did.

Alex stared gloomily at Anna, who was crying silently. 'Try to pull yourself together,' he said. 'Don't make a show of us in front of all these people.'

With a great effort, she drank some tea and collected herself enough to stop crying. She kept her eyes on the sea. The boats were making their way out to the dolphin, the seagulls were wheeling in the blue sky. A seal flipped out of the sea suddenly, swam a few yards in the sunshine, then sliced back through the black skin of the water and disappeared.

She promised herself to telephone Vincy as soon as she got back to her room, and to tell him they had to find a house soon. This situation could not continue.

'You poor thing,' said Vincy. 'It's unbelievable that anyone could behave like that.'

'Please come home,' said Anna. 'I need you. I really need you.'

'I know, darling. Look, I will try, but to be honest there is no realistic chance of that happening for at least a month.'

A month would bring them into August. The baby was due at the beginning of September.

'A month? You've already been there for ages. I thought it was all going to be over in two weeks.'

'Sorcha is still a prisoner.'

'Who knows how long she'll be a prisoner? They could hold her for any length of time.'

'Yes. They could.'

'You mean, you will stay there. No matter how long it goes on for?'

'I don't know. It depends. Look, I have to go now, my driver is waiting. I'll phone tonight.'

'Please, Vincy!'

'Bye.'

He did not say, 'I love you.'

She tried to tell Alex the whole truth, as they drove back to Dublin after the wedding. She began by telling him about Vincy, that she had fallen in love with him. But Alex did not want to know.

'I don't want to talk about this,' he said. 'Not now.'

He was driving, but that was not what he meant. What he meant was that he never wanted to talk about it. What he meant was that he knew all this already, had probably known for ages, but did not want to acknowledge it. As long as he turned a blind eye, it didn't matter.

Penetrating Alex's carapace of denial would not be easy. She sighed and looked disconsolately at her bump, highlighted by the car seat belt. Once he had decided on a course of action, or of inaction, very little could ever dislodge him from it. And he had apparently decided not to accept that Anna had a lover, that Anna was unfaithful. He would do everything in his power to deflect any attempt made by her or anyone else to disabuse him.

The road was not busy, since they had left before noon. He sped along, high above the tarmac, through the smiling landscape. The ditches were heavy with cow parsley and mustard. The grass gleamed with the luminosity of summer, the trees were a clear, deep green.

'Alex, you know what is happening. You know what has happened.'

She could not bring herself to say the words that were in her mouth. I am in love with Vincy Erikson. I am carrying his child, not yours. When she tried to say them, they translated themselves into these vague generalities. Alex refused to understand. It was as if she were speaking a foreign language.

'It is all fine as long as you are adult and discreet. Please think of Rory.'

'I do not understand you,' Anna said.

'No,' said Alex quietly. 'I know you don't.'

They were somewhere in County Laois, passing through a little town that seemed untouched by modern times. How could anyone bear to live in such a place, Anna thought, looking at the little shops, the tiny terraced houses with dirty windows, the café called the Hideaway, like something left over from 1960. Did anyone really live here? What did they do all day? And night?

He had to stop at a set of traffic lights. He used the opportunity to look at her. 'But even if you don't understand me, you can consider me,' he said. 'I have feelings too. You have a responsibility to me too.'

Anna's heart sank. 'Yes,' said Anna. 'I know.'

She had responsibilities for everyone's happiness. For Alex's and Rory's and the baby's. For Vincy's. But, she felt, feeling a wave of pity for herself, nobody was responsible for her happiness, except herself. Another name on the long list.

Alex knew the baby was Vincy's and he did not care. All he wanted was a quiet life. He wanted her to stay with him and live a lie, for his own sake.

She hated him, for pressing her to do this. She hated him for not getting angry and throwing her out. She hated him because he was so dependent on her, because he was calling that dependence love.

Twenty-nine

By the time their honeymoon in Italy was over, Leo had told Kate almost everything about himself, at least almost everything that he could remember and considered of any interest or significance: his childhood in a Dublin suburb; the hard time he had received in the school yard from cooler, quicker classmates; the terrible car crash that had killed both his parents when he was twenty-one, which had plunged him into a long, violent depression, much worse – he believed – than any she had gone through. He had told her about his suicide attempt, his drug overdoses, the incredible squalor in which he had lived. He revealed what he had never told anyone before, that he had been diagnosed as a manic-depressive and instructed to stay on medication for his entire life. And then his moment of triumph: his decision not to be a manic-depressive, his decision to change. Once he sold the family house in Dublin and moved to the country, to the valley, and started again, there was no more depression, or medication.

He told how he had fallen in love with the saxophone when he was sixteen, after seeing a television documentary on the history of jazz, and forced his mother to buy him one. For three years he played it for three or four hours a day. The whole neighbourhood became familiar with his favourite pieces – 'My Favourite Things', 'Night in Tunisia'. Then, suddenly, he stopped playing, because he realised that he would never be as good as Charlie Parker. He told her trivial things as well. How he had hated every vegetable that grows until he came to Kerry and became a vegetarian. About his childhood friends. To her, he had opened up. There had been, in that easy conversation, a great sense of release for him. It was as if he had been storing up his story, his biography, for the past thirty-six years, and now at last he had found a sympathetic listener, and out it had all spilled.

Maybe that was what love meant, he wondered aloud. She allowed him to define himself, in all his triviality, by listening to his story?

And she told him hers, but with less enthusiasm, with fewer details: she was used to talking about herself, was one reason, and another was that she did not believe there was so much to tell. She tended to summarise, to brush over years at a stretch. Whereas Leo, when he got going, seemed to have a photographic memory for the detail of his life. It was not that he remembered every day – whole years he had forgotten entirely. But when he could focus on one incident, he recalled every aspect of it.

There was one thing he pushed out of his memory, however, and did not tell Kate about.

Charlene.

He remembered her as they were queuing for the check-in desk at the airport.

In Lucca and Pisa and Sienna, Charlene had seemed like an unimportant detail, not worth mentioning. But as the plane moved over the clouds and came closer to Ireland, her significance increased, gradually, and then, as they neared home, exponentially.

By the time they were on the small plane from Dublin to Farranfore, Charlene had become the most important fact in Leo's life. She loomed, a giant, smiling scarecrow, over him and Kate. He could see her from the sky, soaring up from the field in front of his house like some supernatural goddess.

Why had he said nothing until now?

Charlene had never moved out. Leo himself had been away so much that it had not seemed to matter that she was there – once he had got used to her, he liked the idea of the house being occupied, looked after, while he was in Dublin. Coming home to a warm fire, home-baked bread and a pot of soup was much better than rattling into a cold, dark house. Then there were the reading lessons – Charlene's own excuse for staying on. She had made great progress, and now could read in both English and Irish. They had moved on from *Noddy and Tessie Bear* to *Coral Island* and the Roald Dahl books – Leo had his childhood favourites on a special shelf. He had taught Charlene to read Irish using his valuable collection of Reics Carlo paperbacks. By now she could read perfectly, most of the time. She had an unusual affliction, however. She still lapsed into illiteracy on occasion.

'This used to happen to me more often,' she said, on the odd days when, out of the blue, the marks on the pages reverted to meaninglessness.

'It's weird,' he said. 'It's nothing to do with your reading ability. You read as well as anyone. It's more like sporadic deafness or blindness or something.'

'Yes,' smiled Charlene blithely.

He wondered what was happening when these periods of blankness occurred – he assumed she was worrying about her horrible husband, or some time of trauma, which blocked her ability to read. 'It's as if you move from one world to another,' he said.

'Yes,' she agreed, looking at the huge sky over the island and the ocean.

'We should bring you to see a psychiatrist,' he said.

Her face darkened.

'Just for an hour,' he said.

But they hadn't done that. Charlene didn't want to go any-where. She liked to stay in the house. Sometimes she sat in the garden, or worked on the vegetable patch in the field, and on rare occasions she walked in the mountains behind the house. But she never went to town, or to the pub, or to the church. She lay low. The only people with whom she had contact, as far as Leo could make out, were the men who drove the vans from house to house once a week: the vegetable van, the grocery van, the baker. Stacey had met Charlene a few times but didn't know she lived in the house.

But she did. She still did. Charlene would be in the kitchen when Leo brought Kate home. She – Kate – would find it incredible. What would she do? Walk out immediately? Start looking for a divorce before she had even started married life? She would think he was crazy.

He got the courage to break the news when they were flying over Tipperary, about a quarter of an hour from their landing place. Kate was looking down at a bright patchwork quilt of green fields and golden fields. She was thinking that Ireland was a beautiful country, even if it did not have as many breathtaking hill towns as Italy. She was feeling glad to be at home, glad to be going to live in the country, glad to be a married woman. She was feeling as happy as she had ever felt in her life.

'Charlene?' Her face dropped. 'She must be the one I talked to when I rang that day after Christmas?' she said.

'Yes, that was her,' he said. 'I forgot to mention her before.'

'It seems odd to forget to mention someone who lives in your house and is like a mother to you.' Kate's voice moved out of the range of confusion and into the range of coldness.

'I know,' said Leo, feeling brave. Lying gave him a strange sense of release, to his surprise. 'The thing is, she is like part of the furniture. She's always been there. For years. She's wonderful but I never think of her.'

Kate shook her head and wrinkled her nose, her forehead, everything that could wrinkle. 'I don't get it. You told me you lived alone.'

'I do!' he said. 'That is, alone, but with Charlene. She does her thing; I do mine. It's old-fashioned. A century ago, fifty years ago, it would have been absolutely normal for a man like me to have a live-in servant. Charlene is like one of those ancient family retainers, you know, the kind who was the nanny once and who stays on forever, until she dies, living in an apartment in the east wing or something.'

'So is your house very big?' Kate was sarcastic. She knew perfectly well it was not.

'No,' said Leo. 'Not all that big.' Two bedrooms and one kitchen. His house was very small, in fact. 'That's an issue. I am thinking of getting one of those wooden chalets, so Charlene could have her own place in the garden. The garden *is* very big,' he added optimistically, hoping that after she sold her flat, Kate could possibly afford to pay for a shed in the garden, one of those log cabin sort of things that people called a Shomera. A shack for Charlene.

Then the plane landed.

They were busy driving home in Kate's car. Kate, of course, had a car. That would be one of the new challenges, and comforts, of Leo's married life. Kate had refused to consider living in the valley without the convenience of a car. She would consider getting a biogas model next time, but in the meantime she would use her Micra.

The sun shone as they left the airport and the whole region looked as if it had been bathed in good weather for many weeks. The landscape had that relaxed look the Irish countryside can get during a spell of prolonged fine weather, not long enough to cause any hint of drought. The fuchsia dripped their crimson and purple flowers into the hedgerows, the fields were bright with yellow celandines. Mauve hills sheltered the deep greens and yellows of the valleys.

Night was closing in, though, and as Kate drove west the atmosphere changed. It was still close to midsummer, and it was never going to get really dark, but the sun had almost set and a misty twilight air began to hover gently over the fields and the sea. When they approached the mountains that surrounded Leo's valley, a strange phenomenon met them. A large white cloud had settled on the landscape. Above this cloud, the tops of the hills, and the large swathe of rich blue sky, not yet night-darkened, were visible. But a few miles of landscape, including a small hamlet, were enclosed in a pure white cloud.

'It's eerie,' Kate said.

'A fairy mist,' said Leo, who had just thought of this. He did not know what a fairy mist was but it must be something like this. A banshee-like veil, a cobwebby wedding dress, flung over the land. 'Something to do with the heat of the day. It's evaporation probably.'

'Is it?' Kate was driving through it. Inside, the white fairy-cloud translated into ordinary fog. Visibility was poor. She put on the fog lamps. 'It looks like a cloud, and it feels like one too.' They had flown though clouds on their way out to Italy. 'We can ask Charlene if it has been like this before,' Kate said.

And Leo felt relieved that she seemed to have accepted Charlene already. He trusted Charlene not to tell Kate too much about herself – the situation was odd enough without the whole truth being revealed. And he felt hopeful that once he and Kate settled in to the house Charlene might consider alternative accommodation. Once the summer was over there would be plenty of vacant summer houses in the valley. It would be easy to lease a place on a very low rent, if she insisted on staying in the area. He had never given much consideration to practical issues where Charlene was concerned, but she must be entitled to some sort of social assistance. A disability pension? Maybe even council accommodation, in the long run. His imagination ran on. He could picture Charlene established in one of the cute little houses the county council had built in the next village, himself and Kate calling in on their way to town, having a cup of tea and a slice of apple pie at Charlene's very own kitchen table. The vision filled him with a sense of warmth and ease.

When he opened the garden gate to let the car in, however, this comfortable feeling deserted him abruptly. He sensed immediately that something was terribly wrong.

The grass around the house was very long. Well, that shouldn't surprise him. Charlene wouldn't cut the grass. In a few weeks it had grown half a foot high.

The house was in darkness. Maybe she had gone to bed?

He went to open the front door to put on the outside light, so that Kate could see her way down the uneven path to the house. All around the stone terrace that surrounded the house were droppings. Some animal had been around, a lot, and Charlene, most uncharacteristically, hadn't cleaned up the mess. The droppings were smudged and Leo could not identify them – sheep, maybe, or a goat. Stacey kept goats; sometimes they got out.

There were no animal droppings in the covered-in porch, but it was spattered with white bird droppings. When he was fiddling with the key, in the semi-darkness, a commotion broke out overhead in the fuse box. Just as he opened the door two swallows darted out of the box, one flying away into the night and the other going right into the house.

Kate had got out of the car and stumbled down the path.

'Welcome to the valley,' said Leo wryly.

They followed the swallow into the house.

Empty. No fire in the grate, no smell of baking bread.

A few books were stacked on the kitchen table. *Noddy and*

Tessie Bear. Matilda. Reics Carlo paperbacks. Charlene's books. A copy of the *Irish Times* lay beside them, neatly folded. Leo looked at the date. It was the date of their wedding day – almost three weeks ago.

'So? Where is Charlene?' asked Kate.

'Oh … I don't know,' said Leo. 'I thought she'd be here.' He felt a tightening fear in his stomach. 'I think she said something about visiting a sister in Cork.' Why hadn't he made some arrangement with Charlene? Why hadn't he thought of the wooden chalet in the garden and discussed it with her? She might have loved that. A chalet for herself at the end of the garden. A granny flat, one might say.

He knew, now, in his heart, perfectly well, that she had left. She had taken fright and left for good and he had no idea where to find her. But he had no time to worry about this problem just now. When he turned on the light, the swallow began to fly around, frantically, bumping into objects and knocking them over.

The next hour and a half, Kate's first in the house, were spent trying to get the swallow out.

But to no avail.

It refused to find the door. It refused to go out the window.

It flew around, demented, but unable to find its way out of the house.

Leo couldn't manage to catch it, even with the fishing net he took down from the attic. Eventually he and Kate had to go to bed, leaving the bird to its own devices.

They were too tired to do anything other than fall asleep.

Just before four in the morning, Kate was woken by a strange noise. Someone was knocking on the door downstairs. She was half-asleep and tried to ignore it. Perhaps it was a dream. She had been dreaming of something wonderful and she wanted to return to the dream, but the knocking went on and on.

It was light already, or half-light. Leo was sound asleep. She got up and went down the simple wooden staircase with the iron banister. The room downstairs, her living room now, was full of a bluish-grey light, a light she seldom saw anywhere: the light of dawn. Now she could see that the knocking was caused by the swallow. Not Charlene. The swallow was banging its head against the window, trying to get through the glass.

She went over, wondering if she could open the window.

She jumped.

Outside the window, staring straight at her, was an animal. A fox.

Although urban foxes were common in Dublin and some of Kate's parents' neighbours in Foxrock claimed to feed them as if they were pets, Kate had never seen a fox at close quarters before, not a living fox – dead ones she saw all the time, on the road.

This fox did not run away. He ... she assumed it was male ... stood perfectly still, like a statue. His colour was unlike anything she had ever seen, unlike any colour in any paintbox in the world. Such a red ... a golden russet, a colour for which she – who had names for many shades and nuances – could find no word. An unearthly colour.

The fox's eyes were piercing. Sharp, focused.

She shivered.

He was really staring not at her but at the bird. Quite clearly he was hoping to eat the swallow. And the swallow was hoping to get out and fly away. It flew against the glass, like a demented thing, again and again. The fox did not move. It did not move at all. It waited for the swallow to come out and land in its mouth. Patient and cunning, it waited.

But the fox was not all that cunning. There was one element in the scene that he was not reading correctly. It seemed that neither he nor the swallow understood what glass was. Understood even that it was there, transparent, but keeping them apart.

This window, she saw, turning her mind to practical matters, could not be opened. It was a pane of glass fixed into its large frame. The other one, its companion, was a door. She did not know if it was right to let the bird out now that the fox was there, but she opened the glass door.

The swallow, which had been stupid in many ways, now used its intelligence and flew out of the house unhesitatingly.

Out it flew, one wing damaged, down the garden and into the sky.

Down on the silvery ocean the islands loomed, dark and huge, whales in the water.

The fox, as soon as the door opened, moved across the terrace, still hoping to catch the bird. Moved not as swiftly as it could –

it limped on three legs, one held aloft, broken.

For a minute every hair on Kate's body stood on end and she felt briefly freezing.

The sky was an eerie white-blue colour. The grass was long, like corn, full of vaguely shaped flowers, their colours pale and indistinct as yet, in the dawn light. Everything was still, but she had the feeling that the grass was hiding a myriad secret lives. She had seen a fox and a swallow, but the grass out there was full of other animals that she could not see, all out there, hidden from her view.

She tried to follow the fox's progress through the grass but that was impossible. As the light strengthened – which it did, very rapidly – she saw something she had not seen before, which seemed to have grown in the field, like a tree, since she had got up. It was a scarecrow, with black wool for hair and a funny old hat with a daisy in the brim, grinning on its scarecrow stick down towards the end of the garden. That must be where Leo had his vegetable patch, she thought.

It was a beautiful scarecrow, Kate saw. It was smiling, benign, not the kind of scarecrow that would frighten anything.

A swallow, a fox, a scarecrow.

What a strange homecoming it had been! The fairy clouds of mist, and then the bird and now the fox, and the scarecrow, had welcomed her, or warned her, as she came to this new place. Were they telling her something about her life here? What would it be like?

The excitement of starting on a new path exhilarated her but it was frightening as well. She was heading into a mist.

But there was Leo, whom she had got to know so well over the last three weeks that she now felt as if she had been with him for years, rather than for months. She went back upstairs and lay down beside him, and soon he woke up and they made love. The new day began.

Summer in the valley. Frenetic activity on every front – the fields and hedgerows were host to a constantly changing crop of herbs and flowers. Leo named them for her. Selfheal and eyebright. Sheep's-bit and meadowsweet. Rough lichen, the colour of old gold on the walls, and flat, glaucous, eerie pennywort. Birds singing all day long – larks, blackbirds, chaffinches, choughs. A resurgence of human activity too. The roads busy with a constantly changing stock of cars and bicycles and tourists. People were coming and going to the B & Bs and the summer cottages. Shorts and bandannas, flip-flops and mountain boots. Horses trekking over the hill, their *clip-clop* part of the afternoon ritual, the sight of them strung out in a black line on the ridge an evening delight. Houses that stood empty for most of the year were now opened up and lively. Their windows let in the air and the light, voices chatted and laughed from the freshly mown gardens. The town was chock-a-block from morning to night. Every shop was busy, selling food and jewellery and leather handbags and jumpers and all the things people wanted to buy and bring away with them, hoping that buying an object would link them forever to the place.

Kate was busy, simply going around looking at everything, for weeks. She wondered about Charlene; she was curious about her, and would have liked very much to meet her. Even Leo's minimal description painted an intriguing portrait of a warm, loving woman. Kate's own mother was kind and loved her, but mother and daughter had grown apart as Kate grew up. Without articulating it, Kate knew that she would welcome another older woman in her life, someone who would be wise and nonjudgemental, who would look after her best interests. As Charlene seemed to have done, for Leo. But Charlene had not returned, or telephoned, or made any contact, and Leo said he had no way of making contact with her. 'Don't worry about her,' he said. 'She will come back sometime, when she wants to. She's not like other people. She wouldn't phone in advance, or anything.' He remembered her, sitting there in the big chair on that first winter night, in front of the blazing fire, and smiled. 'One day, we'll open the door, and there she'll be, with a big smile on her face.'

He believed this himself, and the prospect was comforting.

Leo brought Kate to the beaches, telling her which ones were safe and which exciting, where the water was warmest, where the waves were biggest. She learned to lie on the grass in his field when it was newly cut, feeling the thick rough carpet of it under her skin, smelling the heady perfume of new-mown hay, of clover and thyme, sweet fragrances that were unknown to her.

She lay on it at night and stared at the canopy of stars, more stars than she had ever seen, myriad galaxies, the sight of which, before she even began to think about them, made her head swim.

She enjoyed the town as well, the community of small shops, all novel and fascinating to her. The little streets, spoiled with traffic but if you could eliminate it from view, charming and old-fashioned, with their gift shops and craft shops and art shops, and the more useful health-food store and bakery and butcher. Doing the ordinary shopping was a treat, under these circumstances. Eating became an adventure, when you slipped down a lane bright with geranium pots to go to the bakers, and into a dark medieval courtyard to buy the nuts and sauces and organic vegetables in the health-food shop with its intoxicating smell of herbs and spices. Even pushing the trolley around the supermarket was fun, because you invariably met several neighbours: Leo had quickly introduced her to his friends – and now that he was married he had more of them than he had realised. Everyone was eager to see the new wife. A new, grown-up person coming to live full-time in the valley was an occasion for celebration, a cause for gentle gossip and pleasant speculation.

They got invitations to cups of tea and invitations to dinner and invitations to barbecues. They accepted them all.

There wasn't much time left for work.

'I'll have to get started on things,' Kate said. 'We won't have much to live on.'

'It's fine,' said Leo. He had enough money to keep them going for a while. 'We can take a holiday, for another month, while the weather is fine. I've got some irons in the fire.'

'What about the society?' Kate asked. 'Shouldn't Killing Roads have a meeting? We've done nothing since the march to capitalise on all that publicity and nothing has changed on the roads.'

It was true. Nobody had resigned. A few new penalty points had been passed into law, but there was no sign that the law was being implemented, certainly not down here. Kate had never seen a policeman doing the random breathalysing tests that had been promised, while the pubs were doing a good trade, as always. You wondered if the gardaí were intimidated, afraid to enforce the law lest they annoy the businessmen who owned the pubs. Pubs were the backbone of the tourist industry. People came to the valley and the town for its beauty and its beaches and its Irish, but what was not admitted openly was that they also came for the pubs. What they called the craic. Craic involved imbibing, in large quantities. Alcohol was the lifeblood of the Irish tourist industry, the one thing that compensated for the uncertain weather. How could the local gardaí, living in the centre of the town in an old house surrounded by a garden full of nasturtiums and plum trees, like a tourist attraction in itself, patrol the pub car parks and arrest the customers as they were leaving? The pubs were also the only place where the community could meet; Leo often strolled down to their local, to have a chat with the neighbours over a few pints. He walked, but a lot of people had to drive to get there. If the pub became unviable, if the pub had to close down, the community would lose a great deal.

There were aspects of the problem that Killing Roads had not thought about.

The gardaí did not control the drink-driving, possibly from good motives, but they did not control anything else either. Drivers used mobile phones all the time. They sped along the narrow, winding roads at dangerous speeds, they crossed white lines, they parked on corners where they blocked the view for other motorists. No Garda ever appeared to give them a ticket. The gardaí were largely invisible.

The private firm that had been contracted to act as speed police and promised a year ago had not materialised. Nobody was asking why. Everyone seemed to forget what the Minister promised about a week after the promise was made. He probably forgot himself.

The accident statistics were worse than ever.

Kate and Leo didn't pay much attention to them. They were too busy. But whenever Kate glanced at a newspaper on a Monday, everything was just the same. Three young men killed in a two-car collision on the road outside Buncrana. An elderly female pedestrian knocked down by a truck in County Longford is in a critical condition in hospital. A two-year-old child and her parents killed in a two-car collision on the N11 near Arklow.

'We'll get back to it in the autumn,' Leo said, grimacing. 'The summer is a bad time for Killing Roads, everyone is on holiday.'

310

'It's a bad time for killing, too,' said Kate. 'Do the statistics get worse in the summer or are they the same?'

'Slightly worse, I think,' Leo said, without much interest. He was not going to go up to Dublin during the summer. In fact, he did not feel like going up to Dublin ever again, now that Kate was here in the country.

The strange truth was that he no longer gave a fig for the Killing Roads. He was too content with his own life to bother any more about the problems of the nation, the problems of strangers. The strangers did not care about themselves. Why should he go on bothering? He might, he knew, when he had settled down and become accustomed to his new state, revert to being an activist. But for the moment he wanted to enjoy the summer of love, the summer of marriage, as much as he could. The problems of the world, its disappearing languages, its disappearing energy resources, its Killing Roads, its global warming would have to manage without him for the time being.

Kate understood. She believed he had not changed permanently, and she appreciated that he needed a holiday from all his lost causes. She was sure that that was all it was: a temporary break from worrying and activism. Come the winter, Leo would be back in action, playing out his role as horsefly on the hide of the politicians.

But maybe not. Because in August, when the montbretia had bloomed everywhere and the ditches spilled over with their orange flames, she had news for him.

'Already?' He hugged her and started to cry.

She nodded, smiling. 'I didn't expect it would happen like this,' she said, hardly thinking of what she was saying. 'I always thought I'd be … infertile.'

'Well, you were wrong there!' he said. He hugged her again. 'I thought that about myself too, actually.'

'I feel ready for it, all the same,' she said, smiling.

'At least we're married!' he said.

'It's one advantage.' She eyed him. 'Are you pleased? Or what?'

'I'm thrilled,' he said. 'Of course I am. I am delighted. There is nothing I want more.'

She smiled. 'Shouldn't you try to contact Charlene? Wouldn't you want to tell her about this?'

Leo felt his heart begin to thump.

'I would,' he said. As he said it, he realised how much he wanted to see Charlene again, and how deeply satisfying it would be to let her know they were expecting a baby. She'd be thrilled. 'She'd love to know about the baby,' he said. 'It's funny that you understand that.' Kate kissed him quickly and gently. 'But, as I've told you, I haven't the foggiest idea where she is.'

'You must have some way of finding out,' Kate said.

He shook his head. 'I don't,' he said. 'There it is.'

'What about her sister in Mallow or wherever? Didn't you say she had some relation in Cork?'

Kate had been silent on the issue of Charlene for a long time but now she was finding it more than mystifying.

Leo took Kate's hand and held it.

'Do you really want to know the whole story?'

She nodded without speaking.

'OK,' he said.

And told her.

Thirty

Sorcha Toomey was released from captivity on the 30th of August.

She appeared on the television screens, looking much the same as she had at the time she had been kidnapped.

'I was treated quite well,' she said. She used to smile a lot but she didn't smile now. That was a difference. 'I was isolated most of the time and didn't know what was going to happen. That was terrifying of course. But they gave me food and treated me well enough.'

As well as you treat somebody you might behead at any moment, Anna thought, watching this in the den at the back of her house. The glass wall on the garden side of the room was crowded with flame-coloured dahlias, purple and blue gladioli. The sun was setting behind the thick sycamores at the end of the garden.

'So what are your plans now?' Vincy asked Sorcha.

What indeed? Anna felt her stomach. The baby kicked so violently that a ripple appeared on the skin, big enough to show through the fabric of her dress.

Vincy and Sorcha were standing in one of those Iraqi land-scapes you saw all the time on television: a few ramshackle houses, a tank, a sandy road. One ragged palm tree somewhere in the background.

'I don't know,' she said. She looked like a nice girl, she had a nice girl voice. 'I don't know. I just want to get out of here, see my family and friends, get back to normal.'

Vincy had changed in appearance. He had changed more than Sorcha Toomey had. He was tanned and thinner than before – he reminded Anna of some English aristocrat in Africa, a hunter of lions, Baron Finch-Hatton in the film about Karen Blixen. Lean, lupine in his khaki shorts and short-sleeved shirt, his tight haircut.

There he was, with Sorcha.

She shuddered, not knowing why. She felt frightened, instead of relieved that he would soon come home.

'Will you continue to work at war reporting?' They always asked questions like that when someone was released. And the answer was the same, always.

'I'm not giving up my job because some bunch of terrorists kidnapped me,' she said crossly. 'But it won't be for a while. First I'll take a rest.'

Vincy smiled. 'Well deserved too,' he said.

There was what there seldom is on these broadcasts, a few seconds' silence. The camera hovered on Sorcha's face: pale, with big features – long almond eyes, a lot of teeth. She had long fair hair, the sort of skin that might freckle if it got the sun.

'Would you ever consider returning to Iraq?' he asked.

'I'll have to think about that,' she said.

Anna turned off the television set.

She always watched the bulletins on the main evening news and was glad of the chance to see Vincy, in one way. And in another way, they always made her depressed and angry. It was not easy knowing that the whole country was watching him, your lover, on the television screen, that the moment you were cherishing as your own private moment with him was shared by about two million people.

She opened the glass door and stepped into her garden. She smelt the fading scents of the last of the woodbine, climbing on the trellis in the corner. The summer jasmine was gone already, and the philadelphus with its massed blooms and intriguing vanilla perfume; the giant chrysanthemums were dying on their long, bending stems.

The small solar lights she had stuck in amongst the flowers in the herbaceous border were flickering alight. The sun had set. Nine thirty. It was dark out here in the garden. Soon it would be autumn. Again.

That night, or more accurately the next morning at one o'clock, the labour pains started.

She had been sure he would be home in time. Although her previous dream, that they would by now have a house of their own, that Vincy would be with her when she felt the first pains and would drive her to hospital, had long ago vanished, she had believed he would be in Dublin for the birth. She had planned to telephone him as soon as the time came. He would come to the hospital and be with her, sharing the labour, witnessing the birth of his first-born.

But the baby was talking to her; the warning cramps were telling her that it was setting out on its journey, gathering its strength and starting to push its way out into the world. It was not going to wait for Vincy. It was not going to wait for anyone.

Alex it was who drove her through the dark silent roads of the Dublin suburbs to the hospital.

Alex it was who sat with her in the room while she was waiting for the nurse who would prepare her.

'You might as well sit up,' said the nurse, in a casual tone. 'Nothing will happen for hours yet.'

It was two in the morning when they arrived at the hospital. Everyone was asleep. There was a skeleton staff in the labour ward but no other mother in evidence.

'You go home,' said Anna. She was still hoping that Vincy would magically materialise. 'I'll be all right.'

'No,' said Alex, annoyed. 'I couldn't leave you alone here.'

Ludmilla was with Rory – Luz Mar had long gone back to Spain but Ludmilla was going to stay forever, Anna knew. She would never get rid of her. Tonight, however, she was glad of her. Alex had telephoned and within half an hour she had been installed in the house, triumphant and smug as always, Anna thought, but reliable.

Alex was reading a Sunday newspaper, even though it was Wednesday. He had grabbed it as he was leaving the house.

Anna had a copy of *Anna Karenina*, a thick hardback edition with a portrait of a thoughtful, beautiful woman, who looked a bit like Anna herself, on the dust jacket. She had put it aside, packed it in her hospital bag, for this occasion. She had not read it since she was sixteen and had forgotten it completely, but she knew it would last through the labour, and the days in hospital.

The room they were in was very drab. It had orange plastic seats and a harsh central light.

'You wouldn't want to be in a room like this, on your own,' he said, with more insight into her tastes than was usual for him. But over the last months of the pregnancy Alex had been very attentive to Anna and she had found it easy to accept his attentions. Vincy was away. She was vulnerable. Alex took on the role of protector; knowing she was compromising everything, she allowed him to look after her. She was grateful to him for his kindness.

The pains were not bad, Anna was thinking. She was able to read. When she had been in labour with Rory, she had had terrible pains. She had been in the labour ward, hard at work, almost from the moment she arrived in the hospital, in the middle of the afternoon, on a Whit Monday. And it had been full of bustle and excitement. Several women were having babies. Their screams and the babies' screams rent the air, mixed with the hospital clatter of pans and implements, the sound of wheels trundling along corridors, of laughs and chatter.

Now there was only silence. Muted pains, almost irritatingly lacking in intensity, in the drab, quiet room. And outside, the dim, dark night, lights of the suburb ensuring that it was not ever really dark, a suburban darkness only.

At six or so, before dawn, the pains became more intense at the same time that the hospital began to stir, slowly, with life. She could hear a few cars pulling into the grounds and parking, someone shouting good morning. The easygoing nurse came in and said it was time to go into the ward now.

Anna went into a small labour ward and was told to lie down on a white trolley.

There was no other patient.

This was a very quiet, private hospital.

An anaesthetist arrived and gave her an epidural.

So after that she felt nothing.

This had been her wish. The memory of the pain of the first labour had not gone away. She had promised herself, after Rory's birth, that if she had another child, she would not go through with the pain. She knew what it was like, was her argument. She had had the experience, and once was enough.

But now, after the cold ointment had chilled the skin of her back and the needle found its way into her spine, and she lay in the quiet, white ward, alone and at peace, she wondered if she had made the right decision. The pains had not been so bad. The fact was, she suspected, that the second time round it would have been different, easier, than the first anyway. Her body had done this before. Now she would not experience what it was like, really like, to have a second baby. She would never know if it would have been easier or not, because she was numb from the waist down. Her labour seemed to be happening to another woman, while she observed it from a distance, through a veil of painlessness.

The sun rose and filled the small ward with morning light, delicate as lace. Nurses moved around, tidying things up, occasionally smiling at Anna and asking her if she was all right. Neatness and order prevailed.

Anna, to her amazement, found herself wishing she could just go to sleep. She was tired, and she had been reading for five hours – she had read three hundred pages. Her eyes were dry and she was losing interest in the book. But there was nothing to do, except try to stay awake.

It was as unlike the birth of Rory, that noisy, painful, lively occasion, as anything could be.

At nine o'clock, the obstetrician came in. And then the baby was born – permitted to be born, by the doctor, it seemed. At five past nine in the morning. As thousands, millions, of people arrived at their offices and shops to begin a day's work.

Five past nine.

Outside, the day had become grey and nondescript after the earlier sunshine. It was a heavy overcast day. The last day of August.

Out the baby slid. Anna hardly felt her coming.

'A little girl!' smiled the obstetrician.

The baby cried loudly and grabbed the towel.

'Look at her grip!' He was smiling, admiring. He was old. His hair was white and his face a map of pink wrinkles, and he had seen thousands of babies born. But the magic moment of entry to the world still delighted him. He had not grown tired of the energy of the babies who arrived in the world after their struggle, screaming and kicking and grabbing, ready to go.

He cut the umbilical cord, wrapped the baby tenderly in a pink blanket, and handed her to Anna.

Tiny. A face red and crinkled like a monkey's. Her nose wide, her eyes small.

She's ugly! Anna's heart tumbled. Ugly.

Rory had been a big baby with smooth skin, sallow, a head of black hair, big dark eyes. A beauty.

This little creature seemed hardly human.

Anna pitied her, profoundly, for her smallness, and her redness, and her wrinkles. She had a terrible fear that something would be wrong with her.

They took her away and put her in a cot. The afterbirth came out without Anna noticing it, because she had already fallen asleep.

Vincy came to see her on the third day, at two o'clock in the afternoon.

'She is amazing.' He held the little ugly baby in his arms, gazing at her. His eyes lit up as he looked at the baby, but when he turned back to Anna, they lost their sparkle.

'Yes,' said Anna flatly.

'What are you going to call her?' he asked, in an interested but tired voice. He had kissed her quickly when he came in. Now he was sitting on the chair by the window, i.e. as far away from her as he could be and still be in the room.

'What am *I* going to call her?' She frowned. What sort of question was that? It was the question of an acquaintance, a casual acquaintance. Not like the father of this baby without a name.

He raised his eyebrows. He always looked supercilious when

he did that. 'I haven't had much time to think of names,' he said, rising to place the baby in her iron cot.

'Of course, over there in the war zone, rescuing the captive princess.' Anna felt her blood rise. As she said it, she knew why she felt so anxious. The captive princess. Vincy was carrying on with her, the beautiful hostage with the blond hair, Sorcha. Of course.

He threw up his hands and made some sort of a *moue* with his mouth. 'What is that supposed to mean?"

She started to cry.

He moved closer and hugged her, patted her hair, damp and matted.

'You're overwrought. It's entirely natural.' He kissed her, and hugged her. She could feel his ribs through the thin cloth of his shirt. He certainly had lost a lot of weight over there, his face looked ravaged. She nuzzled the soft bristle on the back of his head.

'Apple,' she said.

'What's that?' Vincy was tired and confused. He had flown in on a direct flight from Baghdad the night before and spent the morning talking to the media. His head was beginning to feel dense, like putty.

'I'm going to call her Apple,' Anna said. Nature, Japan, she had been thinking before. She had thought of the name a second ago, looking at the apple tree outside the window. The hard little apples, oval shaped, were just getting a faint red flush on their green skins. She could glimpse them, nestling among the leaves. Apple trees. Funny, ugly, little trees, with funny, unremarkable leaves, and ugly, wrinkled, little fruits, which became beautiful.

That was the right name for this baby. Little, wizened apple, to ripen to a golden fruit, to tempt the world.

'Hm!' Vincy smiled. 'Apple! That's a fantastic name.' He picked up his daughter from her cot and looked at her monkey face, which to him seemed perfectly beautiful. 'Apple. Little Apple!' He kissed her on the soft crown of her head, handed her to Anna, and said goodbye.

He had come to visit at about two o'clock, and at two fifteen he was gone.

He knew he should stay much longer, with Anna and Apple.

But the media were hounding him. Every minute of the afternoon had been allocated to some journalist or other. If he were lucky, he'd be in bed by midnight.

When he was gone, Anna lay against the pillows and gazed out the window. Behind the gnarled and knotted apple tree, a stand of spreading chestnut trees, majestic and noble, and behind them the Dublin mountains. The view was unimpeded by anything, although somewhere between the trees and the mountain was the M50, with its unending river of traffic. She had become accustomed to its humming in the distance, like the ocean, a sound so constant she no longer heard it. The small, pink room was silent but for the soft breathing, wheezing, of Apple in her little cot, right beside Anna's bed.

She looked at her face, bright red even in repose, her eyes screwed up, her arms wrapped tight to her side. She was wrapped from head to foot in a pink blanket, the same kind they had used when Rory was born, a waffle pattern, cotton. All babies born in Irish hospitals wear these as their very first garments, a nappy, a little white shirt, and a waffle cotton blanket.

She remembered again Rory's birth. The birth pangs had gone on for twelve hours. But when Rory had been born, at the end, when she was almost dead from exhaustion, she had felt more exhilarated than she had ever felt in her life before. He was born just after midnight, at the start of summer. Dark in the inner city where that hospital was. But she saw stars everywhere. Her head had filled with shooting meteors, with sparkling lights. She had been unable to sleep for days, with the excitement of it all.

She had been in a public hospital in a ward with other women. The excitement in the ward was intense. Everyone was having their first baby. They were in pain, they did not know how to do anything, to change a nappy, to breastfeed. But the ward was full of their sense of importance and destiny, and with their delight, which was extreme. And they were busy from morning until night, nursing and changing and breastfeeding, tending their own sore bodies and the demanding bodies of their babies.

This time there was none of that.

She wasn't even breastfeeding.

320

Why she had decided not to do it, she did not know. But she had decided. She had let them give Apple a bottle on the first day and that was that.

Now she saw the trees and the Three Rock Mountain, with its little hut on its side, soaring above her, telling her how insignificant she was, and the new baby. Summer was over. All week had been overcast, and a sad pall lay over the trees and the mountains, over her small, quiet, pink room, which felt more like a room of death than a room of birth.

The thought of going home filled her with dread.

She did not want to go back there, to the house, where Rory waited to be looked after, and Alex too, where Alex waited to torture her with his forgiveness, or his meekness, with his ineptitude in the face of disaster.

She did not want to go anywhere. Not to Vincy's flat either, a place that would be a horrible setting for a baby, all its picturesque charm revealed for what it was: squalor. Owned by Joe.

Or Jo.

Jo was a woman's name as well as a man's.

That was why Vincy had been so secretive about his flatmate. That was why he had never let her meet him. Because he was a she. A Jo not a Joe.

How stupid Anna had been.

But if he was carrying on with Jo, would he be carrying on with Sorcha as well?

It was all so awful, so tortuous, so complicated, that she could not go on thinking about it. All she longed to do was sleep. To fall into a long, deep slumber – that was the word for what she wanted, with its connotations of cosiness, peace, half-sleepiness, its promise of interesting, pleasant dreams. She did not want to wake up until the world had changed completely and become what it had promised it would be, in those days after she met Vincy, or in those days after she was born.

Thirty-one

October. The sun was getting low and shone with the deep mellowness of autumn on the milky sea. The visitors had all gone home. Half the houses in the valley were empty, but the place did not have the closed-up look more lively resorts get off-season. A new life began when the summer was over. The locals settled back into their own routines and repossessed their own place.

The blackberries were thick on the brambles that lined the lanes of the valley. Kate spent afternoons finding more and more, filling a small yellow bucket with the fat fruit.

In the mornings she packed most of them away in the new deep freeze she had bought and put in the new garden shed. She made bramble jelly, using Leo's recipe book, *Food for Free*. He made wine. 'Every year for ten years I planned to make wine,' he said. 'And now at last I'm getting around to it.' He kissed her. The jars of rich purple juice fermented in the shed, bubbling like a river. 'At Christmas we'll be drinking the summer,' he said. 'When the mist wraps us up like a cloud, we'll raise our sweet glasses and say "Summer is coming!"'

Kate was putting her mark on the house.

'It is beautiful,' she said. 'And I like the way you have it.' But it wouldn't do for a child, she said, meaning it wouldn't do for her. They had applied for planning permission for an extension – a new bedroom, and new bathroom, and new spare room, all

322

to the side. She wanted to add a sunroom as well, but you didn't need planning permission for that.

The shed was the first thing. You didn't need planning permission for that either. And into the shed went the freezer, and a washing machine, and a new lawnmower.

'I was slumming it – typical country bachelor,' said Leo.

He was beginning to be slightly concerned about money now that the baby was on the way. But Kate's parents had given her some and there would always be the proceeds of the sale of her flat. Anyway he was working hard and there were new books, new grants, new projects on his work plan. Kate was officially his assistant. In reality, she did very little on the publishing side of things. There was so much to be done with the house, and the garden. She was digging, she was drawing up plans for a patio and a pond and a shelter belt of trees.

The neighbours watched with interest.

They liked Kate well enough. She was a minor disappointment: not as talkative a person as they would have wished for. In the valley, there was a great need for people who had the gift of the gab, who could make jokes and puns, who always had a new story to tell. There was a need for good company. Leo was quiet, and now Kate was even quieter. But they were decent sorts, they were not *muinteartha* exactly – the best thing to be – but they were *macánta* – more important. It wasn't their fault that they hadn't a lot to say. They represented a new sort of person, people from the city who were restrained, not used to expressing themselves, who could not make jokes or tell stories and who spoke a thin, colourless language, peppered with slang they had learned from television. No proverbs, no wisecracks. Kate was polite and friendly. She answered questions as well as she could and did not withhold information. She did her best. God love her.

And they were a young couple. What the valley needed more than anything. Lifeblood.

Thirty-two

Anna had seldom supported any cause for longer than it took to write her credit card number on a website for a once-off donation. (She did not believe in making standing orders for charitable donations, in case she herself became abruptly impoverished and, for some reason, would be unable to stop the standing order.) Like everyone, she had sent a large donation to the tsunami rescue operation; she occasionally gave money to Concern at Christmas, and always put coins in the flag boxes of those people who collected for charity on the street, although fortunately there were not as many of them as there used to be in her childhood, when every day town was dotted with children rattling flag boxes under your nose. On the other hand, there were more of the homeless, the people who were curled up in sleeping bags on every Dublin street. And the Romanian women in the coloured dresses with the babies.

October. It was just over a year since she had met Vincy. She was taking the Luas into town, to go to a reception in the National Library, which had surpassed all other venues as the most fashionable venue for launches this autumn. Tonight was the occasion of a book launch by Lilian Meaney, Anna's good friend, but one she had lost contact with over the past few months when so much had been going on in her life. Lilian, as had been hinted at the last time Anna had met her, had got a good publisher, and, it was rumoured, a substantial advance, such as none of the women in their circle had ever received. But even Lilian would not reveal to her closest literary friends exactly what the advance was, so they were as much in the dark as ever about how much you would really get if you hit the jackpot.

Anna was alone on the Luas. Alex had stayed at home to mind Rory and Apple. The new au pair, Marike, from Finland, was also at home. She was an excellent au pair, much better than Luz Mar had been, and it would have been perfectly safe to leave her in sole charge of Rory and his little sister. But Alex had fallen so in love with Apple that he disliked leaving her more than was necessary. In the household, he was the one who cuddled her, gave her her bottle, talked baby talk to her – although he allowed Marike to change the nappies. Anna had never taken to the new baby, although she did not admit this to herself. She pitied her, the little thing with the red, ugly face and a thatch of blond hair; she reminded her of one of those fledglings you see fallen out of nests, scrawny with no feathers. By comparison with Rory, who had been a robust, cheerful baby, a baby with a presence that filled the house from the moment he entered it, a baby who made his demands and feelings felt from the start, Apple was diffident, silent, lacking in character. She slept a great deal, as if she could not be bothered being awake to face her life. Her cry, when it came, was weak and whining, and she never smiled.

Anna all but ignored her as much as she could. Since she wasn't breastfeeding, Anna was free to leave the baby with Marike most of the time. She was free. That was probably why she had chosen the bottle over the breast on the first day, although she had not been aware of her motivation at the time.

Vincy, for his part, had abandoned his daughter almost completely. He had come to see her in the hospital twice, and once since she had come 'home', to Alex's house.

And in the house, Alex's house, he had demonstrated terrible uneasiness. Alex was not there when he called. Nobody was, except Anna and Apple. But he felt the presence of all the other residents in the rooms.

'I feel like an intruder,' he said flatly, holding Apple on his lap as if she were a bag of shopping.

'You are,' said Anna, looking crossly at him. They were sitting at the kitchen table. The garden through the glass wall was red and gold with autumn foliage. The sun was low in the sky, and mellow. 'And so is Apple.' She looked pityingly at her baby. That was the expression she reserved for her: pity. Akin to love, it is said, but not the best emotion to feel towards one's baby. 'That's why we need to move out.'

They had found somewhere that might be appropriate – a small ex-corporation house in an unfashionable estate not far from Anna's present home.

'Gosh. I can't imagine living here,' said Anna, when they went to look at it.

The house was the usual county council stucco on the outside. Inside, it had been very smartly renovated and redecorated, and the garden was not too small. But there were only two tiny bedrooms, a large kitchen and a minuscule sitting room. The whole house would have fitted into Anna's living room.

'It's the best we can do,' Vincy said, 'on my salary.'

Vincy's was a fat salary, but it was not fat enough to cope with Dublin property prices. What salary was? You had to have a million euro to buy a semi-detached house on an estate, a house like the one Gerry and Olwen lived in, even.

'If only someone would give me a big advance on my book,' Anna said. She added a slight sigh, which was not like her.

He looked impatient. So far nobody had even offered to publish her book much less give her a big advance. And as far as he knew the book was not even written. Anna had been talking about it for months but she never seemed to write anything. He wished she would get a job and earn a regular salary like anybody else. With two salaries they might manage. The book writing was a fine hobby for a rich man's wife but it would not be much help now.

'It's very nice, really,' said Anna, looking at the garden of the house. It was about twenty feet long and six feet wide. It was like a corridor, she was thinking. But it had been decked out with terracotta slabs and big pots. The geraniums were still in flower. There had been no frost, as yet. Or maybe they put them out when the house was on view? 'And it's close to Alex and Rory.'

It had been decided, by Anna and Vincy, that Rory would stay with his father when Anna moved out.

Neither Rory nor Alex knew anything about this. They had no idea that plans were afoot that could turn their lives completely upside down.

As yet, the plans were far from firm. Vincy and Anna looked and talked and hummed and hawed. But made no decisions. Or purchases. They were drifting along, and as they drifted, the situation in which Anna found herself – mother to the child of Vincy, living with another man – became more and more acceptable, to everyone, above all to her. Thus are lives made. Habits, bad or good, maketh the person, and maketh the life, while the person concerned imagines, blissfully, that they are still in charge and have the power to change at any minute.

Anna now walked along by the Green towards Grafton Street. The path under the darkening trees smelt of autumn. The leaves were heaped up under the railings, filling the air with their rich, damp odour. From the jarveys' stand at the corner, the smell of horse manure wafted to mingle with the smell of dead leaves. It was a potent mix, which stirred her soul uncomfortably.

She walked down Grafton Street, taking a long way round to the library in order to look in the shop windows. She hadn't been in town in months. The winter clothes were in the windows – cosy dark coats with fur collars, flowery party dresses. Victoriana was the theme this year – she should get a high-necked blouse, and a tweed skirt.

She had regained her figure, more or less. There was a sag in her breasts and her stomach was flabbier than it had been before but she was slim, her skin was smooth and clear and her hair had not suffered from the pregnancy. She was wearing the same curly, shoulder-length style she had always had, and it glistened with fragrant conditioner and shampoo. The work of looking after a new-born baby had not prevented her looking after herself – thanks to the efficient presence of Marike, Anna had time to bathe and wash, and to go for walks, just as she always had.

A counsellor she was seeing for her post-natal depression had advised her to ensure she had time to do these things.

'You need time, Anna,' she had said. 'Make sure there is something you love doing, and make time to do that every day.'

'What would it be?' asked Anna.

'It might be a bath,' said the counsellor.

Something you love doing. Take a bath.

Anna would have found it more therapeutic to spend hours making love with Vincy. But she had not revealed to the counsellor that he existed, which made the whole exercise ridiculous. Her intention was to tell her sometime, before she moved out … that would be her last visit anyway, probably, since she would not be able to afford the counsellor's fee when she no longer shared Alex's bank account.

She would buy that blouse, cream and lacy, and the browny-gold tweed skirt, tomorrow, while she still had his credit cards in her bag. She should shop and store up for the cold and hungry years ahead, the time with Vincy. He had convinced her that what was in store now was a life of deprivation and poverty. She was giving up a lot for love. You would have expected Vincy to be better off since he was so very well known. But he was adamant. He earned buttons, in comparison to Alex.

'Maybe I will get some of Alex's money?' Anna said. She didn't see why she should, but according to her friends' view of the law, she would be entitled to it.

'Maybe you won't,' Vincy said.

The thought of discussing her plans, her affairs, with a lawyer made her blood run cold. She had never discussed anything with one – all that side of their life had been taken care of by Alex. She did not know how to go about meeting with a solicitor. She was frightened of them – I had an affair, I've had a baby, I want to get out of my marriage.

No, my husband has not been unfaithful, or abusive, or mean.

He is a perfect husband. And I like him.

And, oh yes, we have a child.

She could see the raised eyebrow.

So why ?

I fell in love. I wanted to be happy.

Childish.

Not passionate, overwhelming, elemental.

Not Heathcliff.

More like sex in the city.

Love, even love, was less important in modern cities. It needed other surroundings to ennoble it. Oceans and mountains, forests, winds and storms.

Shops, pubs, museum cafés – these were not the right locus for convincing romance. Solicitors' offices were not the right place to discuss passion.

A solicitor would see her as selfish and immature. Love. That was not a reason that would cut much ice in court.

No, she did not feel like going to a solicitor, and telling her story in broad outline, in legalistic terms.

Anyway, everything would be so definite then, so cut and dried. There would be no going back once a file was opened and her story jotted down.

Whereas, in reality, everything was still ambivalent, ambiguous, indefinite. A mess.

Outside Arnott's the small boy with red hair was singing 'The Fields of Athenry', as usual. 'The small free birds fly,' soared his lusty little voice. He hadn't grown, in a year. Or perhaps this was another boy who looked the same? A younger brother who had inherited the family talent for singing the famous song? 'It's lonely round the fields of Athenry.' The people gathered and listened with tears in their eyes, and some of them dropped coins into the plastic box he had placed on the pavement.

Anna did too.

Minutes later she had to drop more money into the hat of the reading homeless person, the homeless person with glasses, who had settled in for the night in the porch of the Heraldic Museum at the bottom of Kildare Street. He was half-seated, half-reclining, reading a thick hardback volume.

'What is it?' Anna nodded, dangling a five euro note in front of him.

'*War and Peace*,' he said.

'Is it good?' she asked.

'Not bad,' he said. 'And it will keep me going for a long, long time.'

'I've read one of his others,' Anna said. '*Anna Karenina.*'

He took off his glasses and looked up at her. 'How was that?' he asked with interest.

'Pretty good. I'd recommend it.' She dropped the five euro in his hat.

'I might try it when I finish this one,' he said. 'But that won't be for a month. I only read before I go to sleep and the evenings are starting to close in now. Soon it will be dark at five o'clock.'

'It will,' she agreed.

'Then I won't get much time to read,' he said, putting his glasses back on. 'I'll have to go to bed early then, when the winter sets in.'

The invitation to Lilian's launch was a simple white card with the details embossed in gold – totally traditional, although a real cardboard card, with gold writing, was more upmarket than the usual invites. The publisher was a big international concern – the publisher who had rejected Anna's book – so they could afford the best. The title of the new book was, simply, *The Astonishing Voyage of Jonathan Smith.*

The card sparked a strong pang of envy in Anna, but she suppressed it quickly and determined to try and celebrate her friend's success with as much genuine joy, or, if not, faked joy, as she could muster. Heaven knew that Lilian deserved a break, after all these years of writing for small readerships and limited success.

As soon as Anna walked into the launch, she knew that the break had come. In spite of her good intentions, her heart sank. Envy is such a strong emotion, there is no escape from it, no matter how much you want to be generous in your heart. The front hall of the National Library, which is a big space, was packed to capacity, and not with the women writers' groups and Lilian's relations, or not with them alone. Katherine Molyneux, in her long black skirt, was there. John Marvell was there. Seamus Heaney was there. Even Carl Thompson, in a purple shirt, could be seen chatting to a woman in a pinstriped trouser suit and black court shoes, the sort of outfit London literary agents usually wore, so she was probably one of them – probably Lilian's new one.

Lilian had most definitely arrived.

Anna suppressed the green-eyed monster as best she could, and fixing a smile on her face, broke into the fray. She would do her best to be noble and supportive. Lilian was one of her best friends, after all, even though she had not seen her for half a year. Her own chapters were still doing the rounds of publishers, five copies in brown Jiffy bags floating off to various addresses in London, and, recently, in Ireland as well, trying to find a decent home, while Lilian's book was being fêted here in the National Library. The launch speech would be given by none other than Philip Pullman, the famous author whom nobody had even seen before in Dublin, much less had their book launched by him. He was much more important than J.K. Rowling, being the writer for the bright children, the ones who liked their stories set in Oxford, and peppered with allusions to Milton, and Descartes, and Socrates. The sort of children who would disguise their *Harry Potters* in brown paper covers, lest anyone should suspect them of low-brow taste.

'Hi!' Here was Christine. Her long curly hair was a little greyer than when Anna had last seen her, at her own launch, but she was wearing the same long, homespun dress with wooden beads hanging around her neck. And sandals, even in October. 'Long time no see!' She smiled warmly and gave Anna a hug.

Anna relaxed, and realised how nervous she had been at the thought of facing everybody again.

'Not since your launch,' she said. 'I loved the collection, by the way. I meant to send you a card.'

'I've been away,' said Christine. There was something new about her, in spite of her wearing the same old clothes. She looked even more serene than usual. 'I've been away for three months, in Annaghmakerrig.'

'Oh yes,' said Anna. The artists' centre in the country. 'How was it?'

'Wonderful,' said Christine. 'It's the perfect place to be, for us. You've been, of course?'

'No,' said Anna. 'I never felt the need to go up there.'

'You'd like it,' Christine said. 'You'd love it.' She looked at Anna closely, caringly. A scent of compassion wafted across to her, a benison in the edgy atmosphere of the room. Christine continued, 'You'd find yourself there, as a writer.'

Anna let herself slip onto Christine's wavelength. She didn't usually tolerate this sort of language. The 'find yourself' stuff.

'Would I?'

'Yes, I know you would,' said Christine. 'It would do you good. It's tranquil and comforting and beautiful. Art matters there, like nowhere else.'

'Hm,' said Anna, looking at the circular hall, with its stained-glass window paintings of Aristotle and Socrates and

Shakespeare and Milton, its mosaic floor depicting snakes and apples and inscribed with the word *Sapientia*. The tiler had inserted the word four times, making sure you got the message. *Sapientia, Sapientia, Sapientia, Sapientia.* A magic mantra in porcelain.

'Here.' Christine dug into her capacious bag, and pulled out a brochure. 'Take this. Think about it.'

'Thanks,' said Anna, stuffing the leaflet into her own bag. 'Actually, I probably won't be going anywhere for a while. I have a new baby.'

'You have a new baby! How wonderful! Congratulations!' Christine kissed her, spontaneously, on the cheek. 'But anyway … you will be able to take a few days later on, in the spring, maybe.' Her gentle eyes were persuasive. 'You mustn't stop writing, you know, Anna. You are really good at it!'

Anna's eyes filled. It was a very long time since anyone had paid her this compliment.

Anita came through the crowd munching a meatball on a stick.

'Did you know, Anna had a baby?' Christine was very excited.

'I know. A little girl. Apple, isn't it? Fabulous name. I really like it.'

Anna nodded, pleased.

Carl Thompson walked passed, nodding at Anita.

'Lilian has actually managed to drag *that fellow* out of his lair, she must be really going places,' said Anita, following the shadow of the famous writer as he made his way towards the literary editor of one of the big newspapers, an exceptionally nice woman called Clíona.

Anna felt happy. Christine had raised her spirits, and Anita seemed to accept the new baby without question. It felt good to be back in the swing of things; for the moment she forgot about the sad fortunes of her own book. And her other sad fortunes. But at events of this kind, the book problems always seemed much more pressing.

'You had a book almost written the last time we met, I seem to recall,' said Anita. 'Did the baby push that onto the back boiler?'

'Yes.' Anna gave the simple answer.

'That's what happens to us women writers, there's no getting away from it.' Anita launched into a rant on her favourite topic.

Anna half-listened; she had heard it so many times before, although Anita embellished her spiel every time she made it, so there was always some new titbit in the mix of truth, fiction, and indignation, of which her rant consisted.

While Anita was holding forth, Anna spotted Gerry in his usual position, close to the wine table.

'Excuse me,' she said. 'I have to go and talk to my brother over there, I haven't seen him in months.'

Since Kate and Leo's wedding. Olwen and Gerry had not come to visit her in the maternity hospital, or sent a card. She would tackle him on his own now; Olwen never came to this sort of event.

She squeezed her way across the lobby through the densely packed mass of bodies and found him in the empty, if narrow, margin of space around the drinks table.

He kissed her enthusiastically. 'Hi there!' he said, pushing her back and taking a good look at her. 'You look great! Sorry I didn't get in touch … Olwen, you know …'

'Olwen,' said Anna, raising her eyebrows.

'Olwen, as you say. She's … not all there sometimes, I think. Anyway that's all behind you now, isn't it?'

'The birth?'

'Yeah …' He looked nonplussed. He had meant something else.

'It's fine. Apple – that's your niece's name – is healthy and fine in every way. I'm at home with Alex and Rory and I will make up my mind what to do next, soon.'

She felt like telling him she was moving out, buying a house with Vincy. She felt like seizing the moment and telling him everything. But she had promised Vincy not to talk until everything was in place.

'And Vincy?' asked Gerry.

'Vincy is fine,' said Anna.

Gerry was looking at her carefully. 'You're not still seeing him, are you?'

Anna was taken aback. 'That's an intrusive question,' she said.

'Well, you *are* my sister,' said Gerry. 'I suppose I am allowed to ask the occasional intrusive question.' He kissed her again, on the cheek.

'I *am* still seeing him,' she said. Now she blurted it all out. 'In fact we plan to move in together very soon. We're buying a house, actually.'

Gerry looked flabbergasted. 'Anna, I just don't know what to say.'

They had forgotten they were in a crowded room. For the moment, the crowd disappeared and they were conscious only of their own conversation.

'You know, Olwen was right. He is Apple's father.'

'Well, so you say.'

'Gerry!'

'Anna, don't move out. Don't.'

'It's none of your business.'

'Vincy!' He threw up one of his hands, the other being engaged in clutching a glass. 'You can't trust him.'

'What?'

'I've seen him around the place with that girl from Iraq.'

'Sorcha? Well, so what?' Anna's first reaction was to think sensibly. 'He rescued her or whatever.'

'He's not the right person for you. Or for Rory. Or' – he had to think for a moment – 'em … Apple.' He drained his glass and went back to replenish it.

The publisher tapped on the microphone.

'Hi everyone …'

Anna stayed close to Gerry while the speeches were going on, because she had no choice. He stood there, slightly behind her, sipping wine as they listened to the publisher and to Philip Pullman telling them that this was the best novel for children ever to have been written in Ireland. The sort of thing launchers said at every launch. But since Philip Pullman was saying it, it carried some weight.

He did not speak at any length – for about five minutes. But he gave the book great praise. His endorsement was enthusiastic and sounded heartfelt. It was great for Lilian, but how she would have loved to be the author of the book that was receiving such high praise.

When Pullman had finished, and after the rapturous applause had died down, Lilian took the podium and read from the opening chapter of her book. She wore a lovely green dress and matching boots, green crocodile or snakeskin or something, fake hopefully – a dramatic outfit. She read in her clear, high, pleasant voice.

Jonathan Smith walked along the beach, kicking the blue pebbles as he went and occasionally stopping to skim one across the water. The sea was as smooth as glass. The sun beamed down from a blue sky, and seagulls called to one another as they circled above the spot where the fish shoaled.

There was not another person on the beach. It was an ordinary Tuesday. Everyone was at work or at school, which was where Jonathan should be. But today he had decided not to go, because as he left his house with his bag on his back a large grey heron had hopped out in front of him on the roadside and talked to him.

'Do not go the school,' the heron said. 'Come down to the beach, where someone is waiting to see you.'

The heron had beckoned and Jonathan had followed, turning left instead of right at the end of the road, going down the leafy lane, taking the flight of broken stone steps that led down to the deserted beach.

Once there, the heron had disappeared.

Jonathan wandered along the stony beach. Where was the person who was waiting for him? There was nobody to be seen, not a human being, not an animal, not even a boat on the vast blue sea.

Jonathan walked, and kicked stones, and skimmed, and wondered if he should not have gone to school after all.

He was considering turning back and going home – it was too late for school now, he judged – when a large black bird swam up to the edge of the waves and addressed him.

'Jonathan Smith,' said the bird. 'You don't know me.'

'No,' said Jonathan. He had never seen this bird before in his life. It looked like a cormorant but was twice as big at least.

'Allow me to introduce myself. I am the ancient mariner.'

'Pleased to meet you,' said Jonathan.

'And I have come to issue you with an invitation to participate in a voyage around the world.'

'Oh!' said Jonathan, taken aback.

'Of all the children in the world you have been selected for this singular honour,' said the big cormorant, or ancient mariner, or whatever he was. 'I hope you are pleased.'

'Oh yes,' said Jonathan, although he felt a twinge of fear. 'Honoured, I am sure.'

'There is the ship,' said the ancient mariner, waving one black wing.

And out in the sea there appeared a great sailing ship, with red gunwales and white sails and blue masts …

At this point, Anna felt so strange that she had to leave the library.

Thirty-three

Kate was picking the last blackberries. It was the last week in October, and after Hallowe'en they would be useless, according to proverbial lore and to fact, Leo said. She did not need any more, but she liked picking them. The freezer had dozens of plastic cartons of berries now, and there were two dozen jars of jam on the shelf in the kitchen. They looked so homely and welcoming. 'I'm always going to make it every year,' said Kate. 'For the look of those jars alone.'

The sun was low over the ocean, the colour of butterscotch or bronze. That mellow light bathed the road, where the fuchsia shrubs were bared to their reddish branches, and the hooks of blackberries arched out over the tarmac. The stream chuckled and babbled beyond the field.

She was on the narrow road that led over the mountain at the back of the valley to the next parish. Because it was a few miles from their house, she had driven up. Leo had got used to the luxury of having Kate's car and was considering, once again, to learn how to drive. It was so much more convenient than walking everywhere or waiting for the elusive bus.

Her morning sickness had eased off now; she was four months' pregnant. Her hair was glossy and her skin radiant. She felt perfectly healthy.

The blackberry-picking gave her a sense of transcendence. She

337

felt she was at one with the landscape, and with nature, as she performed the simple repetitive task, harvesting the bounty of the hedgerows, as Leo's recipe book put it. Leo had not had to brainwash her into believing that the old-fashioned country tasks were good for people; she had found it out herself, as soon as she had begun to pick the berries. The field around the house she planned to till and fill with vegetables and fruit as soon as the shelter belt was in place – already after a few months in the country she had grandiose plans to become self-sufficient.

'You're a PR girl,' Leo said. 'Don't you want to go back to that glamorous life?'

She didn't, for the moment. She would help him with his launches and publicity, but that would not be so outrageously glamorous. The books of poetry, she liked to imagine, were like the blackberries, or the montbretia, or the fuchsia, the things that grew in a seasonal cycle, patterned, predictable, lovely. The books, too, appeared seasonally, the slim volumes in their artistic covers coming out, like berries, in November and in March, Leo's favourite months for publication.

She filled one bucket. The berries were getting drier on the brambles now, as the autumn drew to a close. In no time they would be withered and white and inedible. Filling a bucket with juicy ones took longer than it had a month earlier. She spent an hour doing it, enjoying the soft sunshine, the feel of the brambles and their spicy smell, the chuff of the choughs, with red beaks, in the fields where she was.

After an hour, when the bucket was full to the brim of shining blackberries, she placed it carefully in the boot. The sun was beginning to sink. At six it would be dark. She was going to drive to the town, where she needed to get a few things in the supermarket. If all went well, she would be home before nightfall.

She drove over the hill road and down towards the town. The flowers had all gone now. The ditches were not bare, but filled with russet-coloured leaves and the red-brown branches of the fuchsia. Even in late autumn the colours of the landscape around here were rich. It had many charms, Kate thought, but the ever-changing colours was the one she liked best.

As she drove down the hill towards the bay, bright blue on this autumn afternoon, with the hills on the next peninsula heartbreakingly perfect, dark blue and pale blue and lilac, range upon range against the sky, she felt the baby move.

It fluttered inside her like a butterfly.

It was a strange feeling, the feeling of a living creature inside her own body. But she knew what it was, immediately, and was overcome with a feeling of joy. It was there, alive, kicking her from the inside, asserting its … asserting its existence.

What are you? she asked, as she came down to the flat part of the road. Are you a boy or a girl? What are you going to be like? What are you like now?

A magpie hopped out of a bush and walked across in front of the car.

You must be bright and strong, she was thinking. You're kicking already. You're quick. You're brilliant.

She came to the white shop at the corner of the hill road. For a second she wondered if she could just get what she wanted there. Then she could get home all the sooner to Leo, to tell him that the baby had moved. He would want to know, as soon as possible. He would want to feel it kicking too. She wondered if she should do her shopping here in the little local Spar and return home. But looking at the shop, she decided not to, she would nip into town. The Spar had such a small range of goods. If she went to town, she would get the rye bread they both loved at the bakery, and the organic vegetables from the greengrocer, and smoked lentils from the woman with the smokehouse.

She drove on.

There was a T-junction just past the shop. She yielded and looked to the right and to the left.

In the field on the other side of the road something caught her eye. A scarecrow, very like the scarecrow in their own field at home. Odd, she was thinking, as she prepared to turn. She looked again. The scarecrow had black hair, red rosy cheeks, a big dotty smile. It was even wearing the same sort of granny print apron their own scarecrow had. It could have been its sister.

Kate smiled.

She liked scarecrows.

She had been upset when the one at home in the field had disappeared. And now here it was, or a scarecrow very like the old one, Leo's old scarecrow. Except that scarecrow had always

339

seemed to smile. 'Should a scarecrow smile?' she had asked Leo. 'Aren't they supposed to be scary?'

She turned her attention to the road, looking left, looking right, looking right again.

She prepared to turn.

She heard a cry, as she pressed the accelerator and went into the turn. Glancing at the field, she saw the scarecrow running towards her … believed she saw the scarecrow running towards her, shouting 'Stop, stop!' The scarecrow had legs, the scarecrow's black hair blew in the wind, the scarecrow looked, not scary, but scared.

'Stop!' screamed the scarecrow. 'Don't turn!' screamed the scarecrow.

But Kate had already turned.

She shook her head, laughing at herself, at the power of her imagination. What a strange place this was that she had come to live in, a place where scarecrows talked and walked, a place where you could still, on a certain kind of mysteriously calm day, understand how people had believed in ghosts and fairies and all that supernatural stuff.

The banshee.

The supernatural death-messenger, Leo called her, quoting from some book he had published.

That was her last thought.

She did not see the big truck racing towards her at sixty miles an hour. The driver had not remembered the junction on the narrow road – the sign warning motorists of the turn had been blown down in the wind last winter and not replaced. The driver was enjoying the October day, the quiet road. He was racing happily around the little bend and saw Kate's bright blue Nissan Micra seconds before he was on top of it.

It smashed like a bag of crisps under the truck.

The scarecrow stood in the field, her arms opened wide. Anyone looking at it would not have known whether it looked like a woman opening her arms to embrace a friend, or catch a bird, or like a woman being crucified.

The scarecrow wept at first, and then, as the driver climbed down from his cab and slowly dialled a number on his mobile phone, the scarecrow began to smile. By the time the squad cars and ambulance had arrived on the scene in a fanfare of flashing

340

lights and blaring sirens, the scarecrow was rigid, and the smile on her red face as fixed as that on a death's head.

A pregnant woman in her mid-twenties was killed when a truck collided with the car in which she was driving on the Dingle peninsula last night. The accident happened at around 4.30 p.m. The woman, who has not been named, has been taken to Tralee hospital. The driver of the truck was not injured. The area has been cordoned off while gardaí are investigating the scene. A diversion is in place.

Thirty-four

Anna half-believed Gerry's story, although she knew his motives for advising her against Vincy were very mixed. He liked Alex, or at least he liked the idea of Alex, and of conformity, and he hated disruption and change. The last thing he would welcome would be divorce, split families. And he liked the idea of being connected to someone like Alex, who was rich and successful. That sort of thing gave people a sense of vicarious security. That would be one of his motives, in warning her against Vincy.

But his main motive was something else: brotherly love.

Gerry's morals were mixed. He made mistakes. He hurt people – especially women who loved him. But he was not an unkind or thoughtless man. He probably really believed what he said, that Vincy was not the right man for Anna. He probably believed she would be happier, in the long run, staying with Alex.

She walked hurriedly along D'Olier Street, that busy, drab street, a street without real shops or charm, which she had always disliked. She was going to see Vincy in his flat over the bridge on Mountjoy Square. She needed his reassurance. She needed to know he existed, and was her lover, and would be there for her, always. She needed to find a house or an apartment where they could start their real life together.

It was dark. A wind blew in from the sea as she crossed O'Connell Bridge. The river was grey and choppy and the sea-gulls screamed excitedly, competing with the roars of the buses. The bridge seemed very wide and she felt she was struggling to get across it. Then the long stretch of O'Connell Street, another unpleasant street, still, for all they had been doing to try to make it look attractive. It was better if you walked along the middle of it, in the new walkway. That was always quieter, and you didn't have to look at the tacky shops that lined the left side of the street. But she went to that side anyway. She would take a taxi. The walk was too long, in her present mood.

Outside a burger joint on the corner of Middle Abbey Street, opposite the shoe shop, she saw Vincy.

She dashed up to him.

She hugged him.

He pushed her away gently. 'Anna, be careful, someone will see us!' he said.

'So what?' she said. 'Vincy, let's stop hiding. We're going to live together in a few weeks' time. What is the point of all the secrecy?'

He looked disappointed in her, as if she were a child who had let him down.

She tried to hug him again.

'Anna, for God's sake!' He looked around anxiously.

Nobody was paying any attention to them. The evening crowds pushed along the street, anxious to get home. A hobo in the doorway of the shoe shop crouched over his cup.

'Can we go somewhere? To the flat?' Anna asked.

'No ... Joe ...'

'So what!' she said angrily. 'Joe! I can meet him, can't I? He must know about me, doesn't he? You're moving out on him in a few weeks.'

'I need time.'

'Let's go for a drink then. I haven't seen you in days.'

'I can't. I've got a meeting. There's something I've been meaning to tell you. Something good.'

'What?' She was suspicious.

'I've begun to write a book about Iraq.'

'Oh.' She had been hoping for something better than this. 'Well, why not? Everyone's writing a book about something.'

'I've an appointment with my agent,' he said.

'You've already got an agent?'

He nodded. 'Oh yes, Jonathan Bewley recommended that I approach his. John Prescott. He's with Wyatt and Wyatt; he's very good.'

'So he's taken you on?'

Vincy looked puzzled. 'Yes, of course. We're discussing the offers.'

'Offers for what?'

A bus roared by. He couldn't hear her.

'Have you already got offers for your book? Before it's written?'

'Oh yes, that's how it's done. I've got good offers.'

'How much will the advance be?' Anna asked. At last she was going to find out.

The tram, the Red Line, the one that goes to Tallaght, came jangling across O'Connell Street.

He shook his head. 'A lot.'

'How much?'

'A lot. Enough to make a big difference. Listen, I'll talk to you later. I've got to meet someone in a few minutes.'

At the far side of the street Anna saw her. The face from the television screen. The long fair hair, the big smile: the face of Ireland in Iraq. Sorcha.

Sorcha was looking around, and when she saw Vincy, she waved.

'You're seeing her, aren't you? You are having a fling with Sorcha Toomey, the prisoner of Basra?' Anna was shouting.

'Anna, please, people can hear!' He clutched her arm.

'I don't care,' she said. 'Let them. You are the father of my child! Listen everybody. Listen Sorcha!'

He grabbed her and tried to stop her talking. 'We'll go for a drink,' he said. 'Let's go over there to the Oval.'

'He is moving in with me next week!' she screamed.

Sorcha looked across the street at Vincy. She noticed the commotion and opened her hands in a questioning gesture.

Anna snarled at her.

Sorcha looked bemused, but shrugged her shoulders at Vincy, and walked away.

Other people had also noticed that something was going on. They moved closer to get a good look at Anna. A small crowd was gathering on the corner under the burger sign, waiting for a green light, and they looked at the couple curiously for a second. But quarrelling couples were not that unusual, so they didn't pay much attention.

'Come on.' Vincy started to pull her off the footpath.

The beggar in the doorway of the shoe shop, the homeless person, who was wearing glasses and who had a fat book in his dirty hand, had got up and was standing right behind Vincy.

Vincy did not appear to see the Luas travelling quickly across the O'Connell Street junction.

The homeless person threw his book out onto the tracks.

Vincy, who seemed bewildered and not to know what he was doing, automatically moved to pick it up.

Then a lot of things happened simultaneously.

The driver of the Luas saw Vincy and Anna. He rammed on the brakes.

Anna screamed.

The brakes of the tram screamed along with her.

As she tumbled into unconsciousness she could see Vincy's head rolling across Abbey Street towards Eason's bookshop. The rest of his body lay on the road in front of Chapters, the second-hand store where the tramp got his reading material. (They gave him classics for free.)

The people waiting at the traffic lights shouted all at once and came running down to Anna. A fat hardback book came bounding back to the footpath, curiously unscathed by the incident. Nobody gave the book, the cause of the tragedy, a second glance. If they had, they would have seen that it was Tolstoy's second major hit, *Anna Karenina* – the tramp was already on page 103. The sirens of ambulances and squad cars began to arrive on the scene. The tramp with the spectacles picked up his book, took up his sleeping bag, and walked away towards O'Connell Bridge. Nobody saw him leave the scene. Nobody had seen him. Nobody sees homeless persons. They are part of the furniture.

Thirty-five

She saw the funeral on the nine o'clock news. It was held at the church in Killiney, for some strange reason, and Sorcha was at it. There was a shot of her, in a black trouser suit, her fair hair spread across her shoulders, weeping. Afterwards in the porch a reporter asked her if it were not ironic that Vincy had been beheaded after virtually rescuing her from a possibly similar fate only months earlier. Sorcha gave him a stony look and mumbled shyly, yes, yes. It was ironic.

Joe, Vincy's best friend, was there too. He was a man, not a woman. How did she know it was Joe? She just did. He was holding Sorcha by the waist, as if he were her partner, or lover. But maybe it was just the sort of touchy-feely thing fashionable people do at funerals, Anna thought, remembering *Four Weddings and a Funeral*, where everyone hugged everyone else all the time, at the funeral as well as the weddings.

Vincy was cremated then. She saw the coffin, which was open so she could see Vincy clearly, his head beside his body – odd that they had not tried to make him look as if he were in one piece, for this last television appearance – being pushed behind the curtain at the crematorium, and then she saw the flames rising and the smoke, over the round tower and the cypress trees, and the rooks circling over the grey walls. The sky darkened and the rooks fluttered across the face of the moon.

Anna opened her eyes. The faces of Rory and Alex hovered above her. Two moons. They lit up.

'She's awake!' Rory shouted. He tried to hug her.

Alex pulled him back. 'Careful! You might hurt her!' he said, in a loud whisper.

'I won't hurt her! Does this hurt?' He clutched Anna in a tight clasp.

She smiled weakly and said, 'No, darling', although it did hurt, in more ways than she could say.

'See?' he said to Alex. But he climbed off his mother and stood beside his father at the side of her bed.

'How do you feel?' asked Alex. He would have liked to hold Anna's hand, but was afraid to.

'I feel fine,' said Anna. 'Vincy is dead.'

She didn't care. She was glad.

'No, he's not,' said Alex grimly.

'He is,' said Anna. 'I pushed him under a tram.'

'You didn't push hard enough,' said Alex. 'I was talking to him this morning. He telephoned me to ask how you were.'

Vincy telephoned Alex to ask how she was? She was a child. They were taking care of her, as if she were not able to do that herself.

'He's fine. Much better than you are,' said Alex. 'He told me to tell you he was asking for you; he's going back to Iraq.'

'What?'

'Soon. Apparently he's got a commission from someone to write a book about it,' Alex said. 'He won't be back here for a while,' he added.

Anna looked around. She was in a small cubicle surrounded by pink and orange curtains. Her bed was high and had steel bars along the sides. All around she could hear voices, low and high; also the rattle of steel and the sound of footsteps.

'Where am I?' she asked.

'In the A & E,' said Rory importantly.

'The Mater,' Alex explained. 'The Mater Hospital. You're in the A & E unit, on a trolley. You've been here for two days. I don't know what we are paying four thousand euro a year to the VHI for.'

Anna tried to remember what had happened recently. She recalled being at a book launch, listening to Lilian Meaney read from her new book, the book that all but plagiarised Anna's own. She could hear Lilian's sweet voice even now, reading the lines that she herself should have been reading. *There was not another person on the beach. It was an ordinary Tuesday. Everyone was at work or at school, which was where Jonathan should be. But today he had decided not to go, because as he left his house with his bag on his back a large grey heron had hopped out in front of him on the roadside and talked to him. 'Do not go the school,' the heron said. 'Come down to the beach, where someone is waiting to see you.'* She could see Lilian, in the wonderful green dress she had bought for the occasion. She could even recall a conversation she had had long ago with Lilian, in which Lilian had commented that women in paintings almost always wore green dresses. It was the most poetic colour, for a dress.

That was all Anna remembered. Had she collapsed then, in the middle of Lilian's reading, from envy and annoyance and righteous indignation?

'So,' said Anna. 'What happened? Did the launch go on anyway?'

'The launch?' Alex did not remember that Anna had been at a launch, that that had been her reason for being in the centre of town when the accident happened.

'Lilian's launch. *The Wonderful Adventures of Jonathan Murphy,* or whatever. In the National Library.'

Alex looked bemused. But he nodded, as if he understood. Humouring her. 'They called me from the hospital. They said you had been knocked down by the Luas,' he said.

Anna raised her eyebrows quizzically. 'I was knocked down by the Luas?'

'Yes.' Alex nodded. 'You weren't seriously injured, but you were concussed. That's what they say here anyway.'

Anna felt her legs to make sure they were still there. They seemed to be in place.

'Are you OK, Mom?' Rory kissed her again, his face full of love. His face smelt fresh, like milk and apples. He was being looked after by someone.

'I should try to get a doctor.' Alex patted her on the forehead worriedly. 'They can discharge you and you can come home then. The sooner you get out of here the better.'

Anna lay back on her pillow.

'I'll get a nurse in to look after you at home, for a few days,' Alex said. 'Or whatever, however long you need her.'

Anna closed her eyes.

The crossroads and junctions become fewer and fewer. She saw them, the crossroads of her youth, softened by hedgerows, white hawthorn, dripping elderflowers. Quite soon you find you are on a straight road with no junctions, leading to an inevitable destination.

'I'm jumping into the forest,' said Anna. 'I need to go somewhere. Alone.'

'Of course you do,' said Alex, glancing warningly at Rory. 'That's perfectly understandable. Would you like to come home now, and then ...' He looked at her carefully. 'Then, when you've recovered from this' – he made a vague gesture that took in the entire A & E corridor – 'then you can decide what to do.'

She looked up at Alex and Rory. They looked at her, on her trolley, with her black hair spread across the flat, white pillow. It was not lanky or greasy, even though she had been knocked down by a tram and unconscious for two days. It still looked as clean and shining as if she had just washed it. Her face was pale but as perfect as ever.

'Thanks very much,' she said slowly. 'But no. I won't go home.' Rory frowned, and turned his face away from her. 'Not for a while,' she said, taking his hand. 'Anyway. Not quite yet. I need to ... do something.'

'All right,' said Alex. Rory was going to say something but Alex silenced him with a nudge. 'That's sensible. You need space and time.'

'Yes,' Anna said. 'Where is this? Where are we?'

'The Mater,' said Alex. 'The A & E in the Mater.' He couldn't remember if he had told her that already or not. 'It's very busy, you've been on this trolley for two days.'

Anna was trying to remember a name, but it would not come to her. It was very frustrating, like trying to get your Internet connection to work when the link has broken.

'There's a nice letter for you,' Alex said.

'How do you know it's nice?' asked Anna.

'I don't. But it *looks* nice. Here.' He handed it to her.

It was a nice envelope, white and thick, with her name and address handwritten in rich blue ink. The envelope was sealed but only just – Alex had probably opened the letter and read it, then tried to make it look as if he hadn't. That's how he knew it was nice. If it had not been nice, he would not have brought it to her in the A & E.

The letter was from a literary agent, to whom Anna had sent a synopsis and the completed chapters of *Sally and the Ship of Dreams* a few weeks earlier. The agent wrote that she had fallen in love with it. They say these things. There were so many good things in it. And it was great that the heroine was a heroine, a girl. A lot of the big successful children's books were about boys – *Harry Potter*, *Artemis Fowl*, *Eragon* – all the rest of them. When you think about it, it's true. *Goodnight Mister Tom*. *Willie Wonka and the Chocolate Factory*. *Charlie and the Giant Peach*. It wasn't like the old *Alice in Wonderland* days. *Pippi Longstocking* ... They say such a lot of crap. If Anna could emphasise the feminine aspect – point it up, make it more obvious – she might be able to find a good publisher, get a good advance.

Emphasise the feminine aspect.

Make Sally more girly.

And more strong and heroic.

'So?' asked Alex, when she had put the letter down. 'Was I right? Is it nice?'

'Quite nice,' said Anna sadly. The agent had not yet encountered *The Wonderful Adventures of Jonathan Murphy*, obviously.

'I'm glad you're pleased,' said Alex, not noticing that Anna was on the verge of tears. 'So now, I'll go and hunt for a doctor ... if there is one to be found in this place, which I begin to doubt.'

He left the cubicle.

Anna reread the letter. Then she pulled something out of her bag. The brochure Christine had given her.

Annaghmakerrig.

A gabled house set in a fringe of evergreens.

A dark lake, green slopes of daffodils.

A retreat, a place to write or paint, to compose. To recharge the batteries. To walk in the forest or swim in the lake. To work all day and all night. To enjoy the company of fellow artists.

Art.

Peace and tranquillity and art.

The gabled house, yellow ochre, the smiling windows.

I need that.

Tranquillity and peace.

I need to see what art is, what artists do. Like that woman in the desk by the window, typing, looking out at the slope of flowers, the wagtail dipping in the pond.

No talk of advances, bestsellers, pricing your book.

I want to write what I have not yet written, something deep inside me, not yet seen, not yet felt, not yet known, to me. Myself. I want to write. Real, I want to write, and unreal.

She felt a bit more cheerful then.

Rory kissed her again. He glanced at the brochure. 'Now you can come home and write your book,' he said. 'And we'll all be happy.'

Anna hugged him.

'What happened to me?' she asked.

'You were knocked down on O'Connell Street,' said Rory. 'You know, that big street where the spire is.'

'Yes, I know that big street,' said Anna. 'But where am I now?'

'In the A & E,' said Rory. 'They brought you here in an ambulance. *Whee-whee-whee-whee-whee*! Then they phoned us. They got the number from your mobile.'

Anna nodded. 'How is your father?' she asked.

Rory was puzzled. 'He's OK. He just went out to look for a doctor. He'll be back in a minute.'

Anna tried to remember the name again. Her head was clear at the front, but at the back it felt like a mass of thick wool, in which all memories were lost. The name would not come to light.

'How is Luz Mar?' she asked.

That was not the name.

'She's gone,' he said. 'Luz Mar. She left months ago. I have another one now. Marike.'

'Marike, yes,' said Anna. 'And your father? Where is he?'

Rory was getting cross. 'I told you, he just went to find a doctor. He will be back soon.'

'That's good. Is there a doctor here?'

'It's a hospital,' said Rory wearily.

'Which hospital?' asked Anna.

'I don't know,' said Rory. 'I forget. What Matter, or something like that.'

'What Matter?' Anna said. 'That's a good name for a hospital.'

She looked around the cubicle again. Her clothes on the floor in a little heap, with her handbag on top.

'I need to go to the toilet,' said Anna, pushing back the blue bedcover.

'You turn right, go down to the door, turn left, go down the corridor, turn right, go up the stairs, and it's just there in front of you,' said Rory.

'I suppose I'll find it,' said Anna, who had not taken in any of his rapid directions.

'You can ask people. I had to ask a few times,' said Rory. 'The natives are friendly.'

'Oh good,' said Anna. 'I better put on my clothes, I suppose.'

'I'll go out for a minute.' Rory vanished through the pink and orange curtain. There was nothing he hated more than seeing his parents in a state of undress.

Anna clambered down from the trolley. Her legs were unsteady but she did not fall, and she managed to get her clothes on quickly enough. She brushed her hair and checked her face in her compact mirror: she looked washy but normal. Pushing the letter into her handbag, she emerged from the cubicle – an expensively dressed woman, who seemed out of place in the shabby hospital. Rory was standing outside the cubicle, playing a hand-held computer game. He pointed along the corridor, not speaking.

Anna walked along as instructed. Trolleys were ranged along one wall, on each one a patient, some old and very ill, some very young. Nurses moved up and down, occasionally stopping to talk to a patient, telling them they were moving up the list and would see a doctor before the end of the day if all went well, or covering the face of someone who had passed away, weary of life on a trolley. Some of the patients looked at Anna with some interest, as she trotted along on her high heels. The nurses did not seem to see her.

She found the toilet after about ten minutes.

But when she had used it, she could not find her way back to her cubicle.

She walked along the corridors of the hospital and finally came to a door that led outside, into a car park. Once she smelt the air, she decided she might as well go out. So she crossed the car park and left the hospital yard.

When she reached the street, she stopped to consider.

She was in a grey place. Stony houses, black roofs. Little streets to her right, a long, dark street to her left. A lot of traffic but not many people walking. No shops.

Seagulls wheeled over the spire of a dark church, their voices hardly heard on the street in the din of the traffic. Still, they seemed to call to Anna. She decided to turn towards them – northwards. It was early afternoon, a mildly overcast day. The sun could be sensed hovering behind the pearly clouds, but it wasn't going to break through.

She walked past the black church, and along some unfamiliar streets, where time seemed to have stood still. Soon she was on a long straight road, lined with big houses. Their gardens were shaded by sycamore and chestnut trees. Drifts of leaves filled every corner, and were heaped up at the edge of the garden railings. The smell of autumn, that mysterious mixture of earthiness and decay, caught at her soul.

She walked along the straight, wide thoroughfare. Now, at the end of the road, she could see an oasis of greenery – the Phoenix Park, although she did not recognise it.

Before she came there, long before, something else caught her eye and caused her to stop.

It was something that was unusual in a front garden in Dublin: an apple tree. They were mainly grown at the back, probably to make sure nobody stole the apples. But nobody stole apples these days. Nobody had even harvested these ones. The grass under the tree was littered with windfalls and there were many apples left on the tree. It had lost most of its leaves but the apples hung there, a bright orange-red, like robins' breasts, glowing on the black branches like toy baubles. The tree was so perfect that it might have been painted by a cheerful child.

Anna stood looking at it for almost ten minutes. It seemed to her that she had never seen anything so lovely.

It reminded her of something. She frowned. She tried to remember what it was – a name, the name she had been trying to remember all day.

But it would not come up.

She could not remember the name, not for the moment.

So she continued to walk up the road.

She walks in a wood. The moss encrusts the tree trunks. Birds move in leaves, shuffling sounds, a white-tailed hare sits in her path, at her approach leaps away. She walks, through the wood to a clearing. Below, the black lake, fringed by feathery evergreens. The sloping greensward. The yellow house rising on the crest of the hill like a rock that has been there forever.

Her room, a large, plain room with green walls, a shelf of old books, a fireplace. Her desk by the window, overlooking the pond. Wagtails dip in the pond, frogs spawn there. First buds erupt on old apple trees. Soon – a month, two months – veils of blossom will lace the orchard.

Anna writes, tries to write, writes, tries to write. Lets the words float to the top like spawn on the water, lets the words sit like a hare on the track, lets the words leap like a trout in the lake, lets the words sing like the finches. Lets the words. Lets the words. Lets the words.